MUNGO, BOOKS ONE AND TWO, REVISED

Illustrated

Keith Hulse

.

Dedicted to scientist as they are never remembered in the honors list.
Three cheers for science, we are going to beat disease and live in caravans on Mars.

CONTENTS

Title Page

Copyright

Dedication

Day three and Mungo led to slave pens to see if his friends were there and   188

Day four afternoon.   192

Day five brought Mungo to Leah for the mazarrats brought him to a castle made of   194

THE END   365

Acknowledgement   366

About The Author   368

Epilogue evolution   370

Books By This Author   374

Chapters

1, Evolution, An Introduction, Frederick Meyers said.

2,The story telling.

3, Leah.

4, Lessons.

5, Lust.

6, Leah Again.

7, Fever.

8, Enkalla.

9, Bait.

10, Cathbadh.

11, Nannaha's Gossip.

12, Hurreva.

13, Underneath.

14, Banishment.

BOOK 2, Seven Years.

1,Year One.

2, What The Elder Told Young Mazarrats.

3, Nannaha's Bites.

4, Year Four.

5, Year Five.

6, Year Six.

7, Year Seven.

BOOK THREE, The Elder.

8, Empress Red Sun.

9, Civil War.

10, Zigaratta.

11,Nodegamma.

12, End.

MUNGO
BY
Keith Hulse
97323 words

K. Hulse
lugbooks@gmail.com
lugbooks.co.uk
Aberdeen

Chapter 1 The story telling

Taken from the captain's log of the Star Ship Bounty sent by the United Nations Geological
Society 70000 A.D.

"I am Captain John Clinton who sought the lost colony New Uranus and place here the papyrus book 'Mungo' which tells all.

The human baby sucked hard on the black lion's red nipples filling its belly with **Deinococcus radiodurans bacteria**. No other young competed because lizard men had taken the beast's own cubs.

Two skinned at their camp and thrown into a copper pot boiling water.

The surviving two strongest sent off to Telephassa the Mighty City State were lizard men flew Pteranodons, reptiles thirteen feet long with head crests to balance the long beak and from their dinosaur tails fluttered their House Carl colors.

So, suck human child to force mother on its side and open legs, so you can take her milk full of **bacterium Deinococcus radioduran** mutated through centuries to protect you against radiation damage **with its own** enzyme Reca.

Needed because in the distance an abandoned damaged nuclear plant surrounded by herds of **grass eating dinosaurs**.

And a mazarrat a cross between a monkey and a mongoose cut into tree bark seeking grubs. And mother lioness remembered when hunting the abductors of its own young it had found the child floating in a reed basket on a yellow river. And the lion given rudimentary intelligence by life saw a cub to replace its stolen young and took the child back to the pride.

Somewhere in the lion memory superstition flashed.

"The Wild One would be found in a basket," and also reason, "The humans send their young downstream away from lizard men cities in the hope they are saved by?"

"*Yes, the Wild One has been found,*" a watching mazarrat called The Elder sang for mazarrats **always sing sweetly.**

Illustration: This is a mazarrat, looks like a cross between a meerkat and a rat, species genning here?

It is the way of their nasal passages, so sing like nightingales, other sparrows and crows but singing together are a heavenly choir.

Now while the baby burped over dinner a strong male voice demanded, "Let us eat the babe for it is man thing," and the voice belonged to a red male lion come to mate in their lion tongue which was grunting, coughing and facial expressions.

And the red lion was a warrior for he wore a brass plated kilt with sheathed copper sword and was handsome, his black mane waxed and curled with heated tongs.

So was his black beard and he was, 'Red Hide?'

"Let Red Hide eat the baby," a male red, black and fawn lion chorused on their hind legs, so their brass plates fell across their loins.

And three other lions with deformed faces and weak legs beat metal tubes hanging from a tree. Deformed because their **checkpoint gene p52** had not repaired their radioactive damaged sex cells because their mother's milk had been weak in **Deinococcus radioduran bacteria**.

And the human babe's mother was disgusted Red Hide showed his adulthood in front of her babe.

"It is the way of the lion pride, I am showing I am ready, I own the pride, hurry and ready yourself," Red Hide the lion creature demanded for he was a mighty king.

And she replied by extending her six-inch claws, spiting, and standing so her yellow kilt fell over human parts and her bosom full of milk retreated within her mammary pouches so only two red nipples showed.

For standing is the first ritual when lions fight in the hope that a challenger backs down and no real damage done.

"I will eat you too," the red lion king boasted but challenged the wrong mother who landed behind him after a mighty spring and raked his bottom so his adulthood must wait another day.

"You have mauled the king," the Black male roared and held a bronze spear with a paw that had three fingers.

And the king hid his shame and pain by licking his wounds and private sores, which is rude for he was in company.

"The human babe is mine," the Black mother lioness roared allowing her paws to drop to a highly polished bronze knife in her red kilt belt.

And from her paws came four fingers from their protective holes and the nails painted purple.

"We are the king's companions, we will kill you," lions, one brown, one fawn and one white and they looked like were-lion creatures in brass chain mail.

"Lion shall not eat lion," a bronze metal worker at his mold and his colleagues agreed and these metal workers kept the secret of fire to themselves so, esteemed by the pride. And the speaker went to a group of skulls placed in a cave and held up one so it could speak.

And The Elder, that Mazarrat was at work on bark carving history nearby.

"Lion shall not eat lion," the soul of an ancestor that taught lions metal work said through the skull, which when alive fitted with **Amulet chips** that did not need a battery to work the **memory chips** in the cranium.

And two **LEDs** bulbs as eyes glowed red by **Amulet chips**.

Chips inserted by lizard men for the ancestors were slaves.

And the mother picked up the babe and fled becoming outcast and the companions did not follow for their duty is to protect the king who was cowering the pride to be humble towards him, for he was bullying, making sure all forgot his shame, for he was still KING.

And the lioness escaped because a silicon chip had said, "Lion shall not eat lion."

"Hey Red Hide, yes you with the foolish expression don't you read anything we write?" The Elder shouted down from seven-foot-wide tomato flowers.

Below Red Hide saw the hated jungle gossip.

"Don't you know who that was?" The Elder asked.

Red Hide did not need to tell his companions to circle the tomato plant and The Elder, did not bother to tell Red Hide who it was but peed Mazarrat fashion on the companions below then fled.

Red Hide roared his anger.

And time stops for no one as rain dribbled down the carving made by the Mazarrat of a mother defending a baby from a lion; **and the child now six** played in a clearing as mother slept under purple rhododendrons as enemy approached.

"Look a slave child," the enemy to one of its own kind and were six feet tall, scaled, wore brass plated kilts, and carried bovine shields and bronze spears.

And pink rhododendron flowers six feet in diameter hid them as the child toyed with a beetle asked a question, he asked all things he found, "Who made you?" And the child never killed an insect if he could help it.

He loved all things and was full of mercy.

And since the beetle did not answer he looked at the yellow sky and asked, "Who made you beetle?"

And the clear yellow sky with white and grey clouds answered, "I did," in the boy's heart and love flowed so his blue eyes watered.

"Who are you?" And his shout awoke The Elder.

And the child filled with joy, and he knew who made all.

"Sa ha lo gr ra," the boy shouted uttering sounds from his spirit and danced naked opening his arms to the yellow sky.

And the mother hearing laughing lifted her head and asked, "Who are you speaking too?"

"I don't know."

"I do," The Elder smiling.

"Wow the child speaks lion," the enemy a warrior named Malachi marveling.

"You are hearing things Malachi," his companion feeling the jungle closing as a trail of solar dust a mile long crashed through their ionized atmosphere.

And he shivered wondering what hell of an effect the dust would have on the climate?

In the distance a bee three meters long flew out off a hole in a nuclear chimney stack.

"Anyway, we are in luck, we can skin a pelt here," Malachi feeling his scales move above rippling muscles as the black lioness appeared, "she is beautiful."

"I don't fancy taking on a lioness with cub, I mean we are just two," his companion Vinki replied feeling a distant volcano erupt and knew it would rain black ash for the next month and groaned.

"I won't take her pelt but will have her as personal slave," Malachi promised aloud.

"If it's a lion bitch you want then hump one in a whore house, let's go Malachi," Vinki urged seeing the black lioness was alluringly beautiful but not enough to stir his loins in her domain.

"We are Fermanians, brave and fearless, masters of this world," Malachi still shocked from hearing the man thing speak lion and dance, and still wanting the black lioness, seeing the possibilities of beautifying her by cross breeding by **shuttle genning** her while she lived.

The results would be electrifying and make her Malachi's favorite. All would be jealous and covert his new lioness and his ego swelled.

Illustration: A typical peanut sized mazarrat singing to the hazy moon: and the song was 'Singing in the rain' for mazarrats had learned to operate human
music players: bring them on, they had choirs.

"Yes, I want that bitch," and after he did sell her for profit to a high-class brothel so all could admire and enjoy his work.

"Malachi maybe we better fetch our Triceratops and bearers then we can be brave and fearless," Vinki answered already sweating worming away, hoping his supervisors had the good sense to close the roofs of his greenhouses against the volcanic soot he could see falling.

And Malachi took one look backwards at his Lord Vinki on safari, spat and stood up rubbing sleep vine extract onto a dart to replace the lance head there. "Yes, bitch tonight I will lie with you," and his actions were deliberate and coordinated.

Whether he stood to force the situation with the black lion and show the young Wonder Lord Vinki what Fermanians were......no one knows?

He was curious, for he was a hunter and the jungle full of tales. "A Wild One reared by lions shall bring judgement upon our race," Malachi remembered a papyrus pulp book, "just rubbish to sell," he knowing the back-street scribes were cashing in on the story, but this human cub had unnerved him dancing naked and singing to the sky; he had never seen the likes before.

"Look mother a giant lizard," the human child jumping running to investigate Malachi.

"Duck child," Malachi ordered with speech like twanging rubber in a duck's mouth and the child laughed at his feet. "What's so funny slave child? There's a lion charging me," and Malachi threw his dart, and the aim was bad because the child was lifting his brass plates to see if the lizard man had a wily like his.

And Malachi felt his thingamabob prodded by a finger.

"Idiot," Vinki running for his life.

"Idiot," Malachi grunted flat on his back with the black lioness's mouth above his face.

"Don't kill him mother, it makes me laugh, can I keep IT?" The boy pushing his mum's mouth from the lizard's skull.

"Get out of the way so I can kill the Fermanian," mother replied, "look his ribs are showing where I clawed, tonight you shall eat your favorite dish."

"But IT makes me laugh."

"I know plenty of good jokes," Malachi offered in lion

tongue.

"His smell is like he who took my cubs long ago," the lioness snarled sitting on haunches now waving an unsheathed dagger, while the other pawed hand flashed claws. *"She really did spoil the man cub!"* A mazarrat sings softly for baby to hush.

So, this action allowed Malachi an opening to survive.

And Malachi took the child and, "Let me go or I will kill the man child thing," and walked backwards towards his camp.

And the child snapped a clawed rib out of Malachi who moaned, "WA."

And seeing what reason the lioness claimed vanish dropped the boy and crawled vines up a rhododendron tree moaning and cursing all the way.

"God Telephassa yak, yam yak," Malachi complained as a claw raked his legs, lifting scales to drop on a foot-long yellow butterfly. "Idiot head," also for a flowering creeper he held was a reared fanged green vine snake, but to Malachi it was SNAKE, and he feared the legless slithering things.

Then the crack of rifles from Malachi's bearers and the lion took her man cub as lances thudded into the giant purple sweet tuber corpse she fled into.

"Well Malachi was she worth it?" Vinki sneered and The Elder sitting on a rhododendron leaf nearby sang, *"Malachi was his friend, Malachi was the corner stone for the temple."*

"Bloody mazarrat again," Malachi and threw a fallen tree mango at the creature. In return a squelching sound as a tree tomato hit Malachi in the face and The Elder climbed higher laughing.

"I don't like the jungle Malachi," Vinki pushing bearers about to shield himself.

"I wonder why I do then." Malachi puzzled over the song.

Mazarrats were gormless with peanuts as brains that sang about everything. No doubt seen with a friend and a no good mazarrat had made a song out of it for mischief, reason apart from stupidity.

And no lizard man had seen mazarrats carving pictures

in tree bark or carrying on a conversation with one of its kind about the dangers of a fast breeder nuclear reactor overheating.

That was because mazarrats kept secrets.

They were just singing baboons to lizard folk that kept them in cages or chained to organ grinders.

And time stops for no one under the fruit bats and like other abandoned **fast 280 megawatt**

breeder nuclear reactors cooled by liquid sodium, the one behind the pride had heat **resisting ceramic corridors** leading to laboratories.

And here skeletons waiting for a finger to activate their **Amulet power pack chips**, also Whole beings frozen in chambers waiting life.

Vials containing chromosomes for inserting into unrelated species and examples of this cross genning seen, apes with human heads for the lizard men folk the Fermanians needed arboreal slaves to collect the gifts of the jungle at prominent levels.

Fermanians hated the jungle that had leeches.

And the human brains here were dim, to collect for their lizard owners for they worked on a reward and punishment basis.

Lizard men hated the jungle.

it was full of things like mazarrats and rodents that ate your woman's eggs and snakes that bit your

ankles, so you swelled and died.

Anyway: *"I will drink this pretty yellow drink,"* a mazarrat the size of a spaniel for it had come through a crack in one of the ceramic chambers, split from a deep quake set off by nuclear explosions, in the nuclear reactor.

And the yellow liquid contained **human smart brain chromosomes**.

And she drank, heard a turbine speed up, fretted so returned to the jungle feeling ill passing a hot house eight hundred yards by six hundred wide and two thousand high with rhododendron trees with purple flowers six feet wide behind its glass walls.

And the trees were as high as cedars bearing fruits like tomato and melon for the rhododendron had their genes spliced into other plants.

And the mazarrat found a tree hollow and slept and it was a trap and taken to a lizard man pet market and sold to a lizard boy who had it frolicking with mazarrats and she told them all about a man lion cub that was wild.Might say the lizard boy had a dirty mind.

And the human brain genes sliced themselves using **p53 checkpoint genes** into the host DNA mazarrat brain codes and the mazarrat remembered better, and the boy sold it for a hover skateboard to surf the red sand dunes about Lake Telephassa.

It was a repeat of what a mazarrat did a millennium ago that led to mazarrats that no one knew anything about being expert carvers of tree bark, *"those types with a peanut for a brain?" A mazarrat eating peanuts.*

The lizards who inherited the reactors did not know reactors hummed away, keeping green houses and labs cozy for mutating genes and bugs for curious creatures too drink the pretty liquids.

And the bugs rode shuttle genes and viruses and found easy access into new hosts like the young mazarrat who thought she was smart but was not, just stupid.

Cathbadh

Cathbadh the mighty man of science in Telephassa was now riding a hired sedan chair peering out the blue velvet curtains. He was watching his paid work.

A hairy hunchback and a little girl who could pass as a human slave playing in the red castle grounds.

Already Telephassa was returning to normal as Lord Artebrates, Commander of the Southern Army set fire to the last house filled with Prince Annunaki's rebels.

The smoke fortunately wafted the other way, there was

nothing as repulsive as burned lizard scavenged, by hungry beggars and Telephassa City was full of beggars, war had ruined the harvests, only Telephassa had wealth. Either you mugged or stole it respectfully by advancing one's position at court.

To Cathbadh a good war was opportunist as both sides employed him to design war engines.

"Science prospers in war not peace,'" Cathbadh mused and signaled his bearers on.

"Artebrates," Cathbadh whispered feeling his strength. "Artebrates," Cathbadh knowing charges of conspiracy to murder Prince Annunai, dropped from Artebrates, and now released from jail, to fight the prince's followers and prove loyalty to his Mighty One, Carman the boy's mother.

"I would have joined the rebels after what she did to me," Cathbadh and there was a crunching as the sedan lurched, so Cathbadh looked out and saw a maimed soldier with no legs.

He would never beg again, the bearers had gone over him, the chair had heavy wheels.

So, Cathbadh closed the curtain and read a new papyrus book, "Wild One and Princess Atora," and groaned. The scribes did not realize what they did writing such tripe. There was no man cub reared by lions as popular imagination demanded.

And he had an appointment with Carman and knew there was other less dangerous ways of toppling the woman than rebellion.

And reading about Mungo made him think about the approaching star he was observing and knew it was a ship but whose? Fermanian or human and Carman refused to believe it could be human.

"There have always been slaves," she meaning humans were igneous to this **Experimental Planet 16A.**

"Humans are escaped experiments," scribes wrote and believed.

Cathbadh knew ten thousand years ago human star ships

fueled here before the Great Atomic War.

"Malachi was his friend," Cathbadh heard a mazarrat sing and peered out and saw the hunter Malachi as Lord Vinki excitedly told people they had seen the Wild One.

"There should be a law against it," Cathbadh and travelled on.

And time stops for no one.

And Malachi never forgot the **man thing now eight** with brown hair reaching his buttocks riding the black lioness's back, pleasing her by plucking fleas, and the child spoke the tongue of the lions of **New Uranus**, which is what man things called the Fermanian Planet Experimental 16A.

It did not matter the lions called **16A, Wonderful**. "They could call 16A, Heaven so what?" Wonder Lord Vinki the Fermanian's mouthed a favorite lizard joke.

And about the child's neck Malachi's rib on a gut necklace.

And the child roared by his mother, cast sharp sticks, and made fire it found in a deserted lizard camp.

"Fire respects no one, it will eat you," mother chiding.

"Mother I have ten fingers and they make the hot coals burn," and mother reminded her son was man.

But The Elder intervened singing nearby; *"He is man thing, wise and chosen, don't interfere Ono of the Lions,"* from the top of a giant red toadstool and Ono shivered.

"Crazy mazarrat, I am lion thing," Mungo roared and ran on all fours and The Elder sighed replying, *"Stupid man,"* and fell asleep

"I will never let him go, my son is good to me, he catches hares and small lizards in traps and gives me them roasted," Ono shouted back at the mazarrat.

The Elder replied with a loud snore and louder windy that drifted to them.

And Mungo kept fire burning outside Ono's cave under a sheltered rock and here one day they headed, smelling the burning herbs to rid the cave of mites never used to, human ways.

And The Elder was happy for the herbs cleared an area of twenty meters of biting insects and so, he slept undisturbed, unbitten, heaven it was, no ticks but still winded.

So, twenty yards and a roar; assassins nearby.

Malachi, one assassin group, did not need to caution his companion silent for it was Lord Artebrates lying beside him on the giant yellow daffodil, not Vinki who Malachi swore wore woman things in private.

"I will kill you now," the voice of Red Hide roared, the other assassin group.

At once Mungo slid off his mother's back and raced the distance to the cave crushing a natural snail.

Now Red Hide chased as his companions sailed out of rhododendron bushes upon the black lioness while Mungo reached a burning stick and held it between his legs.

A swarm of plastic skinned midges melted.

Lo King Red Hide forgot Mungo as he headed for the flame feeling his nose singe before the event happened.

And singe the nose did, and smell and Mungo was winded as Red Hide flattened him, and Mungo accidentally pressed the flame against Red Hide's cod piece that began to burn freely.

"Yak yams help me save me, I burn," Red Hide looking down in horror and fled to find a stream to plunge into. And the king was a mighty beast at least twelve feet long.

And Mungo saw the companions look at their king with his mother under their claws.

"Run dinosaur dung," Mungo shouted throwing flaming sticks at them.

And they fled with fur burning.

"Mother do not die," Mungo running to her side.

"Help me to our lair," and he did for he was strong from climbing trees.

"And Mungo stitched his mother's wounds and she beamed pride for no other lion could use gut and thorns and sew like her babe.

"I love you child," she purred, and Mungo joyed.

"When I am big, I will kill Red Hide and sew his redness into shoes and cloth to hide my bum and a hat and cloak to keep the rain off me," and Mungo filled the forest with a lion roar and joyed for he was innocent.

And love filled Mungo as he danced naked to the Unseen thing that made him part of creation.

And The Elder danced upon Rhododendron leaves, *naked to but had fur to hide his innocence.*

"He is mazarrat," Lord Artebrates to Malachi fitting an arrow to his crossbow as they watched Mungo utter gibberish to the yellow clouds as he sang to what made all things from atop a rhododendron plant.

"The bitch is still desirable," Malachi replied and Artebrates remembered Malachi had met this so called Wild One before.

How much had Malachi got for selling his story to the scribes who wrote such garbage?

And Malachi aimed on the left hamstring of Mungo as, "Those idiotic scribes wrote a great hunter was his friend and betrayed his own race and described me but didn't name me and the damage was done.

I could have made it to Court except for those scribes.

Wild One, just a human cub," and Malachi aimed to put the bolt into Mungo's neck now.

The head was steel, no dart or sleeper juice, Mungo was to die too clear Malachi's name.

But shame entered Malachi's heart so moved his arm.

And the bolt smashed into rock behind Mungo who had knelt at the last moment to help mother.

"He has seen us," Artebrates standing drawing sword that made the five-foot yellow petals wobble, "You missed deliberately, the scribes were right, you are his friend."

And a stone from Mungo's sling hit Artebtrates's skull so he heavily fell thirty feet down the rhododendron onto a four-foot silk caterpillar eating giant mulberry leaves.

"Damn it all," Malachi jumping to the Lord's aid for if the man died, he would have his scales prized off then salt rubbed into his pink spitted flesh for roasting and a grapefruit shoved into his mouth, and head baked in clay.

Such the death of a hunter who allowed a lord to die.

The fruit was optional, dozens used a pumpkin or banana to add ridicule!

And Malachi pulled his lord's face out of the broken caterpillar dripping yellow stinking gore.

"Don't drown in that muck," Malachi seeing himself choked before descaled because his Lord drowned.

"Hey, it's the funny lizard again, got a name chameleon?" Mungo shouted before sending another stone.

And Malachi's brass plates stopped the stone rupturing him.

"Telephassa god he is a good aim," as Malachi staggered away leaving a trail of silk thread behind him, courtesy of the caterpillar.

And the last stone hastily sent hit Lord Artebrates in the right eye.

And it was forty yards away Malachi tied Artebrates across the saddle of his Triceratops, that he noticed the lord's eye and groaned.

So, sadness filled Malachi as he rode hearing a crazy mazarrat sing, *"Malachi was his friend,"* and when Malachi was sure they were heading for camp he took dagger and plucked out his own right eye.

"Good aim boy," he grunted knowing he must remain one eyed if Artebrates
remained such. "Better me do it than some executioner with filthy hands," as his triceratops thundered into camp.

And Mungo's mother purred and forgot he was human.

"Edible protein," The Elder swallowing the eye, *"only thing lizards are good for, getting eaten."*

And time's sands stop for no one under the mosquito swarms of New Uranus and mazarrats black with pink stripes, others pure white came to The Elder who carved.

"For four years he has danced to the power with no name, he has become as omnipotent as life itself. He is merciful and wise seeking not wealth, precious gems litter his yard, now you mazarrats must guard him.

Triceps

But do not look into his face when he dances to the light as causes blindness," The Elder and the visitors now hid their eyes from Mungo, and the bit about blindness was TRIPE, as The Elder had a sense of humor.

"Yes, he is rich," they agreed seeing beasts that were Mungo's gems dancing with him and felt happy for good times ahead must be coming for mazarrats.

And time's sands stop for no one

But **Mungo now twelve** let puberty take him to young lioness seeking harems now forgot to dance so, shine left him.

"Mungo are you forgetting what I have taught you?" The Elder asked frustrated from a red mushroom field for **TIME STOPS FOR NO ONE.**

"I don't know what you mean?"

"Yes, you do, you wear clothes and what is this cod piece, stolen from a Fermanian? You, foolish boy," The Elder prodding the red ornament sparkling with gems.

Mungo covered his shame and said blushing, "I am lion and do lion things and the girls like it."

"The only light shining from you is now lust and the hot breath in your wind, do not forget there is light, and darkness and you belong to light, ah I see we bore, got your own ideas, have we?" The Elder seeing Mungo pull a dull face and cover his ears and

humanoid lionesses watching giggled.

"*Teenagers, well I see you cannot be wise unless you have been burned, go and learn then,*" The Elder wishing he had said things differently, but pride had entered both sides and pride won.

"*Son,*" he sang but Mungo was only brown dust settling on a jungle track used by Fermanians collecting jungle produce.

"*Malachi is right, we mazarrats have peanut brains,*" The Elder and rent his fur so he looked mangy, he was anyway, he was an old wise mazarrat, and gritted his teeth as pulling out fur hurt.

Then threw brown dust on his head and face and could not see and choked so went to wash, and said, "Curse puberty and reproduction," and the cool water calmed him down, Mungo was only following natural ways, he was not to blame, "*the light will protect him, don't lack faith mazarrat,*" and at once became confident and knew the light would be victorious.

And danced and drew an audience of monkeys who, boring of his antics threw fruit at him.

"*Guess I am lucky I can still dance at my age,*" he resigned and left worrying what delights Mungo was finding.

Life was life; Mungo's path was already set before he was born; he just had to open the right doors.

And one delight was velvet furred, beautiful with green deep eyes and human shaped. For her ancestors injected with genes through a **shuttle gun,** so was more human than lion.

Six feet long, muscles, a human female except her mane and pawed hands from which came four fingers.

And this day behind rocks she teased Mungo by licking his body, inviting lion ways but at the last moment fled for in the fashion of females she wanted chased and caught.

And Mungo chased for the gold cups hiding her bosom glittered in the sun promising honey. For her father dotted on her giving gold rather than brass to wear.

And Mungo caught her but behaved as a lad, so, the white lioness became angry, "You are a boy," this white bitch leaving him but wanted him for, "He is more human than I, handsome and tanned, his skin hard bulging muscle, his brown hair long like a mane, it must have been all the running that tired him, I will flirt with other males till Mungo is no longer a boy but adult."

"What happened to me?" Mungo asked knowing he was different now and the air did not answer nor the flowers or singing nightingales, but he was now the man the white lioness wanted.

And Mungo never noticed Malachi watching and his right eye regenerated tissue and he knew it was Mungo for his rib was still about Mungo's neck; and the hunter felt pity for his enemy obviously knew nothing about girls.

So, Malachi returned to tell Lord Artebrates who strapped on armor and rode his triceratops from camp to kill Mungo and end what the scribes wrote.

"A waste of time my Lord, he will have flown," Malachi muttered.

"Remember who is your friend?" Artebrates chided as a mazarrat sang, *"Malachi was his friend,"* and "Dam mazarrat," Malachi answered.

And unknown to Malachi, "Lie with me Mungo," an ape with a human face and front lifting her plaid kilt for Mungo.

"You are not of my kind, go away," Mungo shouted up at the ape.

"Ha I am more your kind than that white lioness. Look Mungo I am easily satisfied, "and the brown ape became a hussy without embarrassment then dropped down beside Mungo.

"Leave me alone, your hands are covered in fruit purée, get off me ape," and he kicked her away.

"WA want to be spotless for that soulless lioness, do we? There's no difference between her and me, we are girls," and again the ape made herself an exhibition.

"You disgust me," Mungo shouted as his body responded for the ape had a pleasant human face and the figure were human and not ape when you looked closely.

And becoming shamed Mungo threw rotten fruit at her and both smelling Malachi's wee in the air retired, Mungo going up cliffs to sit in thought.

He was a lion not a man so what did the ape mean?

And why was his body different when he was about girls?

The mazarrat was right, he should dance more to the Oneness and let his eyes shine again. "My love for Sasha is pure," meaning the white lioness, "no other female will I have," he promised *a boy's promise.*

Anyway: "Hey lizards, want Mungo, he went to the cliffs," the ape shouted at Malachi who it recognized as the great hunter of mazarrat songs and lifted her green kilt to him. *"A woman's "scorn hell has no fury to match!"* The Elder careful as the singer was a woman mazarrat, so a friend of scorn and hell?

"Disgusting beasts kill it Malachi," Lord Artebrates.

So, Malachi unslung his bow saying, "Lord and Master it imitates us," for he no longer feared the future for the mazarrat songs had worked upon him; there was no point in worrying about what was predestined Malachi had become to believe.

"WA The ugly lizard doesn't want to play with beautiful me?" And she threw bananas she had been eating at him.

"Why me?" Malachi asked as his arrow sped towards her splitting leaves missing.

"WA the lizard drunk or something?" The ape shouted and threw hard nuts now with amazing accuracy that comes with arboreal living.

And Malachi quickly gave the order to move on before Artebrates commented on his bad aim; in fact, since he had started listening to the mazarrat songs he did not feel like skinning animals and blamed his recent eye injury for his mood swings.

"Don't worry Malachi, I am not Vinki, whether your aim is deliberately bad is your concern not mine, I kill when I shoot. And the jungle is full of lore, "Malachi was his friend," I understand, you must respect and not kill for the sake of killing, isn't that it?" Artebrates was indeed not Lord Vinki the Wonder Lord who was a dandy.

"It is the same with soldiering," Lord and Master Artebrates said nodding his head.

"The general is actually smiling, if only this moment was recorded," Malachi thought and a pack of armed mazarrats seeing Artebrates 'Stone Face' smile, went to work carving!

Yes, Stone Face knew soldering was killing for the sake of killing. Stone Face had at the Battle of Bayonet Push given orders that any man retreating, "be killed."

Three hundred House Carl's slain by arrows to keep the bayonet push home against human rebellious slaves, and the prisoners taken to Telephassa City and cooked, for its citizens to street party over the great victory.

Three thousand roasts in total.

Artebrates the killer even if he thought sparing a demented nymphomaniac gene altered ape funny.

And the last bearer got a melon thrown at the back of his head and knocked him senseless.

And the mazarrats were more interested in recording that smile and ruining Artebrates nickname for ever than throw things at him too.

Anyway: "Up there my Lord," Malachi pointing at Mungo and Artebrates took from his saddle a powder rifle and fired, and cross currents saved Mungo as the bullet creased his skull, so he rolled down the cliff and lay still, hidden from view by pines.

Half an hour later.

"He is gone, are you sure Malachi this is where he fell?" Artebrates.

"Yes, Lord and Master, see lion tracks," Malachi.

And the lion was Sasha who leaving Mungo wanted to see if he would follow her for, she was manipulating, heard the gun and saw Mungo fall.

"Oh no," her heart ached for she had love for Mungo.

"What did I do wrong? Is it because I am a lion man?"

Mungo asked beside Sasha.

"Ss," and Sasha licked his wounds clean.

And cliff mazarrats heard the jungle mazarrats sing and sang, *"The ape Moragana told Malachi where Mungo hid for Mungo loves Sasha not Moragana,"* and The Elder heard and feared, *"Is Mungo dead?"*

And Sasha hearing felt her heart swell triumphantly, Mungo loved her not that ape.

"What the lizard hunter miss?" The ape Moragana who had scrambled up the cliff.

"Moragana you are a witch and slut," Sasha growled and Moragana fearing she would be lion dinner climbed higher and now safe taunted, "Take this," and threw her plaid kilt at Sasha, "Remember our enjoyable time Mungo," and left laughing over her lie.

"What did the harlot who sleeps with lizard men mean?" Sasha.

"She is jealous of my love for you," Mungo and Sasha's love turned into possessiveness.

And time stops for no one under the Pteranodons flying the seas of New Uranus, wings thirteen feet across as they sought fish.

Lo for two years Mungo did not take The Elder's advice but ran with the pride, being lion one moment and man the next now brought him again to Moragana.

Moragana: "See I am bathed and walk like you Mungo. See the diamond the lizards make humans dig for. See, I smell good for I scented myself with lizard woman perfume they gave me, now I smell of flowers.

Don't you find me attractive now Mungo?"

And the water they had given her was water from their pet cats.

"I am wanting you more than flirting Sasha," and Mungo foolishly swung through vines with Moragana, and apes clapped and hooted, "We are above other beasts for a man thing loves Moragana," for Mungo displayed with Moragana on tree limbs thinking he was smart when he was foolish, and all because Sasha flirted for, she was young.

And below apes who were more human than ape stopped bashing a lizard man against a rock and looked at Mungo and Moragana and shamed, "We are glad we are not man thing and not ape for they are disgusting."

"If Sasha can flirt with lions so, can I," and Mungo threw fruit, monkey fashion at them.

And they shook their heads, so he roared, "I am Mungo of the Lions, and please myself and have no master than who I dance too," and laid a trap for himself with his fancy boasting for he no longer danced.

"*Sasha is lion, and it is time for her to have cubs after the fashion of her kind,*" The Elder said from behind the Y fork of a tree; *he got about.*

"You again?"

"*If not me then what makes you dance, you just ape with Moragana these days,*" The Elder replied tossing a banana skin through the leaves at Mungo.

"I am Mungo and will teach you too insult me."

"*Does your master tell you to kill me Mungo?*"

And Mungo froze the stick above The Elder's head, looking down into the ageing mazarrat.

"*To tell you to be a clown with Moragana in front of all the jungle? Even Sasha flirts in private but YOU? A man thing must twist what is natural and degrade all because you are a man thing,*" and Mungo shamed and swung away, his moon vanishing behind big leaves.

"What have you done tree rat?" Moragana shrieked wanting to bite chunks out of The Elder.

"*Stupid harlot,*" he and prodded his staff into her midriff so she toppled out of the Y and complained.

"*Blooming arthritis,*" as he followed Mungo ignoring Moragana's screams as a python not needing to reach where she and Mungo had been making a public display of themselves snapped her.

But Mungo heard and returned, and The Elder groaned wishing Moragana a lump in the snake's throat, but Mungo with one cut with a Fermanian stolen bronze sword, cut its head off so it landed on the jungle floor as dinner for ants below.

"I am in ape heaven for Mungo is here," Moragana swooned but Mungo resisted saying "I am Mungo of the Lions, but the jungle says I am Mungo of the monkeys, what have I made myself into, go away Moragana, it is Sasha I love."

And Moragana bit him and threw fruit at Mungo as he fled.

"Truly he had to come to her aid, or I would have been wrong," The Elder said and below Sasha looked up hoping Moragana would fall into her jaws.

"Go after Mungo of the Lions Sasha, look after your ward," The Elder advised and Sasha bounded off not understanding, only that she should replace Moragana finally.

And time stops for no one.

And by **fifteen Mungo now danced** again and happy now met Malachi, Vinki and Artebrates sailing down the yellow Yathan River on a raft.

"I will be mischief," and Mungo knocked a Fermanian rower into the river with a sling.

"It is he," Malachi pointing at the left bank.

"Let me at him and I will give you his head," Vinki boasted but ignored by Malachi and Artebrates who knew him as a coward.

And the rower eaten by a Mosassurus, a dolphin creature with toothed beak, legs, arms, and tail.

Artebrates saw death as common place, and the rower was lower than a solder whose job was to die for the glory of Telephassa, so felt no pity for the doomed man.

"Yes Lord," Malachi remembering the sixteen Fermanian heads something staked on the jungle road two days past, and all knew that something was Mungo.

"Mungo do you not feel bad that the oarsman is dead?" The Elder asked.

"Don't you ever leave me alone?"

"You are the Wild One."

"I am Mungo, and my enemy is below."

And Malachi seeing the gossip fired an arrow at The Elder, and Mungo with a stick hit the arrow saving The Elder.

"Yes, Mungo you are brave but lack wisdom."

"I am wise, I leave Moragana alone."

"Yes, by enjoying feeding enemy to the water demon. He is a slave, the dumbest of the Fermanian class system. If you must kill, then kill Vinki who is tender from too much sleep and food," The Elder instructed.

But Malachi's second arrow cut Mungo's right arm.

"You play coup my friend?" Vinki hissed and Malachi knew he was right, he could not get, *"Malachi was his friend"* out of his head.

"I am Mungo of the Lions," and he left The Elder who sang, *"not The Wild One."*

Malachi shivered; he had heard rumors from gossip of a mazarrat who was the wisest of all living things, and not the stupid peanut brain baboon he made himself out to be.

"Malachi was his friend," he heard mazarrats sing from the banks.

"Stupid animals."

"Beach the raft and let us hunt Mungo," Lord Artebrates deciding Malachi must choose whose friend he was?

Now Mungo waited till the Fermanians went into the jungle and then slipped from a tree and came to the raft.

And the jungle watched silently wanting to see what Mungo would do and this is what he did. Seeing pelts stacked on the raft and baskets stuffed with monkeys, mazarrats and meat salted ready as food on safari.

And Mungo cut the throat of the Fermanian guard whose back was too him, and the noise of the carcass splashing the river made the second guard turn and raise, his laser rifle.

And Mungo threw his sword into his neck.

"A bad throw is a quick throw," Mungo jumping over to the

gagging lizard man and pulled his sword out just before his enemy fell overboard.

"Elder that is my mercy, see here Vinci's perfumed sweetmeat, in the half open human female skull. I roar to what I dance too, I kill those who do this and free their captives," and broke open cages.

And The Elder walked on the beach with his staff. *"Yes, Mungo you were chosen to kill them but just remember mercy. Do not be lizard and kill babes, child, and mother. Just kill lizard warriors,"* and left.

"Any Fermanian can put on armor and cut with bronze sword. For that I kill them all," Mungo shouted into the foliage.

And the air filled with ape and monkey tongue as Mungo invited his friends to come for gifts.

And hated The Elder for being right and because he had called out his own future, he had acknowledged his mission and Mungo laughed, his eyes full of light and went into the jungle brushing himself against rhododendron flowers to hide the scent of lion that emitted from him.

Then met Sasha up stream and seeing her bathe in a rock pool surrounded by pink water lilies lust overtook Mungo.

"Sasha it is me, don't be alarmed," Mungo whispered sliding off a purple flower into the water.

"Alone are we Mungo?"

"I had the lizard hunting me, but I am smart and now he is lost in the jungle," Mungo boasted reaching out hands to paw a half-submerged Sasha.

And the light faded within Mungo.

"Bring me lizard gold Mungo and you can touch me when you want handsome hunter," Sasha purred.

"Let me touch first," Mungo lusted.

Now the ape Moragana had followed and sat on a giant red rose watching filled with envy.

"He is touching her; she is a prostitute who utters terrible things not fit for a baby to hear. I will punish them both for their foolishness," and Moragana sought Malachi to do her punishing, hoping he did skin Sasha, so she could sneak into his camp and lie on her skin. As for Mungo she hoped Malachi did beat him good to teach him not to cheat on Moragana the ape woman thing.

Eventually: "Hey lizard man makes me a promise and I will tell you where Mungo is?" Moragana shouted down at Malachi.

"Tell me what I must promise first?" Malachi back.

"Invite me to supper and pick fleas from my back to make Mungo jealous," the ape.

Now Malachi saw the woman ape thing was pleasant to look at since her genes mixed with human, and she did not look like the other apes and monkeys, for she was shapely but her ape traits shown for she walked like a chimp.

Also cultured for she seemed bathed and adorned in precious amulets.

"OK tell me where I can find Mungo and in return come to my green tent tonight," and Moragana told Malachi.

But Malachi had been careful not to promise anything but for the ape to come to his green tent.

"Hey lizard man, want to know something else? Mungo killed the guards on the raft and freed the cages," and Moragana enjoyed this bit of devilry for it affected the lizard man something for he went into a rage.

"Don't miss this time Malachi or your scales will be cut off," Artebrates warned, and Malachi knew thirty scales off by an executioner's dagger: the soldier's price of failing.

And just for an instant Malachi wished he were free like Mungo away from the cruel Fermanian society that was class ridden, and full of Vinki's and Artebrates needing destroyed.

And while Mungo flirted with Sasha growling as a male lion man thing, for he knew no other society, Malachi tracked him down using two lions Abel and Eve reared as trackers from cubs stolen from a black lion-bitch long ago.

"So, man thing I enjoyed Vinki's discomfort as his stolen women clothes went past on the legs of Moragana the ape, but the joke's over," Malachi whispered and fired an arrow.

"Duck Mungo," a mazarrat sang.

"Blooming heck," Malachi groaned seeing thirty scales go.

But the arrow sunk into Mungo's right shoulder, and he growled, and Sasha left the pool for she had quiver and bow herself and Moragana thinking Mungo killed, screamed in horror.

And the jungle came alive with mazarrat songs, and The Elder hurried to find Mungo.

So, Malachi let lose arrows as mazarrats threw nuts at him as the lions Abel and Eve waited to retrieve Mungo's corpse from the pool.

"Stupid mazarrats," Malachi.

And his three-foot arrows sank between tadpoles and Mungo holding his breath swam towards Malachi and each time he surfaced an arrow fell beside him and nuts bounced off Malachi.

And Malachi imagined the executioner, sweated fear, and hit Mungo's right ear for Moragana was now throwing rocks, not nuts and Sasha was sending her own arrows at Malachi too, so obviously his aim was bad.

"Blooming hell," Malachi cursed stumbling behind thorny shrubs.

Then Mungo caught a water snake and threw it at Malachi and his hunting lions.

"Bad boy," Malachi swore jumping into the pool to be away from the poisonous reptile as his two hunting lions clawed up a rhododendron tree for safety.

But mazarrats at the top poked sticks into their eyes to get them down where there was hissing going on below.

Going on about Lord Artebrates feet who was dancing here and there to avoid the snake's strikes.

Now laughing Mungo slashed Malachi's belly and cut sixteen scales from him. Then kicked Malachi somewhere for a joke and swam away.

Leaving Malachi to surface in a pool of his own and Mungo's blood.

It was a good thing he did surface and just in time to see a sixteen-foot snake enter the pool. Just as a watermelon thrown by a mazarrats hit his face disintegrating.

"Hell, fire and damnation," Malachi swore swimming away backstroke to keep an eye on the water Taipan, an unbelievably bad snake and had a memory like an elephant for it never forgot who annoyed it.

And Mungo escaped riding Sasha back to her father's pride met Moragana, before the jungle became red grass plains.

"I saved you Mungo, come away and give me babes as reward," Moragana pleaded without any pride, and she was an ape who had travelled through the treetops to meet him.

"Cannot you get it through your thick skull I am Sasha's, and she will be my first female of my harem and I don't want a harem anyway, I just want Sasha," Mungo moaned much in love, "in fact I don't want this Wild One thing the mazarrats sing about as I don't understand, so go away Moragana."

"I told Malachi where you were, I will again till you swell me with man thing babes that will be beautiful man things like you are," the ape hotly.

"You are a monkey not an ape," Sasha insulting for monkeys was known for their foolishness while apes were not.

"Malachi promised to be mine tonight," and Moragana swung away on vines believing her lie.

"We must stop her as Malachi will put her in the Pot Market," Mungo pained at the ape's future plain to see.

"We can free her later, being ready for the pot will teach her some manners, any way let me help you," which was just an excuse to cuddle up to Mungo and get him red in the face and because he had said those nice things about her, she forgot about her promise to lie with a black lion so Mungo's wound was seen to; stuffing it with antiseptic moss and putting ants on it to bite it close. *Yes, it hurt but, he could not show pain in front of Sasha.*

Later:

"The man thing, I will eat first and belch then that stupid

lioness," Red Hide the red lion who had been sitting on a wooden tree stump shaped to resemble a throne upon seeing Mungo.

"Mungo has triumphed over Malachi again; he does lions proud, and I claim the protection of the pride for him," Sasha growled, and Red Hide saw she loved Mungo and he, Red Hide was wrath so, beat her.

And other lions pulled him off, those lions that had agreed with Sasha.

"What is this, does Mungo claim my throne as well?" Red Hide prophesied.

"Mungo is leaving," and he walked away painfully.

"Man thing," Red Hide cursed, and his companions repeated his words.

"Wait," Sasha and ran after Mungo.

"I will banish you," Red Hide and did not specify whom? "Are you The Wild One?" He with an afterthought afraid for he had heard mazarrats sing.

As for Moragana she went to Malachi's green tent that night.

"Malachi it is I Moragana come for my reward and your promise," she called from a rhododendron tree.

Now Malachi was sore and confined to his hummock for lizards slept on them for their tails to hang free and he thought, "That ape has some cheek," and summoned Artebrates to ask him to catch the ape who was a prostitute, with no brains. And Artebrates was with the executioner when asked for he was saying, "Malachi is friend I hope, so make sure with this gold coin your dagger is sharp and clean when you take thirty scales from his back."

"Surely come to me Moragana and make Mungo jealous," Malachi called out to the ape.

And Moragana came down from her tree knowing Malachi was a man of his word.

And he had promised her nothing.

"Here drink the stuff Fermanians are made off and be

strong and brave and fearless like us," and she wanting to copy those with intelligence allowed Malachi easily to get her drunk.

"Is this the human ape that mimics her betters?" Lord Artebrates entering the green tent.

"Another lizard wanting me?" Moragana foolishly.

"Give her to the slaves," Artebrates ordered, and 'House Carls' carried Moragana the nymphomaniac human ape on a pole to where the slaves ate, and they knew of her and spoke aloud, "Thank you Lord Artebrates and Master for your kindness," and Artebrates hearing said to Malachi, "it does no harm to spoil the poor."

And the poor in their minds cursed Artebrates for sending them Moragana and not a real human woman: and knew Artebrates and his kind saw slaves as monkeys or worse, rodent scum.

And Malachi did not break his promise, he had told Moragana JUST to come to his green tent so was still a man of his word.

And Moragana got what she wanted, men, the foolish drunken ape.

*

Cathbadh

Cathbadh allowed The Mighty One Carmen to wipe her sandals on his red pig tailed head.

His audience was over and again rebuffed over the approaching star ship.

"It is Fermanian, slaves existed before I was born," she told him. What could he do? To argue his point now would be dangerous as Lord Vinki and his Wonder Lords who formed the Modernist Party held favor, were present.

And Vinki meant to stay influential as Cathbadh knew he was fleecing everyone of what they owned.

"Now, if the scribes tell true The Wild One will bring judgement upon us, then we better get rich quick," Cathbadh quoted Vinki sourly as he walked out of Carmen's rose garden.

"WA let me die Cathbadh," a lizard man begged nailed to a wind wheel turning slowly in the summer breeze.

But Cathbadh ignored, the man was a fool to get drunk and demand Prince Annunaki's son be emperor.

He deserved what he got.

"I had better play a middle game," Cathbadh to himself, only Artebrates whom the army followed can rid Telephassa of Carmen and he is loyal to her; but change was coming, and it would slap those unprepared. Humans in a star ship and if The Wild One was true, judgement also? But Artebrates had changed by calling Malachi friend instead of servant, and that was as far as any of the established ruling elite would concede to change.

"Foolish Carmen, the civil war would continue," Cathbadh.

And it took the safari forty nights to get back to landscaped plains where Fermanians watched humans plough soil with wooden yolks, and all the time Artebrates drank with friend Malachi who thought, "How can he be jovial with me, soon the executioner will come, is he so high and mighty he sees me as a toy to break at will?"

And when Artebrates reached the first military fort he gave instructions for Malachi to have thirty scales removed as punishment.

Nearby a Fermanian who had one hundred scales taken so had run out of back scales, so flesh taken, so died on his wheel, now hummed to the sound of insects.

"His crime?" Malachi asked the executioner.

"He spared human children, when their camp was raided but Artebrates had ordered 'kill,'"
and Malachi's soul cried in disbelief, and gasped when the first scale flew off him and a mazarrat sang, *"Malachi was his friend."*

Lord Artebrates hearing came to the executioner and said to both; "A reminder Malachi who are your friends, executioner make those fifty scales," and at that moment Artebrates hated all that was lizard for Malachi he really did like, but an example needed seen.

And Moragana fainted as soldiers placed bets if Malachi would survive.

And time waits for no one while crane toads hunt frogs in the radioactive rain of New Uranus.

And that was the first time Mungo slept with Sasha the beautiful lion woman. For he saw himself as a lion man and for the next six months did not dance naked to the sky and become one with the Oneness, for he was content to be with flesh.

Dreaming of cubs and not serving the Oneness that made his eyes shine.

And Sasha was more lioness than Mungo, so she was not faithful and loved watching young males fighting for her.

You see her lion genes were too strong and overrode her human side. For she thought, the strongest will give me strong cubs," and momentarily forgot Mungo till he found them all, and he would shout "Let me challenge the winner for I am the strongest here."

"You are man thing and will be eaten, now come and comb my fur like no other lion can for you have five fingers, then maybe I will be kind to you," and the foolish man would eagerly comb and forget The Elder and the ways of Light.

But Mungo was man so suffered from guilt and often told the mazarrats this during this six-month period when Mungo sought the ways of flesh than spirit.

"Pray tell us your guilt Mungo," a small mazarrat would prompt.

"My guilt is I did not seek Moragana the ape human female for now she is in Telephassa a pet in a lizard brothel.

"Why did you fail to free her as you wished?"

"I had to wait for my wounds to heal," Mungo replied lying and mazarrats sang far and wide, *"The shame is Malachi's."*

"Mazarrat dogs," was Malachi's angry reply and caught handfuls and beat them good to stop scribes hearing them, but mazarrats were in thousands, so failed. And the scribes of Telephassa made Malachi out to be a liar and cheat, an unworthy lizard man who broke his promise to Moragana.

B *"Well, they needed trash to sell, and it sold."* And the mazarrat sang in high notes.

Also, "And Mungo tried to free Moragana but for his wounds," while Malachi tore hair from his mane and drank shouting often, "Mungo I should have killed and hate all mazarrats," over his drink very intoxicated.

And lizard men did not feel sorry but laughed at the drunk behind his back, and when they got drunk, laughed in his face.

And since the lizard law prohibited Malachi regenerating new scales for six months to remind him and others of their place, he decided to hell with it and hired a surgeon to insert bronze scales and hired a shoe shiner to rub them up to catch the lavender sun's rays.

Also, The Elder feeling his age used this as an excuse not to visit Mungo saying, *"Mungo needed time to think for himself."*

"He is man thing and can reason," he told younger mazarrats come to learn how to carve history into tree barks.

And time waits for no one as a Star Ship approached New Uranus and at **sixteen Mungo**

courted white Sasha seriously for she was ready for his cubs, for he had not seen his own human female kind really.

Cathbadh

Cathbadh closed his eyes and extended his mind out to the star ship bridge. "Captain Clinton we have woken up too soon, it will be another forty years before we reach New Uranus," Cathbadh heard and groaned.

"There is a mental probe, and it is not human," a ship's computer and Cathbadh was amazed it could detect him.

"Can you get a hold on it and ask about the human colonists?" Captain John Clinton but Cathbadh broke contact.

Cathbadh, you see had the ability to cast his mind, and kept it a secret which helped him survive since Vinki sought continually to destroy him, fearing he might influence Carmen.

And that day Cathbadh sold his pork belly company to Vinki, a spaceship was coming; and with the money he bought diamonds and gems which were small and not bulky like gold bars; war was coming in a big way and Fermanian society was about to collapse.

Chapter 2 Leah

And his mother forgot Mungo was man thing and was glad he wanted a lion bride but afraid he had chosen Sasha, King Red Hide's daughter which meant trouble.

For there was a saying, "Don't go looking for trouble and trouble won't come knocking at your door."

"I have brought you a rabbit and a rose," Mungo at a water hole offering the white lioness Sasha both and she was pleasing in his eyes with gold cups and slit ruby satin kilt and flowers in her combed flowing blond mane and she played with a scent bottle, taken from a Fermanian unfortunate woman, unfortunate as she ended her life *in a belly.*
And Sasha had put blue powder on her eye's lashes.
And in her lair, Fermanian chests of silks and gems, presents from Red Hide a dotting father.
"The meat I will eat but the flower what do I do with it?" Sasha accepting the hare while crumpling the small rose for she had gone the way of a lioness and been with four lions that day so was not in the mood for Mungo romantically.
And Sasha made fun of Moragana the ape woman thing "Mungo's girlfriend?"
"I am Mungo and don't need to fight over something I love but do you love me?"
He asked, "I will go away and find my own kind for you toy with me always, and that is cruel. *His love was as a crushed rose, poor boy. It is mazarrats adding the italics, just to let you be aware.*"
Now carelessly Sasha responded, "Think I care?" And she felt fear in her heart in case he did leave for good.
"All you want is me to comb your fur," and Mungo combed, and she purred lying in a provocative fashion for she wanted attention for the female had awoken in her.
And she wanted Mungo to comb her body, but he did

something new, he massaged instead, and she wondered where a man thing got the wisdom to think up such delights?

But at that moment a young black lion roared a challenge to Mungo, and Sasha became annoyed that Mungo had stopped what he was doing and was roaring back.

Then two more lions appeared both wanting to go away with Sasha in the fashion of lion culture.

"Will you fight them all for me?"

"Yes," Mungo and attacked and knew he was being foolhardy as to fight one lion was dangerous but three was looking for trouble, *well suicide.*

Now what Mungo promised now he told The Elder later who then had great trouble carving a promise as hieroglyphic drawing?

Mungo's promise: *"Too you, who have no name that makes me dance, make me* strong and I will obey. As a sign between you and me I will not cut my hair.

So, Mungo filled with strength from an inner glow and beside him a dinosaur bone and he picked it up.

"Leave Mungo with me for you soothes me," Sasha told the lions who were trying their best to maul Mungo and themselves, to the victor the spoils.

As she ignored so left saying, "You bore me," and the lions seeing her depart had nothing to fight over.

And Mungo took to the trees and followed Sasha leaving the others to quarrel over something new to see who was the mightiest amongst them.

And Mungo caught Sasha up and she pitied him seeing claw slashes dripping blood so, licked them clean and Mungo lusted, *if he had been older, he did be ill.*

And something inside him had changed when the inner light had made him strong, "Way a ha, what am I doing, I am a man," he cried and looked at her and no longer saw her desirable but as lion creature akin to a were creature, but worse for Sasha's had a developed mind so as a hideous monster.

"Run Mungo run," A mazarrat sang and soon all these

talkative creatures singing this advice.

And Mungo ran away from Sasha knowing she was different and, "for her I would have killed those lions and that would have been wrong."

"Mungo now knows different," those arboreal scribes sang at once from rhododendron trees.

"Man, thing if you ever want to be king of the lions you must prove yourself a great giver of cubs," Sasha called out to Mungo for she was following, "and I know you must kill my father in battle and make a broth out of him and drink from it to get his strength and virility. And since I will be your first wife you must provide me with lesser wives to be my servants."

"She is right; I want to be king of the lions for I want things in life. I have I have," but there was no word in lion talk for ambition, so said, "Good things," which to lions was harem, cubs, and good hunting.

And Mungo went back to Sasha and lay with her and gave her life through shuttle genes.

"Moragana was no competition, she was ape harlot and now Fermanian whore," mazarrats sang; *also, Sasha was blonde, gentlemen prefer, but with mungo she could have been red head, rainbow maned, he was a boy still with a one-track mind.*

"Flowers are for man thing women," and Mungo wheeled recognizing the voice of Red Hide and saw two companions circling him and Sasha.

So, Mungo picked up his bronze spear and faced Red Hide who climbed a Rhododendron tree.

And then next Mungo knew was the brown companion of Red Hide had dropped on top of him.

But Mungo pushed up with spear through the flesh that joins leg to body and twisted. And Red Hide made the mistake of jumping at Mungo instead of just biting and Mungo stabbed his pink nose and Red Hide howled away to the water. Then a claw raked Mungo's bottom and he turned to stab a brown companion in its right eye.

"Yak yam help," Red Hide called from the water as he fought a crocodile, and the last companion went to his aid.

Of Mungo the brown companion ran with his spear till exhaustion claimed. As for Sasha the three other lions who had fought Mungo gave her gold amulets taken from Fermanian women they had eaten and Sasha who thought of Mungo wished him back with gold for her, to fight off these three lions and then comb and massage her limbs.

And Red Hide, "I will never call her daughter for she has brought the Wild One to me and death."

But he was a doting father? The mazarrats understood such family matters.

"Mungo has blinded and killed for a woman," a mazarrat sang shrilly and The Elder said, *"What do I do with that cub?"*

And at once logic entered him, "He is man," and The Elder knew man never obeyed nature's laws. You could get apes like Moragana obeying as the songs said she danced in frilly pinks on tables for if she would not, prodded with lizards' swords: and would dance without the prodding for she had been born that way and had her own path to follow.

"She has little choice," The Elder rubbing his greying beard, and that is the difference between man and beast, choice."

But mazarrats choose to eat the grub or sleep, a mazarrat somewhere.

And a wind blew and the mazarrat shivered and saw, sniffed, felt, and touched by unseen hands and knew that all are born with doors to open, all predetermined, all different choices so all do indeed have choice through a door.

Now as Mungo slept exhausted, he dreamed blackness and himself speaking, "I want a female to call my own, not Sasha for she is lion, a female like me, man thing but woman thing with bosoms to touch and the other bit to give me real man thing cubs.

Playing with that ape Moragana taught me something as she looks like me, that it was wrong currently in Oneness to play with others that are not like me.

Illustration: A singing mazarrat, the gossips of the planet.

Sasha, I love dearly but will push that love behind me for Sasha flirts with any powerful lion who lets his mane out like a kite in the wind.

Especially if the lion has lizard meat and gold for her. *Blame the dotting father.*

And how will I know the cubs are mine? Am I to stay there all day combing her, spying on her?"

Then light entered darkness as a still voice, "I will give you what you want." And Mungo awoke not to find his mother helping him but a girl with a hunchback covered in scales.

"Lie still slave," the lizard commanded but Mungo did not understand as he was too interested at looking at the girl.

Can I own him please, I don't have a slave, please?" The girl pleaded and blushed as Mungo stared for it made her conscious of her beauty," *yes, a girl all right"* the mazarrat singer accompaniment.

And Mungo found by reed ropes bound and his left sole hurt as it burned.

"Your name is already on his foot," the hunch back answered, and the girl smiled and offered Mungo a grub which he refused but instead sniffed her lion fashion filling himself with her scent and she laughed.

"Humans don't know what's good for them," the

hunchback sitting back admiring his work eating the offered grub after taking the fancy wrapping paper off.

"You better get used to it, full of protein and fresh from a grub farm," and he reached into a pouch and stuck one in Mungo's mouth and laughed when Mungo spat it out.

After brushing dust off the wrappers, the hunchback ate them all up.

As for Mungo he looked at the black stitches in his fight wounds and grunted satisfaction for the lizard man was a good sewer; *never felt a thing, doped to the gills.*

But at that moment Ono came and the hunchback holding the girl's left hand jumped into a machine hovering over Mungo.

"I must have one and fly also," Mungo promised and himself, the girl.

"Always man things dream," a whisper.

Anyway: "The black lion has taken the man thing into the trees," the girl using hand signs prodding the hunchback lizard for attention.

"I will ask your master and Lord Artebrates for a slave for you. I am sure he will agree, he likes you and treats you as a daughter and not tissue numbers," the lizard man replied and flew the shiny yellow machine away.

And the speechless girl investigated the jungle feeling sorry for the slave that no Jungle monsters ate doubt, nothing deserved that, and he was a handsome man thing wasted at that. *Yes, it was girl thought, poor Mungo.* **And The Elder took note he had coemption, for his words were not in italics.**

This was the first time Leah met Mungo and her fears for his fate were false as she learned later while watching the hunchback speak to Malachi his friend in Telephassa City.

"That was Mungo and you had him tied?" Malachi agitated and the girl when left sought the privacy of her chambers and read all her papyrus pulp fiction books written by scribes on Mungo and dreamed strange fantasies such as Mungo capturing her and flirting with her. *Whisking her across the red dunes to his lair, littered with skulls and bones, from his meals.*

And Malachi's agitation passed to the hunchback who, returned to his laboratories deep in Lord Artebrates castle.

"I have much work to do, The Wild One exists, judgement is coming," and he with latex gloves with scalpel slit open a conscious human female and removed things.

A man thing slave looked at him fearfully as the hunchback pushed deep into his body via an abdominal cut.

"Slaves don't feel pain, they are like lobsters, just drop them into a pot of boiling hot water to get the perfect taste," the hunchback and did not finish sewing the wound closed but sat down. Since making the speechless girl, he was concluding humans did feel pain, and Fermanians did not want to accept this so could still whip human slaves unrestrained; to make them work harder.

Also, dishes demanded the human flesh thrown into a cauldron of boiling water to keep the porky taste fresh and succulent, *just like a lobster.*

"I must hurry," he and closed the wound, next he would induce self-fertilization.

TIME WAS RUNNING OUT, the first to transfer such knowledge into Fermanians would be a hero, one sexed, a savior of a dying race poisoned by radioactivity.

More babies born, more warriors for Telephassa to extend its borders.

Somehow the hunchback knew with The Wild One here, it did not matter, TIME HAD RUN OUT.

"All pulp trash made by scribes seeking gold coins," he spat. **AND TIME DOESN'T STOP** on New Uranus as a crocodile crept up a beach and gobbled up a monkey stupid enough to drink there and not from a pool in a Y trunk in a tree. *The wind had carried loose tobacco into the Y trunk, so the water was bitter. The tobacco was also halogenic but poor monkey reached Dream World the brutal way.*

And Mungo six months later saw the flying machine hover land on the jungle.

"Malachi can you get that rare monkey out of the trap?" The hunchback asked pointing up a rhododendron tree.

"Watch me," and Malachi gave the hunchback his laser rifle and climbed.

Now Mungo was coming on the back of an ape for the primate could swing faster on vines for these beasts were his friends and he came upon Malachi who bitten by the monkey was cursing and doing his best to lower the trap down.

And Mungo put a finger to his lips for the ape to be silent as he hurriedly made noose out of a vine and after he did this went above Malachi.

And the girl next to the hunchback saw him but was unable to utter any warning for she was dumb.

"What have I caught?" Mungo in lion tongue.

"Catarrh," Malachi answered as Mungo pulled the vine lasso, secured it about a branch, and dropped as the hunchback below let lose white laser that felled violet flowers, sending feeding bees angrily into the air that returned to sting the cause of their discomfort.

Oh, bloody hell," the hunchback getting stung heaps.

And Mungo hid behind Malachi and the hunchback stopped firing in case he killed Malachi for his aim was bad as he had come out in hives from the stings.

And Mungo fascinated by the girl moved close to the choking Malachi and edged him off the branch, so his feet hit the hunchback's face and his body stopped there jerking.

Now the girl drew a little dagger with intention to cut Malachi down and in her efforts made the lasso tighter, and Malachi went blue.

And Mungo watched as his primate friends freed the monkey Malachi had trapped.

"Is he your friend?" Mungo asked the girl who ignored, and she senses Malachi doomed, went for the laser rifle to cut the vine above his head.

"No," Mungo dropping and snatching the rifle and with it butted the rising hunchback in the back.

"Oh, bloody hell," the hunchback gasped.

So, after coughing and grunting the hunchback asked, "Why me Why me?" And Mungo stood on the little man's chest with his left foot as he had seen Vinki and
Artebrates do for photographs.

And the girl, "Bully," but the words were silent, and she could kick so in the end Mungo lifted her up so she could touch the lasso and then handed her his knife.

She could have killed Mungo but cut the lasso, so Malachi dropped heavily dragging all down upon the hunchback who pleaded "Please," which was an atonement to get off him as he was asphyxiating from the crush; *blue also, it was catching.*

And did not know about Mungo's dream and Mungo believed the girl had been given him by the Oneness he danced to.

And Mungo laughed for he was not mature since he did not socialize with humans and laughed as he tripped the girl up and laughed when he brought his clenched fist down upon Malachi's rising head, so Malachi seeing stars fell back on the hunchback, whose limbs seen now.

"Please," the hunch back under Malachi.

Then the girl managed to stand, and Mungo stopped laughing for she was indeed beautiful. Indeed, she was the female after his own kind that he longed for as well as that yellow flying machine, *for he was still a boy.*

And her hands spoke for her, "What are you staring at baboon?" And with Mungo's own knife slashed at him and if Mungo had not sucked in his belly, well, but he did and held her knife hand and kissed her, so she bit him.

This was not in his dream and spat out blood for his tongue was now sore.

"I really like your green eyes," he told her taking his knife back.

And she full of pride arched back her head so Mungo could dispatch her quickly and cleanly and since she had seen Mungo before, touched by his jungle beauty so knew he stared at her, he was not going to harm her, *"Girls know these sort of things"* a *mazarrat sang advice to the know all Mungo.*

She also expected Mungo to ravish her for she was a civilized person.

And Mungo touched her soft skin and was amazed it was unbelievably soft scales but still was flesh like his.

And Leah still full of Fermanian imperialism stood in her arrogant pose, found his rough hands gentle and now felt really insulted Mungo was examining her as if she was a human slave. But under her mind a part of her tingled at his touch for this was The Wild One; *"What would he do next?"* These mazarrat singers can be boring.

But Mungo only knew he was a lion man thing and wanted to know if this girl was the same as Sasha.

And Mungo smirked and Leah wanted to hit him and did for she knew she would get away with it and was testing Mungo to see if he would hit her back and had judged him wrongly.

And being a lion man thing did what he knew male lions did, he scented so covered Malachi and the hunchback in hot pee.

And the girl was shocked, and because he did not look like a beast, well he did in a way, for he had long brown hair fashioned as a lion's mane and was dirty looking saw him first as pervert or idiot or a man without Fermanian manners or civilization that was nearer the truth.

"Little dung head," Mungo heard the hunchback who cocked the laser rifle so Mungo quickly cut the cups from Leah's chest and fled into the bush with them as a souvenir and a laser light-streaked fern leaves and cut a giant red and white toadstool in half and singed tree bark beside him, *but he had a souvenir.*

And civilized Malachi had a good look.

Mungo also did not see The Elder shake his head and say, *"That is no way to treat the wife."* **Cathbadh**

"My grandfather once told me you had royal blood in you

from King Sess?" Artebrates.

"He was wrong," Cathbadh lied, "why should he have told you that?"

"Because he was fed up being ruled by a Mighty One which always has to be a woman," Artebrates investigating cautiously.

"I heard you hung the last of Prince Annunaki's males' cousins?" Cathbadh.

Illustration: Such an idyllic setting but genes to change you lurked nearby.

"Yes, just leaves female lineage alive, but we will get them. Carman doesn't want a challenge to her son Hebat when it is time to become Emperor," and Artebrates smirked at Cathbadh who did not show his shiver.

And Artebrates knew Sess had died during the Atomic War and since then there had been only female Mighty Ones.

"There is no female heir," Artebrates.

Before that no one wanted a male on the Rose Throne of Telephassa as King Sess started the Atomic War with the humans, blamed him for failing to exterminate them and the war had cut off contact with their home planet.

"No one knows where we come from?" Cathbadh.

"I come from Telephassa," Artebrates answered.

"Why don't you make yourself emperor as people want a male Mighty One these days for the times are troubled?"

Cathbadh asked.

"Vinki and his Modernists have got changes, the civil war is ending, I can now call Malachi friend and see me as the equal of noble women of the court, why get hung for nothing? Besides that, is why Carman keeps her son Hebat alive, an appeasement to defuse the situation for he is her puppet," Artebrates but Cathbadh saw by his face Artebrates had thought about it and was doing so again.

"There will never be total change as long as Carman continues her reign and the human wars," and Cathbadh stood up, "a ship is coming, it is not Fermanian, we must have peace with the humans now before that ship arrives and its weaponry exterminates us. Artebrates you as emperor could make that peace, you must
Artebrates."

And Artebrates got up too and just before he shut the door leaving said, "You have served me well Cathbadh making war engines and Leah from your vats and since there isn't no mazarrats about we will pretend we never had this little talk, goodbye friend."

Cathbadh showed no fear, Artebrates would never talk, and Cathbadh had made Leah and knew whose lineage she sprung from; it was their little secret.

"Ha, ha, ha what a jolly joke, human star ships," Artebrates chuckled to shake of Cathbadh's prophecy of doom.

And behind a crack in a wall a mazarrat heard everything and soon told another
mazarrat and eventually The Elder heard, "*Right gossips.*"

Chapter 3 Lessons

"Rapist, dung head, barbarian, bully, a sad day when he was sired," the hunchback comforting Leah in the flyer leaving Mungo behind.

"I should have killed him long ago," Malachi grunted rubbing his skull, "the next time I will hang him from a tree and, cut him into pieces and make him eat them," *for Malachi smelled of his friends pee."*

And only Leah with silent lips understood Mungo was none of these, he was a curious handsome boy needing lessons on decency that was all, "A*nd she knew he liked her, a lot, girls know these things,"* has this mazarrat a name?

Besides all he had done was look and there wasn't anything wrong with men having improper thoughts, they did all the time, and she, used to manly ways; no doubt they had these thoughts when they slept and, even before they were born? *Especially a handsome boy who fancied her,"* my name is mazarrat.

"You had better bathe when we get back, your Lord and Master will want his Number One Comforter tonight, and he wants the snake dance, and don't worry about the python, it's well fed this time," the hunchback reassured Leah.

" On the fool that forgot to feed it, so dance well child, Artebrates is honoring Wonder Lord Vinki's birthday," Malachi and Leah shivered, she didn't like Vinki who was cruel, rough, and made her do perverse acts.

"And what is unnatural anymore?" She asked silently and

both lizard men seeing her Lips move, read her thoughts, felt pity for an instant, she was Leah, a Comforter, and it was her job to please by giving.

And as Mungo ran through the ferns, he roared and Leah, looked down from the flying machine and, saw him break cover often and wondered if he was truly The Wild One, the deliverer of slaves and he was? *"Deliver me also for I am a slave too,"* this mazarrat sang for her.

And Mungo becoming frustrated thought of going to visit Sasha but changed his mind, she had a litter of cubs, and they were not his.

Instead, excited over meeting the wonderful girl thing again, he danced to what sang in his heart, Sasha besides was a long way off, *and could not hear.*

"He is insane," Malachi observed high above heading for Telephassa City.

And Mungo stopped leaping in mid-air and felt guilt for he still loved Sasha and knew he had thought wrong of her, she was lion thing and he a man thing, with more wisdom than beast so, should know better.

"A roar of pain, maybe a yellow cobra lurking in the grass, let's see if he is dead," the hunchback taking the image analyzer from Leah.

And saw Mungo running for Sasha.

"Your experiments going well?" Malachi asked.

"One successful self-fertilization," the hunchback looking at Mungo.

Then looked at the girl, she was to be the next guinea pig.

And Leah smiled a beautiful innocent smile back.

"I cannot," the hunchback and kept looking over the side, Leah was like a child to him, been associating too long with her, become a friend, a parent?

"Artebrates would never allow it, she's his favorite," Malachi lied thinking he was protective.

Anything that could stop the infertile rate amongst their kind rising were welcome experiments.

And was Vinki's idea to use Leah, a perversion if any; Leah was from the vats, and was as close to a Fermanian lizard, so to experiment on would not risk any lizard folk: she was expendable.

"It's dangerous, hormones and heart failure, go blame the makers of the fast reactors, it's their fault our race has a low fertility rate, blame King Sess and his war.

What about you Malachi? Want to father your own child? Volunteer to replace Leah, it would be like cloning yourself, as if you were ensuring your own survival after death, in another body," the hunchback inquisitively.

"I am Malachi and there is nothing wrong with me, and many an Inn Keeper's wenches has born me eggs that hatched fine young lizards.

"Well, I am just an ugly hunchback so don't know," the hunchback jealousy.

And over the next four years' **time did not stop** for Mungo as cocoons became butterflies and, Mungo had encounters with Fermanian lizard men and his own kind, so was known by his roar and during this time he caught a Fermanian and kept him prisoner for four months to learn their tongue and it was Malachi.

And then the slaves revolted and crushed and nailed in the forest for the putrefying stench made Fermanians afraid to breath in the cities and Appian Ways.

And round ups of humans, held by Cities like Telephassa throughout New Uranus, to replace the nailed ones.

And the power with no name knew Mungo, needed to save humanity.

And the other he caught with Malachi was Leah, the speechless girl, and her captivity was not as long, only four weeks for she escaped, and it was Mungo's fault for he adored her. Leaving Malachi behind to rot.

It went so, "I have given you much freedom to win your heart, many rabbits to eat, and made you a sleeping bed on rhododendrons safe from creepy crawlies, and yet you refuse to speak," just before she escaped.

Now Malachi a wise hunter had forbidden Leah to let Mungo know she was dumb, and her status in life.

"Only his interest in you keeps us alive," he instructed her so, did not teach Mungo the word Comforter.

"He worships the cups he stole from you in the past," and Leah thought Mungo was no different from Vinki until she saw Mungo revered them as relics because they were hers; something special to remind him of her.

"Vinki can go and wash after being with me, and he will always be dirty for his mind and spirit is unclean," Leah silently.

And she remembered she had not wanted the job Comforter, but she was a product of the vats, and a Comforter was a step up the social ladder, and if she refused then back to the vats? She understood FEAR and was a sensible girl.

And time stops for no one as rats sneak into granaries and Leah began to enjoy her work, it brought rewards as Artebrates Number One. He dotted on her and was kind, but she hated it when he offered her out to his friends, such as Vinki.

She saw Artebrates an unofficial husband which she would never accept.

"Play the role of chaste virgin for if he ever realizes you are a Noble's bed Companion, he will treat you as Vinki does and cut my throat to boot," Malachi advised.

And Leah silently "So what, Mungo is just another man and more moral than her owners who say they have morals, and Mungo none, but they are wrong," "*And only her spirit heard her and communed with the Oneness about her, for being downtrodden and she believed there must be more to life? And the Oneness that is the Universal Spirit heard her, and touched her spirit and she was silent, listening to unspoken words for the Spirit communicates by spirit*", The Elder as knew this was too much for the singer to understand, as she was a woman, even if he knew he was wrong, but wanted to down the singer who was after his job.

And Malachi beat her to make sure she understood, for she was only a comforter, a slut handed out by her Lord and Master to his friends, like a slave girl with no soul because his Fermanian god could never love her? *"And Malachi hoped Leah would be given her for a night, for her beauty made him lust,"* the mazarrat sadly sang knowing who was at fault.

For that Mungo beat Malachi good and rubbed vinegar root juice into Leah's welts to make the redness go, and Leah joyed over his kind act.

"But he threw salt onto Malachi's," **the mazarrat sang loudly so the land applauded.**

"That white lioness bitch is jealous of you, string Mungo along to keep us alive," Malachi but Leah no longer really believed him, Mungo she knew would not eat her, him?

And Leah, by looking at Mungo knew why the lioness was jealous, *"Afraid you steal his love for her to you,"* the mazarrat sang sweetly, and flowers opened so perfumed scent filled the air.

"Apart from that salt, he feeds me well so let him paw, our lives are in your hands," Malachi also.

Now Leah let Mungo paw but not for Malachi's reasons but, because she was female and a law to herself.

And because of Malachi she urged Mungo to tell her the way to Telephassa from where they were.

"It would take forty days to walk to Telephassa from here," Mungo, "but it would be quicker by road the lizard men built with slaves, then it is only fourteen. Now come ask me why I would walk forty days rather than fourteen?"

And she could not speak, "So be silent then, it is because of the Fermanian patrols, and they have block houses along the road, from which the road guards speak to each other."

And Mungo told her too much for he was still a naïve boy.

Mungo daily took Leah to bath in a pool. Of course, after checking for water snakes, and did pretend not to watch, but she knew he peeked and was pleased, besotted.

And she remembered Malachi's advice and did pick up a

water lily and put it in her hair, so would deliberately expose her charms by stretching her arms, upwards.

At times Leah forgot Malachi when she did this and did it out of female ways, and she was pleased, "*So was the boy,*" and a mazarrat giggled and listening wildlife also.

Mungo had swallowed her hock and was about to swallow her float as well.

And often Leah would spit at Malachi silently, "he treats us better than you do our human slaves."

And Malachi would reply, "He beat me good over you so do what you are told."

But she thought Malachi a pig, for it was not him who was the center of Mungo's

attention who brought her sweet fruits, and even gave Malachi, but not as much as Leah's portion, and were not ripe so were still hard and green, and bananas were brown and squishy, all that went to Malachi. *"And bad fruit gives tummy ache and loathsome wind,"* that mazarrat and laughed while singing and all listening laughed too so minded not the interruption of the song.

And when she bathed, Mungo began to stand up and eventually approached her and washed her hair and back.

Illustration: Malachi would find his tail hung him.

And when she bathed, he began to stand up and eventually approached her and washed her hair and back.

And found her scales were as soft as his skin.

And it was different from Lord Artebrates owning her, who handed her About, because he owned her as a slave, with no rights, then she disliked them touching her; but remembered the Vats, *"So allowed it,"* the mazarrat almost whispering and the Spirit of Life saddened.

"Why must I obey Malachi?" She would ask herself often, and answer, "Malachi says humans will be extinct soon, so better know what side the butter is buttered on the bread?"

For Malachi had promised, "Do as I say, and I will ask Artebrates to free you, and then you can pick your own to comfort."

And she felt cheap then for Malachi must have a low opinion of her, and all Fermanians would remember her past.

Leah was only for drunks who would force themselves on her. No one loved her, it was in the books, a whore belonged to everyone.

But the books were wrong, she belonged to what Mungo danced too, and The Elder knew, and she thrilled, that Mungo loved her for herself. *"Love knows no boundaries,"* the mazarrat happily.

So, Leah played a cat and mouse game with Mungo, but never slept with him, part of her training for years to obey, and Malachi had told her to string Mungo along.

And Mungo gave Leah the choicest cuts of meat and Malachi, just fat.

"Many times, cold fat, which clung to your fingers, so when you wiped your face, fat got there," the mazarrat sang and the listener's thought Malachi was lucky to get even that.

Just to annoy Malachi a young mazarrat let The Elder know Mungo's heart seemed closed, as it was full of infatuation and was not living up to his calling, 'The Wild One. *'Perhaps a young mazarrat should be chosen as The Wild One, never too late."*

And Mungo made a necklace of lilies and began to bath and was amazed how different he looked without dirt.

"Don't get too involved girl," Malachi warned, "slit both our necks," meaning Mungo and his mother Ono the lioness. For about Mungo's neck, Malachi's missing rib on a necklace plucked out long ago.

And Leah sighed, in the bubbling vats spawned her Fermanian genes floating, and so sided with Malachi; Mungo did hate her for being an experimental creation.

And one day in the pool a snake slithered into the water and Leah saw but could not tell Mungo of the danger. So, it bit his left ankle and pulled him below the surface.

And Leah ran out of the pool and into the cave where Ono, Mungo's mother was, but could not make her understand the danger but Ono knew something was amiss by the girl's frustration so hurriedly descended to the pool.

"Quick free me," Malachi commanded seeing a chance to escape.

But Malachi face muscle's slagged when he saw Leah could not free him and resigning himself to captivity ordered her to escape and bring help back.

And both stared into each other's eyes knowing she was going to obey from years of servitude. So, Malachi stared her out for he knew she wanted to stay, for Mungo treated her well.

Now while Leah fled Mungo found he was in the coils of a python, and he cut its neck with his short sword, and Ono pulled him from the pool, or he did have drowned.

And Mungo could not walk for the ankle wound was deep, so Ono carried him into the Cave, and Malachi hearing them knew what had occurred in the pool and offered to stitch Mungo's wounds if they did promise to free him after.

"My hands are torn from that reptile's mouth so cannot work the thorn needle, and you have only three fingers mother," meaning Malachi would need to sew.

And the blood from Mungo ran freely across the cave floor, and Malachi's hands Ono knew needed to stitch the wounds.

"We promise," Ono said.

"I promise you freedom," Mungo added when Malachi looked at him, therefore Ono climbed a rhododendron tree outside the cave to cut the vine that stretched down to hold Malachi about his tail, so he just dangled off the ground; so, he would bounce up and down so cursed his own lizard tail and

Mungo's ingenuity.

Now Malachi did have a thought to kill Mungo, but instead took a fire brand from the campfire and cleaned Mungo's wounds.

And Mungo did not scream or faint.

And Malachi lingered the hot stick more than he should and was so impressed with Mungo's pain threshold he gave up torturing his enemy.

Then sewed with these words, "I know many a Fermanian who would have fought me to stop," and remembered Lord Vinki.

And Ono was close to Malachi and that sobered him up, and wished Mungo were a Fermanian for he was brave.

And when Malachi finished Ono put him into a pit and closed it.

"You promised freedom," Malachi shouted.

"First I seek Leah," Ono replied and bounded away. Now Leah was easy to find for Fermanian scent was strong. And Leah climbed a tree but still Ono found her.

"Mungo desires you, and that is a terrible thing, for you are not a lion," Ono and Leah understood Ono could eat her, and saw Ono did not understand Mungo was man, not lion.

"Come down and I will take you to a Fermanian Road, but never tell Mungo I let you escape for I owe you for bringing me to the pool to save Mungo from drowning." But Leah did not for she was afraid; "*Who said the girl was stupid?*" The mazarrat shrilly.

"Mungo will harm anybody that hurts me," Leah hoping to bluff Ono the lion away.

"I know lizard woman thing so here is my short sword from my belt that wraps my kilt, come and use it on me if I lie," and Ono withdrew to allow Leah down to get the sword, but still she would not for she was afraid of lions, "*Especially big lionesses,*" the mazarrat laughing.

Leah was like the monkeys above on a tree branch who would soon hoot and throw ripe fruit down on Ono.

"Listen Leah, I will rub the sword on crushed red thorn berries and that kills quick, we have no medicine like you lizard folk, so come down and hold the sword against me, and be quick for I smell dinosaur."

So, Leah seeing a better bargain descended; but in truth she too could hear the flesh eater Tyrannosaurus coming. And Leah marveled over the strength of the sword and wondered who had made it, it was not Fermanian, surely lions never made this?

"Human man things beyond the Red Grass Valley," Ono and crouched down for Leah to ride her back.

"Get on," Ono as Leah like anyone else was hesitant to get close to a lion.

"They ate people, didn't they?" Truthfully said by this mazarrat and the land agreed with hoots, yelps, howls, and barks.

Then the monstrous flesh eater broke cover and Ono fled, and Leah hugged her neck so, she would not fall off.

""*The danger is past, now what would Malachi do?" Leah asked herself and knew "slit her throat," but she was not Malachi, and this was Mungo's mother,"* the mazarrat asked and the listeners argued amongst themselves, what she should do?

""*I do not like Mungo," Leah's silent voice, "he disgusts me,"* and she lied to Herself" the mazarrat knew.

Also, "*What am I? I am three quarter human and was slime in a vat, an egg bought from a hungry harlot and added to a Fermanian gene. I want to be sick; I am the product of green sludge."*

"*Who am I to look down upon Mungo, at least he knows his parents, here is Ono," "But Leah was wrong, Ono had found Mungo floating in a basket and forgotten The Wild One stories,"* the mazarrat remind listeners.

So, Leah believed she had no soul for she was from a vat, "*Very interesting,"* a young mazarrat.

And Leah rode Ono's back for six days and began to meet the corpses of escaped slaves crucified to trees by Fermanians bounty hunters, who just took their scalps as proof.

The nailing done for effect; slaves needed to know who was boss.

And in the distance a Fermanian block house where guards peeked at the jungle
through slits in the cabin walls, ready to work the highly polished signal shields high above on posts.

Shields **that bounced straight radio waves** up, ducted back to the next block house and then Telephassa City.

"Now give me back my sword and I will tell Mungo a Fermanian patrol found you," and Leah again thought "What would Malachi do?" But she was not Malachi but a girl.

And the crucified shamed her for the Fermanians were a cruel race.

Now Ono sheathed her sword and was standing on two limbs to do to so when Leah stroked her mane, then hugged her out of impulse.

"You are not all bad girl, but Mungo is fated to take Sasha the king's daughter as wife, and enough hell will come out of that union without Mungo tangling with a lizard woman thing," Ono and smiled.

And Leah let tears flow as was a 'lizard woman thing, a plaything of Artebrates and others.'

"Made you more human than lizard must have for you to cry so. Do not worry I never told Mungo what you really are? A Comforter, isn't you? No different from Sasha and her suitors but she is royal, and you are not, and she is lion and you lizard.

Old Ono knows more about jungle tales than Mungo cares too listen. I won't tell him, but you had better go now, the guards have seen us," and Ono bounded away on all fours into giant red ferns.

And time stops for no one under the red moon and Mungo freed Malachi because the lizard man pined for freedom promised, and Mungo had stopped teasing Malachi about his tail, since it was an insult, and he knew insults hurt from experience growing up a man thing amongst lions.

And began to treat Malachi as a living being not a Fermanian by giving him good meat and fruit to eat, so the Oneness returned to Mungo and Mungo did a magnificent thing, when he had taken Malachi to Highway Set, the road home to Telephassa, **he shook Malachi's hand.**

And because Mungo had started to treat Malachi decently, the latter had grown fonds of his enemy and so saluted Mungo and walked down the road.

"Malachi was his friend," mazarrats sang and Malachi said, "No, no, no, no, no," a hundred times so when he finished, a Fermanian patrol found him.

*

And Lord Artebrates was happy to have his number one comforter home, and Malachi whom he now regarded as FRIEND, and Leah wished she were back in the bush where there were no scented baths, but fresh pools and flower perfume, were Artebrates could not give her jewelry and attention, where she had had the freedom to say a silent "No," and owned by no one.

But she was back home, and with that freedom gone.

"All female things want that glamour, the softness and gems so they can sparkle and attract us," Artebrates told the hunchback who said nothing but thought, "Yea, it is nature's way." *It is the way men things think girls think,* that mazarrat who has ambition.

And to show friendship to Malachi, Artebrates had collected all his plucked scales and had them sewn into a green alligator jerkin.

"To protect you from slave arrows," and Malachi allowed Artebrates to hug him as a Lord and Master publicly, claiming an inferior an equal, for Malachi was proving his worth scouting for the army under Artebrates's command hunting rebel slaves, but the crucifixions sickened Malachi, for they polluted the air with bad vapors.

And it was about now Malachi joined Artebrates household as hunter.

And time waits for no one under a lavender sun seen by the captain of an approaching spaceship.

"Mother, why am I called Mungo?"

"Because you are beloved," and **the twenty-year-old smiled** never wanting to leave the black lioness, eager for motherly love, proud to walk in front brandishing a solid bronze spear, and that the ageing red lion King Red Hide feared him, for he was now a fully grown man thing.

And The Elder ahead with his staff and Red Hide roared, "Who does Mungo think he is?"

At this age Mungo killed Fermanians come to claim glory over his death.

And Mungo often visited Sasha now her cubs had gone, that allowed his lion side to dominate, and he groomed her.

Sasha was still beautiful.

"You will never make me your first wife Mungo," Sasha enjoying the smell of wild rose bush nearby for she knew Mungo was now a man and wanting his own kind, even if he did not know it.

"I am a man thing."

"Then why seek me?"

And Mungo stood up, saw a snake slithering towards them and it rattled a warning, and Mungo threw his bronze dagger through its neck, so it died.

"I will always protect you, Sasha."

"It's not protecting I want."

"Don't lie Sasha when I leave, others will come courting and the next, we meet you will have cubs."

"Maybe yours?"

And Mungo laughed and Sasha hurt for she did really love him, but knew he spoke the truth, already she had heard a lion roaring for her, returning with promised spoil from a Fermanian merchant.

"I will have none of them as my king," Sasha said tearfully and Mungo wiped, then roared a challenge to the newcomer who thought twice about visiting Sasha at that time.

And Sasha wished Mungo were not a man thing.

"I must go," Mungo.

"To seek the Fermanian harlot?"

"She is not a harlot," and Sasha saw in her mind Mungo sought Leah, the Fermanian comforter who had crawled out of a vat.

So, Mungo bent to kiss Sasha, but she kept her lips shut, and looked the other way to woods where the challenger waited for Mungo to depart.

"If I was more human woman thing, perhaps the answers lie where the metal workers came from," and Sasha looked at a distant smoke flume, an abandoned nuclear power plant where **P53 checkpoint genes** waited splicing into her DNA for the insertion of female human chromosomes to give her body her wish, and Mungo.

And a mazarrat peaked out of a bush and she gasped for the face was human female.

"What are you?"

And the mazarrat sang about drinking a yellow drink in the old lizard's man's house, about how its face changed and how its own kind did not know it anymore, but said she was a dwarf human disguised as a mazarrat.

"If only I could?" And Sasha dreamed and saw herself a woman female thing with Mungo, her pride king.

"Come with me?" The mazarrat and Sasha followed a dream to be a human female to win Mungo for good.

And Mungo returned to Ono, "Mungo I smell death, we must turn back," Ono warned hurrying to ward him away from the nearing water hole.

"I fear nothing," and Ono knew it was the pride of youth so got in front and growled showing her six-inch claws to stop him.

Now Mungo did not like his mother chiding, for it made him feel like a naughty boy when he was a man.

"Mother I am full grown."

"They are Fermanians."

Now any remorse over the chiding vanished as he was curious if the Fermanians had heard of him, and if not, why not?

It was indeed the pride of youth, ego and what he danced to saddened!

"I will pass you and see these lizard folks for myself."

And Ono leapt upon him to stop him, but Mungo caught her and rolled so she somersaulted into a bush.

"Mother," Mungo running to her fearful of what he had done?

"Son, when I move the thorns hurt, pull them from me I beg man thing," she for she saw him as a man thing now, who could better her.

He had come of age and the slave sayings about a Wild One come to lead The People, for that is what humans called themselves against lizards, now fulfilled.

All knew about Mungo's wild naked dances to something he felt and thought him crazy, touched by the gods.

But Ono had heard The Wild One as reared by beasts and be close to them gods.

A ruler and Ono knew he was fated to be king over Red Hide and was already a King of the Jungle and saddened for both. For he would make brother fight brother, give judgement of life or death, and sacrifice himself for all.

"Have you not heard Red Hide call you man thing?" Ono remembered asking from the past.

"That is because I am ugly and look like a frog."

"No, my son, you are handsome and strong and one day I will tell you about The Wild One," Ono sighed and knew the time had come since she saw him as a man thing.

"I found you floating in a basket and claimed you as my own, you are not lion but man," and Mungo saw clearly what bothered him always, his difference from Sasha.

The gossip and taunts of the adolescent lions was true, he was man thing and saw his offspring as hideous beings with fur and orange manes, catching Pha antelope by the neck with their claws.

Beasts.

That Malachi had spoken true when Malachi had asked, "Why is a man thing a lion?"

"Leah is Fermanian and human," Ono meaning she must feel like a human in a lizard world as he was a man in a lion's world. She was also telling Mungo to get her.

"My world has collapsed," Mungo and saw why he wanted Leah for she was human, even if she had soft scales under her flesh, they felt like his skin, looked like his skin.

Her cubs would look human.

They would not have soft scales. Maybe have a neck thrill like those dragon lizards that ran on two feet.

And he saw his mother struggling to free herself from the bush, and shaming helped her as she told him about The Wild One, and a Fermanian investigating the noise hoping for an easy kill appeared.

And saw a dirty human slave kneeling over a black lion with a deer loin cloth.

And she was a girl.

And Mungo smelt her strawberry perfume before seeing her, heard the scraping of gold bracelets and rustle of silk and deer hide boots and knew she was rich.

Now Mungo could speak Fermanian but kept kneeling and turned at the last moment to face the lizard woman, who wore gold plates of armor above her long skirt of red velvet.

"You must be hot?" Mungo fascinated by what he saw for she was all Fermanian lizard woman.

And the female Fermanian hunter found Mungo had pushed her laser rifle down, and his strength kept it pointing elsewhere.

"Who are you?" She asked fearful of the answer.

"Mungo and you?"

"Carman the Mighty One," and Carman had heard of the man thing and wanted him mounted on her trophy wall for all to see, Carman was a great hunter of humans and to stop the rumors about The Wild One. And was not surprised Mungo did not bow, *"fat chance with Mungo,"* the mazarrat and the jungle nodded agreement.

"You are what I have heard," Mungo all coiled muscles and as Ono now free, Carman faced a new threat.

"My mother will not harm you."

"I will kill you both with sword and spiked shield," Carman and tried to

draw out a short sword as she tried to pull a shield from her back.

"No, you won't as you interest me," Mungo stopping her, beginning to paw her to see if a Fermanian woman was like Leah, so ignored the hurt he felt in his spirit for his spirit being part of The Oneness knew Mungo was doing wrong. But knew also he was too weak when flesh was concerned.

"Insolent pig," Carman looking at Ono licking her lips showing lots of teeth.

"No mother, I am not done."

And Carman saw the big black lion squat waiting for the word to eat her.

And Carman regretted ordering her servants to wait behind so she could show all she was The Mighty Carman.

"I like your red eyes, full of spirit," Mungo and he stroked her hair next to see if it was as soft as Leah's.

"Was just the same and Sasha's, no difference," Mungo amazed. *"For girls washed and scented their hair, unlike some,* advice for a smelly boy," and the mazarrat sang joyfully.

"Filthy minded pig," Carman and this made Mungo stop and think, *'What was wrong with wanting to see what a Fermanian lizard woman thing looked like, and then play with her?'*

'Because that would be by force which is wrong,' The Oneness answered his spirit and Carman grunted, "The tales you are mad is true," for she saw he spoke to himself But at that moment other Fermanians had begun searching for Carman as

they worried.

And one richly attired for his metal sparkled under the red sun for it was gold, and he was Lord Artebrates and behind him Malachi the Hunter.

And in a barrow cage, Moragana the ape with ribbons, and The Elder stirred his limbs to stand from a tree to have a good look.

And behind them Mungo saw Leah, who had been with the hunchback lizard in his laboratory, and was more human than before, as the soft scales under the skin not seen and her eyes a solid green, and hair long blond-haired twisted through gold bands, and she was pleasing to Mungo's eye.

"No scales on the young then," he is meaning his cubs from Leah who being woman understood and blushed.

And Carman took the opportunity to crawl backwards away from this crazy man.

For Fermanians feared the insane and threw them out of their cities, and they eventually killed others for they had to eat, *cannibals.*

And Leah's legs and arms adorned in gold, and she wore a short silver kilt while her bosom fully formed showed in the fashion of ancient Cretans and Cavalier women.

And she stood curious wondering how Mungo had changed, for he was no longer dirty and smelly but seemed bathed and scented with flowers.

"Something she had taught him while she was his captive," a mazarrat reminded and the jungle agreed.

"Kill it," an important lizard man on two legs not Lord Artebrates said to Malachi, disgusted seeing Mungo, who to him was a bad copy of civilization.

"You must forgive me, but Wonder Lord Vinki has ordered your death, for you are human," Malachi told Mungo," and my master Artebrates has agreed with a blink."

Now Malachi had formed an admiration for this man thing that always outsmarted him, and knew Carman had come to kill Mungo, and was sad and knew Mungo would react but how?

"Why must it die?" The girl Leah asked with hand signs of Malachi.

"No one will kill me or my mother," Mungo replied in grunting lion tongue, for Carman's benefit and then did worse, he winded loudly, picked his nose and, and,
flecked it at Carman and scratched if plagued with fleas.

And Leah giggled, and Carman slapped her lips so that they bled, and Mungo slapped Carman so all gaped, that the Mighty One Carman, a man slave had bled her.

But Mungo was not a slave, he was a free man, a savage beast.

Now Carman's House Berserkas advanced with shields and throwing axes to slay Mungo, but out of the bush came growls and Sasha with lions, and there was stand off.

"He is beast," Carman angry for Mungo flicked nose stuff at her, and any opinion she had of him as a handsome wild man to keep as a toy vanished, *"For gooey stuff dripped from her cheeks,"* a mazarrat pointing out gooey stuff.

She would chain and subdue him; teach him he was SLAVE.

And Mungo laughed with his hands at his sides, for he was still the same mischievous Mungo.

"The girl Leah asks you to lift your left sole for her mark is upon you, and if you are her slave and if you are, you cannot be killed without her assent," Malachi translated for he understood Leah's diplomacy, but kept two eyes everywhere there was a lion, which is pretty hard thing to do if you have two eyes and there are scores of hungry lions wanting to eat you.

Illustration: Leah captivated Mungo with her solid green eyes.

"MMMM, her brand is upon me and painful too it was," showing the sole of his feet, "but I belong only to mother and what makes me dance and sing naked," for Mungo knew flesh made flesh ugly, and dirty not The Oneness that made him and flowers needing insects to have seeds.

And flowers waved in the wind and were glorious to see and so was the flesh glorious for LIFE to see that made it unashamedly."

Now Carman had had enough and strode forward in front of Malachi not afraid of this lion human thing with bad upbringing, and curious to find out more since she had Berserkas.

As for Mungo he knew his wish, he was indeed famous.

And Carman's red velvet dress now open from her fall and showed her chest and had gold body piercings.

"Why?" Mungo not understanding why one wants to modify their bodies loaned to them by what he danced too.

"And Mungo saw his body as a survival suit so he could run in and out of thorn bushes while less nimble lions got stuck there; those who followed him in who he had managed to annoy in the past, and more lately Sasha's challengers," The Elder.

"So, my lovers can admire them," Carman and so Mungo pulled the one on her lower lip and the mighty empress howled. *"Howl, howl,"* a mazarrat copied and *"howl, howl,"* the listening jungle came alive.

And Leah took a diamond studded dagger and faced

Mungo for it was her duty to protect Carman.

Malachi raised his spear.

The House Berserkas stared at the lions who stared back, whoever flinched and broke ranks first was dinner on both sides.

But Mungo had slung his sling and the pebble hit Malachi on the skull, and he swayed, falling flat on his face.

Then dinner arrived amongst the Berserkas and lions, for hell broke out.

Also, Artebrates remembered after, that a black lion running at him and his shield Bearer, running away with his shield, "*As fast as the wind,*" a mazarrat added laughing.

"Nothing more I can remember; Malachi tell me what happened" Artebrates much later did ask.

"Mungo felled me and your guards he did horrid things to, so others seeing fled in terror.

And the black lion when it leapt did not land on the spears put up for it but sailed over them and landed behind so attacked raked our bottoms.

This foul trick Mungo taught it, and Mungo threw the heads of your slain guards at our faces. I told you he did horrid things; then armed mazarrat came out of the jungle and rained missiles down upon us.

The jungle had gone crazy; why we build block houses to keep it out of our society.

And your slave vat girl, Leah stood above Carman not allowing The Mighty One to crawl like a worm, prepared to give her life for her against Mungo."

And Artebrates was glad then pondered, **"Armed mazarrat, are you drunk?"**

"No, my Lord and Master," Malachi but Artebrates only half believed for he was of the master race and arrogant.

"What of the House Berserkas?" Artebrates.

"A white lion more pleasing than any seen before led other lions to attack them, so these Berserkas could not help," Malachi humbly, "but killed four lions."

"Ah good, four lions we got."

"Yes, my Lord, before they were killed and eaten."

And Artebrates was silent before asking, "Why did Mungo not eat Leah?"

"My Lord and Master I never lie to you, as Mungo did not eat me when I was captive, he did not eat the vat girl Leah. When I came too, I found Leah tending Carman whom Mungo had stripped of her red dress and given it to the white lioness to wear as a trophy stuck in her gemmed belt that holds up her green velvet kilt.

And Mungo promised Carman another opportunity to hunt him if Carman would promise to lie still.

And Carman did my Lord.

See my Lord, Mungo thinks this is a game and is laughing at us," Malachi.

And Artebrates wondered how often Malachi lied to him and knew Mungo did not kill Leah, because he wanted her, just as he was fascinated to see what Carman were. *"He was naughty and not fit to be Wild One,"* a young mazarrat wanting to replace Mungo and be famous, loved, adored.

This Artebrates believed was Mungo's Achilles' heel.

His weakness was Leah.

"Mungo did not eat us, he is a man thing," Malachi.

"Rubbish, those humans who escape eat us," Artebrates in disbelief Carman had lain out as a trap for Mungo human slaves, and mungo freed them, not ate them.

"My Lord Carman's executioner is coming for us," Malachi pleased his Lord as well getting punished. "Mungo does not eat things that think like him, he is a man thing," Malachi.

"A man thing reared by a bitch lion Ono," Artebrates knowing the story staring into his warm red wine, wine to soften his coming agony, not the beer that Malachi drank made from fermented bananas and sometimes had fermented insects in it too.

"I am The Wild One," Artebrates said, now if Malachi had said this?

And Artebrates remembered Malachi carrying him from the slaughter as Mungo fed his lion friends Fermanian livers on the end of Carman's personal lance.

Mungo ate Fermanians for they tasted like chicken according to Artebrates.

""*You will get sick child,*" *Ono chided for the liver of Fermanians was bitter and not sweet like a human.*

"*It is pha liver given me by Sasha to restore battle strength,*" *Mungo and offered his mother some which she ate and found it juicy and sweet,*" that mazarrat who eves dropped told all for a smile.

"Carman the Mighty One is ready," the executioner in red cotton from head to tail commanded and Malachi and Artebrates went with him.

And Carman Mighty One sat on her sedan carried by sixteen human slaves.

And all about House Berserkas so Malachi and Artebrates obeyed.

"It is a long way down my friend," Artebrates said as they climbed a tower.

"As Carman fell so must we," and Malachi walked off the plank heavily falling thirty feet into brown dust.

Artebrates landed on top of him, why he had gone second.

And both remembered The Elder, "*The jungle beasts will protect him.*" meaning Mungo.

Then their clothes stripped as Carman was, so her red dress could be Sasha's trophy.

And Malachi suffered a broken leg, then hauled to his feet punished now for Lord Artebrates sores.

As two lions had clawed Artebrates his Lord, two stolen cubs from Ono's litter now full grown came for Malachi; called Abel and Eve.

"It is a stupid law, "Artebrates whispered to Malachi, heard so dragged to stand with friend Malachi as punishment for that.

And Abel and Eve enforced the Fermanian class system and

the divine position of royalty and nobility that you must be prepared to die for; or punished.

"One day I will raise my house flag in revolt," Artebrates.

Cathbadh: Cathbadh was furious, Carman had scorned him and all he had said was, "Now you believe in a Wild One believe me when I say a human star ship approaches.

"Do you want the same fate as Prince Annunaki's female cousin ten times

removed?" Her reply and Cathbadh fell to the floor for her to wipe her sandals on his red hair. The girl had garroted on a public square.

One less claimant against Hebat, Carman's son.

Now Cathbadh promised he did work for her fall; she was evil and had to be destroyed if Telephassa was to be prepared for the star ship's arrival.

And what Mungo danced naked too as he already knew about Fermanian ways, "*they tasted like chicken,*" a cheeky mazarrat we know.

*

And Artebrates now feared what Mungo man thing was capable of and would reach for the soft hands of his Warmer and she would hold his hands and her name was Leah, and one night.

"So soft like Mungo's," Artebrates, and she smiled and wondered if she was truly Fermanian or something escaped from a biology lab?

And Artebrates undressed Leah for she did not have Freedom to be her own person.

And he put a ring around her neck so, a chain attached to it so he could chain her to a post to remind her that he owned her, and others to gloat. So much for his ideas of calling Malachi FRIEND.

She was comforter, and lately been thinking which meant she envisaged herself as something higher in station.

"My Lord and Master, Mungo fancies this girl as his own," Artebrates remembered Malachi and, "Mungo would kill both for Leah's shame," Malachi was sure of that.

And Malachi looked for mazarrat and saw that human ape Moragana, now shaven of fur and body tattooed after the latest fashions. Mungo did come back and slit throats when they slept for Leah's shame, as no mazarrat, or ape could help singing the news.

"Why beloved bodyguard?" Artebrates asked Malachi who was present as he pawed Leah. And Malachi joined, for he was FRIEND and to remind Leah of her place, a comforter.

And Artebrates made a musical rhythm from the wrist and ankle amulets found.

"For Mungo gave her the choicest meats and me the fat, I tell you Leah is the first human he has seen in his life, he is besotted with her my Lord," Malachi refusing.

"And her beauty will give me Mungo's head on my wall over my fire," Artebrates and sought comfort and Malachi being lizard did not mind as he stared into the fire, remembering Mungo, fingering his lost rib, but Leah being human shamed.

"She is Mungo's, he will eat us, "this is what disturbed Malachi only.

"This is Telephassa, here I am Lord and Master," Artebrates.

Then Malachi got up to sharpen his weapons.

Mungo was no longer boy, he had seen a woman, and like all men would kill for a woman.

And a woman of sort called Moragana went ape fashion to the barracks to comfort the drunks there who would throw her coins to do silly things, and she would drink the drink to be able to cross the boundaries of decency.

She was Moragana the stupid ape woman thing, with human genes.

And preferred alcohol to fruit.

And blamed Mungo for her present position in society, "If he was my man thing, I did be a respected lady, but he does not love me but that creature of the vats, Leah, so I behave like a fallen woman."

"It is Moragana's shame not Mungo's," listening mazarrats

sang and Moragana Rattled her cage in anger. *"My, mazarrats get about,"* the mazarrat added.

But the anger was Moragana's for Fermanian dandies came and tormented the troopers there saying, "What you young men with this ape Moragana? See the lame beggar at the barrack doors? Aye the one who spews gruel down his scales, well she sleeps with him for a copper farthing."

And the dandies would roar with laughter, and the troopers beat poor Moragana who screamed, "This is Mungo's doing."

"Moragana likes being beaten," mazarrats replying in nightingale voices.

And as Malachi rubbed olive oil into his spear head a papyrus book lay upon his table next to uneaten meat.

Malachi was not in the mood for sweetmeat boiled in vinegar, for the opened head reminded him of Mungo, and the fact he turned the plate round so the brown human eyes in tripe in their sockets, would not haunt him, and the slack hanging lips do not whisper, "Mungo will avenge me."

So, looked at the barbecued ribs and slices of cold meats, and felt ill for he saw in the dinner remains, Mungo.

"From this day I eat other things," and kicked his dinner elsewhere.

A brown rat watching from wooden beams knew dinner was coming, and Malachi felt collywobbles for Mungo was coming.

"What have you done to me Mungo?" He and read the papyrus book's first chapter again.

"Cheap fiction about the man thing reared by lions on the red grass plains. Mungo who swings from giant rhododendron trees to lasso lizard men," he read the scribe's words aloud, "to lasso me?"

And new books written by back street scribes eager to cash in on Lord Artebrates meeting with Mungo.

"Well Master you were ordered to find Mungo and found him, now you must cut scales off in front of Carman for failure, better you than me, and something ought to be done about these scribes stirring up nightmares for profit," Malachi tossing the book away.

Now across his room's wall were drawings of Mungo, and maps with dates of sightings for Malachi were obsessed.

Anyway: Leah lay on a gold table as Artebrates sought his comfort; he had paid dearly to have her out of the vats.

"Fermanian or human, so long as they are female, they can comfort me," Artebrates reasoned and Leah thought of Mungo who pleased her eye, and wished it were he, and not Artebrates who she saw him as an ugly lizard these days.

Then Artebrates sucked hard on his opium pipe and put it down, and seeing Leah so well formed, realized it was time she should have life in her belly, and provide him with sons who would join his house guard, and be his personal Berserkas; and dreamed of becoming emperor.

And his dreams spoiled for he heard a roar, a lion's roar.

And the roar came from the throat of a human.

At once Malachi returned to his Lord and Master Artebrates and shut windows looking across the mangrove swamps circling Telephassa City ignoring the drugged semi naked Artebrates, who he got away from Leah, the tethered goat for the lion.

And while Malachi herded his Lord to safety, Leah went in search of the hunchback and found him at a table in a room lit by a beaker of glow worms.

Hunchback

"Child," he asked seeing her.

"If I were a child my Lord and Master would treat me kindly and not as his comforter," she with hands.

"It is a cruel world and only the successful are happy, come and have a candy," he replied knowing she had a sweet tooth for the red and white striped rock.

"Mungo is here," she told him, "He is coming for me."

"You are the bait," that has been decided between Malachi and our master," he said.

"It is my time to give young," she told the hunchback.

"Live young and not eggs for rodents to crack open, and eat, much expense has been put into your child in the vats," he softly, "be glad Cathbadh's latest idea has stopped you coming to me," and he meant in experiments in self-fertilization.

"Will my young be soulless slaves like me?"

"We are all soulless slaves here and I withheld your infertility wine. Child don't you realize what you are?"

Leah covered her ears.

"Bought merchandise, where is your predecessor? Sold to an inn for she could only lay eggs, a failure, your fate child unless; see men pay dearly to hump the likes of you, noble comforters are always the prettiest.

And her eggs sold for she carries good genes, and all her young are beauties, merchandise.

Do not look at me like that? It is not I made our society, blame the gods on Mount Tullos," he defended.

"But I do see girls more beautiful than me?"

"Aye but they aren't a Noble's *comforter*," he said the last word slow so she understood.

"Artebrates loves me," Leah not wanting to face facts that she might sold off.

"Our master doesn't like his nightmares *comforter*," and the hunchback knew he was being cruel to be kind.

"You mean he doesn't like the scribes writing he runs from Mungo, and returns to Telephassa covered in banana skins, and mazarrat thrown down dung," she was angry.

And he took her hands to silence her, remembering when Artebrates gave him this embryo to nourish in a vat and now Leah was full grown and her round tummy
demanded swelling, and tears fell from his eyes for she was like a child to him, his daughter: but he knew his place in Artebrates household.

"I changed your nappies, didn't have too but I saw then you were different, something in you what it said on your label, your DNA codes had wisdom, beauty, and promise," and remembered a papyrus book, "The Wild One's mate is Fermanian but human," and wished he never read it as he explained himself to Leah.

"Child, I value you even if you are a replaceable number," he said, and she sought trust in his eyes and found it absent and remembered Mungo's freedom and wished for it.

Looked at her hands in his and saw his were lizards and hers human and knew she was different from her own Fermanian race.

"We make your kind with human genes for softness and the next models won't have scales," the hunchback knowing her thoughts, "I am Fermanian and disgusted being one, but I am one for Mungo broke scales when he used that rifle but for, he knows I am one and don't forget you're Fermanian," and he took from a drawer a numbered gold ring.

"What is that?" Knowing.

"For the ring ceremony and I will do it while Artebrates and Malachi watch," the hunchback holding out the ring and it was numbered; *"She was a number, like the stars above, numbers are names,"* the mazarrat sang.

And Leah ran from the room knowing she had been bubbles in Cathbadh's oily vats for Fermanian pleasure only.

"The Wild One's Mungo's, you won't be ringed, the mazarrat don't sing that Mungo's woman is ringed," he shouted after her.

And Lord Artebrates found another comforter who would not remind him of Mungo, as Malachi got drunk and found a scribe who next day found amongst water rats, on the banks of one of Telephassa's sewers; revenge was at work.

Cathbadh

Cathbadh sighed, the ape Moragana had just left him on her way to tell all what she knew. Cathbadh also knew he was not her first visit.

She had told him she had visited Lord Vinki's.

"So, one of the general's secrets is out," he mused hoping fear would make Artebrates act now before Carman dismissed him to the gutter.

Artebrates had slid into a dream world where there was no more butchery and Wild Ones.

"He liked his opium," the mazarrat pretending to suck opium from a twig, and copied by other beasts, mazarrats, apes and monkeys.

"My fault gentle friend, I pushed too hard with my warning of the star-ship, and you don't have pork belly to sell Vinki, just your soul."

And these days Cathbadh stayed in as Moragana had heard Carman cursing his name and star ship and shouted, "If we don't have enough to worry about now, we got to worry about humans falling out of the sky," and Cathbadh blamed.

Chapter 4 Lust

And Mungo left deep tracks in the mangrove mud that was a natural defense for Telephassa City, and now stood below a sixteen-foot clay wall no longer roaring. Lions roaring yes, for his roar had set of challenges and those Fermanians who did not recognize his roar, thought the noise commonplace. *"Just dumb lions, go back to sleep,"* the sentries and snoozed, dreaming of beer, women and sung, as a mazarrat singing sleep melodies to help the Fermanians sleep deeply.

And mazarrats added to the din, just to be annoying of course.

Also, the hum of a **crystallization plant** where crystals filtered brackish water feeding city water pipes.

And the wall cheaply made by an army of thirty-six thousand slaves, who lived in barracks on the Telephassa side of the wall, a mile away on drier soil.

And Mungo noted where the pipes went but did not know it took the slaves twenty years to build the walls of Telephassa City, and he stood on slave graves, and one skeleton exposed covered in osteophytes, bony outgrowths caused by heavy labor, and the spine crushed by a falling limestone block.

And Mungo wrinkled his nose for the mangroves stank of sewage.

An unhealthy place, and small bull sharks swam amongst the shallows for they could live in both fresh and salt water.

And in the summer plankton came with the tide carrying hitch hiking cholera.

And swarms of biting insects left Mungo alone, for he had berry juice rubbed on and as jungle talk had it, *"Telephassa City was rife with Purple Fever,"* so he ate red mangrove melon to protect himself as advised by The Elder, a mazarrat of course.

Another had been here under the red moon, the hunchback overseeing the refilling of beakers full of jam made from white

Calceolaria flower containing **naphthoquinones,** to kill bugs naturally resistant to Fermanian insecticides.

The bugs carried liver flukes and other nasties.

He had also checked a **pseudomonas bacteria meter** for they ate leaking oil in freezing conditions for winter was blowing in from the North Pole.

"This is easy," Mungo spoke to Ono as they heard the armor of guards above fade, as then he climbed after the fashion of primates.

"You are a foolish young man; you have Sasha for cubs so why sniff about the skirt pleats of a Fermanian witch?" Ono angrily wanting to tell Mungo that Leah was a Comforter, afraid Mungo might succeed in capturing Leah, and then he did leave his mother who said cruel things about Leah; "*But I am a mazarrat so can say what I want?*" Yes, that mazarrat and the land agreed wanting the latest gossip.

And six times Mungo stopped as guards passed, and then Mungo was above and **"Wow a man thing,"** and Mungo faced an adolescent Fermanian in cotton armor from a poor regiment, as the Fermanians put their expendables up front.

And Mungo sailed through the air landing both feet on the lad's chest, so fell together on hay below with Mungo just missing, a pitchfork.

Now Mungo could have killed for the youth was Fermanian but saw terror in those pink eyes and knew the soldier was a boy, not adult.

So, Mungo with the boy soldier's own sword hilt clubbed, and Mungo's spirit gladdened he had not taken life he had not made for once; "He *was not all lion thing but man,*" the mazarrat sweetly.

Now while Mungo approached the lighted trench that was the third defensive line of Telephassa City, Sasha came to Ono.

"What has the lizard woman have that I do not have?"

And Sasha stood erect, so Carman's red ruby dress fell alluring about her limbs.

"She is made after his own kind," Ono replied.

"She is made from slime scooped from middens," Sasha spat, "why cannot he take this human woman just as Comforter instead of wife, and come with me?" Sasha bitterly.

"Mungo has seen man things, freed them from their lizard masters but never seen a female of his own kind," Ono looking up the wall, and fell silent as guards passed.

"In my belly is young," Sasha and stood to open her dress and rub her belly, and Ono saw Sasha was grotesquely human in appearance, what had Sasha been doing?

"And a mazarrat knew who had been drinking potions in a power station and talked," the mazarrat singer, *"we just do not how to keep a secret."*

"Mungo's," Ono afraid of Red Hide for she had seen Sasha lie with lions to make Mungo jealous.

"Of course," and Sasha then bounded up the wall and vanished.

"Enya what shame Mungo brings me to abandon Red Hide's daughter with cubs for a vat prostitute," Ono screamed and rent her fur. "Ouch," the mazarrat emulating but stopped.

Now Sasha followed Mungo's smell to the young youth tied up.

"I will kill you because you are lizard and Mungo's young are hungry," and ate until she realized, she was too heavy to run, so lay down for an hour.

"She ate him because Mungo had rejected her for a piece of slime. He was only a boy, a child, in cotton armor, of a poor regiment," the mazarrat sang to make Sasha feel guilt.

Now Mungo's act of kindness had not gone unnoticed for mazarrats, those creatures possessed with intelligence and sought after by civilized races of New Uranus had watched with their many-colored eyes.

They also saw what Sasha did.

And it would take three months before a trapped mazarrat would sing about it from a cage in a Fermanian household, and what happened become the possession of back street scribes and papyrus books.

"The Wild One's Cubs," a sample title, and the pulp fiction would argue seriously that Mungo was whom they stated him to be, "He will come from jungle royalty," but there had never been any mention of him having cubs; never mind the scribes had papyrus books to sell, and a bit of smut always went down with the buying public.

Mongolism was fashionable as citizens followed him as, "He will bring judgement and feed us to his lion friends," it was written by the scribes as the mazarrat prophecy sold books, for it was they who sang about it first from large bird cages, "*Had to be large as mazarrats are big, furry, and cute,*" the singer and "*O,*" the land agreed.

Anyway: At the trench, the scribes would again have opportunity to spread Mungo's fame, for here a centurion of archers was allowing a shaman priest to call upon his ancestors to help his ill child.

For the Fermanians believed that on the '5th of Sead Leaf month' the underworld opened its purple gates and allowed spirits freedom to the real world from springs.

Now Mungo seeing no enemy allowed himself to slither down one side of the Trench, for he feared no obstacles and would solve the problem of getting out the other side of the V sided trench when he got down.

This is the way Mungo worked.

And Mungo looked up the twenty-foot mud trench and began digging holes in it with his dagger to make steps.

"Hiss a man thing," a voice and **Mungo now twenty** knew no fear and stuck his dagger under the serrant's throat.

"WA I will kill you man thing," the serrant hissed.

"No beast with stumpy legs I will slit your throat unless you help Mungo of the Lions of Ono," he hissed back.

" Holy rainfall, the man thing speaks," the serrant and Mungo pushed its coiling body away and stamped its tail.

"I will give you three seconds then I slit," Mungo added and counted.

He got too two.

"Agreed Mungo," a hiss but Mungo kept his dagger where it was.

Illustration: Mungo got the better of the serrant

"Now dinosaur droppings with the rest of your body pass it upwards so I can climb this trench," Mungo instructed.

"Are you crazy, Fermanians above will kill me?"

Mungo counted again.

So, the serrant obeyed this crazy man thing who it now loathed.

And Mungo made the serrant raise its head as he climbed so he could cut a throat if treachery arose.

"Anyway, *it seemed hungry, and Mungo wasn't going to be supper, and I am hungry from singing,"* the mazarrat looking for grubs in the bark he sat on.

Now at this moment the silent shaman with the centurion carrying his son came to the wall to summon the spirit folk where the boy lay.

And the moon was crescent and under it flew a vampire bat.

"God Telephassa protect your shaman as he calls upon the ancestors of the centurion **holy warts a man thing,**" he blurted as Mungo jumped off the serrant's head and kicked shattering the shamans' pearl cod piece, so the shaman fell the escarpment trying to stop those expensive pearls escaping, black pearls.

"*And because of that did not break his fall but broke his neck,*" the mazarrat watching.

"I will not kill you if you keep silent," Mungo told the soldier holding the child, for Mungo had pity in him.

"Spare my son?" The soldier begged, and Mungo saw the child was gravely ill, so sheathed his own short sword.

"Centurion of Centurions it is I Mungo, and I will kill him for you," the serrant hissed as it held the top of the trench with stubby fingers, and Mungo slapped its face, so, it fell backwards towards the shaman.

Somewhere black pearls.

"Wah Mungo, you are a latrine cleaner," the serrant hissed falling.

"Mungo," the centurion, "only a man thing as you would come here," and still did not draw his sword, for Mungo did not threaten the child.

Now Mungo lifted the child up and gave him to his father. And the centurion could have attacked but did not.

"The priest cannot save him, but I have seen this fever on lions for the face turns purple, and they eat mangrove melon," Mungo breaking a bit off his red melon, destined for Leah, and mashed it in the boy's mouth, and the centurion allowed for he wanted his child to live and would try anything for it was his child dying.

"Mangrove melon? If this is so you have saved our city for the sickness is rife, everywhere, scores die as our scientists seek a cure and when Flood month comes, the virus goes.

Will you kill me now?" The centurion.

"I go my way, you go yours, I passed melons on the way in, feed them to him and your boy will live," and then Mungo vanished as the boy began to open his mouth for melon as it eased his swollen throat.

"Truly there is mercy in the world," the centurion and carried his boy to his Barracks, where he ordered a company of soldiers to follow him into the swamps for the healing mangrove melons.

And the centurion's name was Enkalla, brother to the hunter Malachi.

As for the shaman with chicken bones Sasha added his to them and was belly huge.

And the serrant it lay unconscious in the trench for it had landed headfirst, so a vampire bat full of disease sucked its blood. And Sasha was too full to eat the serrant, besides the bulge of the shaman amongst the coils was off putting, *"Reminded her of what she looked like now from desire,"* the mazarrat thinking that funny and half the listeners decided not to sleep with desire.

Now there are many walls surrounding Telephassa that if a human slave walks from north to south would take forty days, and likewise from west to east, and Mungo avoided further walls by walking open sewers for he was heading towards a castle on a hill, and it belonged to Lord Artebrates for mazarrats told him, *"Leah was there,"* and *"For mazarrats in cages got around, they sang like nightingales all the latest gossip."*

And Mungo saw two hunting lions tethered to red posts ready to warn House Berserkas at the drawbridge of danger.

"I am Mungo a lion like you, let me pass?" From the shadows.

And the lions growled alerting guards.

"Why betrays another lion?" Mungo asked.

"You are a man thing yet speak our tongue, and stink of cats urine," the black bitch Eve answered, and she looked like Ono and squatted and made her scent.

"My mother is Ono," Mungo answered, and the white male Abel stopped growling, "Ono was our mother, but you are man thing," and he made his mark too, as he was as excited as his sister

"It was also the stinky way of cats, mazarrats are too clean minded to do that," the singer already marked.

"I was raised by Ono," Mungo replied and as House Berserkas approached, he allowed darkness to swallow him.

"What ails you, you flea ridden cubs of cows," a Berserka

for a lion to have a cow as a mother is insult, and these hunting lions humiliated enough, for not allowed clothes or gold ornaments that the Lions of Ono pine; so were naked.

The only things allowed spiked collars and limb studs and when in battle body armor.

"Mazarrats," Abel and Eve agreed, and the guards left.

Then, "Mungo," Abel whispered but Mungo was climbing the castle wall following Leah's scent.

And when The Elder heard from mazarrat songs Mungo had not killed but shown Mercy, he was glad for one chosen by the Stillness being must be kind and forgiving to be able to have the eyes shine bright, then dance unashamedly naked to the Unseen maker who made all bodies naked in the glorious act of creation.

But for how long would Mungo show he was a responsible man thing and because he was man thing; The Elder knew it would not last. Mungo he knew had a weakness, the flesh.

Cathbadh

For forty nights Cathbadh had watched the funeral pyres blacken Telephassa's yellow clouds. Now he had just left Carman pleased, promoted to Chief Judiciary with emergency powers to stop the food and fever riots; power was his.

In his left hand he carried papyrus parchments banning books on The Wild One and "About time," he knew.

""*Why hadn't you thought of this Lord Vinki?*" Carman had asked and Cathbadh would have liked to say, "Because you are an idiot Vinki," and now he knew Vinki would hate him more," the mazarrats recorded history too, so could cast facts up during arguments to win, shame and made others foolish.

He also knew Vinki had employed troublemakers to make the mob demand an electoral senate of which Vinki would control; "*Vinki could dream, and dream of ice cream too.*" Oh, I am such a cheeky young mazarrat.

Now Carman's answer had been to send House Berserkas to silence the mob, and those who had not died decorated metal cages at crossroads while roof top ravens waited for them to die.

But the blow to Vinki would come from Cathbadh for he had the power to open Vinki's granaries to feed the poor.

Making Cathbadh extremely popular with the mob.

There was no other way to do it, Artebrates was on sick leave raking fever but Cathbadh knew he was smoking poppy seed, as was his restful fashion between wars.

"What was that?" Cathbadh hearing Mungo's roar and shivered as thoughts of Mungo came to his mind, so looked for a star ship amongst the stars.

"We Fermanians cannot even kill one human running loose in the jungle, so what hope do we have against a ship load of them?" And Cathbadh sighed for he knew the new human arrivals, would have modern weapons, not a dagger that Mungo carried.

And Cathbadh showed his despair with a deep sigh.

A black rat on the hunt for scraps heard also and ran for cover.

A serrant could not hear, it was still unconscious.

A shaman would never admire his black pearls again.

A vampire bat heard and being full crawled into a crack in the wall.

A good thing the serrant had not been able to see what had been feasting on him or would have died of fright.

A dreadful thing now as the serrant full of disease would die slowly and spread it.

A centurion with his men collecting melons heard and looked towards the roar, "Thanks," the centurion, and his men did not complain, the centurion told them why they were here.

A great hunter heard the roar and felt his ribs wondering if he was too loose another?

A mazarrat sang, *"Malachi was his friend,"* as answer.

A Wonder Lord called Vinki heard the roar and from fright loosened his bowels, so furious sought a toilet and a change of silken underwear.

A great general instead of dreaming of killing human

rebels saw lions coming to eat Him but could not wake up as he was full of poppy seed.

A queen heard and hoped The Wild One would come, so she could have his head on her wall.

A hunchback heard and understood and hoped Mungo would spare him for the kindness shown Leah.

Cathbadh heard and dreaded the human starship.

A vat product, Leah smiled, she knew why a lion man thing was roaring about Telephassa.

A black lioness added her own roar to confuse the issue.

A white lioness awoke and was silent, she was on the wrong side of the wall to go roaring alerting the enemy she was here. Bones of a boy solder were evidence he never deserted his post.

Leah Again

Chapter 5 Artebrates

Lord Artebrates was happy; his number two comforter had new life in her belly, he hoped. Also, he was happily delirious too because Mungo had stopped howling and roaring.

"Tomorrow I want you Nannaha to make Leah beautiful, for we go on safari and will bait Leah out for Mungo to see, and Malachi will kill him and now I will sleep" and Nannaha hated Leah for her soft human complexion.

"Yes, I will make Leah beautiful and when she is staked out, I will cut her wrists for blood will surely bring Mungo to eat her, then I will be first comforter," for she read papyrus books on Mungo and not all said he was a tolerant jungle lord, but a cruel sadistic eater of Fermanian livers stuck in lances; *covered in sweet chili sauce. Now where did they get that idea?* And a young mazarrat seen and heard gigging as it went up a banana tree.

And Artebrates dreamed on poppy seed seeing Leah adorned in strips of silver, for these lion folks pined for such trinkets, so Mungo would come to steal them.

And Leah scented in flowers and not properly attired, so Mungo could see her tantalizing flesh: "T*hey had forgotten he had seen that already snort,*" and The Elder was becoming annoyed with this youngster who wanted his boots, so shamed for he knew he should be grooming the youth to be a critic, not planning his fall. SHAMED he was The Elder, SHAMED.

Then Malachi would take steady aim with his laser rifle, never mind his hunter's bow, he wanted Mungo dead.

And Mungo said, "I am man thing," and Artebrates awoke screaming.

Now Mungo heard Artebrates calling for Leah, and had brought him by the hunchback. And better, Mungo heard Leah speaking to the hunchback from behind red silk curtained windows on the castle wall.

"Leah, Leah are you man thing woman?" Artebrates asked from his bed his Fermanian tail swishing, disturbing flying insects, flies.

"Most of me my Lord and Master," she is using hands and with good sense knelt with bowed head which subdued Artebrates.

"He will come for you, won't he?" He, and Leah warned by the hunchback agreed.

"Let me see her as she is going tomorrow, yes that is what you must do Nannaha, and make Leah stand on her veranda with Malachi ready to strike Mungo when he comes," and Artebrates fell back on his bed full of poppy, and Nannaha prepared more poppy seed to smoke for she was bad.

"Let us arise and do our bidding," Nannaha told Leah and they left Artebrates alone and Leah did not trust the other woman, so did not want to leave.

Now Nannaha was glad she was to dress Leah, for she would beat Leah so pushed Leah, so she fell.

"Why so rough Nannaha?" But Leah knew Artebrates had forsaken her and her position was vacant.

And Mungo overhearing raced ape fashion on the castle red wall to Leah's room and entered and hid under the bed for Leah did not have a tail so did not sleep on a hammock.

"You are privileged our Lord has chosen you for this honor," Nannaha lied, and the door slid shut, activated by voice and palm print.

"I am not afraid of Mungo," Leah answered which made Nannaha furious for she was.
So dressed Leah roughly and with a blade cut Leah's right arm as she was dumb, could not scream.

"Good red blood for the lions," Nannaha smirked, and Leah replied with hands," I will dress myself," but Nannaha stronger dominated and tied Leah's hands behind her back.

So Artebrates could not see the cut.

And to enforce upon Leah she was a lion bait to trap Mungo. Nannaha was now favorite comforter.

And Leah cried for she felt betrayed by her Lord and Master.

"Not ringed yet either," and proudly Nannaha showed Leah her numbered belly ring, which meant she was slave of Artebrates. And Leah was glad she was not ringed as she did not want her body pierced.

She was the way she was and liked her body the way it was.

Now Nannaha was a cruel bully and began to paw Leah as if he she was Artebrates, saying dreadful things about Mungo eating her, how when she was dead Malachi was to skin and stuff her, so she could sit in a corner of Artebrates room, remembered as the girl from the vats who had trapped Mungo.

And began to hurt Leah so Leah fought her rope, until Leah could take no more and kicked Nannaha hard between the legs, so she fell.

And Nannaha **gazed under the bed and**:

"A man thing is hiding under your bed, what evil do you do behind our master's back?" Nannaha shrieked, ignorant of Mungo's identity and prodded Mungo with her dagger.

A bad mistake.

Illustration: Lord Artebrates believed in setting examples.

For Mungo rolled out the other side and stood with a smile for Leah that vanished as he saw her state, and roared forgetting where he was, and ripped apart the vine rope against Leah's soft skin and wrapped silk about the cut arm.

"Yaa I am locked in with a were-lion creature, may the gods

help me," Nannaha shouted and ran for the door to unlock, but forgot it only opened to Leah's palm print and silent voice which she did not have.

So, banged like a crazy on the closed door.

"WA I am being eaten," as Mungo took her long black hair pulling her backwards.

"I am Mungo foolish woman," he is locking her in a silver cupboard and Leah dressed and armed herself with copper cutlass.

"WA, I like games," Mungo thinking wrong that she had been playing with Nannaha, for he had no idea how man thing woman things got close, apart from kissing and how Sasha got cubs.

"*Which was a rather clever idea then! Yaeko, The Elder approaches, I am off,*" a mazarrat we have come to love or loath?

And Sasha said the Fermanians did it with snakes in public, against walls, in toilets, anywhere, there was no place scared from a Fermanian on heat. "*So, Mungo had the wrong idea, didn't he?*" That mazarrat climbing walls to distance from The Elder.

"Mungo, Leah, we do now?" Thinking his luck was in, silly boy.

And Leah was horrified.

"*And that's what happens when Mungo listens to biased interests and something else which isn't his head? And a young mazarrat I am looking for,*" The Elder.

Now Leah pitied Mungo for she was a comforter trained in the use of weapons for she must protect her Lord and Master against assassins, so could have fought Mungo.

But stood and cheekily let Mungo have a good look, after all that is what he had come for.

"*But he had come for more,*" that mazarrat on the move, "*Mungo came for more,*" copied by the night.

And she slapped his face.

And Mungo jumped back imitating Nannaha.

And Leah cut the air with her cutlass, of course missing Mungo.

"Also contradicting herself, she guessed Nannaha had been correct, Mungo would eat her? Both idiots," the same young mazarrat.

And Leah cursed the day the geneticist had foiled her speech genes, for he was drunk.

And an awoken mazarrat sang sweetly about what was going on for it was excited.

"It was no way to treat the wife," it was one of the night creatures copying that mazarrat.

And Mungo jumped high as Leah swung the cutlass at his ankles.

"Wah, I love you more, I like the Fermanian way of doing it but when do we kiss," and Mungo puttered out his lips.

And light entered one of the two coconuts and Leah comprehended what Mungo was up to.

And she was heartbroken.

For Mungo saw her as comforter only.

Now she swung the cutlass with deadly intent to cut Mungo too shreds.

And Mungo rolled under the bed and jumped across the table.

"What is going on in there?" The hunchback demanded for mazarrats were singing everywhere *"That is no way to treat the wife."*

And a young mazarrat took confidence The Elder had not caught her, so sang like a songbird, *"You cannot catch me old man, I dance to the sailor's horn pipe, and sing to a soldier's pipes, and from treetops spread the news, for I am a mazarrat born free."*

"Mm, well I must admit you are doing a decent job," The Elder overcoming his SHAME.

Is this The Elder or the other one, they all look the same?

Chapter 6 FEVER

And the hunchback sat quietly at Leah's bedside watching her thoughts on the
encephalograph measuring p300 brainwaves made by brain 0.3 per sec as Leah had lost movement even blinking.

"Purple fever is a thief in the night like meningitis that you had long ago, can you remember child? No, well the doctor refused to come out, almost died, well I slit chicken necks on god Telephassa's alter that night.

Did not work little girl, what did was ghostly. I remember looking at the stars and something entered my heart, a voice from a recess of my soul. "She will live," and at once met a living intelligent force greater than that stone idol Telephassa.

And I see you think Mungo? Hurt you? Well, I 'll tell you a secret, he and you are bound like chromosome strands and that voice that night, is the same telling him to dance naked under the moon.

Bet you did not know that?

Those stinking scribes do everything to turn into papyrus books for cash. They speak the woman man thing, is for The Wild One, meaning you.

If I blow my nose, they did oracle the contents and author a book about the future from them.

They are farts and control our fantasies. See one found floating in a sewer? The Prefect of Police thinks Malachi did him, lucky I went down and found the bottle Malachi was drinking from, don't won't that found?

Do not want any cells from fingers going under the electron microscope and having Malachi's DNA linked to their computer memory banks? Took the murdered eyes out as **we do not want the dead's retinas read either,** or see Malachi there throttling him?

Malachi likes you, those scribes say a hunter will help The

Wild One, so do not worry.

Gad, I am believing this rubbish," the hunchback spat and fiddled with a **gene gun** full of **Agrobacterium tumefaciens**, his **gene shuttle vehicle, a soil bacterium** altered to Fermanian needs and on its chromosomes the code for a protein, which would surround the purple fever bacteria thus, strangling it.

And slowly he lowered his glasses; microscopic lenses wired to a **plutonium portable battery cooled by coils of liquid sodium and** saw through the layers of Leah's cells her chromosomes.

And deftly inserted a needle he could not even see at the end of the gene gun and fired.

Saw the **tumefaciens bacteria** enter and watched it slicing her DNA codes and insert its own.

Saw the bacteria stimulate her **RNA polymerase** that started straightening kinks in her chromosomes put there by fever.

Kinks that stopped her healthy cells breathing.

It was a new idea his using the bacterium, was dangerous as never given to lizards, and he was at his wits end for Leah was dying. It worked on rice then it would work elsewhere; it was a natural organic product.

The gene gun had cost him his mother's diamond tiara, everything in his labs below the product of his secret inheritance.

"From his mother, he was a mummy's boy who dressed in sailor outfits or cowboy boots, with 6 guns and all with a difference, he had bowed pigtails," that female young mazarrat, so, even The Elder giggled at this cheek, he did not like Fermanians anyway.

Yet his powerful father gave him nothing, blaming his son's deformity for the death of his wife in childbirth.

Anyway: He had tried the conventional **electroporation** method of inserting genes
into Leah but they failed to kill the fever, and no one had told him about red mangrove melon as something nasty had

happened to the centurion, which he had not heard about as he only moved from his dungeon laboratory to his private cooking cubicle to Leah's besides, catching sleep on a dog's floor mat nearby, so that explained why he was scratching. *"Which he spreads to his pals and other citizens,"* oh what a mischievous mazarrat I am?

"Did it hurt her?" A smooth voice.

"I give painless needles," the hunchback responded afraid Wonder Lord Vinki might do mischief.

And Vinki smoothed the little lizard's man's long black hair tied behind his head, "Then you should serve Artebrates for his hands shake."

"Only Nannaha feeds his habit," the hunchback gritted knowing since she had advanced up the comforter's scale his Lord and master's addiction to poppy was now chronic.

Had stopped using antibiotics to counteract the poppy drug, had become degenerate and typified all that was stinking in Fermanian society.

"Nannaha," the hunchback venomously as he pictured her in black leather surrounded by fawning human slaves, crushing, and heating the poppy seeds for Artebrates.

And when Artebrates dreamed, she and the slaves would play chess?

"Erath," and the hunchback spat out green stuff into a chamber pot. Something splashed out of the pot onto Vinki's soft pink moccasin made of finest human hair.

"Leah on Nannaha's orders had been denied servants during her sickness," a mean one that Nannaha," the mazarrat being a girl knew girls.

So, very slowly Vinki wiped it off on the hunchback who did not protest, to do so would invite a whipping from Vinki's red alligator belt.

Vinki who took magnificent pleasure in handing out the whipping to a friend or slave to Continue, as he easily suffered fatigue being of gentle stock.

"So, Malachi killed the scribe, I wonder how much you know?" Vinki as he fingered orange rouge on Leah's bedside table for, he had overheard.

"A bright color my Lord."

"Yes," Vinki rubbing orange on his cheeks and then played with Leah's blue lipstick.

He also rummaged through Leah's smalls, and the hunchback said nothing; Vinki was Head of Army Purchasing and only a fool crossed him.

Why the hunchback did not move, did not dare too or he did attack Vinki for defiling Leah's clothes.

So, Vinki stole Leah's blue suspenders and wore them: it was fashionable, silk stockings added, and these dandies pranced and popped up all over Fermanian society. They powdered their hair and cheeks, sniffed herbs and drugs from snuff boxes: gambled fortunes on cards and frequented brothels, *"And stuck false black moles on the cheeks,"* a mazarrat copying and soon most creatures that listened to her sprouted at least one black mole.

"Earache," and this time the hunchback swallowed.

"I want Mungo brought back alive, I want to kill him personally, and for this favor I will arm Artebrates regiment in steel swords and laser rifles for his forthcoming campaign against the humans along the Red Grass.

They say Artebrates just wants rid of Leah, for she gives him nightmares about Mungo?

Nannaha says you would like to go with Leah because you are kind to her?" Vinki was a Wonder Lord, "And someone found a blood-stained glove tucked in the murdered scribe's belt, it seems it is Artebrates?" *"Of course, a lie as we know as the glove was blue velvet, not the choice of a great hunter.?"* The mazarrat and the wild answered, *"Malachi did it drunk."*

And the hunchback thought of turning Malachi in to break the influence Vinki would have over Artebrates for planting such evidence.

"Pity your Lord and Master is a poppy freak? He dreams of

civil war?"

And the hunchback hated his master for his weakness and prayed to god Telephassa to send him to hell where Vinki was destined, so he could torture Vinki for eternity.

"Give Leah this," Vinki putting down a vial full of red juice.

"What is it?" That was a brave thing to ask.

"Seems Mungo has given us the cure for purple fever, why I don't know, we are always spreading illness amongst the humans to keep their numbers down?"

And the hunchback knew Vinki would not understand, he could, and it came from loving and caring someone who was always on the receiving end of the stick.

"Because Mungo cannot bring judgement upon us without knowing mercy," the hunchback looking at the vial thinking how Vinki shamed Fermanians, by reducing Mungo's kind act to that of a man thing only fit to clean toilet bowls.

Why Vinki slapped the hunchback's head, so it bounced off the soft mattress Leah was on.

And Vinki held the head down on the mattress so, the lungs suffocated.

Three times the hunchback raked Leah's body gasping for air.

"I don't bloody well like you," Vinki shouted at the weakened hunchback who he now held up by an ear.

The hunchback's mouth swallowed air like a fish out of water.

"Don't let me ever hear you speak well of Mungo," Vinki who twisted the ear he held so it ripped, and the hunchback screamed falling to his face, and Vinki stood once hard on the back of that head.

This effort of busting the hunchback's nose so infuriated Vinki he kicked till overcome by exhaustion, then backed away panting, gasping.

The little hunchback represented all impurity to Vinki, unperfumed and stinking, ugly, and deformed, dark and living in the gutters and under floorboards with the rats; a creepy crawly.

Even the clothes the hunchback wore did not fit, the legs bent, no fashionable clothes could fit.

Ten minutes later Wonder Lord Vinki finished patting down his disturbed hair and tucked Leah's personal items into his pouch.

He also sprayed himself with flower scent to hide the body smells of the hunchback.

And when the door slid shut, the hunchback moved cursing Artebrates for being so weak.

Illustration: Lord Vinki was corrupt and so was Nannaha.

Quickly ignoring his bruises, he forced the melon into Leah's mouth as watery pulp.

Then waited.

So, sat against a wall allowing the cold stone to sooth his aches, and Leah moaned, a good sign, life was returning to the girl, and he would be here when she opened her solid green eyes to see, a friendly face.

*

"No one cares except for me, and Malachi and it must be done," the hunchback alone with Artebrates on the lord's bed.

"Ha, Ha, ha little monster I see someone has given you a good beating," Artebrates reminding the hunchback of his place in society.

And the hunchback wrapped the rubber tube tight about his lord's left biceps to make a vein swell up good.

They looked all red and sore from too many needle pricks; Nannaha was a rogue, selfish and wicked, thinking she controlled Artebrates with poppy seed, but, if, Artebrates fell, so, would they? Who wanted a second-hand comforter? Brothels at the harbor perhaps or, she could earn a living giving quickies to drunken late-night revelers in dark alley ways.

And the hunchback prodded veins and Artebrates howled; infection had set in.

And the hunchback fought for sympathy as, "You have given Leah to Vinki, why my Lord?"

And Artebrates swiped with a hand the hunchback's face to give deliberate pain. Artebrates like Vinki belonged to society, the hunchback belonged to him.

"Hell, fire and dinosaur dung I see Mungo in my dreams using a sword fish on my spine," the reason Artebrates wanted rid of beautiful Leah.

And the hunchback had confidence in that Artebrates under the influence of poppy would not remember done to him.

"Mungo waits for you, you have harmed Leah, given her to the dandy Vinki to harm, Mungo is coming with a swordfish my Lord," and hoped he would too, giving Leah away was the last straw, so he thought! And injected **naltrexone** into Artebrates, could have done it so it scraped a vein but felt since Mungo had given a cure for purple fever for free, so did it painlessly and the drug would stop the poppy producing excess **dopamine**, a **neurotransmitter** inside Artebrates's brain that gave him his high.

"That's torture enough," and "you won't need this," the hunchback clearing a table of needles.

Then left and locked the door, for he had a cloned hand of his Lord and Master, Artebrates, stolen when Artebrates was on a high.

Now he was taking a risk for Artebrates could have him

served up as a selection of sliced meats in his House Berserkas Barracks, "But it need be done to save Leah from Vinki, besides the fool's dream of being emperor will boil him soon enough."

Anyway: Now sometimes later he returned to Artebrates room ready to give

naltrexone again and opened the door with the cloned hand.

"Wah, you almost made my heart stop freak," a lizard in a leopard skin robe

attended by a human slave in a silver stretch one piece said.

"You here?" The hunchback feeling hope crumple and realized he was not the only one using cloned hands to open locked doors.

"Crawled out with roaches, have we?" Nannaha replied, "The deformed come to ask Heaven to escape his back?" Nannaha said pulling a white packet from a pocket, "for you no charge."

And the hunchback looked at Artebrates and was obvious he had a high dose.

"Nannaha?" The hunchback sickening.

"My Lord and Master asked for 'Mr. **Drupe,'** I am loyal and serve his cravings" and the hunchback, *"Gad you bitch of darkness, crawl back to the pit you flew out off?"* A thought only, "Nannaha you are his loyalist servant," and with that retired from the room wishing her dead as 'Drupe the human slave laughed his head off.

An hour and a half layer 'Drupe' left the room, and the hunchback noticed his hair was newly wetted and the zip on the human slave was open at the neck.

"And I know every corner of this castle," the hunchback and followed the slave to a nasty figure, a seller of poppy seed and the hunchback, recognized by the seller, who thought he would sell more; and rewarded with a dagger in his stomach?

"Spare me," the human slave 'Mr. Drupe' begged.

"Help me," the hunchback and together dragged the seller through a secret Doorway, down a flight of stairs and, the place was full of crossroads, but the hunchback knew which way to go.

"And the slave trusted him entirely, silly lave, the hunchback has a dagger, run," a watching mazarrat, see they get everywhere, and soon HER above would sing about what goes on below.

And they came to the hunchback's laboratories, looking like any school lab' but had a difference?

"They say I am a great anatomist, independent of the medical school and the priests; Artebrates backs me in the hope of finding immortality. And slid the seller

of poppy seed down a shaft to waiting crocodiles below.

"They must have been hungry for the splashing was much? My rooms are full of vials, books and empty

cages, empty because what was in them waits for you."

"Arg," the human slave gasped as the hunchback used the dagger again to good effect.

And the slave, pushed down the shaft into the mouth a crocodile, that had the limbs of a dash hound.

"Yaw a aww," the hunchback uncoiling the slave's vitals from his feet and threw them after the body to the crocodiles.

"Go rot in hell scum bag," for the hunchback had no mercy for his type.

"What goes around comes around.

"And that's what you get for trusting a partner in crime," the watching young mazarrat from a hidden wall corridor.

"I don't believe it?" The hunchback hearing the mazarrat.

But in a way he was a slave too, used to death and slaves had no rights, even him, just things that existed for instructions and as food for another.

"I have no remorse, death awaits me too, I have sent them both to a better land, and I want no repercussion from killing the poppy seed seller, slaves know how to

talk, they get it beat out of them."

And after rummaging about his vials found a sedative for Leah, Artebrates could go cold turkey, he deserved no less.

"But another vile returned that night, the vile creature type,

Lord Vinki," a singer.

"How is Artebrates tonight?" he asked Nannaha.

"He sleeps my Lord," and allowed Vinki to wipe his sandals on her black hair:

she was a comforter only.

"Good, keep him on poppy seed so when Leah is well, I may do as I please with her," and he fondled a handful of rings for he planned to pierce her ear, nose, lips, and belly so, all could see Leah was owned by men and tattoo her flesh on shoulder and bottom with inviting signs, so all would know at once she was a

comforter.

And while Vinki dreamed such cruelties, cruel because Leah had no opinion in the matter, the hunchback found his father.

"Wake up father," he shouted as he pumped **naltrexone** into the old warrior in another room. Now and again, he hit the old lizard hard.

"I should let you die, so I can claim my inheritance, all my brothers are dead, and you killed them with your stupid wars; now only I live, and a good lawyer can fix anything."

You disowned me so I live at the level of slave, so am childless," and spat at his father repeatedly.

"Yes, Lord Artebrates was the hunchback's father," a mazarrat already knowing but the listeners did not so gaped astonished.

"Because you are so dam ugly you did have ugly children, and I did disown them in case folk saw I carried bad genes.

I know 10% of children born are not their father's, something as ugly as you could not be mine. What I know before a baby's year is out, the real father see's himself in the child and I do not see me in you, nor when you were a baby. Your mother cheated on me and with what? Ha, ha, ha, ha," his father Artebrates was cruel.

The hunchback felt a volcano erupt in him and knew who the real monster was.

"She never cheated; her servants swore to me before you realized, they loved me with Kindness, so you cooked them," the hunchback replied calmly, how he managed to hold his wrath is Heaven's secret?

"Their sweet meats were good," Artebrates and his deformed son compared him to Mungo and sighed disgusted, this **was** his father.

"Now your legal male children are dead, burned by humans to ensure they cannot be cloned, now the only seed left is mine," the hunchback.

"Not so monster, I have whore sons, many," his father seeing a way out and looking for more poppy seed and, "You killed your mother."

"You are lying dinosaur dung head; it wasn't my back that split her so in childbirth, so, she bled, it was you, where were you that night?

Sucking poppy seed and you left Vinki and his quack to her needs; you killed her dinosaur dung head," and hated his father even more so than he already did.

Artebrates checked his plate of poppy seed, he did not like anyone belittling him about his habit and put on a stupid face, as if he could not care, but he did, deep down, just was not showing the hurt.

"If it wasn't for Leah I did have left long ago," the hunchback continued.

"And I did set the hunting lions Abel and Eve on you, as is my right as your Lord and Master, slave because you would be an escaped slave because I owe you."

"Stuff you," the hunchback shouted unable to absorb any more punishment and just before he shut the door, Artebrates called out, "I suggested to Vinki she die."

The hunchback's heart murmured; his father had ordered mummies death under the hands of a sadist. "Hail Emperor Artebrates," and went straight to Leah's room and used the cloned palm print on it b*ut it would not open. Was father lying to wind him up?*

"Someone outside," Nannaha to Vinki who was admiring his body piercing work and Nannaha flicked on a video screen, and they saw the fuming hunchback outside Leah's room.

"Let him wait," Vinki as he hung yellow silks from his swishing lizard tail, and Nannaha turned down the door volume so never heard "Mungo will eat your livers
for you."

Two hours later the hunch back stopped crying outside the door and swore he did burn down the rotten city of Telephassa with every foul lizard in it.

"According to the prophecy this isn't supposed to happen. Dam scribes and them lies," he screamed.

Illustration: Abel and Eve invite you to supper

He also realized if father was telling the truth, he had murdered mummy legally
by letting Vinki at her over a lie she had cheated on him.

"Why?" He asked and answered "Because you are Lord and Master, why not let the hunting lions Abel and Eve at her, it would have been more merciful than
Vinki."

He also remembered it was Vinki who had boasted he had caught his mother in bed with a House Berserka.

"A no one House Berserka who wouldn't be missed when he was quickly hung from a beam in the great dining hall, as an example to others to keep their place in society.

And his mother's tongue cut out to stop her telling her side.

If daddy got his poppy seed, he could not care what happened.

And never heard Vinki boast, "I have Artebrates' new will, I will inherit everything, and he can live here in his castle till his death, *which won't be far away, does that please you Nannaha my girl?"*

Again, Nannaha fell to her knees so Vinki could wipe his feet on her hair, "I am loyal to my Lord and Master, and give him anything he so desires as I am his number one comforter," and as for Vinki would pump the old foolish warrior full of poppy till he burst.

Vinki loved her, and the more powerful Vinki was, the more powerful she became, and one day she would be the power behind the throne Nannaha believed.

"You speak wisely child," and led Nannaha to a bedchamber, "and feed my pha well with that hunch back."

"Lord and Master the feed will be mixed well with him," and Nannaha comforted the wondrous Wonder Lord Vinki.

And much later Leah's door opened and these two, departed and the hunchback asleep, Vinki wiped his feet on the little man's head.

"What goes on here?" The hunch back rising and realizing what had happened anger consumed him.

"Dinosaur dung head," the hunchback and leapt, so he planted both his feet into Vinki.

"Gad that hurt," and was the hunch back whose bandaged ribs hurt from Vinki's earlier beating.

"Slave," a priest shouted as both holy men tried to pull the hunchback away from Vinki. Now these two were bodyguards for a third priest behind.

But the hunchback, "I aim well even with black eyes," and hit both priests in the throat, killing them.

And the third priest shouted, "I am a legal scribe so protected by the law."

But the hunchback had just crossed the law's boundaries. *"He was now bandit, outcast, robber, murderer, swindler and more,"* a mazarrat warning listeners who might be the next victims, for mazarrats know how to make an audience listen.

And this man ruffled under his black robes for a laser pistol, and the hunchback intuition filling him landed upon him, twisting the pistol down and against the
priest, so cut off both the man's legs so he fell and balanced on the stumps left.

"Mercy," the priestly scribe begged.

"Man, of the law I am now my own law," and used the laser to open the scribe's sweetmeat to the world.

"Surely a son of Artebrates," an admiring mazarrat.

"Awa," Nannaha screamed fleeing to her own room whose door she bolted, just in case a cloned hand was in the possession of the deranged hunchback?

"Vinki's safety was far from her thoughts." The mazarrat telling the story.

And muttered brave words to herself because she primed the laser pistol, she kept in a draw for emergencies.

"Not much good having one if it isn't ready for use?" The mazarrat knowing it needed charged.

So, never heard the hunchback cry over Leah or return to his father's room.

Here he left a note, "Father, this was Leah's."

And left the rings he had carefully removed from Leah. Leah was not into body piercing: she knew her body was beautiful enough.

At that moment, a black fly bit Nannaha and was full of **onchorcerciasis** which was river blindness, but she did not know that.

And Vinki escaped, and deep in his heart he wanted Artebrates dead for as legal heir, he could have Artebrates green houses, for his own had shattered during a **cosmic**

storm that had brought radioactive ions into his cotton crops within.

He was now penniless; just a greedy lizard man; and Cathbadh had emptied his granaries to the mob.

And Lord Artebrates dreamed of successful civil war.

And that is all it would be, thanks to poppy seed, dreams.
Cathbadh.

"You are blood?" Carman.

And Cathbadh knew there was no point denying so shrugged.

So, Carman studied him good.

She saw much of King Sess in him and was pleased.

"Come and eat," and Cathbadh accepted sitting beside her on a lounger ate vinegared human sweet meats.

"Vinki is useful, a monarch needs an unpopular minister for her people to hate," pause, "they love you."

"I fed them in your name."

"Why didn't you throw in your lot with Prince Annunaki?"

"Dead, isn't he?"

And Carman laughed, "I like you Cathbadh, they say you are a wizard, show me some tricks"

And Cathbadh put his head on her feet, and she wiped her naked feet on them.

"He was no fool," a watching mazarrat behind a plaster crack.

The election for the new Senate is in two months. I will show you how to put your people there and not Vinki's," Cathbadh and rose and opened his mouth to accept a morsel of sweet meat from her.

"Serve me well," Carman and he did, and **time stops for no one,** not even for the black domestic beetle that crawls out of floorboards to eat food remains under the red moon. **"So Cathbadh returning home found the frightened hunchback waiting for him.** *"What will happen next, more murder,"* a mazarrat sang and the wild held its breath anticipating, what?

"How did you get in?" Cathbadh *"A silly question?"* The

mazarrat and the jungle and red grass laughed.

"Master teacher, you gave me a cloned hand when I was your student," the hunchback on his face for Cathbadh to wipe his feet on his hair. And Cathbadh did

shaking his head, making a mental note to retrieve the hand, and to who else he had given his cloned hand too?

"I need help, I have beaten Wonder Lord Vinki," and explained and Cathbadh grinned.

"I will seek Carman and get her to grant you immunity from Vinki, anyway tell me how your experiments are going?"

"Well soon the question of our infertility will be a nightmare of the past," the hunchback still flat.

"That will go well in your favor for Carman is relying on us. She knows only you and I can solve the problems that decline our race, but you must promise not to harm Vinki again, after all he is a Lord and what are you?"

"A monster," the hunchback quietly.

"Yes, quite so."

AND BOTH THOUGHT OF THEIR RACE'S BIGGEST PROBLEM,

The Wild One.

And when the red sun rose the hunchback was in front of his Mighty One who had no sympathy for him.

An attack on a ruling noble was an attack on the ruling class of which she belonged too. The aggressor punished to discourage further attacks on her divine enlightened position.

"You will be taken to the poultry market and beaten with sticks till you faint and left there till the next sun. Count yourself fortunate little man that Cathbadh speaks in your favor," Carman.

The hunchback crawled forward and kissed her sandaled feet in gratitude.

Carman smiled; she always liked her mercy appreciated.

"Oh, Mighty One please hang him from my kitchen so he can see the pots and cauldrons ready for him," Lord Vinki complained and his Mighty One cast a stony look at him, and bent forward, "Artebrates is our only hope of crushing the humans, harm him not, but slip the executioner a gold coin to make sure the hunchback does not faint too soon."

Vinki smiled, she was indeed cunning, worthy opponent and was satisfied.

He would slip gold coins that way and the hunchback restrained from fainting all day.

"Now Vinki trembled "I lost the mob when Cathbadh gave my grain to them, but soon the senators you have never heard of will demand your banishment, and as for Artebrates, I own him, and his gold will pay my expenses." The mazarrat quoted Vinki's thoughts who gasped in horror they were now song.

And allowed Carman to wipe her perfumed feet on his hair as a sign of submission.

And mazarrats sang for Leah and The Elder heard, and said to young ones, *"There are many false prophets such as scribes, only listen to me for I am The Elder he that is to lead our people to light,"* and the young ones understood; *"except for one," "yeh it is me,"* and sang sweetly.

All knew one day they did live above ground where there was sunshine, and no recycled air. Did hear birds instead of lathes and fountains than a turned-on tap.

They could toilet where they pleased like other wild beasts instead of in steel drums, which went for fertilizer for the vast vegetable burrows, heated by abandoned nuclear reactors.

And they need not fear the reactors exploding. *"We will only listen to him that is close to the light,"* meaning The Elder.

"I am the way," and The Elder smiled, and Mungo is the chosen instrument, protect him.

"I am an alternative way," she now risked her life as
The Elder knew there was only One Way, his.

Chapter 7 Enkalla

And that serrant, a primitive cousin of the lizard people begged of Mazarrats, "Give me help for I am sick, and I will tell you what you want to know," and the mazarrats gave him berries and red grass to eat, and the serrant spoke of the centurion of archers and the mazarrats sang and Enkalla arrested.

For all young mazarrats sing, *"Enkalla cages mazarrats as singing pets, revenge is sweet for he will be caged now."*

As for the wicked serrant, berries and red grass did not cure it of hepatitis, so was ill six lunar months. For as all young mazarrats sing, *"Mazarrats are serrant snacks."*

Now Enkalla stood proudly as his silver armor stripped from him by red robed executioners in tyrannosaurus masks. *"If it was me, did have wet myself giggle,"* yes still singing away.

Malachi his brother stood holding his sobbing seven-year nephew, who could not care Fermanians were brave and fearless, just father manacled at the ankles by chain to a post at Executioner's Bay.

And executioners' emptied chub into rock pools that waited for the rising tide.

"And the mazarrats are the media of this alien world, and as all young mazarrats know, the only good Fermanian is a dead one. They do horrid things too mazarrats, firstly, eat them, train them to fight each other in gambling dens, put them in cages to sing like nightingales and skin and stuff them full of saw dust to sell as ornaments," she sang, and the listeners were dismayed mazarrats were treated badly.

And as for the rock pool, first would come the crabs and small dinosaurs, and if Enkalla was lucky a giant flesh eater to end his misery quick, for the manacle was long for him to run from predators, and to swim when the tide rose, but not long enough to escape.

And with the tide a following Mosassurus to gobble what left all up.

Not a trace for the crabs to finish off later either!

But as this was winter, and the seals and tuna gone, with the Mosassurus, Enkalla might last seven days before exhaustion drowned him, before eaten.

And it was official tourist policy to encourage boaters and surfers around the winter shores of Telephassa City, and when they vanished, strong currents blamed.

"In truth, Mosasaurus was feeding." A mazarrat and a hush fell upon her listeners, afraid to breath.

And a red robed executioner threw the key to his locks into mangrove mud to sink, and left, and Malachi led the boy away who kicked and screamed, "Daddy." *And a spare key existed as they needed the lock open for the next victim, not fools these lizards, giggle,"* the mazarrat knows Fermanians.

"He is a good soldier," Lord Artebrates looking down from the Royal Observation tunnel and he did not feel well, in fact dam right shaky.

"He let Mungo live," Carman replied.

"He showed how to quell the sickness," Lord Artebrates trying to save the life of a good man.

"He is Mungo's friend," Carman and retreated to the comfort of cushions were Wonder Lord Vinki served her wine, and by this act, showed Artebrates he was out of Favor about Enkalla.

And Artebrates looked at the honor guard about her and could not read their eyes, staring unfocussed in front of nothing but read their minds.

Knew each Berserka personally, only the bravest went into the honor guard and they came from his regiments.

Smelt the pity in their minds.

Knew they waited for him to become Artebrates again, *"If ever,"* the mazarrat laughing so, the listeners laughed and Fermanians looked to the laughter with distort minds.

But part of Artebrates could not care anymore, arthritis

had set in and was waiting for new joints in his fingers, but the operation put off because of campaigns against encroaching humans, like the war he planned now against them along the Red Grass Plateau.

And he knew Nannaha with poppy seed would be coming too. The war was set, there were good officers and willing soldiers to die for Telephassa's victory: they could die without him.

He was only a needed figurehead; this time he would not be up front freezing his tail off in furs, but in one of them new flying machines, warm watching Nannaha light his poppy pipe.

"He was a fool; soldiers loved him because he was up front with them freezing tails off!" The mazarrat and the wild nodded agreement.

"Mungo," the scream of victory came from Enkalla and made Artebrates come out of his dreams.

"A good man," Artebrates sighed as one executioner cut deftly Enkalla's limbs to make good chub.

"I have a seventh cousin removed and recommend him as new Centurion of Archers," Vinki.

"One of yours, a weakling," Artebrates who did not know he had signed his

possessions away to Vinki. *"That's what the fool gets from salivating over Nannaha, giggle,"* the mazarrat parading on a tree branch in Nannaha's stolen lingerie, and wild things went, *"Get them off"* in imitation of the Fermanians.

"You are on your way-out sunshine, too sinewy, Carman likes us soft and perfumed," Vinki smirking and returned to The Mighty One to massage her shoulders for the day had been strenuous.

As for Artebrates, dismissed by Carman who sighed as Vinki's fingers stroked down her back.

"My friends scream you are divine, and should have a temple built in your honor," Vinki.

"My shoulder aches here," Carman replied letting Vinki

114

think the idea of divinity came from him, and not god Telephassa. "To make your religious subjects submissive in more ways than one," he said, and then she examined his soft gold torc with three faces on one head and marveled at the human artisanship.

"Where did you get this?" She asked.

"A human called John Wrexham," Vinki pleased she liked, "*a right stinker, giggle,*" the mazarrat knew Wexham.

"Artebrates," she relayed, and the old general returned finding his legs stiff from drug withdrawal.

"Bring me more like this," and Artebrates understood, gold kept everyone happy. So did Vinki who planned Artebrates would never come off his poppy seed.

"Gold is power, gold makes the world go around," Carman hoping the Berserkas loyalty bought with better weapons; the gold was hers.

And Artebrates dismissed, ventured down to Executioner's Bay where he saw Malachi with his nephew, Akkad on a cliff.

And Artebrates watched a good man dying, and understood why the condemned had shouted, "Mungo," in defiance of everything that was Vinki in the empire.

That there was one, The Wild One who would destroy Enkalla's enemies and satisfy vengeance was worrying for vengeance was a human.

"And the good man dying is me, "Artebrates just before he saw the man thing.

"Remember me," Mungo to Enkalla as the tide flowed in, "W*ith flotsam from sewer outlets, phew, dirty lizard folk, not clean like us house trained mazarrats giggle snort giggle,*" was this mazarrat snorting opium?

"Mungo?"

And Carman did not hear as she was far away.

And Mungo threw a lance into the back of a Mosasaurus, then jumped on its back and stabbed with a short sword.

"Die water lizard," Mungo shouted as he pulled his sword out and thrust again, seeking a heart.

"Daddy," Akkad shouted.

"Dam Mungo," Malachi seeing himself as the next offering on the tide.

And the Mosasaurus floated away, and Mungo started to dig Enkalla out of the mud.

"Hold man thing," Malachi and pointed a laser pistol at the post and cut it in two.

"That was close," Enkalla.

"I am doomed," Malachi's reply.

"You are free centurion," Mungo.

"Were too, I cannot return to Telephassa?"

"No one saw us, I am still safe," Malachi.

"I will take you and the boy to Hurreva City, the lizard men there need good men," Mungo offered and by now the three were on the rocks and Akkad joined,

"Daddy," he sobbed.

Illustration: Mosassurus

And Artebrates watched understanding why Malachi had helped Mungo. It would not do for the hated man thing to save the life of the centurion, as brave and fearless Fermanians stood by doing nothing.

"But I must see Leah, then we go," Mungo.

"You mean your lion nose has not scented her?" Malachi.

"What do you mean?"

"If it had not been for my brother's execution, I would

be there armed waiting for you. She is bait for you off Set Highway," Malachi warned.

"I must go to her," Mungo.

"Wait, we will all go together," Malachi's crazy idea, for he was crossing the RED LINE.

"Traitor," Artebrates sighed and left meaning he was the traitor to himself and swore he would change his ways and cried sin out of his eyes.

At that moment something good filled his heart, and he fell to his knees and talked straight to himself.

"The old fool has fallen, let me replace him Carman, and I will crush the humans," Vinki boasted watching from her palace.

Now the Berserka lines advanced uniformly to protect Artebrates their commander.

"They dislike you Vinki," Carman seeing, "*hate more like it,*" the mazarrat and the wild rattled branches that sounded like, "*hate.*"

"Traitors too you mistress, boil them all, throw their cooked meats into Executioner's Bay," Vinki hoped.

Now Carman remembered she had not paid the Berserkas, and chilled, seeing corruption to blame, and all that was corrupt in Telephassa seeped from Vinki.

And Vinki shivered from her look.

And Carman called out, "Artebrates I have punished you enough, good men are needed in Telephassa," and said this to mollycoddle the Berserkas who stopped and looked at her.

"Artebrates is hero," she shouted and the Berserkas cheered.

Now nearby a fearless and brave mazarrat listening soon would tell her kind what it saw and heard and in two months one recently caged, would sing of it and ordinary Fermanians would wonder what sort of man thing Mungo was.

"*Carmen is not daft,*" one of the mazarrat songs.

"*Artebrates knows Mungo's unseen God,*" other mazarrats would sing.

For Artebrates on his knees mumbled, and the spying mazarrats with their good
hearing heard, "It is inside me, I know Mungo's secret, and we inherit Light at birth on a gene. It is logic and common sense, and mops darkness which is cruelty.

God Telephassa cannot hear us from a stone seat in Heaven. We hear ourselves; the light hears us and grows inside with logic and straight living.

I believe in Mungo's God who is the life that flows through all of us, it is omnipotent, it is light.

The omnipotence is water, and we live in that water," so Artebrates sang.

"Look the old fool is dancing," Vinki hoping to belittle Artebrates more.

"No, he dances with life, he will lead the campaign," and Carman shoved Vinki out of the way, and he tripped falling exposing navy-blue stocking clad limbs, and carmen was disgusted she allowed him to massage her, *But was alright, he longed for lingerie and not her throne,*" a mazarrat choir and added, *"Maybe is Daft."* And Carman trod over him, and he protested not and the Berserkas cheered.

"To each of Artebrates heroes a barrow of this human gold, take Artebrates and march to the Red Grass my heroes," Carman shouted needing the gold.

And honor guards beat their shields and advanced and trod upon Vinki deliberately and Carman said nothing but not, "Us, and the nailed boots shredded Vinki's stockings, ripped his thin flower print jacket open, showing Vinki had grown small breasts.

This was not the time to be absolute but to give them something they hated; Vinki.

And these men put Artebrates upon a shield and carried him.

And Vinki from his position watched little red land crabs scuttle over his nose.

And crabs' bit Vinki.

"Let there be a feast to honor General Artebrates return," the men shouted, a feast and quarter moon cycle holiday, then the Great Artebrates will lead the Berserkas of Telephassa against the humans," Carman promised but showed them no gold for Vinki had stolen most of it hidden under bad army purchases.

"I am not great, Life is great," Artebrates and men saw he was not boastful like Vinki.

Now Carman ever the show woman put Artebrates in her chariot and went home followed by cheering Berserkas.

And when Artebrates had mounted the chariot, he had stood upon a little red land crab and said, "Who have I stood upon."

"*Surely he has met Mungo's God,*" The Wild before the mazarrat we love could sing a note in C minor.

And Vinki lifted his face and said, "The gods exist upon Mount Tullos, they reward us with harems of humans. All know to kill a human while dying is to gain entry to Mount Tullos, Artebrates will not gain entry to Naja as he will die from the poppy seed not in battle."

And marching Berserkas trod over Vinki, pushing him into yuck, so he stunk giggle, foul lizard, better run chameleon as Carmen will give you cooked to her guard," the mazarrat quickly singing before The Wild or listeners could be first to sing.

Chapter 8 Bait

Now Leah was bait, and her perfume wafted to the forest, and she hoped Mungo would come before a flesh eater.

"What have I done to thee my Lord and Master that I should be eaten?" Her silent mouth.

"You were better than me," Nannaha reading her lips and the House Berserka bodyguards gave their hearts to Leah, but Artebrates had commanded, "Guard Nannaha my new Number One Comforter."

And these Berserka were Artebrates offspring from comforters, whores, and slaves and they numbered a hundred under a centurion, and all treated kindly by Leah.

And butterflies flew about Leah, and the Berserkas witnessed saying, "God Telephassa knows she is good and Artebrates does wrong."

"Fools do you think rabbit feet cures your pox?" And Nannaha swatted yellow

butterflies killing two and a third she pulled its wings off.

"Nannaha has the dark god Arawan in her," and distanced themselves for Nannaha was ignorant of what had happened at Executioner's Bay, but not of her darkness for she selfishly gloated in torturing insects, thinking she impressed the Berserkas.

"She is a bully," so impressed and Nahanna went to Leah and cut Leah's arms so blood would bring Mungo the lion man thing and killed.

"What you do is wrong," the centurion of her escort complained.

"I am Nannaha."

"So?" And Nannaha slapped him, and he led her away all saw the satisfaction in the soldier's faces at her discomfiture.

And the Berserkas loved Leah, had she not stopped lashings ordered by Artebrates?

Had she not sold her gold trinkets for their children's medicines?

Sent the hunchback to sew their wounds.

 Found homes for their orphans.

 "Lady Leah they whispered behind Artebrates for he was a real Noble.

And the cheeky mazarrats saw and sang about kind-hearted Leah.

"Say again favorite Nannaha what title Leah has given herself?" Artebrates amongst his poppy clouds.

"Lady," wicked Nannaha and pored warm oils over his back to massage and, "You will make her legally your wife."

"I love her dearly, why has she done this to me? Does she not know this is a capital crime?" Artebrates his mind sliding away where he saw Leah sitting on the Rose Throne and all mighty men shouting, "Hail Mighty One Leah,"

And Nannaha knew it was a capital crime!

 "She must surely die to teach us comforters their place," Nannaha crooned and "When Carman hears of it, she will ask why you have not cut off her arms when Leah held them out to welcome you to her bosom.

"Gad Telephassa Carman will use my innards as fishing bait," Artebrates groaned.

"Not if you send Leah out as bait for Mungo who fills your mind with nightmares.

 You must protect yourself Lord and Master."

"You comfort me always Nannaha, why do I always overlook you for Leah?"

"The soldiers whisper she is a witch."

"The mazarrats don't sing of this?"

"She has cast spells on them, but I have found one she has not harmed," and Nannaha pulled a cloth off a bird cage and there sat a green mazarrat ready to sing.

"Leah boils newts for potions to seduce Artebrates and

Berserkas," the mazarrat sang as it did not want beaten by Nannaha anymore the more.

It was a young mazarrat and inexperienced so did not realize Nannaha would eat it anyway, to keep it silent.... forever.

And Artebrates was afraid of Leah and wanted her dead.

"You are lucky my Lord and Master Leah has not given you something from a Berserka, you know what ink pots they visit, Moragana!"

And Artebrates looked down at his groin and feared.

"And she may carry Mungo's brat within her and lie and say it is yours Lord and Master."

Now it was too much for Artebrates; escaped, now on a shield to inspect his troops.

"Artebrates," they chanted, and he felt good and swelled with pride, he would lead them against the humans and let them loot and rape, for humans were not Fermanians and outside the law.

Above floated jelly fish inflated with methane gas and controlled by kite handlers below.

And Artebrates smiled imagining their four-hundred-yard-long trailers stinging and pulling into their mouth's human warriors.

And Artebrates saw flying machines overhead with colored smoke, and behind Pteranodons with brass armored plates and their warriors holding lances high.

A wagon creaked, Artebrates looked, in it a six-hundred-yard-long worm to go underneath the human walls, so the earth would collapse entombing them.

"Death to the Red Plains," he called.

"Artebrates, Artebrates," the Berserkas thinking of gold, glory and drink, human wenches, and food, after fun, and Carman smiled from her Royal Observatory, and behind her cowed Vinki. Below French horns played Telephassa's anthem, and Berserkas saluted Carman. "Gold buys Vinki," meaning the gold he stole from Artebrates which she stole from him.

And threw him a gold torc, she would be getting more soon.

Vinki brightened.

She also shared a tray of sweetmeats fresh from the slave pens.

Vinki was smiling as he ate, Carman had forgiven him?

And Artebrates had no thoughts on Leah, she was part of his nightmare and his sweet Nannaha would make sure Mungo would not hunt him again.

And The Elder explains: *"While Artebrates sucked his poppy seed he thought he dreamed the above, but it was real, he was on his way to the Red Plains on poppy seed, unable to distinguish between reality and dream worlds.*

And Nannaha wanted Leah out of the way in case she was with Artebrates child and as she emphasized to her Lord, 'it is common ten out of every hundred are not their father's, Mungo's perhaps?"

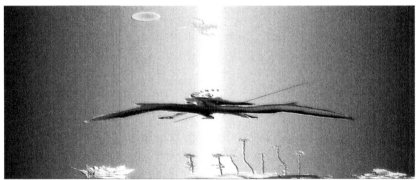

Illustration: Pteranodons with brass armored plates and their warriors holding lances high.

"And easy because she is a comforter and whore Artebrates reasoned," forgetting it was he who ordered her to comfort his friends? "If she is innocent god Telephassa will bring her back as number two comforter, if not she will be eaten by the wild beasts of the jungle," also, "I will poison her flesh so when Mungo touches her, he will die, and this pleased Nannaha much.

And while Artebrates drifted into a dream world, Nannaha whispered to him, "Leah sells your secrets to your enemies in Hurreva City State and poisons your food, only eat what Nannaha gives you."

So Artebrates still had nightmares for the food he ate, poisoned.

And Malachi showed Mungo where Leah was.

That Sasha had her.

So, "What about you beloved Sasha?" Mungo wondering about her feelings, would she eat Leah from jealousy?

"Not me craven man thing *but the killer of killers,*" she replied, and Mungo knew she spoke of tyrannosaurus who was forty feet long and called Mungo craven for he wanted Leah. "It came for your woman but if I had not allowed it to chase me this vat would be eaten by now. Why I saved her when I wish her destruction?" Sash sadly.

"Praise be to what I dance too Sasha spared Leah," Mungo.

"I don't want to dance like you for your God scares me Mungo, and if you know what is wise, come back to me and your lion ancestor spirits," Sasha looking at Leah who had skinny limbs compared to her?

Now, Nannaha and the Berserkas had fled to a blockhouse when seeing the killer of killers' approach.

"Kill them all even Malachi who is Mungo's friend," Nannaha screamed from the blockhouse.

But the Berserkas did not throw their pilums at Malachi.

So Nannaha, "Give me a pilum," and the Berserka refused for Malachi was a good man, so she took a short sword and thrust it deep under his chest armor, so his blood gushed out.

And she threw his pilum missing Malachi.

And the Decurion surgeon came and unstrapped the Berserkas armor and saw the wound was deep and the man would die.

"Your body will be preserved, and you will be cloned when we take you back to Telephassa City," the surgeon.

"No, he will not, I have Artebrates attorney, and I give death to all whom refuse my commands," and she stood upon the Berserker's windpipe and the man's face blued.

And not one Berserka stopped Nannaha for what she had said was true.

But at that moment Mungo threw the pilum back, so Nannaha had to duck and roll to save her life and the man could breathe again.

"Attack them, attack them," Nannaha called and the Berserkas fearing Executioner's Bay formed a shield wall, and advanced upon Mungo and his party.

"The world has gone crazy when I fight next to Mungo my enemy," Malachi
fingering his laser pistol and cutlass.

"Brother he is a good man thing, better to die by his side than under the feet of Nannaha's orderings," Malachi's brother Enkalla.

"Daddy," Akkad howled but Mungo called out in ape tongue and picked the boy up and climbed up vines into a tree where primates took him.

"Hold Fermanian officer, Mungo saves your child," Sasha growled stopping him climbing the vine too.

"Give me copper sword Malachi," Leah and he gave, and a flash grenade for stunning wild beasts which she threw at the shields, and it exploded breaking the shield wall that would close again; but not before Enkalla and Malachi charged the gap.

And Malachi's laser reflected off the crystal shields for they were prisms, and Enkalla swore, "Bloody hell fire Malachi throw the gun away and use sword before you blind us all."

"A clever idea," and Malachi used a hammer he had swinging at his belt.

And shattered the crystal shields.

Now at that moment there was a roar which froze all for the *killer of killers* attracted by the din had returned for supper.

"Run," was the advice of a Berserka, and they fled to the

blockhouse, but one caught by the monster and shaken like a doll from side to side, for swallowing more easily by the dinosaur.

"Taste this tick hide," Malachi shouted and shot it with laser, but it was only a pistol, so only opened wounds and the *killer of killers* stamped the ground in fury, and some brave and fearless Berserkas, as is the Fermanian way attacked the beast and chopped with their throwing axes, and one was crushed so his bile splashed open his fellows.

"Come Leah," Enkalla to make Leah retreat for Malachi was able to care for himself.

And the roar of a mighty lion came from Mungo upon the tyrannosaur's neck, and he cut the spine, tissue, nerve and bone and the beast ran off with Mungo.

And armed mazarrats appeared from nowhere following. To the Fermanian the world was ending for mazarrats were but singing birds in cages, good to eat barbecued, and now they had seen them armed as men, like themselves?

"And girls for mazarrats are neither patriarch nor matriarch, except for him, The Elder," a certain female mazarrat sang.

Now those Berserkas who had not fought but hid reappeared ashamed, from the blockhouse with Nannaha.

"Kill them, kill them all," Nannaha but ignored for the Berserkas believed they owed Mungo life for blockhouses had crumpled under the assault of the **killer of killers**.

As every soldier of Telephassa knows, Wonder Lord Vinki is Head of the Army Purchasing Department and buys cheap cement and pockets the difference.

Whispered Nannaha was Vinki's whore.

"Lady Leah are you alright?" Their centurion taking courage from Malachi who had defied Nannaha.

"What about me?" Nannaha complained and a soldier passing pushed her into a bush, where thousands of midges found her and fed.

"Holly sparrows," Nannaha screamed forgetting Leah now.

"That bitch will have us all in glass cages in the arena full of bees for that," a Berserka voiced as Nahanna was Artebrates number one comforter, and what done to her done back to the oppressors.

"Come with us," Mungo dropping from a tree with savage apes that looked man thing.

"Are you a forest nymph?" A Berserka asked and temptation to be something he wasn't entered Mungo, and his mouth opened agreement, but then his mind saw a silence and he, "I am learning to be man thing and am flesh like you. We are all the same mold under the sun, let us not fight."

"Such wisdom from a forest dweller, where does he come from?" A Berserka asked.

"He comes from the latrine house," Nannaha shouted and a Berserka threw clumps of dung left by the *killer of killers* at her, and others copied so, Nannaha cried for she now stunk so, hundreds of flies sought her for a snack, as well as the midges. *"She was a honeycomb to them buzz bite buzz."* Our mazarrat again still alive.

"Where are you going Mungo?" The centurion asked keeping his hands away from his swords.

"To Hurreva of course," Mungo happily walking up to Leah and he said, "I am sorry."

"Oh, Mungo how can I hate a lion cub?" Leah's mouth silently.

Now this confused Mungo for he was doing his utmost to be man thing, so in the end he smiled and shrugged his massive shoulders, and Leah fell upon him sobbing, *"so the blood from her cuts ran down him to form pools, and an army surgeon came and worked on her, painlessly of course",* our beloved singer and the listeners, The Wild, the jungle, the red grass all sighed for romance was here.

"What about me? You cannot leave me here?" Nannaha hotly as a disturbed giant tarantula reared up to bite, but Mungo caught it.

"Roasted they are good to eat, have some Leah, no, Malachi?"

"Cub, it is time I taught you something about women," Malachi promised.

"What's that?" Mungo suspiciously. *"Mungo knew all there was about girls." They liked combed, massaged and precious commodities Fermanians owned, gold, silks and a Fermanian steak,"* and the listening laughed at a mazarrats humor.

"About the finer things man things are."

"What does finer mean?"

"Good things," Malachi replied.

"Giant tarantulas are finer things."

And Leah cried.

"I see I've much work," Malachi allowing Leah to sob in his arms.

And a mazarrat from a tree did toilet on Nannaha, as it copied its betters the Berserkas.

And Nannaha said nothing she had poisoned Leah but waited patiently for Mungo to eat Leah.

*

Now it was a long trek to Hurreva City, for the empire of Carman would take a human three thousand days to walk from west to east, just the direction Mungo was

going. *"It was sure to give you blisters,"* and that mazarrat blew upon its feet and her audience loved her, even so the Fermanians had to laugh.

And it was upon this great trek that Mungo met his own kind, warrior's intent on killing lizard men, women and children for lizard meat tasted good roasted, broiled, or barbecued if it was Fermanian.

It was also now that Nannaha did wrong, "This embalmed body stinks of the urinal," she often sprinkling perfume on herself and the Berserkas laughed, for she carried he, whom she had killed, with the sword, remember the Berserka promised cloning by the surgeon?

Then one day the embalmed vanished and they said, "Nannaha could not carry him, someone stole him who was to be cloned."

"It was Mungo, I saw and followed, and he cut the liver out and ate then climbed a tree to watch dinosaurs come to eat the rest," Nannaha said lying.

"I am Bennathan Centurion and I know a man or lizard thing of honor so answer Mungo, did you do this?"

And Mungo drew a picture in the dust of a man thing taking a rib from a lizard Hunter, and put the rib on his necklace, then saw the hunter dead and the man thing give the rib to a lizard doctor, and next the hunter cloned.

"The rib is Malachi's and about Mungo's neck," and the soldiers left alone and saw Nannaha as dirt and treated her as such.

And Malachi he said, "Blow me over my rib will be my insurance, better to trust Mungo than my own kind."

"Malachi was his friend." A mazarrat sang nearby.

"Now I understand and curse fate," Malachi also.

But Mungo sent Sasha to find the dumped soldier's body and they followed.

"Ashes, he can never be cloned again. I thought Nannaha said Mungo fed him to our cousins the dinosaurs?" Ben Nathan and his men suspected one of themselves of helping Nannaha for the reward of her body.

"Any who call me liar will answer to Artebrates in Hurreva City for extradition can be arranged," Nannaha haughtily and not harmed but a week later at camp.

"Nannaha you should change, be like Mungo who dances to something Unseen and powerful," Leah with hand signs.

"Go eat dinosaur dung," Nannaha and waited for the next Berserka to drag her into his green army tent.

"Why don't you ask Mun go for this too stop?" Leah.

"Ask that naked squirrel for a favor, are you mad?" *"Now that was rich since she was naked in the tents visited,"* and the mazarrat showed her moon to Nannaha and listeners copied, and from jungle edge beastly moons, winded so the Fermanians gasped for air.

"If you want this to stop, I will tell Mungo."

"Listen Lady Leah, I don't care what happens to me these days. This way Artebrates will know I did not join you, that his Berserkas forced me to lie with them, besides there is not anything better than a good tumble to pass the time before I am back in Telephassa City, and you lot crucified."

"Even in Mungo's eyes you are worth something, that thing he dances too knows that."

"Maybe I just like men," Nannaha.

"Mungo likes women," the mazarrat joked to lift the atmosphere.

"So, the lion monkey is straight, well I like anything to do with a tumble, bosoms full of milk and babies in a tummy put there by strong Berserkas.

Yes, I love men."

"Maybe Nannaha you speak wisely, I knew an alcoholic who got implants to stop her ways, but always got them removed so she could drink.

Enjoyed drunkenness, no responsibilities, plenty of guilt free fun, always can blame the drink, don't know what I am doing, it's called the **"Throw it syndrome,"** yes Nannaha, you like being wicked and having a tumble," and Leah joined Mungo at the fire, and Nannaha threw a clump of red grass at Leah's back.

"But Leah ignored the clumps as hurriedly thrown, so missed and hit a spying young female mazarrat square Face on, so worms wiggled down my mouth, spew it all.

Why this watching mazarrat threw rotten fruit at Nannaha's face and it soiled and flies already visiting sweaty Berserkas got a treat.

Oh, what a vengeful mazarrat I am," our hero.

"Yes, she is and has much to learn about calmness if she is to wear my shoes;" but knew Nannaha deserved what went around came back. He just did not want to admit the young mazarrat had what it takes to be in his shoes.

And a Berserka offered his hand to Nannaha who accepted,

threw back her black mane and went with him.

"I want all Berserkas," she whispered to him, and he gave her his scarf to clean her face, and later that night the whole Decurion passed through the tent and promised her a gardened house with fountain, slaves, and gold income in Hurreva City, for they doubted Artebrates would want her back after what had happened.

"Not all of us are like her," Malachi defended his race to Mungo.

"Not all lions are like me," Mungo apologized putting Malachi at ease, and all marveled at Mungo's words.

And a mazarrat sang, *"The soldiers are whores, worse than Moragana the woman ape thing for they sleep with Nannaha."*

And the soldiers inwardly cursed themselves for being men but outwardly put on an act of bravado over their manly acts with Nannaha.

"Do you think you are better than us common soldiers?" A drunken Berserka and Enkalla, Ben Nathan and Malachi drew swords.

The situation became tense.

Officers, against enlistees.

"Not all are warriors," Mungo seeing the soldier's friends willing to fight for him, "before Leah I ran after Sasha and bitches, and even swung the vines with Moragana for I didn't know I was a man thing.

As Fermanian House Berserkas, I know you have honor and are men of valor, so if Nannaha said no you would respect her.

"And if I don't," the drunken soldier wanting to fight.

"Then you are a thief," Mungo and the Berserkas marveled over his wisdom.

"So, what, both these women are Artebrates' concubines, given to his friends," the soldier, for the drink had him and drew his sword.

He also held Nannaha by a lead, so she went on all fours, and she purred against Malachi's legs and sickened, pushed her away.

"No," Mungo halted his Fermanian new friends beating the drunk senseless, even if they did not realize they were now friends.

And Leah fell to her knees, her secret life revealed; Mungo would treat her as Lord Artebrates did, as the soldiers did Nannaha.

"For they were men," our mazarrat wondering if Mungo would and the land was silent.

"What does she mean friend?" Mungo asked Malachi.

"She talks of the finer things men things can be," Malachi sarcastically but Mungo was too innocent to understand except that she used to be Artebrates woman; Artebrates had thrown her away and Mungo did not mind, Leah was now his, Artebrates had made a bad mistake, Leah's past forgotten, the future lay ahead.

And a Night Skull Moth landed on Mungo's hand, and it was glorious to see.

And at this moment The Elder walked amongst them, and the Berserkas wondered, none had seen a mazarrat use a staff before and besides, his eyes shone as if a god was upon him.

And the drunk's friends became ashamed for the shameful things they did.

"Where are you from Mungo?" A Berserka meaning not from this world.

"A nut house," Nannaha called from a green tent.

"Here stands a chosen one," The Elder and the superstitious Berserkas were silent as an abandoned fast reactor switched on, by a timer switch hummed, and a volcano erupted.

And Mungo eyed the drunk with sorrow, and he a mighty giant of man said to Mungo, "I kept a woman and her brats from another, and she took me for every coin I owned to furniture her house for her man's return. Taken for a ride Mungo I was.

Women are cheats," the drunk shouted.

"Shame not Fermanian women and men in front of the

man thing Aralwan Giant," Ben Nathan the Decurion.

"A woman's a port of call for a soldier," Lug another soldier with drink added.

"Tell me," and Mungo left out 'brave soldier,' "is this moth not beautiful and naturally made?"

"An insect come to make holes in my winter underwear," Aralwan Giant.

"And if I put it in cage, it will lose all its right things," for Mungo was ignorant of the word behavior.

"So?"

But others understood except the other one Lug, who was mischief by nature and had drunk for encouragement to go with Nannaha in the green tent.

And Nannaha moaned and wailed like a Fermanian unclean spirit to distract them from Mungo.

"Should I let this moth go that took time to make, or kill it so it will not eat your hidden silks?" And the soldier stood still, and then understood the insult.

Mungo

"What? Woman suspenders on me?" And he lifted his sword, but Mungo took it easily and pushed the lizard man onto his back, and the fall made wind come from his bottom and all laughed except him, "*of course, and was loud too,*" the mazarrat holding her nose and her audience out there did likewise.

And all lizard men saw Mungo was within his rights to slaughter but had not.

"This fallen man is drunk and does not know what comes out of his mouth, take him away," the centurion and done, so Nannaha left alone till, she screamed for attention.

"I come," Aralwan Giant answered from a bush where he landed thrown and Lug, also came out of the shadows, and Ben Nathan then realized who had helped Nannaha dispose of the soldier, who hoped for cloning.

And while these three drunks did things reserved for comforters and their masters, Mungo danced naked under the moon and his eyes shone.

"Who is this man thing, a witch?" A soldier asked afraid of Mungo.

"He has shinning eyes," another said.

"He dances naked for he has no shame," Malachi looking at the stars. *"I grin, for Mungo's body is handsome,"* and *"Oh, naughty girl, time you were married,"* her listeners joyfully.

"When he gets up from sleeping on the ground, a hole is left for so heavy is the demon inside him," another Berserka.

"They say he floats when he sleeps," another.

"He has wisdom," the last and all had read papyrus books on The Wild One.

And the books said he would betray his maker and the Berserkas knew his maker was not their god Telephassa, but something greater and Unseen.

"He is The Wild One that is who he is," The Elder and the Berserkas trembled for they had read the scribes papyrus pulp books. *"Making the scribes rich,"* the mazarrat.

And one seeing Mungo as human emptied his rations out of his bully tin, he wanted to eat but it was slave sweetmeat amongst noodles and to eat them in the presence of Mungo seemed wrong.

And salted human meat emptied out, crackling fingers a delicacy, and eyeballs in brine and pickled vegetables.

He feared Mungo and what Mungo danced too.

And others copied him.

"What shall we eat?" A Berserka.

"Berries and tubers," The Elder and that night they did until the fear for Mungo waned; then went about while others slept picking up their thrown away food.

"Oh, so many sleepy solders next day," our mazarrat having a pretense yawn, and of course, the audience yawned so all froze thinking the heavens had fallen on their head and looked for a Tidal Wave coming to drown them.

And Leah felt love in her for Mungo, for she had read the papyrus books too, and read one such as her would be his woman; and she wondered if that woman was her? And she knew it was true deep down and, knew she had influence over Mungo.

"*And the woman from the vats will bear Mungo Mighty Children,*" and ignored the fact the scribe wrote it drinking at a pubs table, "*Some things best kept secret,*" our girl mazarrat.

"One child shall be a mighty man and another, rulers shall kneel at his feet to hear wisdom," for Malachi also had read.

"His God is a man thing maker, not a maker of lizard men," Leah quoted and the Berserkas shivered for the papyrus books only spewed forth doom for the Fermanian race.

"I should kill him now," Malachi putting a hand on his sword hilt, but Leah stopped him; "If he is fated to be your master then nothing you can do will stop it happening."

"My god Telephassa is cruel and fated to be forgotten under grass where her statues will fall hidden," and Malachi went to relief himself for he was nervous.

And that night Nannaha screamed for previously an insect had bitten her and given her River Blindness.

And her screams hid the advance of man things that ran through their camp slaying five Berserkas and Malachi held off their attack, for he was not sleeping but gone to watch the stars, in the hope of seeing the God of Mungo amongst them.

And armed mazarrats dropped out of the night to shield Mungo, not the lizard men.

"Rally to me," Mungo shouted near the campfire waving Ben Nathan's Decurion's standard.

And none argued except for Nannaha and Aralwan Giant and Lug of course, who hurried back into the green tent, where moths flew about the oil lamp and bed bugs crawled up hammock ropes.

Here they hoped Mungo slain.

*

"Peelock, that is a man thing who has killed ten of us," a young human said to Peelock. "Why does he fight with lizards?" "*And knew why?*" The mazarrat with answer.

Illustration: killer of killers, tyrannosaurus

"**Mungo**," Peelock and at once the young man left the older and walked to Mungo throwing his weapons down and fell on his face.

"Master," he and Mungo helped him up and bade him stand next to him.

"Amazing," hundreds on both sides so stopped fighting. **Even The Elder climbed Ben Nathan's standard just as a comet burned New Uranus's atmosphere and the sky went orange and yellow.**

"Mount Tullos has opened its glory upon Mungo," the Berserkas and hid under their shields.

Now humans did likewise but not all, handfuls hacked the superstitious lizard warriors, chopping off tails at the chance to try and maim and kill their enemy.

And Berserkas slain so even Mungo threw pilum and drove these human attackers away.

And the humans decided they had had enough of this Mungo and to kill him.

And thunder clapped and green lighting hit the ground so many humans flew into the air and somewhere burned.

"He is chosen, he is The Wild One," The Elder shouted appearing green as the comet crashed, and the ground quaked and peat opened below Mungo and bituminous tar gurgled out.

Rising with its dinosaur bones and their gaping skulls grinned so the humans said, "Hell has opened and eaten those who oppose the gods chosen," for he who had fallen at Mungo's feet were sinking in the open ground.

"Our ancestors rise to defend Mungo," the Fermanian lizard warriors.

And hundreds swore the thunder was the voice of gods and fell and the lighting struck rhododendron trees instead.

But dozens ran and the lighting found them, and all saw green lighting strike Ben Nathan's standard, and both Mungo and The Elder were unhurt for the standard had earthed igniting the pitch about them.

"They live," dozens amazed.

"Just," Mungo whispered to The Elder.

Who said nothing, he was shaking, and none smelt his burnt fur apart from Mungo?

And Peelock the human leader crushed the tarot cards in his robe pocket and cursed the day he read the stars concerning a Wild One.

Now Peelock believed he created The Wild One tales to frighten Fermanians and keep his humans under control; with a future hope in a savorer, but was wrong, the tales existed before Peelock kicked within his mother for mazarrats sang in human towns.

And the armed mazarrats melted away.

And before the night was out five more fell on their faces before Mungo and one woman who was totally woman thing in gold kilt.

And Mungo's loins stirred for she was attractive and had skin not soft scales like Leah: and saved any more lust because he wanted to dance to the Oneness of the universe.

"Leah," he called, and she came red eyed from sleep.

"Here is my first choice," and Mungo felt good and forgot he had said the same to Sasha for truly he was a man thing.

And Leah sobbing fell into his broad chest, "My Lord and Master I come to you willingly," and thought I am only his first choice like Artebrates women are cattle to him.

"The stars say Mungo is a demon from hell," Peelock as he lied to his men.

And Mungo shamed when he held Leah and looked at the

human woman at his feet.

And wished Leah would go back to bed with his guilt.

And a mazarrats sang, *"Mungo's shame is Leah. For Mungo is man thing that think with what is between their legs. For this young mazarrat gets about and does not smell of singed fur."*

"It is written The Wild One must marry a virgin, that thing who clings to you is a comforter of Artebrates and his legions," Nannaha to make trouble.

And Mungo hurt for he wanted Leah all to himself, and had wondered into the domain of possessiveness.

And he forgets he was not perfect, and what made him dance was for all, perfect and imperfect.

"Whether given or rented out by Artebrates it was not my wish. What difference between them and you that you all see me as harlot? I too want to dance to the Unseen One that you dance too, for it calls me and does not see me as harlot," Leah and her words cut into Mungo. *"One point for women and none for Mungo,"* the singer clapping.

"The fool, the woman loves him," Peelock meaning Leah and that Mungo lusted for the human woman at his feet. Now he Peelock did not like Mungo, but if he were truly the Wild One, lizards would die, and his people saved.

Mungo to Peelock was the sacrifice to save humanity.

"Kill Mungo," Peelock for if he were the Wild One, he would survive so three men with guns ran towards Mungo to shoot him dead.

Now Mungo pushed aside his friends to face them, and static from green electricity stored in him came forth.

And the bullets missed; his sudden green appearance startled the aim of his attackers.

Their mistake.

"And Mungo leapt upon them like the lion thing he knew how to be and hurt them all.

But one stabbed Mungo in the chest.

And Mungo killed him and threw his parts hither.

"I will grant you mercy," he said to the other two and killed them quickly with his teeth that were sharp like a lion, for he had that milk in him.

And then he calmed down.

"I have killed out of anger not necessity, I have done wrong, my mercy was death, when mercy is life," and Mungo saddened over his behavior.

"Mungo has killed wrongly, his mercy is death, we mazarrats know for we are the scribes of the law," and the attackers and defenders, even Nannaha fell silent as all peered into the bush for the thousand mazarrats who chanted this thirty times.

Now Ben Nathan's surgeons stopped sewing wounds, both lizard and human and ran to Mungo.

"The surgeon is a good man unlike Mungo," a mazarrat sang and copied by its kind, and then all fell silent.

And a cicada deciding the mazarrats dominating enough called a love song for a mate.

A green chameleon hearing stalked cicada.

The cicada mated and the chameleon ate them and was satisfied and went to seek a mate.

A green vine snake ate it and it eaten by a night eagle and next day did droppings on the land which benefited from the nutrients and grass seeds finding the soil rich germinated, so the cycle that was The Wild One continued.

"And his enemies are given him to die," The Elder shouted and humans and Berserkas feared Mungo.

And a human and a lizard died while the surgeon worked.

A useless waste of the gift of life.

And scores sought to see if Mungo would rise from the dead because he had a chest wound, that had made him kneel looking pale and gravely ill.

"Holy Fire cannot a man have solitude for nature," Malachi relieving himself in bushes as men went to see Mungo pushed past him.

And he was highly embarrassed.

And Mungo stood up, and roared lion fashion and proved the tales about him true, he was a forest nymph and other wonderful spiritual things being true about him; all forgetting his physical strength, and the skill of the surgeon and his wound was not life threatening.

"Kill them all," Peelock to his remaining men and none did so.

And in the end Peelock threw his tarot cards away.

Later:

"This Mungo loves not our gods but something else and has women like they weren't in production," later in Peelock's Barracks by a man called Angus Ogg.

"Yes, but the difference between Mungo and you Angus Ogg," an answering mazarrat sang *"Is that he has innocence, and you have electricity taken from a solar plant while poor about you use candles."*

"Angus Ogg, we saw you fall at Mungo's feet, so why the change of heart?" Another soldier asked in the barracks.

"Mungo wove a spell about me," Angus replied truthfully for at the time spellbound.

"You are a small fish swallowed by a massive fish," the mazarrat sweetly.

"He said he is The Wild One," Angus defending Mungo had bewitched him.

"And Malachi was his friend," the mazarrat.

"Well, he stopped us killing and getting killed and that takes all," a soldier in the barrack room.

"He is Mungo," Angus and thought of the other five who had not come back and was glad he still breathed.

But Peelock was jealous Mungo had drawn away his best warriors with fancy words.

And Peelock went back to his Red Castle built by men out of devotion for him for he was a soothsayer and feared Mungo would destroy his standing in the community.

And Peelock had a **SOFIA** stratospheric observatory, for an infra-red astronomy and he had no idea, how **this flying telescope saw 70000 kilometers away**, and travelled stars or how it got up there in the first place?

Nor that inside a droid worked starting its twenty-year life span anew, so it was truly immortal.

But he could see a black hole, and its mouth in Galaxy NGC 4261, and knew it was matter compressed as gas emitted from the back and propelling the hole at speed across space.

"And nowhere in the astronomy books does it say divine hole that you are an angel of death coming to give judgement to the lizards," Peelock and wrote his words down for insertion into the seventh day prophetic announcements he made every seven days, to astonish the humans who knew about the Wild One and he had much to lose if the tales were true.

And near the black hole he saw the approaching star that winked red and green navigation lights, and knew he would have to wait patiently for the star to reach his
SOFIA before he could divine on that subject.

And about his castle tulip gardens tendered by young children and his women and he knew the wind of change was coming as the star was feeding his imagination, so read about star ships and went to the main Red Temple of god, took off his fur boots, went into a private steam bath rather than the public unisex, and bathed ten times to be clean and holy.

Then dressed in white smock with slits for eyes and entered the

Temple Courtyard.

Now beside him ordinary folk on their stomachs asking God and other god's favors, but Peelock passed dozens crawling to his shadow, and one cripple grabbed his helm for healing but almost tripped Peelock, so he turned and burst the cripple's mouth with a foot.

"*Peelock is not a healer but a troubled man thing, a giver of boils, leeches and bad breath,*" the mazarrat and The Wild inches back from Peelock, cutting him off from what flows about all, "oneness."

And the cripple was happy, Peelock had put a holy foot into him, he deserved it for he almost tripped Peelock.

And worshippers trampled the cripple to touch Peelock.

And eventually Peelock managed to enter the inner courtyard where a young man circumcised screamed out in pain.

For it was Peelock's law, anything entering the inner courtyard of God must be circumcised.

He got this idea form reading the Bible.

And being a holy man realized it meant the circumcision of the spirit that only God sees, but those about him failed to see this so wanted it done physically.]

And eventually got to the Virgin Corridor were virgins sent by their mothers to serve the priests and priestesses and the worshippers in the Outer Courtyard, and so give their earnings to the priests. "*And rich Peelock of course got a share. It was all about sex, cash and the fear of not complying, of being cut off, kicked out from human villages, bad Peelock,*" the mazarrat angry.

Which idea Peelock had from reading history books on the Temples of Rome, prostitutes and he was just a pimp. "*PIMP,*" the mazarrat and the listeners spat "*PIMP*" at Peelock who stood still shivering and blamed it on a coming pooh.

And he saw an empty cubicle, where the girl Wendy should be waiting for someone to show them themselves from the Outer Courtyard for business.

And he knew all the girls' names, especially Wendy.

And at last, he entered the Holy Chamber of Knowledge where the Bible was, and a computer that ran on solar power.

Just like the Fermanians this human folk had suffered much during the atomic wars.

And Peelock's handprint worked the machine, so all its knowledge was his but not the understanding he needed to decipher it.

"Incorruptible."

Printed over a female body in a glass cage in the center of the computer and wires came from her head.

And this was the main reason Peelock's followers thought him God's seer for the machine was God. And scattered about bones of The People who came to see their God, for Peelock divined sacrifice them while praying to the computer, their God, and Peelock with sword pierced their back, so his secret was safe, God was a machine and so spread fear about and people said, "Only Peelock can speak to God."

And before Peelock pressed fax Intake he saw a young mazarrat up above on the wall, and *"she was uncircumcised for she was me, a female with a voice like a lark.*

And Peelock pressed fax Intake as he foamed anger because I knew God was a machine, SOFIA a telescope and Peelock a murderer" so called to him, *"what goes around comes round, murderers hang."*

And SOFIA saw star ships used by humans to colonize New Uranus.

And Peelock read while the Incorruptible One's eyes watched him.

"One day I will take your place," Peelock to the woman.

"The makers of this **IBM LOGOS** put me here so the computer could have a Conscience, and you by accident found OVERRIDE and me, but still, I won't give you the doomsday bomb for at least OVERRIDE stops there," the Incorruptible One.

And Peelock did what he always did, took a red fire axe, and hit the glass that did not shatter.

"Give me the weapon to exterminate the lizard people," he demanded rubbing his sore wrists.

And the Incorruptible One laughed and to Peelock seemed went back to sleep.

"Holy bitch," he screamed and closed the computer and never heard a cripple beg for mercy under a tree, as the infuriated crowd shouted, "Fool," we know Peelock gets God's offenders punished," and ground their boots into him.

"Peelock will praise you, give him that eye when you see him, and he will accept you into warrior school," a proud father to his nine-year daughter who had an eye on the end of a stick.

And Peelock saw on leaving the Temple the cripple hanging from a tree, his face blue, and one eye gone, and tongue swollen from his mouth and Peelock averted his eyes for the cripple was a sinner.

"Look holy leader?" The nine-year-old and Peelock remembered his teachings and rewarded the child with a blessing, "here is a faithful and shall become a warrior of mine and reach Heaven for serving me."

"Peelock was incredible, he was a lying son of a gun, he was huma n thing," the mazarrat shocked.

And he went to his castle as the nine-year-old threw the stick at a stray dog that ate the eye.

"I will be like Angus Ogg and slay lizard men and roast their babes and crack their crackling with my teeth," and saluted Peelock and stopped playing with her toys.

From that day on her father bought her a bronze chest plate and copper sword for practice.

Her new toys and went about shouting, "Kill, kill," and hit lesser children pretending they were Fermanians.

Anyway: Peelock went to his castle and had his drummers bang skin drums summon The People.

He also ripped the soiled hem from his silken white robe and threw it out a window, for that beggar had dirty fingers.

And a young girl took it from her head and ran home and her mother not knowing its holy origins, made silken lingerie from it, and praised God and her gods for it.

"Who amongst you is the fairest girl?" Peelock asked the assembled and the ugly made way till at last a fair young woman stood alone, and she was Wendy.

"Sacrifice her to God this very moment for his judgement is coming upon us," and the people pulled the clothes of Wendy and beat her body till it bruised.

"Take the blasphemous parents that bred this whore and drown them," and Peelock watched the girl beg for mercy, as her plough people to the yellow river Yathan to drown.

Now none protested for Peelock to enforce his spontaneous

dominant whim let loose a stream of laser from a finger.

"God's power flows from Peelock," one youth, ignorant Peelock had this assassin fingernail laser by the Wonder Lord Vinki as a birthday present?

And Peelock had his bearers carry him in a chair to the river Yathan, and other parents were thankful, it was not them, being, drowned. *"Here he mumbled prayers and blessed the waters, waters were drunks at night peed in and fell in and drowned,"* the mazarrat singing sad melodies.

"I will do anything to save them;" the beaten girl and Peelock "Take her to my chambers for further questioning," and they were in his castle where he returned,

"Safe, cozy, secure, wait I get him?" The brave mazarrat.

Now the silly ogled for they knew Peelock's reputation and spat at the girl, now taken to his castle from jealousy.

"God always demands the fairest," they whispered amongst themselves.

"We must always give God's seer Peelock our fairest to save us from the Fermanian onslaught," others.

"Water courses are gateways to hell, so the damned won't hunt us," another at Wendy.

"Didn't Abraham want to cut his son's throat to God?" Another rearranging her blue cap with Peelock's feathers in its rim, then a drew sword to stab Wendy forgetting herself.

"Better she dies for us than us for her who thought she was better than us," this woman and stabbed and wiped hands, on her multicolored robe.

And the truth was, Wendy never thought she was their better but was.

"I hope God tells Peelock to take me," a young stupid girl in the crowd.

"I hope Peelock dead," another who did not want to end up like Wendy for Wendy had said NO to Peelock earlier, and why she chosen this day.

No one said No to Peelock.

And dozens in the crowd hoped The Wild One would

deliver them.

And inside Peelock's dark castle the girl now chained to a table leg, so her whelps cooled with the air conditioning.

And droids came and worked on Wendy, so life returned to her eyes for her conscious was now on the internet.

Another wonder of Peelock's God.

The stab wound had been fatal but the Incorruptible One had drained her mind into the computer to live.

"Surely a wonder for mind and brain are separate. I can crawl through the smallest wall hole," a mazarrat warning just were crawled into?

And Peelock came to Wendy later and when he saw her bruises was wrath with the droids for not healing them and beat her more for her ugliness hurt his eyes.

"Even in death there is no escape from me," Peelock boasted.

And her screams heard through the computer's internal speakers.

"A demon is trying to get out of her, beat her harder Peelock," a woman in the crowd below the castle.

"Peelock is wrong," one of the warriors who had been at the meeting with Mungo.

"What can we do? The priests of the Holy Books give him their backing, I don't won't burned as a witch," his friend fearing.

"We take some of this to chew," and both chewed on green leaves that made them numb to their surroundings.

"When is he finished with her think we might get her?" The friend.

"No, not even her clones, it's all fixed, a racket between Peelock and those damned priests."

And in Red Castle Peelock "No one cares about you, hundreds of us are taken by the Fermanian yearly, tribute to the lizard men and in return they give me technology; and what I care about is that you have made me dirty," and he pulled a cord and two females entered and they took Wendy out onto the balcony and put her onto the cup of a catapult.

And the cord had sets of bells that drew the townsfolk back into the square.

And the two girls were robotics and showed no emotion as they drenched Wendy in inflammable liquid and pulled a lever, so Wendy alight shot towards the stars.

"And her consciousness is inside the internet and her DNA on file that the computer operates so is not dead, only the shell that was her body.

I am clean now," Peelock and "the Incorruptible One must tell me how to clone each Wendy with a different consciousness, so each clone looks the same but has a different personality, like twins, one for a different day of the week?"

"Oh dear, his followers outside the castle walls heard everything, would they revolt or be chickens?" The mazarrat.

So attacked her glass cage again and still it would not break and the Incorruptible One looked at him and smiled.

A smile of pity. *"I give Peelock more than a smile, smell this man thing,"* and the young female mazarrat winded a green cloud towards Peelock.

"What is the internet?" A big woman who had born sixteen children hearing below.

"What tribute do we give the Fermanians," her friend wondering what had happened too many of her fourteen children?

And the two warriors laughed leaning on their spears for they knew the secret but feared Peelock so said nothing.

"He gives your children as sweetmeat gifts to his Fermanian pals." The young mazarrat not afraid for Peelock could not scale the wall to catch her; instead, below covering his nose.

And Peelock knew the people below were asking questions, they could ask all they wanted, he was too strong for them. His men wore Fermanian lasers, and it was the approaching ship, he worried about. His world of gods and technology threatened by the unknown. The known to him was familiar, dinosaurs who liked to eat them and Fermanians whose delicacy was their sweetmeats.

And a bell heard, prayer time for Peelock and the devotees of the gods.

And Peelock went to pray, secure in the knowledge that he was going to paradise.

Wendy however was already in paradise.

And about Red Town people read the Bible and other religious books and took from them sentences to justify their cruel ways.

And in cages human boys sang, mazarrats those wicked gossipers not wanted here.

"*Chick, chick,*" the mazarrat meaning the people were chickens, so stayed Peelock's.

And the two-robotics returned with a silver tray with refreshment for Peelock for when his prayer finished.

And a spider dropped onto one of the robotics and Peelock had a fear of these insects.

And he hit the robotic till she fell.

"Go and bath five times then return to me clean," Peelock.

Then Peelock on his knees took drugs to enter purple dream world and speak to the spirit folk that lived there.

"Now I have given all that is red in New Uranus to humans and all that is not red to the lizard folk. Now I make a new covenant with Peelock my servant, I give to you the Fermanians who eat your sweetmeats, and insert remotes into your spines, so you cook yourselves at their banquets.

I give you their lands so have my people multiple, so they number the grains of sand in the sea.

And give you The Wild One for war and afterwards when he has slain all the lizard folk give him back to me," god who was red told Peelock in dream land.

Now the robotic girl returned clean, and she wore muslin and Peelock stirred and wondered why he did not send the ugly people on the fire rainbow as Wendy had gone?"

"I demand the pure and fair but hurt when I see the ugly for, they are a blight upon the land," god who is red told

Peelock. "I wanted Wendy as I possess you and she said NO. That is why you sent her to me, as an example to the others; control must be kept through fear."

And Peelock saw in a vision that no more Wendy's burnt, but those who did not fit into society, the cripples and loonies, the ugly ones could.

And Peelock smiled for he could hear them screaming louder than Wendy.

"The fatted ones are fatted cattle, and their fat will burn as incense longer in my god's heavenly house," Peelock believed then lay with the two robotics.

And the Incorruptible One knew if it was not for the prophecy of The Wild One, she did set the Doomsday Bomb upon these humans who had become monsters.

"It is his inner self, his super ego he speaks to, loosened free by dope, that or an unclean demon ha that would be something deserving this murderer," the mazarrat not singing.

At that moment, a servant arrived, "Master, Lord Vinki has arrived seeking tribute."

"He is a month early," Peelock.

"We are late Divine One," the servant and bowed and Peelock checked the lunar calendar and knew the tribute was late. "Dam Mungo for he and the star ship occupy my mind always. Go and arrange the tribute then, then bring Vinki here for talk, also fatted calves for his liking," so Peelock instructed meaning fat people reared on milk.

And Vinki came surrounded by Berserkas armed with lasers for he was Head of Army Purchasing.

"Nice and tender ready for the pot?" Vinki enquired.

And silver trays given Vinki and his Berserkas to eat from

And the trays had the remains of the slaughtered cattle that had gone into the Inner Courtyard, and never returned. *"Murderers,"* the mazarrat audience before she had a chance to sing, so became peeved, then sat on a giant toadstool and thought, *"Why am I annoyed, I have taught them right from wrong."*

Vinki needed gold and Peelock needed weapons; did not matter what happened elsewhere.

"Come girl," Vinki to one of the robotics and pawed her, and done to show Peelock, Vinki asked his own favors.

"In return," Peelock eyeing a laser pistol.

"Yours friend," and the word friend used in the neutral, not lost upon Peelock, who took the gun anyway.

And the girl, passed around and the Berserkas joked and pawed her much.

In the end, Vinki made her sit next to him, and then he trepanned her and dug out the fresh sweetmeat for she was just an animal for slaughter, a cyborg.

"And was lucky for Peelock she did not blow a fuse, smoke, and spark." The mazarrat pretending to do just that, she was an actor with an audience.

And Peelock did not tell Vinki he was eating robotic bionic flesh and summoned servants to remove the sitting corpse that technicians would resurrect later.

Now defiled as Vinki pawed her any way.

So later that night a mazarrat seen crawling down the castles wall.

"Peelock hates Mungo,
Peelock feeds the Fermanians well.
Vinki is Peelock's friend," it sang.

Also, a beggar saw the Fermanians leave but escaped attention because he slept under cardboard boxes.

"Thank the real God who isn't red and isn't inside Peelock that I am still alive," the beggar prayed.

A fat woman returning with loot from Wendy's house saw them too but made the mistake of shouting, "Fermanians," so beaten and gagged, then thrown over a saddle, the journey back to Telephassa was long.

As for Vinki he took flight back to Telephassa in a new flying machine, happy he had gold and cattle again, after his granaries emptied on Carman's orders.

And one last also saw the lizard men, Cadfael, a warrior

from the outer tribes who lived on the Red Grass. And he saw all and realized Peelock was darkness fled into the plains to tell his people what he had seen.

*

And Angus Ogg knew why they followed Mungo; they were ill of Peelock.

"When I joined warrior school, it was to be a slayer of lizard men but instead I am a robber of my people, so Peelock has power. If I desert, Peelock will send his pet killer of killers after me.

I am close to Peelock, and he listens to me, this new Wild One Mungo will never listen to me, for to him I am just another warrior. He listens to a lizard called Malachi, a jumped-up skink, which has crawled out of a decaying tree stump. And thinks to order us about, well in that case I stay with the devil I know who rewards me with what I want.

If I want this woman I take, if I want to sleep in that house I do. If there is food laid out, I will eat, and if not give orders for all know, **I am close to Peelock** and all fear me suggesting that they become an offering to the gods, on the flaming rainbow.

And always the River Yathan that is haunted. Dozens say they see the spirits of the sacrificed here demanding justice against Peelock in the name of God they demand, but what God, Peelock already speaks to our red god, so I know what side the butter is on.

Chapter 9 Cathbadh

And time stops still for no one not even for Cathbadh nor the hippopotamuses in the yellow river Yathan.

"Deewana," Cathbadh screamed opening a secret tunnel under a memorial stone that would lead him to Carman.

"Die cousin," a Serrant hissed and lunged with its mouth to rip Cathbadh's throat.

"Die yourself cousin," Cathbadh replied as he raised his left arm to take the force of the serrant's teeth.

And did not grunt for his first scream was a summons for help, but who would hear him amongst the graves of the ancestors of Telephassa?

"Yeah," the Serrant moaned as Cathbadh's right hand stuck a two-foot-long bayonet into the serrant's belly and twisted. "Let me live and I will tell you who sent me?" The Serrant pleaded.

Now Cathbadh was not known for his viciousness and did not pull out his dagger that twisted around innards that would follow.

"Vinki the woman and don't kill me for even Mungo spared me cousin," the Serrant moaned and Cathbadh threw the beast away from him.

"You met Mungo?"

"He is my friend and the lover of Moragana the woman ape thing, and she can lay a trap for him, so spare me cousin?"

Now Cathbadh picked up the serrant's gall bladder that had hung out and plucked and ate it.

"Wah don't eat any more of me please," the Serrant begged.

"You and Moragana will lay a trap for Mungo," Cathbadh and stuck the dagger into the jaw of the Serrant and took him back to his house.

And the Serrant was afraid, it was a dinner.

"I am a master surgeon **who taught the hunchback**

everything he knows, and when I give Mungo to Artebrates, Carman will reward me by giving me Vinki, that girl who wears pink frillies, and I will slay him, and I have never known a Serrant to die from losing its gall bladder."

"Wah I will obey Cathbadh and capture Mungo for him," the Serrant.

And Cathbadh only stuck the Serrant together with sticky tape to ensure it would obey.

And the Serrant saw and was wrath.

"Why should I help you, at a moment all of me will gush out, why have you done this too me?"

"For insurance that the naughty Serrant does what it is told," Cathbadh who was indeed, a true Fermanian, cruel and wicked. "Woo ah you are moaning beastie I have told Carmen; I know you and that ape can bring me Mungo? See cousin reptile," and Cathbadh pulled some of the silver tape away so things behind threatened to tumble out, "bring that harlot Moragana here."

"First I must find her," the reply.

"I have to the end of time, go now," and Cathbadh knew that time was near for he often cast out his mind, and saw Captain John Clinton on a star ship in suspended sleep as his ship, a sphere within a rotating sphere to keep the gravity within the inner sphere, at Earth g approach Experimental Planet 16A.

"Even in her bed I cannot convince the woman a human star ship is coming, and that all Fermanian cities must unite to meet the threat. There is only one solution: Artebrates must join Prince Annunaki's sympathizers.

And then who knows a relation of King Sess may be found and made Emperor?"

"*Maybe a mazarrat should be queen of this planet and put all Fermanians in the highest tax bracket, for even mazarrats have learned such matters eves dropping.*" The mazarrat and her audience where glad they were not Fermanians.

*

And time stops for no one under the red moon as insects skate ponds, teeming with mosquito larvae and beside such a pool sat Angus Ogg, smeared in berry juice.

"Old Peelock did turn Angus Nero my cousin into something nasty? He lies at the bottom of his cage a dried toad."

And Angus Ogg remembered Nero cut about his skin, and a strange smelling gel rubbed into the wounds, and during the summer he became a toad and knew not a shuttle virus had carried amphibian genes into his cousin to take root and grow.

"Feed well on flies Angus Nero who defied me," Peelock to The People and Nero starved for he refused insects and cried, "I am not of The People who are no longer human. I am human and believe in The Wild One and a God with no name too."

"We have the red god," The People but it was clear The People were not all behind Peelock who ruled with terror and employed mind control teachings." *Interesting, yes?"* A mazarrat thinking might be the way to rule when she is The Elder?

"The Temple and Peelock get a tenth each out of us," a common complaint for not all obeyed for they were human.

"I was wanted by Peelock and so gave him my land," a warrior before sent into battle against Fermanians and had his bronze helmet opened by laser fire.

And Peelock divided the spoils with his loyalist warriors who were not much better than he.

Illustration: Angus Ogg at the pool

For there were hundreds with consciousness like Angus Ogg who joined Mungo that night, and there was John Wrexham who lived outside the walls of Peelock's Red Town.

And he read much and headed the Pioneer Settlement Association and knew of

Mungo of the Lions.

"The spy says you are too late to save the girl Wendy," the man Cameron Black

riding a Pha antelope told John.

And the man dressed in reptile skins instead of furs and clothes for riding long distances on the range.

"We will show not all follow Peelock," John replied and mounted his Pha and led one hundred men who called themselves Freemen to Red Town, where Peelock lived.

Anyway: Yathan Bend Crossing.

"John, lizard men," Cameron Black warned, and John gave the signal to dismount and went ahead with an escort to investigate and saw a human with lions and a girl he swore was the most beautiful girl he had ever seen, ever.

"Who the hell rides lions?" But knew the answer so stood up.

John, are you trying to get killed?" Cameron Black asked following suit.

And a growl from the naked human greeted them and they saw lions circle and a large lizard hunter stands protectively in front of the human.

"Malachi was his friend," a mazarrat sang nearby.

John Wrexham grunted and walked purposefully up to the lizard that held a laser rife to his belly.

And Malachi slowly returned the smile thinking the man brave but loose in the brain.

"Mungo I presume," and John held out a hand and Mungo sniffed it.

"Excuse me," Malachi to Mungo as he shook the hand and when finished Mungo shook it too.

"Yep, there sure was as hell plenty wild stuff in you," John told Mungo.

Malachi groaned; this new human was as crazy as Mungo.

Now the hidden one hundred human riders seeing the lions circle John came riding hard in.

And Mungo roared, and John shouted for his men to stop, and Malachi shouted at the lizard Berserkas to form a wall.

And out of the confusion came order with both sides facing each other eager to kill.

"You are like Moragana the ape," Mungo said to John.

"I am called John, and we are on the same side, and where the hell did those armed mazarrats go?" He rubbing his throat staring at the bushes. *"I know and isn't telling."* A mazarrat thinking she was in opera.

"I could ask the pha my cousin what they are doing with men things?" Malachi. Meaning the pha two legged dinosaurs the men rode.

John grinned, "For a lizard I could get too like you?"

Malachi laughed, "For an ape that walks I could like you."

At this moment, The Elder appeared having wisely hidden in a badger's burrow during the fracas. Fortunately for him the burrow was vacant.

"By gad its Moragana the ape," John Wrexham gasped.

"Where?" The Elder.

And John Wrexham got the feeling he was an alien on his own planet and that *"mazarrats had been hiding something from him?"* A mazarrat chorus.

Now Mungo again given the opportunity to show his greatness for out of the dark came again the killer of killers, and it stood no chance against all these armed beings, but it was arrogant and the hundred charging pha had scared game off.

It could have waited; the game would have returned in an hour or so.

And Mungo took a lance and ran forward, confident in killing one in the past he could kill another.

"Dam man thing," Malachi spat following him trying hard

to fix a three foot long, poisoned arrow to his bow.

And The Elder stood waving his staff.

"I haven't seen no mazarrat like that one boss?" Cameron Black looking back.

And John swore it was waving a bone necklace, so shook his head and said, "Let's go boys," mounting and the killer of killers seeing all this coming stopped, then focused on The Elder who froze and nervously, peed.

He was only a little mazarrat, a tasty snack but easy to gobble up.

And Mungo drove the sixteen-foot lance deep into the killer's heart, and the beast roared, and Mungo somersaulted away on a broken lance.

Then Malachi sent the arrow near the lance so, only feathers showed.

And the killer of killers fell dead.

John whistled, Cameron Black gasped, and the Berserkas had expressions of, "we could have told you so."

The Elder nervously winded relaxing.

"Mungo you, OK?" Malachi finding him in a rhododendron tree hanging upside down.

And Mungo dropped, and then roared and danced under the red moon, and John and the others stood bewildered by Mungo who ended up roaring on the tyrannosaur's back.

"He is an evil man, I can tell you things about him no one else knows," and John turned to investigate the beautiful poisonous face of Nannaha.

"Why does Mungo order Aralwan Giant and his friend Lugh to beat Nannaha?"
John wondered why anyone could treat a lizard woman as good looking as this like that.

"Don't listen to Nannaha, she is Lord Artebrates First Comforter," Leah said, and John whistled over this new beauty.

"Do all belong to Mungo as booty or something?" John asked and tried unleashing Nannaha thinking this was no way to treat a noble's woman, especially Artebrates.

And Leah stopped his hand and John finally noticed soft scales under her skin.

"You are a lizard female?"

"So?" Leah.

And Nannaha kicked out at Leah and missed by a foot and John realized she had river blindness.

"We got medicines," he said and out of the corner of his eye saw The Elder

scratching something on a termite block turned into rock by wind, bird pooh, rain, dust, and green lighting.

"Grubbing for termites," John dismissing the idea mazarrats had enough thinking power to write.

"Many humans couldn't read or write." The mazarrat singer being insulting and defensive.

Peelock only taught his followers.

So, John never saw The Elder carve Mungo killing a killer of killers.

John Wrexham had human prejudices, so never saw the work of art.

*

And a mazarrat sang from dark rhododendron trees and copied by his kind, "Peelock sells humans to the Fermanians," and Mungo heard.

And a lone warrior neared Mungo who rode Sasha and shouted, "I am Cadfael, let me join you, John Wrexham?"

And the ex-warrior of Peelock told that human thing on the white lion was Mungo.

"I am delivered," Cadfael gripping his bronze spear tighter and followed. He also told all he had seen concerning Wonder Lord Vinki.

*

So, it was then a puzzled John Wrexham rode into Red Town and again, The People came into the streets.

And were amazed and frightened, hoping to see excitement for lions and lizard men accompanied John.

Mungo was also amazed for he had never seen a human

town so sprawling, and as large as Telephassa City. "If men build like lizards, why are they slaves?" he asked.

"Because they feel secure when others tell them how to live," Malachi also amazed for although he had eaten Red Town citizens, he had never visited.

And The People knew of John for he survived assassinations opposing Peelock the Astronomer. And The People gazed upon a man thing sitting upon Sasha's white back, as she ran with Carman's red velvet dress open revealing brass armor plates, and   sheathed   weapons   underneath.

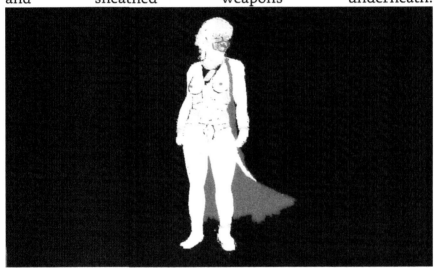

Illustration: Sasha, daughter of Red Hide

"He is Mungo," Peelock for all when they eventually met.

"I have brought you something back," Mungo and dismounted and took the back of a pha fur and opened, so the burnt body of Wendy seen by all.

"I am ashamed to be a man thing," Mungo and then drew in the sand.

"What did he say?"

"Quiet I can't hear."

"What did he draw on the sand?"

But Peelock saw.

"A picture of a man riding a lion, what does it mean?" Peelock crossing his arms annoyed that Mungo had rode into Red Town displaying obvious threat.

"It means he's The Wild One," John loudly and at once electric anticipation flowed through The People.

"We are all the oppressed and yet you do worse things to each other than the Fermanians would do you, why cannot you love one another than burn and mutilate each neighbor?" Mungo asked loudly relaxed.

"We do, why everyone here loves me Mungo," Peelock boasted and trapped himself.

For a tramp in a cardboard box called, "I saw Peelock give humans to Lord Vinki who dinned in his castle on human sweetmeat?" *"Yes, I saw too,"* a mazarrat screamed.

"Yes, we all did too, many mazarrats added.," and the shadows of warriors drew close, and Mungo growled with the loins and the pha whistled after their kind nervously.

"Is it bloodshed you want Peelock?" Mungo smelling Peelock's men and suddenly a flint dagger pressed into Peelock, who could not withdraw for Mungo held his head down.

"Kill me and you won't live," Peelock warned.

"It's a good night to die," Mungo and cut Peelock a little so he bled.

"You are insane, let us rule together," Peelock begged.

"I don't want to rule, and I know I don't like you so tell your men to sit down," Mungo ordered and Peelock feeling his blood soaking his under shorts obeyed.

"Take their weapons," John barked, and men things and lizard men obeyed but isolated fighting broke out.

When it went quiet the armed mazarrats vanished.

"Was that a mazarrat holding a dagger?" Someone asked disbelievingly.

"Not all love Peelock but their own hides," Mungo hissed sliding his blade two inches further into Peelock.

Who felt something throbbing, then cut, and he quickly went faint?

As Mungo said, "It is a good night to die."

Poor Peelock wanted home to his robotics.

"Go back to your barracks and await commands," Angus Ogg shouted, and men did not want the humiliation disarmed by lizard men and strangers, obeyed.

Then Mungo did to Peelock what Peelock did to chickens, so the man staggered to his castle.

"John is astronomer now, and no more killing each other like you did to Wendy," Mungo roared.

And he walked up to a fat woman plucking a chicken for supper and Mungo took the carcass and threw it to Sasha who ate it.

"*Lesson learned upon the crowd who was Boss*" us *mazarrats of course.*

"What about us?" The fat woman asked, and she wore a multicolored robe.

"Peelock's missionaries are disbanded," John and pushed past Mungo, and digging angry fingers into the fat woman who hated him anyway said, "To the victor belong the spoils."

So, she saw an end to her looting bullying ways as she sat in the front row on the Yathan River watching Peelock's enemies drown.

And always kept knitting scarfs and such.

And a young girl who had spoken earlier said to her friend, "I won't have to go to Peelock's anymore," and her friend cried with relief as they remembered Wendy.

"We must go to Hurreva," Mungo resting a hand upon Malachi's shoulder, and Malachi looked close at Mungo wishing he had never met him, for he was trouble just as The Wild One is supposed to be.

But in the meantime, they followed Peelock into his castle, and to the inner chamber where the Incorruptible One lay.

An easy trail to follow for Mungo knew how to work a knife.

"The end of time is upon us," Malachi coughed seeing the Incorruptible One. And robotic women had slid Peelock into a tube that sent shiny probes into his body's secrets.

Also, a shatter proof glass shutter slid down to separate the intruders from what happened next.

"Wheel the cage to me," a metallic voice ordered the two women, and they took from an adjoining room a caged naked man, and the rooms were set at body temperature.

"Put the cage in the slots in the floor," the computer and the women obeyed and stood back.

"Let me out, the man screamed as metal hands came from the computer operating on Peelock and seized him.

And made him ready for transplant for Peelock's liver ruptured and they took out the man's parts for future needs, and a hole appeared below the cage and the corpse fell through to Peelock's pet killer of killers that ate.

It needed fed too.

And because Peelock's walls had **an inner chamber containing a duplicate**
atmosphere all sounds, and radio waves ducted back to their source and thus soundproof: so, none heard Mungo scream, "Is the world full of evil only?"

And not once did the two females speak for, they feared the machine god they could not understand, and knew Peelock a wizard could turn them into toads like Angus Nero.

And about themselves vials full of mutated versions of the shuttle virus vehicle the **soil bacterium Agrobacterium tumefaciens** that put its own genes into a host and whatever Peelock wanted carried.

On a microscopic level of course.

And the computer inserted **Rec A** that spliced and cut DNA fragments to rebuild chromosomes damaged by radiation leaking from the damaged fast reactors outside Red Town.

And wrapped Peelock up **in arglaes the silver dressing that kills bugs** that antibiotics cannot.

And John Wrexham took pity upon Nannaha giving medicine that stopped the river Blindness and killed the parasitic worm causing it.

"We want to wash for we are women," Leah also, and Wrexham sent an escort with them to fresh water, and they bathed and washed their clothes.

And only The Elder dull of misgivings saw John and Cameron Black ride out.

"They are beauts," Cameron to John not believing lizard women could be desirable.

"Yes, they sure as hell aren't described like that in folklore," John answered.

"No, things big and fat with fangs hanging from purple rubbery lips and udders
dripping kids," Cameron.

John nodded; he needed a stiff drink like men did when their world went crazy.

"I work hard and play hard," he to Cameron on the way back, "I am a fair man, never hurt no kid and treat no woman kind unfairly," and remembered what he had seen bathing and he stirred and now coveted Nannaha and Leah.

They were not human so came under a separate set of rules.

Chapter 11 Nannaha's Gossip

And John Wrexham took pity upon Nannaha giving medicine that stopped the river blindness and killed the parasitic worm causing it.

"We want to wash for we are women," Leah also and Wrexham sent an escort with them to fresh water, and they bathed and washed their clothes.

And only The Elder saw him, and Cameron Black ride out with misgivings.

"They are beauts," Cameron to John not believing lizard women could be desirable and available at the spring.

"Yep, they sure as hell aren't described like that in folklore," John answered.

"Nope, things big ad fat with fangs hanging from purple rubbery lips and udders dripping kids, those ones are almost human, man I need a drink," Cameron replied.
John Wrexham nodded; he needed a stiff drink like men did when their world went crazy.

"I work hard and play hard," he to Cameron on the way back, "I am a fair man, never hurt no kid and treat women kind," and remembered what he had seen bathing and now coveted Nannaha and Leah.

"I agree John," Cameron and none said fair to human kids and women, lizards was something else. And Fermanians liked human kids as veal.

And women for fun and dinner after.

Let us face it, the races hated each other and tried their hardest to exterminate bugs.
A human was slave and sweetmeat to lizard; their gods said it was OK. If it was human.
Lovely.
Sweetmeat.
And to humans a lizard was alligator belts and a stinking

carcass under the red sun.

To Peelock humans were tradeable merchandise for Fermanian goods.

To Peelock Fermanians were only good dead when they were not looking.

Both sides raped when they looted and burned each other. They sometimes made the husbands look; something was wrong on both sides.

"*Could John Wrexham and Cameron Black, be forgiven? Nope, hang them,*" a singing baboon.

*

"I am grateful to a human, something I have never been for I must learn we must share this planet in peace," Nannaha to John standing submissively in his tent, alone and full of evil intent.

And her painted blue eyelids closed so the human could not see the lie twinkle there.

And John Wrexham who stood tall amongst man things felt his heart melt for Nannaha, and swallowed drink to hide it; she was woman even if a dirty lizard.

"I must learn to respect your race," and he held out his hands in friendship and was a lie for his below parts were thinking for him. He needed to reproduce, with anything if it was female.

And Nannaha understood, the races would be equal if humans were masters and had nothing to fear. She also knew it was the Fermanians who were the established primaries here, and if it remained that way, they would be equal with the humans when it suited, like when it was fashionable.

She also understood this man never paid for what she had offering, he was too important in his own heart for that.

She saw in his eyes that John wanted to know what it was like doing it with a Fermanian called Nannaha? She looked real human except for the scales.

"I am beautiful, Lord Artebrates will pay a ransom for me, I am a Noble's woman," Nannaha closer and unclipped the gold fastenings to her washed white silks and took John's hands.

He could have said no, but then he remembered Leah at the pool and was weak where his flesh was strong.

Later...." Why does Leah hate you?" As he drank again to wash away the taste of lizard for, he no longer lusted; she tasted like chicken.

"She is Mungo's woman although she was a court whore. She hates me because I know her filthy past and am her better. Now I am her slave because she is Mungo's harlot and beats me, or when I was blind led me amongst cacti so I would stumble and hurt," Nannaha lied for she was frail and lost from the light in her genes.

And John thought Mungo something else and Leah a strong cruel woman needing conquering, by a strong man like himself; he was letting drink do his thinking. *"Yes, he was drunk, and I caught up at last, darn The Elder leaving me behind, it's as if he didn't like me spying."* The mazarrat and *"he fears you,"* her audience.

He also never noticed Nannaha lace his drink with rape date drugs and nasty mind-bending additives, but they did make him high and feel like a man again so in the end ask for more; and she had a price, NAHANNA.

"She got scales yet is human?" He asked meaning Leah and Nahanna knew what he meant so hurt.

"We can make her type without cloning from shuttling genes in viruses in a vat bubbling tissue," Nannaha looking up at John's stubbly chin, "arms and bones sticking up and the stink is bad, neither lizard or human and has no soul, does not know what love or pain is?

That ape with the walking stick is crazy to say she is Mungo's woman; Mungo is lion yet man thing and for future kings of the humans Mungo's woman must be a human. I read the papyrus books, and they did not write this.

How can Leah's son sleeping on a hummock for his swishing tail, rule you?" Nahanna said these things to John.

"Gad you telling me she wasn't born natural like I was?"

"Notice he didn't include Nannaha for she was a Fermanians hatched from an egg." For the drugs made him want Nannaha again pleasantly our darling mazarrat.

"Out of a vat, no mother or father, she is like the walking dead."

And a mazarrat sang, *"We are all the children of the Oneness of the night so* Nannaha lies, even the walking dead and werewolfs."

"What sort of man is Mungo?" John feeling the heebie-jeebies from listening to the mazarrats.

"He is not man but lion thing and will be your master," Nahanna meaning harm but told the truth; *for once.*

"No freak is going to be my king. I am my own master; I fought lizards for my land.

I do not believe in kings; damn what has come upon me! I just lay with a lizard," and beat Nannaha for he did not feel clean and was the first time he had ever hit a woman, but Nannaha wasn't woman, she was lizard, *"a sex toy, so much for the drugs,"* and the mazarrat laughed at Nannaha's foolishness.

"Destroy Mungo John," Nannaha wailed, and he liked her idea, "it's Mungo's fault you defiled yourself in my arms," she and he knew she was right and enjoyed kicking the reptile some more, for she was just a reptile slut. *"And what was he?"* The audience while the mazarrat had a break.

It made him feel sexually powerful. He had to have her again to prove who was Master, and who lizard. His last words, "I got a lizard as a mistress, I am as crazy as this Planet New Uranus."

"But never mind do not feel sorry for him for all that exercise, Nahanna fed him poppy seed, crushed of course in drink so he wouldn't notice.

That was all right, he was not a Fermanian so in her gods eye had done no wrong," the mazarrat feeling sorry for the new addict.

"Nahanna didn't mind anything that happened to her, she had plenty practice enslaving General Artebrates, *"but if I ever beat her, she will know a difference"* The Elder sang but John spent ignored the ape with a walking stick that was a mazarrat.

Mazarrats did not know how to write or use words, they were stupid mongoose.

Later Nannaha went to the number two human boss, Cameron Black.

"You are a snake with legs so what makes you so sure I want to lie with you?" He is looking at her putting down his drink; men were men who rode the pha who knew how to work and drink hard then play hard.

"I saw it in your eyes," and with that she advanced upon him disrobing in the dim light and he saw she had a human body and because it was dim, did not see the scales, and did nothing to stop her; Nannaha was right about him, he was a man and never noticed she had a tail.

Later......" Mungo will kill me if he knows I slept with you Cameron Black, you must protect me?" *"This lady sure did get about."* The mazarrat.

"Possessive, is he?" The drink asked for him, "I had a sneaky suspicion he was taking you, someone pretty like you always has someone," and he stroked her tail thinking it turned her on; and he was wrong, it was a cooling mechanism provided by what made her.

They were both aliens living side by side for years and never said, "Hello."

"More than that, Mungo sells both lizard and human women to Fermanians, don't tell anyone I told you this, I don't want you harmed Cameron Black for knowing that" and Nahanna did not feel bad about lying.

But Cameron Black decided to tell John which was what Nannaha wanted.

Later.

The Elder walked with Leah who was swelling a bit from child when John and Cameron met them.

"The comets say one will be a warrior and another full of

wisdom," The Elder as one of New Uranus's moon satellite planets glowed bright green.

John looked at Leah and even carrying child found himself wanting to find out what her soft scales felt like. She was a lizard, a sexual plaything.

And Nannaha seeing crept through red moon beams to get closer for she was wicked.

"She must not lose the child, it is Mungo's," The Elder to himself, who saw he hadn't made an impression with the humans, *"after all to them he was an ape with a walking stick, a mongoose that ate snakes."*

And The Elder resisted the urge to throw ripe juicy fruit at him.

"Yaw ah she carries eggs with human babies in them, WA WAH scaled humans with tails and snake tongues," Nannaha moaned.

And The Elder promptly used his staff on her and stopped by men who saw proof of Nannaha's beatings, and they did not like it, "Mungo beat Nahanna," but they wanted Nahanna so would protect her, OK.

"Man look at the baboon fly," for they had roughed The Elder up and swung him by his limbs and then let go.

"Zoom," he went.

They were men and it felt good to protect a defenseless lizard female, especially one who was free with her charms?

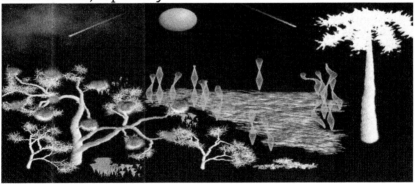

Illustration: The red moon

Here The Elder made a bad mistake, he told Leah to leave

fearing for her unborn for Nannaha was wailing Mungo would kill her.

"No one will kill you Nahanna, come with us," John **ordered**, and they left as warriors attracted by the nose began to approach.

"This way," Nannaha, "Leah went this way," and the humans sheepishly followed for she had cast a spell upon them, it was available sex and they had been drinking.

And Leah found by Nannaha in a rose thorn bush circle finding the peace within good and the flower smells uplifting.

And this was The Elder's bad mistake, telling Leah to leave for now she was alone.

"What do you want?" Leah asked angry her privacy invaded.

Nannaha answered for the humans, "You."

Now the humans had drink in them and disgust for Leah, who was a lizard female carrying human babes in eggshells and saw her as something needing put down.

Leah, a monstrous parody of humanity deserving no respect.

Why they respected their lizard enemies more than they did Leah at that moment.

So, showed themselves for she was not one of them but a plaything.

"I carry child," Leah protested disgusted, and the Giver of Life in her making woman special would remember all when they passed over.

But they were drunk and showing themselves and stripped her caring not to look at the sky and see all the stars and wonder what worlds there where?

They had listened to Peelock perhaps?

"Then be good to the human men," Nannaha and gave the men more drugged spiced drink to fuel their passion. Never mind these were men who would blame the drink and not themselves?

Their god was on their side?

And if things got sticky, Nannaha, "*she was just a lizard any way."*

Tasted like chicken.

"I will avenge Leah," the mazarrat and the listeners agreed.

"We going to cut those monsters out of her John?" The men not liking the sounds of the Wild Things.

Leah collapsed into a fetal position defending her babies.

She had a womb, and it was an oven of life, so the men were wrong.

Why that born wicked Nannaha drew Cameron's dagger and lounged at Leah but John stopped her.

He had drunk enough for this butchery; he wanted to sleep with lizard Leah, *"that is why he stopped Nannaha,"* the mazarrat singer disgusted.

"Cut her belly open and destroy the monsters in her," Nannaha urged Cameron and seeing John had not agreed took back the dagger.

"Guess we will leave camp," John knowing they had done wrong, and hell did follow.

"Did you not enjoy me, I am Artebrates Noble woman, Leah will kill me for sure now, take me with you?" Nannaha shouted which made it easier for The Elder to find them.

"You are a lizard," John replied slobbering and drooling.

So Nannaha exploded in a frenzied rage and clawed the man.

And that is when The Elder arrived and beat Nannaha with his stick for Leah.

And the two men watched Nannaha hit and did nothing to stop, only Leah stopped it: *"no one scratches big John Wrexham."* The mazarrat taking the micky.

"No lizard out of her belly will be my king," Cameron.

"Another time, another place," John knowing Mungo was nearby, *"for I was leading them, yes me,"* for I am a hero.

"One will be warrior, one will be wisdom," a mazarrat sang somewhere nearby.

Why men wondered if their future king was at their feet.

"Damn this world, I want home," John meaning Earth.

And the answer lay in a fast-approaching bright star.

And when Malachi and Mungo returned from a scouting trip, they found the humans and their riding pha gone.

"Leah for you I will kill them," Mungo promised then roared and his roar heard by those who had left, now mazarrats a hundred at a time copied the roar and made sure Mungo's anger heard.

Now Angus Ogg and the remaining human warriors looked at Malachi and the lizard Berserkas to see if they were about to fight each other.

"They are full of Nannaha 's lies and drugged drink, leave them Mungo," Leah and was why she was called Lady Leah, "*she was forgiving like me*?" The mazarrat and "*forgive me, no me, I*" and her audience confessed the wrongs they committed.

And hands holding weapons, relaxed and relieved sighs heard.

Then Leah picked up a grass grub and gave it to Mungo saying, "Do you understand there is more glory here than in one strand of your hair Mungo?"

The Elder smiled, of course he saw where the unborn ruler with wisdom would come from, and he looked at Mungo, poor Mungo was only the vehicle of change and felt pity for him, "*Mungo was a shuttle gene.*"

Mungo's life already mapped out before he had been born.

Illustration: Riding pha and rider

"You also need John Wrexham's men to help destroy all that is evil in Telephassa City," Leah again, "and you show all men and lizard can fight together, so die together, so now show can live together."

"I need no one, I am lion thing," and Mungo roared and went to sulk alone.

He wanted to kill the men who wanted to defile his Leah and had stopped. And a grub was more beautiful than him, what was Leah talking about and maybe if he had stopped sulking and danced, he might have understood, because once he did.

"Lady Leah," a Berserka and kissed her hand and soon all the lizards had walked by kissing her hand, for she was saintly to them. *"Just kissing her cured their pox and addictions."* *"Oh dear, hope Lady Leah has rubbed germ killer on her hands,"* the cheeky mazarrat.

"I must try this," Angus Ogg and kissed her hand for the wrong reasons. He found her hand soft, not scaly, and sweet smelling, for Leah rubbed flowers on her body.

And because he was close managed to see Leah curved in all the right places.

He also saw why John and Cameron had desired her; Leah could stir a man's loins and did.

"Men lack discipline, unlike us mazarrats. We are the night shadows you think are spirit folk, spying on you, always a mazarrat nearby, I wonder why?" Mazarrats knowing why.

Chapter 12 Hurreva

Now Hurreva was a floating city built upon connecting tubes filled with the gases of dinosaur methane and hydrogen. *"In reality was the caged mazarrat methane that was the gas,"* and she held her nose and the Wild started gassing so, the stink was unbearable.

And it was a mighty city and needed flying beast or machine to enter it.

"It is from Heaven surely for yellow clouds float across its silver houses," Enkalla Centurion in awe.

"No, it is Fermanian," Mungo in wondering how they would climb up to the gates?

"How do you know man thing?" Malachi grumbled for the papyrus books said god Telephassa lived with the Queen of Hurreva here, and it was a gateway to Mount Tullos where the gods lounged, and all lizards that died as martyrs got there, served by maidens, truly Heaven

"The air is full of Fermanian dung," Mungo replied and walked onto a roadway.

"Dung?" And Malachi sniffed before he felt he had 'been had' and gave an indigent snort.

The Elder rolled about laughing and scratching fleas.

"The Hurrevians will think we are invading with our numbers," Enkalla warned seeing signal flags.

"They do," Mungo shouted, and Malachi cursed for above came warriors in baskets held aloft by gas filled seeds, and large drums beaten in them. *"It was a din, worse than them farting,"* the mazarrat jerking a finger at The Wild.

"Why didn't I think of putting the fern swamp tree seed to such use?" Mungo asked as the first basket hovered fifty feet above, "then I could fly."

Malachi tapped his head then drew an arrow.

"Put this on slave," a voice above the owner of manacles

thrown at his feet.

"I will not," Mungo shouted up and an arrow replied.

"Wait brother Fermanians I am Malachi, you must have heard of me, I know I am Famous, as there is trade between Telephassa and Hurreva. I come in peace and seek service within your city as a hunter.

We all do, we are all mighty men wishing to give our shields to the glory of Hurreva."

"I didn't know you were famous Malachi?" Mungo.

"Not know Mungo."

And a mirror flashed from the basket to Hurreva which answered.

"I don't like the look of their faces, maybe my fame hasn't reached here?" Malachi and winked at Mungo.

"The Fermanians must put on manacles, and their truth established in the Arena of Criminals when they get their weapons back," the voice shouted down, "but the man thing will go to the slave pen."

"They are crazy; don't they know who I am?" Mungo complained walking away from Malachi waving up.

"Obviously, but in case they don't, don't tell them," Malachi warned too late, and Mungo greeted with laser, arrows, and lances so, he fled.

Wise thing to do.

"You have killed one of us and wounded two," Malachi shouted up and those above seeing Mungo gone into the jungle stopped killing.

"Malachi's arrow killed too, and nets dropped that had pythons coiling them, making freeing oneself a nightmare.

And Mungo roared and came to free Leah, then the others but a python's coils dropped over his body.

"Python's cousins of the serrant without stumpy legs," mazarrats in the jungle chorused.

And the last to help was Sasha come to aid Mungo and when trapped too, her lion kind came to free her.

And Mungo did not fear as the python lifted him into the air but took in all the detail of the land below, and the approaching city, and threw a decapitated snake's head at his captors, and it fell below amongst armed mazarrats who had appeared from nowhere.

"Armed mazarrats?" Heard shouted, by the captors.

"Mungo," was Leah's silent warning as a Pterodactyl flew out of the yellow clouds and attacked his net, and here the decapitated python's body dropped upon lizard men in a basket below Mungo, knocked overboard screaming as the headless giant torso thrashed. *"It did not know it was dead, unlike me who lives with gaiety, fun, and color,"* the singer in operatic silks borrowed from Madam Butterfly.

And the Pterodactyl seeing the lizard men an easier supper flew for them.

"Shoot it down, shoot it down," a centurion shouted to his men in the baskets and Mungo was able to think.

"Mungo fly," Malachi proclaiming his belief that Mungo was capable of anything.

It was now the time for The Elder to stare disbelieving at Malachi, *"What faith?"*

He added and dared to look to see if Mungo flew.

Leah screamed in terror for her love for Mungo was a woman's logic.

"Please fly," Nannaha gloating and "You read too much pulp fiction," Nannaha laughed as Leah swooned seeing Mungo fall, and then he was out of sight, as their baskets flew into an empty plastic sphere surrounding Hurreva City, then a second sphere which had parasitic plants **emitting antibiotic gases** and then a third which heavily armed Fermanians rode tamed Pteranodons covered in brass amour plates.

"To the Arena of Criminals then Malachi?" Enkalla joked, hugging his son full of worry breaking the stunned silence.

"He **was** The Wild One, wasn't he?" Akkad asked.

The Elder did not reply, he had devoted his whole life to Wild One tales and Prophecies, and it was a lie for nothing, none said Mungo would die like this? And then the timing of the armed mazarrats had been late, and he blamed them for his predicament, he should be free.

And was smart enough to realize the armed mazarrats had come up against flying Weapons and had been ineffective against them. Therefore, a new weapon needed to combat these Fermanian trapeze artists, *"flying mazarrats of course!" I aided the old bugger tee he,"* she was asking for it, please dear keep out of reach of that staff.

And The Elder was the only one amongst them that saw IF the lizards could build a floating city, they could travel the stars if they woke up one day, it was a frightening thought.

And Nannaha laughed for she saw their predicament; they had given their lives for a joke.

But Mungo was not dead as he fell, he caught trailing vines underneath the floating city for he was thinking. *"Certainly not daft fools, what do you take Mungo for, The Elder?"* She lives dangerously.

Nor was afraid and as he leapt his heart calm as, he scrambled down an uncoiling net and the python living there tried to bite him.

"Ugly legless brute with no brains," Mungo shouted at it, "leave me or I will kill you," but the snake was hungry and shot its head out which Mungo stuck his dagger in.

And it was it that fell as a blur to his watching friends and others.

"He is falling, the damn man is truly dead," Nahanna saying epitaph.

"Mungo," Leah screamed.

And the python hit the ground below as a puff of dust.

And The Elder shook his head in shock.

Now Mungo swung underneath the floating city of Hurreva with these words, "I have much to thank Moragana for she taught me how the apes do this," and he made ape and monkey talk for he joyed at being alive.

He swung with no safety net below.

And saw sewage openings and jumped for one and caught

railings and hung there.

And watched the net he had left fall hundreds of feet to the swamp below made from what came out of the openings!

"Leah and my friends need me," he said and climbed the rungs into darkness.

Illustration: Wicked lizard woman Nahanna

"Will I ever know true happiness?" Leah asked.

Malachi said nothing.

The Elder threw his arms out so the power of the universe, Mungo's unnamed God could tell him what to do for he was at a loss.

It was fortunate John Wrexham and Cameron Black were not there to see or they did burn the baboon for blasphemy.

Only humans could be the Lord's anointed prophets.

Hurreva City.

"My Lord Artebrates trust not Carman," the hunchback whispered to him with his back to the security cameras.

And Artebrates knew he did not need reminding.

And behind him Wonder Lord Vinki doing his best to win the sympathy of Queen Ishtar of Hurreva as all waited for the captives to arrive.

"Mighty One," a herald careful not to let his excitement make him shout, fell at their feet, "Mungo has fallen to his death; a detachment of guards has left the city to search the swamp below for his body."

"Our common foe The Wild One is dead?" Ishtar said looking at Carman and happy took off her red ruby ring and gave it to Carman.

Carman kissed it.

Noticed by all.

"The alliance is still needed Mighty One for the subjugation of all humans," Vinki quickly pointed out to Carmen, fearing his new commercial ventures in Hurreva would collapse without a common threat.

And Lord Artebrates felt a twinge of regret that Mungo was dead. Deep down he envied Mungo his freedom, and had wanted to be the one to cage him and then what?

Let him go for Artebrates knew without Mungo an era representing his own life would be over.

"Don't believe it till the body is found," the hunchback advised.

Queen Ishtar smiled over crackling fingers and joints and threw one at the hunchback, for she had taken pity upon his deformity.

"Gracious majesty," and the hunchback made a show of noisily extracting marrow and did not enjoy for the human bone made him think of Leah, who loved Mungo.

"Curse the day my seed marries a slave," he thought knowing the Fermanian
genes inside Leah came from him and wondered if his father Artebrates remembered sending him to the vats, and gene banks as a donor, for he was full of poppy at the time and thought it a jolly good joke.

"There are carnivorous creatures down there," Artebrates hoping they would not find Mungo and the legend could survive, and he Artebrates would lead safaris into the unmapped parts and receive glory from the Geological Society.

"Fear not the alliance, we are equals Carman, sisters," Ishtar Mighty One to Carman who returned her stare and Vinki saw desire there, and glad he could vanish into warehouses and inspect contraband.

Tactfully he backed away.

And Carman thought, *"Witch of the floating city I will have you make me joy and no other. Agree to the signing of wills to make both cities one in case of death and the death shall be yours."* For Carman knew Ishtar was mightier in arms than she and why she had kissed the red ring as a sign of submission, the younger sister awaiting the command of the older.

And Ishtar thought, *"Carman I am dominant in all I own, and I shall chain you to the end of my bed and there you will grow old emptying my chamber pot."*

"These were nice people! Should be like mazarrats, don't use chamber pots, we are like birds," the mazarrat and birds dumped upon her for mazarrats stole their eggs, thieving mongoose.

At this moment Malachi, Enkalla and Leah, all brought in, as trumpeters drew attention to them, and Leah found Malachi held her chains to protect the young she carried, for he was saying to all she is no danger, she is mine, leave her, show her mercy, and the chains he hoped would stop the Queens ordering Leah chained so hurting her.

"Malachi was his friend," a mazarrat in a cage sweetly sang.

And The Elder acted ape so, all saw mazarrats had peanuts for brains, he sang and picked fruit from a bowl.

And Nannaha broke from their ranks and fled to Artebrates.

"Well, my famed hunter seeking sanctuary?" Carman and Ishtar blinked, and a guard slapped Malachi's back with a halberd so, he crumpled.

And all-seeing Carman understood why they were not welcome; the witch Ishtar did not need her.

Now Leah sank to her belly to protect the fetus or fetuses from a blow for she was part Fermanian who could bring forth young.

"Leah beat me, and Malachi raped me, even Enkalla his brother," Nannaha lied.

"Enkalla and his little one, a shame they must be separated

for the law states a condemned has no rights over his young," Carman hissed and Enkalla pleaded the
rights of the Arena of Criminals hoping to win his freedom and son.

"Even Akkad sat on my back and rode me like a pha degrading Lord Artebrates
comforter," Nannaha again.

"But you are going to the arena Enkalla, all of you except Leah and Akkad," Ishtar replied as she stroked Leah's soft curling long blond hair.

And Enkalla pained and felt like strangling Nannaha who was pulling Akkad away, proclaiming she would be guardian.

"In a week's time," Ishtar added, and the brothers saw themselves weak from malnutrition and torture unable to defend themselves against laboratory mutants.

"Oh, Mighty One, Leah is innocent of all Nannaha's claims," the hunchback giving rose water to Leah to sip.

And Carman stopped slapping the porcelain bowl by Ishtar, who never broke a beautiful object, whether of stone, China, or flesh.

And Artebrates said nothing, earning loathing from his son the hunchback. More when Nannaha clasped him like a squid and shouted, "The Elder knows many secrets and mazarrats are an intelligent race spying on Fermanians."

"The red sun has touched your head child," Ishtar sympathetically and when Nannaha protested Artebrates silenced her, two Mighty Ones were present and
Nannaha was a Comforter.

So, The Elder threw a banana skin at Nannaha and sang *"Nannaha is a mazarrat,"*
courtiers laughed.

*

"We cannot escape," Malachi looking out the open veranda as no bars were necessary. If they had wings, they might fly as pigs could fly.

"Come away from there brother, this city shakes from

methane build ups," Enkalla warned which made Angus Ogg look out and got dizzy by the height. Mungo he knew was not a pig.

*

"That mazarrat had wit," Carman to Ishtar eating grapes as they lunged on cushions and why she was more cunning than Ishtar for she sensed Nahanna spoke truth.

"Nonsense, it is argued they are a cross between an ape and a mongoose," Ishtar replied and shut her eyes as a fanner fanned with peacock feathers.

And the fanner was human.

"It takes intelligence to make wit," Carman troubled wishing she were in her own city Telephassa; her dungeons would make The Elder speak.

"My sister in desire, give orders to have its tail snipped, fur burnt and then thrown from our walls if it pleases you to make it talk like us," Ishtar for this Mighty One hated men: even a mazarrat male with a peanut for a brain.

"I will," Carman who never let an opportunity pass to be cruel.

"As it falls, we will all listen to what it screams, usually the sight of the ground rushing up makes them say things they would not say. Better than getting the truth out of them when they are drunk. Men are all the same, yes, we shall throw that baboon off a wall and listen, also watch, it is good sport.

Such a Mighty Queens of the Fermanian cruel race.

Chapter 13 Underneath

And the **first day** Mungo met a mazarrat in a drainage pipe and it had four arms, and a gigantic bald septic bald head and was mangy, and Mungo saw lice and ticks the size of his nails sucking blood upon the beast.

"Yah a slave for dinner," the beast sang as it saw Mungo and opened jaws to show black and yellow teeth, where they were teeth. *"For it, unlike other civilized mazarrats, its cousins, did not brush teeth,"* and the singer flashed her teeth and that started its audience showing each other teeth, scores still had dinner remains, so much audience vanished.

AND THERE WAS PEACE FOR TEN MINUTES.

"I am in the other world or something worse?" Mungo replied finding a slime covered stick which he then stuck deep in the beast's mouth.

"Gag a ga," the beast could not speak now so made these sounds instead.

"Why eat me singer of songs? Your kind are fruit eaters," Mungo pushing the leprous thing away from him.

"I still sing but I learn from my masters above."

"Fermanians did this."

"I am from the cages and escaped by flushing myself away," the mazarrat explained.

"Don't let me kill you then for I am Mungo of the lions."

"Mungo's shame is Leah."

And Mungo felt his heart break, shook his head, and said, "Even baboons know?"

"Yes, they know for we sing loud," and the mazarrat missed the insult for baboons have big red bums and nothing between their skulls.

"So, great singer, will you lead me out of here to some friends?"

"Come and meet friends then?" And the beast skipped away

scraping knuckles leaving pus behind.

"I meant my friend," Mungo shouted and followed avoiding a clump of fallen fur and the things that lived upon it.

And the friends were mutated mazarrats used for experiments and humans and other beings from around New Uranus, and Mungo was angry for science had perverted life.

And he roared and danced throwing his arms and head this way and that.

"Mungo dances now we have seen this too," the mazarrats sang.

And it was not joy but anger that filled Mungo.

"I must rescue Leah," he loathed aloud.

"Mungo's shame is above," the mazarrats.

"Don't mazarrats ever stop?" Mungo grunted covering his ears mockingly.

At this slight encouragement mazarrats jumped and sang, holding the tail in front and train fashion circled Mungo.

Human mutants beat a rhythm on metal drums, *"and not a tail came away"* I heard from the singing outside.

Other beings downed masks and imitated beasts.

Then one lay beside Mungo shouting, *"I am Leah, I am Mungo's shame."*

"What have the lizard folk done too you, gentle people," Mungo disgusted.

"We are mazarrats fearless and brave and want a Mighty One," and began squabbling as who this should be?

"We will help you if you help us get down," a human said quietly with eyes on the end of stalks.

Mungo stroked the stalks gently.

Then there was a scream as a female mazarrat thrown down a waste flume that dropped her to the swamp below.

Unfortunately, there was no net to catch her!

"We don't want her as Mighty One," the mazarrats chorused.

Mungo thought all crazy and wistfully, "I got in so we can get down," and the listeners wondered at his wisdom which was none. "I must destroy life in Hurreva."

"Yes destroy," the mazarrats copied Mungo who saw clouds full of cuckoos above their heads and grey metal walls elsewhere.

"The Unnamed One does not live here, it is free and wild," Mungo.

And the **second day** Mungo, led to laboratories by mazarrats where he saw from the ventilation grills beings in cages; freshly arrived while others twitching death waiting experimental cures.

And a Fermanian in a white coat and mask stood with his tail to the grill Mungo hid behind.

"I am Mungo," and *"We know you are Mungo,"* the mutants behind agreed for they were dim.

And the first the Fermanian technician knew was the kicked grill heading for him.

"Dung," the lizard a second before impact and Mungo was down and running at him.

"I am Mungo, give me the keys for these beasts," and the technician did for Mungo held a dagger to his throat.

"Come with us brothers," the mutants urged the freed and all fled into the drainage chamber.

"The only reason I don't kill you is that I want Leah to know I am alive," Mungo pushing his enemy away and went back to jump high into the shaft.

But taken from behind for Mungo had forgotten Fermanians thought themselves brave and fearless masters, of all, especially slaves.

But the man watched as Mungo bent down and cut here and there.

"Bloody hell what has the beast done to me," the lizard man screamed disengaging, and Mungo still ignorant of science then showed mercy by slicing the man's throat and stabbing the heart.

"That was Mungo's mercy for he knew not of wondrous surgeons so believed he had done good. Better not visit him sick ha, Ha, tee he," and the audience copied.

Now Mungo cleaned himself and saw pictures on the wall of a man thing riding a lion, "Not bad," he said as he had drawn the picture in the slain warrior's blood.

He also said nothing as the mutants cut up the lizard man to eat him all up later.

Especially the liver.

The sweetmeat they cooked in the fashion of the Fermanians, and the smell made Mungo shelter elsewhere till the feast was over, with these words, "They are no longer mazarrats and I will avenge the wrong done Life here by Fermanians."

DAY THREE AND MUNGO LED TO SLAVE PENS TO SEE IF HIS FRIENDS WERE THERE AND

found them not.

"Most are for the pot," a mazarrat told Mungo who saw most were human and saw barrows full of sweetmeats, innards and limbs and a mincing machine hummed grinding bones into powder for lizard farmers.

"I am Mungo," and kicked out the grill in the ventilation shaft and landed on a startled supervisor, a thing with two tusks with green scaled skin who was not Fermanian.

And Mungo at once realized there was more to New Uranus than he knew of.

"Who are you?" The supervisor grunted as Mungo opened his scales from groin to neck.

"Mungo, I am Mungo follow me," and slaves ran to the opened grill while others so badly starved shuffled.

"The slaves are escaping," another supervisor to another and immediately they stabbed the slower escapees in their backs with copper swords.

And Mungo raged when he saw a copper sword split an

infant girl's head.

"What have we here?" One supervisor afraid for Mungo was on all fours growling advancing upon him.

"*Mungo,*" a mazarrat sang which was fortunate for fear paralyzed the supervisor now, who might otherwise have slain Mungo? But instead with his friends turned to flee and Mungo was on their backs.

What goes around comes around.

And Mungo's lungs filled with stink for large cauldrons bubbled and saw hooked carcasses on a conveyor belt like cattle, and the humans were exactly that, this place was slaughterhouse and kitchens.

And seeing armed guards coming he spilled the cauldrons of boiling broth, so the feet of the guards burned, and they jumped hither and thither.

And Mungo took cleavers and sunk them in the jumping bodies and strung them up on the conveyor, then swung across the belt ape fashion, which he owned the harlot Moragana the ape woman thing teaching him how a favor.

And he roared like a lion.

Illustration: Mutants they were victims of shuttle genes.

And then he cut off the Fermanian tails and shouted, "I have brought judgement upon the Fermanians as foretold and obeyed."

And the last cook he put headfirst into a cauldron too boil away, and then flipped the cook in and shut the heavy lid on.

And about Mungo sixteen wiggling tails seeking where they had come from for lizard tails can live without a body.

Six cooks and ten guards and three evil supervisors.

What goes around comes around.

And Mungo barred the exit doors with empty cages as the last human child was lifted to safety.

That night the mutants divided up the cooks, and still fought for pieces even though there was enough for all. And Mungo now joined by the latest freed slaves, and these were not mutants so refused to eat what the others gobbled.

Even non mutated mazarrats were shocked, at seeing their mutated cousins eat parts of Fermanians fit for the bin.

"We ate them as they eat us, and we get Fermanian wisdom in our tummies," a mutant explained happy.

"They are crazy," Mungo tapping his head.

"No," they are human," a freed human and Mungo remembered Peelock and saddened.

Day Four am. And Ishtar and Carman were now aware something was wrong within Hurreva and told why.

"Did no one tell me about the picture drawn in Fermanian blood?" Ishtar asked and there was silence and Lord Artebrates drifted away in a dream world and imagined six guards, two technicians and a microbiologist hanging from hocks, as descaled prepared for cooking as punishment.

In case you have not guessed, Fermanians are cannibals. *"Waste not want not,"* one of their sayings a spying mazarrat.

"Ah well at least something tasty will come out of this," as his mouth savored lizard flesh roasted and smeared in thyme butter.

And the flesh served in their empty craniums containing their hot and sour sweetmeats.

And Artebrates hungered but not the hunchback who no longer ate anything intelligent, not even roasted mazarrat in orange sauce with cranberry gel stuffed in the mouth till it came out near the parson's nose!

"Lentils and fish are my limit now," he muttered and Artebrates looked at him saying nothing.

DAY FOUR
AFTERNOON.

A platoon under a Decurion, a leader of tens, ambushed entering the drainage tunnels seeking Mungo, by armed mutant mazarrats and other beings.

"I have fought as a Fermanian and die with honor," the Decurion standing next to his trumpet blower who fell with a mazarrat at his throat.

"Die foul thing," the Decurion running his copper sword across the beast's spine and then stood alone to take Ishtar's enemies with him, for he remembered pictures of Artebrates facing humans with his sword.

An inspiration for any brave soldier facing death alone.

"A brave man deserves life," the Decurion heard and saw a dirty man thing and bowed his head for he knew it was Mungo. But the bow was an acknowledgement that he was brave and had nothing to do with servitude.

But the mutants still hummed their pleasure, silly things.

"Go and tell them I want Leah and my friends freed," and Mungo pointed the way out where the Decurion had entered hell in the first place. And the Decurion walked as a Decurion should, within his plumed red helmet high and his back straight and his sword sheathed and found his nerves breaking, for he was trusting the word of a human beast.

Then a mazarrat threw its dung at his back, and soon covered, and Mungo did not stop this show of hate, understanding mazarrats wanted revenge.

"They were also crazy and numbered hundreds and were

enraged they couldn't eat the Decurion, and Mungo wasn't crazy, he wanted to see another day," the singer after hearing from the mazarrat spy.

DAY FIVE BROUGHT MUNGO TO LEAH FOR THE MAZARRATS BROUGHT HIM TO A CASTLE MADE OF

crystal the colors of the rainbow, and Fermanians said it was the gateway to Mount

Tullos, and the crystal were a weapon, for Ishtar knew it was a prism bending light dividing one ray of laser into a hundred upon any advancing enemy below or in the sky.

"Here you will find Leah," Mungo advised, and he opened a grill and entered and found the crystal warm, for the crystal stored heat like a radiator.

And Mungo heard the grime leave his soles and saw he left a trail and knew he must hide his nakedness.

And a House Berserka saw the grime and hefted his axe over shoulder and followed, past where Mungo hid amongst a room littered with papyrus books.

For Mungo had walked backwards over his own footprints so was now behind the warrior.

And the enemy could not scream as Mungo covered his mouth as he cut the lizard's heart out and threw it across the room.

For Mungo still raged over what he had seen in the

laboratories and Mungo wronged, "*did he*? **What goes around comes around,**" **the singer.**

And then a mutant mazarrat ran in and out again with dinner?

And the lizard berserker body Mungo skinned quickly in the room and the blood he wiped on papyrus books, and were priceless, but he could not read so the books were just paper to him, and Fermanian paper at that.

"*Just as well he didn't need number 2 giggle,*" and she laughs at her joke and the audience also.

He was just skinning a rabbit for the pot, which is how he saw the Fermanian and the Fermanian saw him as a rabbit too.

"Now I am a lizard," meaning he wrapped the lizard skin about him and left seeking Leah as mazarrats sang, "*Mungo's sin Leah is here.*"

And as soon as he was gone the mazarrats were back and ate the lizard Berserka.

"*Sasha pines for Mungo,*" they sang also.

"I love Sasha too," Mungo replied wishing sometimes they could stop singing.

And Mungo had put on the man's armor and helmet and stayed in the shadows.

So avoided his enemy in the corridors and the deeper he went into the crystal noticed the Berserkas carried lasers as well as axes.

"Blood there is blood," Mungo heard and hurried on for the mazarrats had started throwing books at each other in the corridor and blamed for the Berserker's death, not Mungo.

And Berserkas passed him carrying nets full of slain mazarrats to show Ishtar their excellent work.

"I smell Leah," and followed her scent which came from air vents.

And found her.

"How do I get in," Mungo again?

"You don't," the door replied, and Mungo jumped and sunk his axe into it.

"You are not authorized to enter, you have no palm print," the door and Mungo took off his skinned right foot and put it on the square where a red hand glowed.

And the door laughed and answered by Berserkas with lasers.

"Decurion?"

"Mungo and the lizard man slapped him for he remembered the thrown insults and tripped Mungo, so he fell.

"What noise disturbs me?" Ishtar from the now open door and looked down and saw scales and blood, fallen from the hide covering Mungo and recoiled in horror.

And one used a hand to say his name and it was Leah, and Mungo saw pity in her eyes, and she was as a yellow bird whose feathers the Mighty Ones had been plucking to belittle and embarrass the girl.

For they were not good women.

"Stand him up," Carman barked like a dog as she had come to the door also, "It is Mungo the slave."

"But Mungo had never been their slave, always free on the plain and jungle," a mazarrat from a hanging cage.

And a Berserka took down the cage and threw it hard against a wall.

And Carman swung a right into Mungo's jaw again, till her knuckles bled for she wanted his teeth loose, of which she managed to pull one free for rage gave her strength.

"What no howl from the beast man thing?" Carman gloatingly.

Instead, Mungo smiled to give Leah courage.

Now Carman seeing took Leah by the cheeks and kissed fully, and Mungo kicked the queen's rear, so she fell upon Leah.

"Take him away," Ishtar fearing the destruction of the beautiful man thing for she had not the same dealings of experience with Mungo as Carman.

"Wait," Mungo shouted, and Ishtar signaled curious.

"I have found Leah but where are my friends and Sasha who pines for me?"

Now Ishtar marveled at his cheek while Carman raged.

"Sasha has been given to the hunting lions Abel and Eve as reward for serving Fermanians," Ishtar.

"Let no harm befall Sasha for she was my first love," Mungo.

"Ah what crazy talk is this, a man thing saying a lion thing is his woman? Is this whom they call The Wild One, let Mungo throughout Hurreva City known as The Crazy One," Ishtar.

And Leah understood why Mungo thought of Sasha so did not hurt too much.

And Carman knew foolish Ishtar had just told Mungo where to find Sasha.

And Mungo chained and beaten in his own cell, and they did not take the hide from him, and the blood congealed, and Mungo now felt unclean for flies found him.

And a screen spoke to Mungo who marveled when he saw Leah and licked and sniffed it, became angry when he found it lifeless, for he lacked the wisdom of technology.

And the screen's microchips responded with a self-protect program and allowed Leah's scent out and changed to a 3D image of her, which infuriated Mungo more, instead of calming him, for he had tried to put his hand into the hologram.

"Leave me alone," the screen's computer howled as Mungo raked but taken over manually as Ishtar and Carman appeared and began to abuse Leah and Mungo sickening looked away.

And because there were cameras in Mungo's room, the queen's and Ishtar observed him knew fury for Mungo would not play their sad game, and shouted, "Give the man, lion hell," and it was so for blades came out of his cell walls so he could not sit.

And left him so for hours.

And Mungo knew Hades as his body ached to straighten but could not so when the blades departed at last his body knew more pain just to straighten, for it cramped.

And the Mighty Ones were not mighty for they debased themselves by abusing beautiful Leah and reminded her she was only a Comforter, made of bubbles in a vat.

And Leah saddened that such cruelty could exist in a world so full of diverse color and evolved animals! For Huverra had proven The Elder correct, these Fermanians were much more advanced than Telephassa's and could have reached the stars?

And the Mighty One reminded Leah of her past from the perversions they acted upon her for, they had the power but not conscious, and after they were satisfied left Leah, thinking they had destroyed her spirit. *"To destroy her is to destroy Mungo, but this is one whose first love was a lioness, Sasha,"* so Mungo would survive.

But the queens were wrong, she had come to believe in the Unseen and knew nothing could harm her soul, it belonged somewhere else.

But was a lesson that slaves existed and who was master.

Day six and Mungo slept but hundreds of cockroaches kept crawling over him nibbling away so, he did not sleep well, for these animals can eat through cement so Mungo was like a box of chocolates to them.

And he crushed the insects and hurt inside when he did so for, they were life and existed at a lower God consciousness than him. And he understood this from what he gained when he danced for Mungo was a *"Shinning One,"* a mazarrat sang nearby.

For he did not understand he was in tune with life, so hurt much when he killed a lowly bug.

Then hunger visited him and that was a lonely ordeal.

"Eat," something whispered to him.

"Eat what?"

And saw the cockroaches.

"That is mazarrat food and unclean," he replied to the Unseen.

And the spirit that is wisdom and sees inside you replied in his mind, "What is unclean to one is clean to another."

And Mungo ate and apologized to the creatures that he must eat or starve.

And flies had laid eggs in his cuts and the maggots kept his flesh from rotting.

And he ate these too.

So, Mungo refreshed from their nutrients.

Then ants came, hundreds seeking food they had come to expect, and he was the food.

And he flattened scores of ants and felt like the supervisor in the Arena of Criminals as the ants and roaches fought each other, for the privilege of eating him, *"and mazarrats know big words," and the music notes drifted to the clouds.*

Then scalding hot water flooded in and washed all away.

And even Mungo burned, as the cell sloshed with hot water.

Day seven, and Mungo taken to an arena with seating for seventy thousand and he marveled how the Fermanians could build such for they were lizards? *"With tails,"* and the singer had wrapped a toy tail on her as was *"Fermanian."*

At this moment what he danced too did not forget him as he often forgot It, for he was full of lust for Leah and Sasha these days, but his hair was still long.

"If it was not lion woman, then it was lizard woman Leah," Mazarrats would sing and *"We will dance for Mungo,"* and they did and found animals could enjoy the Unseen also.

Is it not written by Isaiah, "Even the beasts of the field will know the King of Heaven?"

Anyway: "Mungo?" Malachi shouted and Mungo smiled seeing his friends crowded in the middle of the arena and hobbled to them on blistered bitten feet.

"Take this," Enkalla offered a blunt copper sword and Mungo took it and shook his head, "My hair is uncut," he still had his hands and what made him dance in his heart.

"Truly The Wild One," Malachi as he saw Mungo's long dirty hair, greasy and louse infested now from contact with the laboratory life, also, "God of Mungo remember Mungo's friends," and felt joy and knew even a lizard could joy also, for lizards were beasts of the field too.

"Don't forget me," Sasha and Mungo went to hug her but she seeing the lice held him back.

"My first love," Mungo and Sasha beamed and made sure she was beautiful too the watching Fermanians.

"I am Red Hide's daughter," and her lion companions straightened their brass plate body armor too looks smart, they would not die shamed as uncouth unkempt beasts.

For Mungo's presence had electrified them into not accepting their fate with courage and valor, *"for they were just 300 Spartans", this mazarrat knows her human history.*

Mungo was hope, Mungo was life.

"Well man thing you got old Malachi into a right mess this time?" Malachi.

And all followed Malachi's gaze to an opening gate and behind the gate an emerging deinonychus.

Now these deinonychus were just lizards running about on hind legs that possessed a foot with a flesh cutting claw, and each animal was about nine foot long.

"Are you in a hurry to die Mungo?" Malachi joked as Mungo forgetting his pain had run to the gate and as the first beast saw him it jumped, to open Mungo up with its claw.

But Mungo rolled under the beast and used the short sword on it, so innards fell out and trailed about, so the other deinonychus gobbled them up except for a lone kidney, that hung lonely from the belly of the doomed monster.

And Mungo ran up this creature's tail and with pressure in its eyes with his fingers, used it to defend his friends by making it jump with its claw.

"Run for the gate, we can shut them in and us out," Malachi ordered, and they ran but not all made it, three Berserkas died split by claws and then fought over.

So, they gave their lives for the others to make the gate, *"no greater sacrifice than this, sniff,"* the singer and loud sniffs were heard from The Wild, so Fermanians ask themselves again, *"Why do we put up with this?"* And mazarrats answered, *"Because we outnumber you."*

And here Mungo made his beast stand at the gate entrance defending till it was dead.

"What type of man thing is he?" Ishtar marveled and the watching Fermanians went quite with fearful admiration of Mungo, and the Unseen Helper who always helped him.

"He is Mungo," Carman and Leah beamed pride and put a hand over her womb.

One or a dozen inside her were all Mungo's.

At this moment, a nuclear reactor exploded and shook the ground, and Pteranodons flew above seeking the smell of blood, and lizard folk took this as a bad omen.

"Take Mungo alive," Ishtar and Berserkas armed with lasers entered the arena and commanded Mungo to come with them, and he looked at the guns and looked for Leah.

And she sensing his meaning stood up allowing the wind to carry her sent to him.

And Mungo roared and ran to the wall below Leah

And the remaining deinonychus followed and attacked the Berserkas who killed a handful, and one went after Mungo, who had managed to scramble Moragana fashion up cracks in the plaster towards Leah and The Mighty Ones.

And the following deinonychus bounced off a fallen sister using it as a springboard followed Mungo.

"Kill him"," Carman demanded but the Berserka beside her looked at Ishtar for he knew she had ordered Mungo be taken alive.

But he did throw a poisoned lance into the deinonychus behind Mungo.

And Mungo knelt and leapt so he sailed into the air.

And the deinonychus still alive leapt also, *"for cruel folk use slow poisons,"* and the singer gasped her last, poisoned, pretending, an actor for she had an audience that clapped her short performance.

Illustration: deinonychus.

"Move," whether Carman meant Ishtar who had fallen on her or the dinosaur that was, stabbed, lasered and poisoned by other Berserkas.

And hell came to The Mighty Ones as other deinonychus copied the one who had followed Mungo and the royal box was mayhem.

"Where do we go?" Leah asked Mungo as they fled down a corridor now empty of Fermanian candy vendors.

"Nowhere," Nannaha appearing with Aralwan Giant and Lugh with Berserkas armed with lasers.

And Mungo answered with a roar and Nannaha took intense pleasure in firing a suction cap at him, and it stuck to his chest and rewound towards her and the Berserkas.

"Take this," Nannaha panicking giving the suction gun to a Berserka as Mungo neared, salivating at the mouth for he was a lion man thing now, for she slapped his face.

And more suction caps fired, and Mungo stretched ways and became unmovable.

"A present," Leah who had silently walked up behind Nannaha and slapped her hard.

"What do you smirk at?" Aralwan Giant demanded from Berserkas for Nannaha's reputation had spread.

And only when Leah began kicking Nannaha did the Berserkas obey for Aralwan Giant, and Lugh now thought it their position only to give orders.

For Nannaha had made Vinki promote them centurions. "It must not be seen I sleep with lowly privates my sweet handsome Vinki," she had complained and maneuvered.

"They know many gentlemen's destinations in Hurreva and as officers will know more for, they can visit places as officers?"

And Vinki saw the extortion and promoted the flotsam.

And Mungo was ignorant Malachi had fought his way to the docks and take a flying machine, and escape with six Berserkas remaining, also Enkalla, Akkad, Angus Ogg, and his friends.

Or the hunting lions Abel and Eve trailing them.

*

"Mungo what do we do with you?" Ishtar against butchery as Carman wished, for she still marveled over Mungo's physic.

"Give me Leah and I will go away," and this brought laughter from the courtiers except Artebrates and the hunchback.

"You must be obedient if you wish Leah," Ishtar told him and Mungo understood, "I promise you Mungo I will let Leah visit you; am I not kind Mungo?" Ishtar but Mungo thought she was a cruel wicked woman so, said nothing.

"Take him to the galleys," Ishtar and the galleys were warships that floated in the air, built of wicker plated with brass, woven with tubes of helium gas.

And propelled by blades worked by slaves sitting on lower decks.

And the ships strapped to giant squids plated with brass for the squids could eject wind for speed and clouds of ink for cover when needed.

And the upper deck sails for wind and steering and crystals embedded in the wicker to deflect laser from enemy ships, *"more for moral than practical reasons, and who were the enemy, mazarrats ha, Ha,"* the mazarrat wondering too."

And the Decurion who suffered mazarrat insult was

captain of Mungo's vessel for Ishtar saw he hated the man thing which was good.

NOW: Ishtar had Mungo come to her that night before he went to the ship in chains, and in them bathed him in primrose water. *"I never get that treatment,"* a jealous singer and beasts came out of the jungle offering her service for that pleasure.

"So strong," Ishtar crooned sweeping a hand over his shoulders.

"I think of only That who I dance to naked under the moon," Mungo to her.

"What is his Name?" Ishtar.

"There is no Name," Mungo.

"Then he cannot be a god," and Ishtar made Mungo lust and wrapped herself about him for he was vulnerable in chains.

"I will not joy," Mungo and forced himself to be calm.

And Ishtar called for Carman to join her so they could overpower Mungo's determination not to lust with them.

They wanted his light, and for hm to darken like them, and so worked hard on the chained lion man thing like vampires.

"Is my body separate from my mind?" Mungo as Carman injected him full of hormones to make him lust.

And he roared and his body wanted the queens.

In his mind an image of Leah remained, but he was no longer his own person as his mind crossed boundaries because of what Carman had given him.

And still bound they had him put in an open seed bag, and lifted Mungo away by tame Pteranodons. Dropped in a public square, where all could see The Wild One lust chained, and roar for, they had overdosed him to humiliate him.

And at last, he exhausted slept and when he awoke cried in shame, "Why have I done these horrid things when I only wanted Leah? Where was what I dance too, why was I not helped?"

In reply to his prayer a galley expert came for him and whipped him hard.

Lo, at the end of the week The Mighty Ones visited with

Leah dressed in spiked leather and purple hair dye with body piercings.

And Leah prodded with an electric stick to make her jump and obey.

Now Mungo looked at the yellow clouds and, "Remember me," for he knew his hair was long and he grew strong and broke his chains.

"He is not human," Ishtar screamed, and Carman drew dagger and held it at Leah's neck.

And Mungo crumpled defeated and beaten for Leah's sake, and next awoke chained again ready at his oar station.

"Remember me Mungo and Mungo saw Ben Nathan, Centurion now ship's master who picked up a swill bucket and emptied it over Mungo in return for the dung thrown at him by the mazarrats.

Of course, the lizard marines laughed, and a supervisor lashed Mungo to make him also laugh, but he did not.

"Hold taskmaster, there are better ways to break the lion, starve him good and no sleep," Ben Nathan and left.

And Mungo drew upon an inner spiritual strength and slept with his eyes open when the oars were silent.

"What seven days without sleep or food and the lion lives still?" Ben Nathan furious and ordered Mungo above to wash the decks of squid stinks.

"Here is a tar stain Mungo," for Ben Nathan had smudged the washed spot with his sandals and the supervisor whipped.

"Beg for food Mungo?" Ben Nathan.

"I beg to dance," the reply and Ben Nathan would have refused but for his crew demanded a dance from Mungo.

And unchained Mungo danced to the Unseen and his eyes shone and men covered their eyes.

"Wah a demon has possessed him," they said.

"Give him a sword," Ben Nathan brave fearless and master of slaves and one thrown Mungo.

"Fight man thing," and Ben Nathan sliced the air, and Mungo, cut across his ribs so smarted.

"Afraid?" And Ben Nathan gloated.

"Not so, I have seen men whipped to death and others given to the squid, why should I add you to my sins?" Meaning he did not want the death of Ben Nathan added to them, as a caged mazarrat suddenly sang, *"Leah is his shame."*

And Ben Nathan pushed his sword into Mungo's left arm and finding Mungo nonresponsive raised his sword to cut off Mungo's head but remembered Ishtar did not want Mungo dead but broken, so stopped his intentions.

"Take him to the oars."

And Mungo danced when severe weather approached for the demands of the superstitious crew, hoping Mungo's powerful Unseen presence would quieten the storms.

And the storms did quieten.

Now even Ben Nathan began grudgingly to respect Mungo and allowed him food, water, and sleep, "We killed an albatross, bad luck will come, let all men pray to their gods."

And the bad luck came when three pirate ships sighted and set course to attack the galley.

"Beat fast the drums drum master," Ben Nathan commanded, and Mungo rowed, and his muscles ached.

And Mungo heard brass plates roll down the ship's side as battle joined.

And slaves died when a steel ram's head smashed through oar seats as the ship was rammed.

And rammed twice more.

"I die for Ishtar," Ben Nathan forced below decks with the surviving marines, and Mungo remembered his hair and stood and broke his chains and slid them off him, and slaves freed themselves.

Now a pirate with horns was to gore Ben Nathan who had slipped on blood and lay exposed.

And the tusked one heard a lion roar and turned to see Mungo bite his throat open.

"I am Mungo, I am The Wild One, come and kill me," for he wanted to die for *"Mungo's shame is Leah,"* a mazarrat sang

from a cage.

And the pirates hesitated for they knew of him.

"He is a slave, kill him," their captain shouted and pushed his fellows forward.

A bad mistake for Mungo lifted from its screwed position a bench top and swung it about killing pirates.

Then tossed it at the pirate captain.

And Mungo got his strength not from flesh but spirit.

"Wah I am wounded," the captain groaned pinned by the bench top and his men

seeing him fall sought to escape.

And Mungo gave Ben Nathan his steel sword and helped him up. Lo Ben Nathan drew his Decurion's second sword and men on all sides wondered if he were to open Mungo's bowels, or if Mungo would allow him too?

"Defend yourself against Ishtar's enemies Mungo," Ben Nathan turning sword about so, Mungo took hold of the hilt.

And a lion's roar came forth and Mungo with sword rushed and followed by freed slaves and marines, all knowing they needed a seaworthy ship to stay afloat in the sky.

And great splintering heard as a squid tore planking apart.

And Mungo's charge was so furious they pushed the fearful pirates back onto the ships left; two.

Of these the ships squid squirted an ink cloud and began to rip the pirate masts down with its tentacles.

And Mungo saw unfired catapult scythes and fired them into the pirates trying to kill the squid.

Now one ship was burning because its cauldron full of hot coals for catapult work spilt.

"We are victorious," Ben Nathan shouted and cut boarding ropes and the ships drifted apart.

And Mungo fired again and burst balloons, so the pirate ships dropped from the sky.

"Man, the fire hose," Ben Nathan and men ran over the side hoses from which burning paraffin jetted out upon the descending pirates below.

"Here is Ishtar's mercy pig scum," Ben Nathan also, and had his marines take pirate prisoners to the railings, and here he cut open their bowels and threw them over the side.

So, they fell past the doomed ships below trailing all out so those pirates still alive saw their own doom.

"Ishtar's mercy and why they were pirates in the first place, for they hated Ishtar," the mazarrat sighing and aloud sight came from her audience.

And a roar stopped Ben Nathan who heard, "Forgive them, give them a landing on the promise they live decent lives," for Mungo was naive.

"You are a lord and demon of the bush; I know you give death to Fermanians who come and hunt lions?" Ben Nathan trapping Mungo with words.

"I saw a tunnel of light and golden city at the end, and it is coming to lizards as well as men when I last danced. It is mercy, judgement, and new order, to Ben Nathan once I would have eaten your liver but now, live in peace human and lizard must, let the pirates live, enough have died."

And Ben Nathan's reply was to stuff pirates into cages at the ship's side and swing them out. Intent on opening the cages so ridding his ship faster of scum.

But Mungo he sat and drew in the blood a woman in an exotic embrace with a lover and because he was a poor artist explained.

The next he drew the woman covering her bosom before red masked priests.

And red dots came from the red priests stoning.

Then Mungo drew the priests with women in erotic stances.

It was obvious to the crowding crew and marines that the priest had killed the couple for having a liaison when they themselves enjoyed women.

"Who is guilty?" Mungo asked.

And Ben Nathan was the only one shooting arrows into the caged pirates as the crowd understood none were free of sin to kill another.

"Even Mungo knew as he did not create, he had no right to kill the created things, like mazarrats," the singer getting an oar in.

Now Ben Nathan exhausted came to see what had taken his men away, suspecting Mungo again.

"A man and a woman follow their desires put in their bodies by what made them, so a pirate seeks riches and escape from your brutal laws, and you Ben Nathan kill pirates in disgusting ways in the name of the law they escape from," Mungo, "enough killing for one day Ben Nathan, forgive the rest and put some light into them."

"For Mungo wanted rid of his own guilt over Leah." Truthfully, the singer.

"By the laws of Ishtar, I am allowed to grant you one wish for helping us," Ben Nathan replies still not a changed man.

"Let the pirates then take the place of the slaves till we reach Hurreva since we slaves are now free?" Mungo.

And Ben Nathan knew Mungo was wise.

"And have hot tongs stuck some place, no I did rather die here," a pirate in a cage shouted and six others joined his chorus and Ben Nathan ordered these men given to the squid and they were.

"I am not you, nor do I dance to the Unseen as you do," Ben Nathan warned Mungo.

So, Mungo grunted and went to the bow to wait the ship's pointing to Hurreva and Leah.

He wanted his Leah; the rest could hack themselves to death.

"You make me feel bad Mungo," Ben Nathan later at table alone with Mungo.

"You speak of Leah?"

"It was Nannaha's idea; it was she who brought Leah to me as she is a comforter."

Now Ben Nathan was taking a risk here was he not? But then he had not changed so perhaps wanted Mungo to hurt.

But Mungo shrugged the pain away.

"Nannaha tells me Leah plots to destroy you."

Mungo shook his head to rid it of Nannaha's wicked tongue.

"I did wrong; forgive me Mungo lion man thing?"

"You were my enemy, now you are one of the chosen," Mungo.

"What do you mean?"

"Malachi was his friend," a mazarrat sang,

"Don't you listen to the mazarrats sing; you will follow me to the final conflict," Mungo meaning, he would be like Malachi till the end.

At this Ben Nathan drew sword wanting to pierce Mungo's bare chest.

"Malachi was his friend, so were many others, Ben Nathan too," the mazarrat sang and the Decurion went top side to think.

"I am an imperial officer, Mungo is my enemy," Ben Nathan replied to the mazarrat.

"Give me your sword?" Mungo from behind startling him and Ben Nathan at first refused till he saw dozens followed Mungo and were behind the lion man thing.

"Many of my men are behind you, they will cut you too pieces and there will be no final conflict Mungo?" Ben Nathan.

Now the soldiers nervously, sheepishly drew their weapons.

And Mungo took Ben Nathan's sword and held it above his head to the red moon and then placed his teeth on the blade and bit.

Then spat out a piece of sword.

All marveled at this and did not know that powers were at work protecting Mungo.

How else the stories of boiled alive and come out untouched? How else men fly with no machine aiding them.

The message was obvious, Mungo could slay them, and he went alone to the bow again, and looked towards the lights of Hurreva on the horizon.

"I am coming Leah," the mazarrat sang and added, *"Ben*

Nathan was his friend too."

"Who are you Mungo?" Ben Nathan screamed in fury and got no reply.

And as Ben Nathan went to check course, he heard twenty mazarrats below deck, *"The Wild One,"* from crews' pets in cages and their song heard sixty feet below amongst the forest tops and mazarrat free here repeated the song.

So, Ben Nathan covered his ears, then took pilum to cast at Mungo, then feared the Unseen above him in the red moon and cursed this unknown God, Mungo danced too.

So, went below decks and got drunk as he listened to mazarrats.

"Ishtar will be punished for Leah's shame by Mungo," mazarrats.

"Carman is wicked, and her judgement day is soon," mazarrats added.

"What do these baboons know of the future?" Ben Nathan asked disturbed by the boson.

"Master a bright star has been seen approaching in the night sky, come, and see?"

And Ben Nathan saw also the crew cowed afraid of this aspiration.

"It is Cathbadh's spaceship, is it Fermanian or human?" Ben Nathan.

And all hoped Fermanian yet Ben Nathan knew in his heart it was not.

And Mungo appeared and Ben Nathan seeing him cast his pilum, but a mazarrat fell from the rigging and took the weapon instead.

Mungo shook his head.

"Ben Nathan is Mungo's friend;" also *"Ben Nathan murders mazarrats,"* now sung.

"What are these baboons?" He asked aloud again and feared

the cargo he was
bringing back to his Mighty One Ishtar; the cargo of Mungo.

And he crossed himself with a T, the sign of his god Telephassa.

But he still shivered.

And the question was, did he cross himself for protection against Mungo or them baboons? And if The Elder heard him, did have something to say labelled "a baboon," with a red bum?

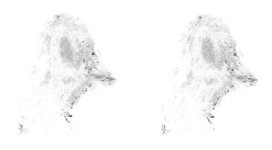

Chapter 14 Banishment

Nine months passed, and the Decurion with Mungo at his side raided the enemies of His Mighty One and today now brought his war galley back piercing mauve clouds to Hurreva City.

And news of their exploits went before him.

So, when his galley descended out of the lavender sun, the marina flying boats of Hurreva decked in bright flags released air from reed horns so, there was noise, and Fermanians crowded the wharves eager to see the Decurion who had slain their enemies allowing tribute and trade back into the city.

Flying machines, baskets hanging from gas seeds and tame Pteranodons carrying citizens filled the sky throwing streamers.

Illustration: The galley with squid in the rigging.

The scribes needed a hero to match Mungo, and they wanted the Decurion who stood at the prow of his ship full of pride at this honor, as the pilot took his galley through the marina into the war docks behind.

He was full of dread for Mungo wondered freely on deck staring back at curious faces looking for Leah. And in the Decurion's heart a struggle for light planted, and it fought everything taught about his gods and god Telephassa!

"Can I expect Mungo's mercy from the Mighty Ones?"

And the scribes who filled papyrus books answered, "No," and the Decurion shared his fame with The Wild One for without him the Fermanians would be nothing, also, "The fame of these two out shone the Mighty Ones who were filled with jealousy," the scribes wrote and the mazarrats could read so sang about it. *"And singing about mungo made me famous to, giggle."*

But the Fermanians if told mazarrats could read did laugh at you thinking you silly.

And Ishtar and Carman sat on two thrones of soft human gold from the red plains and not of equal height and weight.

"Who is mightier than the other?" A mazarrat sang.

Also, both women in yellow robes bedecked by gems and ruby crowns, for they emphasized that Telephassa and Hurreva were one city.

At their feet Moragana, as a ballet dancer, emphasizing all other life was slave.

"Doomed," the Decurion as his ship approached the royal quay seeing no warmth in his Mighty One's eyes, even if they were smiling for the crowds.

"The law is the law, they live by the law so are judged by the law," Mungo told him reading his fears.

"They are above the law for they make the laws."

"Then they have judged themselves when they die>"

And Ben Nathan looked at Mungo and hoped this crazy lion man thing's God would help him out of this fix?

"The laws of Telephassa and Hurreva say we are owned by our Mighty Ones to die as they please with us, we are the clay and they the potters so can break our baked shells at will," scribes and mazarrats sang freely.

And Carman whispered to Ishtar who frowned and Fermanians and mazarrats saw.

"Decurion you have made us proud, stand on the honor scales and your weight will be matched in gold," Ishtar and he did, while Carman pored a pouch of gold onto a scale.

After those human slaves, came with more gold.

"Hurreva and Telephassa welcomes heroes," and Ishtar bade the crew receive gold and they were happy, and the crowd cheered, the crew would spend it with them in inns and restaurants and of course, women.

"The slave oarsmen are free," Carman and the slaves were the slaves and pirate prisoners who thought of red grass plains, alien worlds and a ship to join; and there
were no cheers for Fermanians did not know how to accept them as equals? It also meant they did be free to kill Fermanians riding with John Wrexham's pha riders.

"Even The Wild One," Ishtar and there was silence for the crowd wanted him dead so, they could sleep at night.

And Mungo walked on for he did not trust her, saw Abel and Eve, and smelled Sasha.

"We harmed not Sasha for she is Mungo's lion," Abel and Eve and Mungo shamed over Sasha's love for him, so did Fermanians who saw the lions had more honor than them.

"She has cubs by you," and Mungo rent his slave clothes in pain for he carried natural shuttle genes inside him from drinking Ono's milk as a baby.

"I have two women, am I lion thing or man thing?" He asked and did not know the answer was that he was a spiritual being first, and since flesh decays that secondly.

"Leah has also cubs from Mungo," they told him.

"Yaw ah WA I am master of none," meaning he was not his own master, used, by something Unseen and became confused and wanted a harpist to sooth his mind.

But it was shuttle genes at work again and, *"The Unseen he danced to trying to show all that all life was divine, for it was made of the same spark of light; that none had the right to say this was unclean or that person was condemned for none present had made a sole star,"* The Elder.

"Windbag;" that mazarrat out of stone throwing range.

Now the slaves followed Mungo for they knew not how to

get home for Hurreva floated in the yellow clouds, and that was their freedom's irony, they could not escape for the law said, "Only Fermanians could ride anything that could fly."

Doomed to work for food which meant to beg a Fermanian to employ and where again slaves?

And Carman whispered to Ishtar.

"Decurion," and he looked at Ishtar who spoke his name.

"You are a traitor," and he shivered, "lay down your sword," and he obeyed unquestioningly as Ishtar had taken counsel from Carman.

"What is divine Ishtar doing?" A man in the crowd.

"You have brought The Wild One to destroy two great cities, how do you reply?"

Ishtar asked and Carman remained silent.

"Our queen is right," a shout from the crowd, "The Wild One who eats our livers has been brought into our city,"

"I brought him back alive, he is impossible to kill," the Decurion.

"To kill us," a senator in the pay of the queen's yet a moment ago had cheered this hero, Ben Nathan.

"That is your charge then, The Wild One walks amongst us an equal, we Fermanians are heads of all, and your gold shared amongst the crowd.

And citizens outraged by their hero's arrest saw the weight of the Decurion's Gold, and watched slaves begin to hand it out to them.

It was now their gold.

"That is not fair," a mother in defense of the Decurion, "ships can now bring grain to us because the pirates are defeated," but no one listened to her, she could not read or write; besides the crowd sensed free entertainment in the arena and a holiday atmosphere was setting in.

"Strip the Decurion of his rankings and then cut off his tail so now he can act, as a human beside his friend Mungo," Ishtar commanded.

And the crowd went silent, and the silence of the city made

Mungo return to the quay, growling aside those who barred him.

Then he heard a huge rush of sighs from mouths and did not know what it meant.

Then saw a tail wiggling on the quay that would live for days without its body.

And the Decurion branded, with a slave mark on his back, so the air smelt of burnt flesh.

And behind Ishtar, Carman shook her head deliberately playing a double game, so the crowd saw her putting sympathy with the Decurion, *yet it had been her idea.*

She still dreamed of being the only queen for two cities.

"Much is wrong in Hurreva since Carman came," was a common whisper and the mazarrats sang it louder than a whisper.

"We go now," Ishtar to Carman and one throne had forty-foot-long poles slipped under it and lifted by slaves. The other only thirty long foot poles and was Carman's.

"Who is mightier than the other?" A mazarrat sang.

Hundreds of slaves and one slipped on the cut tail and a foot behind stood on his chest, and because of the weight of a throne, sank in killing him.

At once a task master pressed a remote and these two slaves released and replaced immediately.

And Mungo roared and went crazy and cleared a space about the Decurion's gold by bashing the crowd this way and that.

And not one Berserka came to help the crowd, for they thought the fate of the Decurion wrong.

"What is the lion man thing doing now?" Ishtar asked Carman.

"He is taking a galley," for it was Carman who had looked back and by doing so had accepted she was not equal, but a vassal of Ishtar.

And Mungo had led the freed to a war galley carrying the Decurion and was not opposed by Berserkas who saw Ben

Nathan as a hero, worthy to lead them, another
Artebrates.

And the mother with no education held the helm of
Mungo's kilt for a moment and Mungo saw in her eyes the
goodness that was in Malachi, goodness found in both races.

And he smiled.

"Kill Mungo," Ishtar repeated to the Berserkas on the quay.

Then by ones and threes whole ranks ran to Mungo
shouting, "Lord and Master," and knelt and joined Mungo.

Even mazarrats on leads bit their Fermanian owners and
ran to Mungo.

And sewer grills splintered, and hybrids and mutants ran
cheering joining Mungo, biting any foolish lizard person to get
too close to them.

And the mother with no education joined Mungo.

And the crew of the stolen galley joined Mungo.

And the largest albatross seen landed on the galley's
crow's nest so joined Mungo.

"Good luck has joined Mungo," said by thousands.

"This is Mungo's doing," Carman shouted at Ishtar, but the
scribes knew, "Carman has poisoned Ishtar with greed who
makes new laws to break our backs," they wrote often.

*"She is the mouthpiece of Mount Tullos and we mazarrats
don't believe in god Telephassa,"* the mazarrats would reply.

And fresh Berserkas came from barracks having witnessed
none of the proceedings and were loyal to the queens.

"Kill, kill, kill," they chanted as they advanced.

And Berserkas who had remained beside the two queen's
undecided were slain by the newcomers who did not
distinguish between them and those, that had
joined Mungo.

For they were standing still when they should have been
fighting.

And Mungo now on the ship sent a scythe into the
advancing ranks slaying twenty, just like that.

And Ishtar and Carman took jitters covered in gore and felt

unclean.

And the easy slaying of the Berserkas triggered slaves to throw down their litters,
and quickly killed their masters and mistresses that tumbled out, but these slaves killed, by the Berserkas. But those more interested in freedom than revenge quickly ran to the ship so, saved their lives.

"Where is Leah?" Mungo shouted asking all for an answer.

"With Nannaha," the Decurion answered so, Mungo cut a bow line and the ship floated and the stern line cut, and nets put over the side for stragglers to climb to freedom.

And one that climbed was Moragana, the ape woman man thing in her ballet dancer dress.

And his crew threw flaming torches amongst passing rigging.

And smaller ships and two galleys followed staffed by anyone wanting away from the two queens and these rebellious souls raked the streets and houses with laser, and missile fire.

This was wrong, but amongst the crowd were Berserkas firing at the fleeing refugees.

And those like the mother with no education fled to safety on the ships.

"Oh no," Ishtar groaning seeing death as a scythe blade came towards her.

"The potter can do what he wants with the clay," Mungo and the Decurion looked at Mungo, "Are you a god?"

"No, I am clay."

And the Decurion saw the scythe cut all in its path as it raced to Ishtar and *someone* close to this queen, instead of pulling her towards safety, pushed her directly in front of the spinning blade.

And Ishtar even though see did not see who pushed her knew who did it, as she
fell forward in the last few seconds of life remaining.

"*What goes around comes around,*" mazarrats sang loudly.

"All mine," Carman now sitting on the highest gold throne amongst the gore that had been Ishtar.

And the Decurion saddened for the death of an era had just occurred and change was on the wind.

"I will return for my Leah," Mungo and roared and made his departure from his

ship as the ship's squid above, clouded the enemy with an ink cloud.

This is the end of Book I and the seven years of Mungo's banishment begin.

"Carman pushed Ishtar," a mazarrat whispered to a scribe who now feared for his life.

"Carman pushed Ishtar," the mazarrat sang more loudly and all his kind sang the song so all in the city heard.

"Our Mighty One is a murderess, bad luck will befall our city now," one

whispered.

"The Mighty Ones have murdered us daily and that is why The Wild One is here," another soul whispered.

"But she is mighty and we low so what can we do?" Another quietly.

And the whispers showed Fermanian society was not united but ruled as if it was a collection of cities bribed to destroy the other, in the quest for material things.

"And that is Fermanian for you," The Elder.

And Carman ordered the extermination of all mazarrats, and thousands in cages euthanized, but still, she could not stop the mazarrat songs about the murder of Ishtar for these wily animals climbed walls, trees, roof tops and forests and hid amongst grasses and sang about a murder

"Carman murdered her sister to be a murderer."

Book 2 Chapter 1 Seven Years

John Wrexham shouted, "They are lizard seed bags coming our way and I guess we are in for a thrashing," then cleared his throat.

Cameron Black did likewise, then bolted his riding pha with John to rally the defenses of the ranch.

Now a ranch on New Uranus was not like one on Earth.

Illustration: Hurreva City

John Wrexham had built his in the killer of killer's graveyard, and the reptiles crossed the red grass plains to die here, and it was only foolish Fermanian lizard patrols

sticking to, "We are brave and fearless and masters of this world, so go where we please," that ventured this way and got eaten all up, *"every tiny scrap giggle"* the singer wiping her mouth as if just eaten.

"There isn't no more vicious thing than a dying tyrannosaurus wanting a last nibble of lizard meat," John liked to joke watching a gas seed basket fall from the grey sky.

Fall because Cameron Black's anti balloon crossbow had brought it down. And the ranch house was on a plateau looking down upon tyrannosaurus bones, and nuclear power chimneys.

"We can see the killers coming to die miles off, better close the gates to keep the pha in," John **and the gates were one of the Wonders of New Uranus for they were**

pink sandstone slabs worked by hydraulics and carved with history.

Knowledge squeezed out of Peelock whose Red Town faced starvation one winter, in return for a herd of pha, and the Incorruptible One had given the instructions how to build the gates.

Anyway: "They are coming mighty close John," Cameron complained waiting for a signal to fire a bolt.

"They aren't all lizard, if I didn't know better, I did say that was Mungo on the prow and Cameron do not say I am crazy, but there is them blasted eve dropping mazarrats clinging all over the rigging.

Have a look," and Cameron did and whistled.

"Yep, mazarrats peeing all over the side right on the heads of our riders."

"Let me, see?"

And when Mungo landed, he walked straight up to John and Cameron Black who feared he did do a savage act for they remembered their night with Leah now.

"I bring gifts," and Mungo's motley crew brought baskets that John saw each contained a lizard head.

"Welcome me," Mungo and John hugged him, and Cameron Black noticed, there were no warmth in Mungo's eyes.

Later: "They were brave Berserkas," Mungo at dinner with

Malachi as John made toasts in front of his men, meaning the enemy berserkers treated with respect

"and were killed by my Berserkas who died for me," thus showing Fermanians were the friends of humans, of Mungo.

"I understand and that is why I eat this," and Malachi held up mashed potatoes signaling he was not eating any human.

"Ugh," Mungo replied but ate the same and sat with Malachi showing he ate no more livers.

And a fly landed on the rest of Mungo's green bushel sprouts, the fly was welcome to eat the vegetable bitterness, they were not baby button sprouts covered in melting butter but, *"was so crunchy mmm, the potato here is full of marshmallow texture bites, the sprouts yuk, bitter as the pee mazarrats peed over the side of the ships onto these pha riders,"* oh dear, what will become of the singer?

"I am a Fermanian and want sweet meat," Moragana demanded but ignored as she was just an ape woman man thing in a soiled ballet dancer dress making her look cheap.

And that is how Mungo started his seven-year banishment from Leah but not from Sasha his first love, who with Malachi and the others had now taken up residence in John Wrexham's ranch, *"and just as well The Incorruptible One gave John plans for a good sewerage works, I mean we mazarrats using the wilderness, will soon smell the place up, so are house trained mazarrats as we watch and learn, giggle,"* and she held up a loo paper roll.

And war was war; Malachi proved his hunting skills leading Berserkas and humans burning Telephassa blockhouses, and looting agricultural stations so was respected by all.

"Malachi was his friend," mazarrats and his reply, "I did like to quieten the giggle."

And Malachi always gave back to the poor, human or lizard and yes, even mazarrat.

"I am showing we can all live together," Malachi to John who saw why Mungo liked the lizard, tail, or no tail.

"Yep, just don't include them tyrannosaurus alright?" John meaning, he drew a line when friendship and reptile was concerned, and Malachi was lizard, reptile.

"They are our cousins," Malachi seriously, "like apes yours."
"*Moragana*," sweetly sang.

At this John fell silent thinking of what he knew of Earth where humans pinned their cousins on tables and pickled their innards in the name of progress.

Also remembered what they found in Peelock's castle and regretted, vials of pickled this and that and specimens shot dead Ape like creatures but very human, from far off lands.

Even books which he saw as occult but knew better, knew it was science but had

just been reacting how Peelock obtained it.

It had disgusted his humanity, which destroyed the knowledge gained at a suffering

price by others, them that did the suffering, for knowledge challenged his world; "*Why it was destroyed, but we mazarrats are quick and rescued the books in the fires, and learned, whoops telling too much?*" The singer, "*Yes, stupid singer, shut up,*" The Elder.

Why humanity hunted dolphins and anything competing on the intelligence scale of

evolution into zoos, better the kitchen, and he was ashamed; goodness was in all and **just needed reaching.**

"Yep, we sure as hell won't make that mistake here," he did reply and Malachi

having undergone this conversation before knew what the human meant?

Humans killed everything just to be the primary species,

and Malachi remembered

The Wild One's purpose and pained.

And never forgot he and six remaining Berserkas were lizards, and had changed

their diets and started wearing top hats, even donning human clothes and lizard skin jackets.

They also ate human food.

To be human, "*just like some mazarrats did, they were now human dandies*" and she whistled, "*Yes, be like Morgana,*" The Elder insulting.

And Mungo led war parties against Telephassa and Hurreva and soon humans from the red plains, Cadfael's primitive wild and free joined, and deserters from Peelock.

So, one late autumn when the leaves were rusty, Mungo to please Malachi and Berserkas who had joined them, bringing the lizard band up to three thousand, Mungo had human prisoners from Peelock in front of him. Was now to shame his Unseen invisible benefactor........." He's more famous than you John," Cameron would often speak.

"Better war leader also, dam lion thing has a knack about war," John did answer with a hint of jealousy or admiration?

"He hasn't forgotten about what we did to Leah either?"

"I know."

"Better kill him before he kills us?"

"I know."

"You going to do him?" Cameron asked as Mungo drove a lance through a captured warrior of Peelock's.

"He's going to kill them all, at least thirty, our men aren't liking this," Cameron.

And John rode over to Mungo shouting "Enough, enough," and "What did Mungo think he was doing?"

"Yes, what was Mungo doing?"

"Once I gave you lizard heads and Malachi and Berserkas said nothing, now I give your human heads to make it equal," Mungo for he knew the lizards were unhappy that only Fermanian prisoners seemed executed later in gruesome ways.

And a Berserka held up a head, for once not a lizard head but human dripping stuff.

"Want women Mungo, drink, lasers to kill Berserkas in Telephassa? Better than killing these men Mungo," John but Mungo cut off another head and gave it to a

Berserka.

"They are enemy, they kill us," Angus Ogg knowing Mungo was trying to pacify the rising number of Berserkas, *"to show there was not one rule for humans and one for*

them." Mungo will not rule me, yes her again, The Elder had failed to shut her up, too good a singer anyway, and the truth, she was too fast and he an arthritic fool.

And Mungo walked away with his axe and the Berserkas seemed satisfied, and John said no more as, the remaining twenty-four human prisoners became jittery with nervous relief they were still alive.

"Bloody savages all of them," John and Angus wept in his soul for he felt he had betrayed his human race. But deep down he wanted accepted as a great warrior

by John, an equal not something that followed a man lion, a were creature.

"We do not need them, those Berserkas are becoming too numerous, better do something now John before that lion cub lords it over us?" Cameron.

"But how?" John answered.

Later that night, John allowed a woman lizard to pour him drink, had followed the deserting Berserkas; and John remembered the softness of Leah and electricity of Nannaha.

This was New Uranus, men lived short hard lives so drank and played rough, that was their excuse to be what they accused Mungo of a beast thing.

Human women were for marrying, having kids; lizard women were for fun when you were drunk, of course, so did not mind the tail.

And if you did not like the tail, well cut it off!

"What's that noise?" John asked.

"Moragana demanding a man? Ha she is going to chase him till she gets him, dam disgusting what we become since Mungo arrived," Cameron forgetting his own past?

And The Elder in skins for his own burnt skin was bald arrived on a litter by young mazarrats his disciples.

"I never told them we were smart, so they threw me down a fume in Huverra sooner than expected Mungo," The Elder telling his story, "I walked nights across swamps

shutting my mind to pain. Went into purple dream worlds until swamp mazarrats rescued me and now I am here to counsel again."

And Malachi and Mungo wondered who New Uranus belonged to?

Mazarrats were everywhere, they had underground cities, and was just waiting for Fermanians and humans to slaughter each other off, before coming topside?

"I am your friend," The Elder glad he was home for Mungo was home, *"I knew you could fly."*

Cathbadh.

Now in Telephassa City, Wonder Lord Vinki now made no effort to hide he was feminine for in senate he wore colored silks, and all saw through the silks and saw

what he wore under them.

But he was power, and so none said anything to his face.

He was now the Modernist Party Leader and thought he was invincible for the Senate passed a law stating its members were above the law, now he was the mouthpiece of the mob.

The mob would protect their senators Vinki believed, and had learnt from Cathbadh for from his red sedan, he showered the mob with coin. And what made his head swell was that he had successfully ordered the assassination of Loyalist and Legion Senators, and thought he was all powerful, a demigod upon the planet.

He was wrong, for one hated him enough to poison the mob continually against him, and murder Modernists.

And he was Cathbadh and The Mighty One profited as her opponents killed each, other off.

And it was rumored the Legion knew Cathbadh was a descendant of King Sess, and Carman's spies heard, and her love for him waned. And Cathbadh had a visitor, the

Serrant......" Moragana is with Mungo."

"Mungo still lives?"

"Yes, Lord and Master for he is not dead!"

"Return to Moragana and remind her of my bidding what she must do," Cathbadh ignoring the serrant's humor.

"Yes, Lord and Master and what about me, when will you heal me?" And Cathbadh not a cruel man by Fermanian standards removed the silver algae bandages, and healed,

"I work with Serrant cousins without my ability, so grant them mercy for I understand them." Meaning they had few brains so must put up with their bumbling ways.

"Moragana is your cousin?" And Cathbadh sighed.

"The Fermanian world was crazy," mazarrats sang.

Chapter 2 Year Two

Now Leah gave birth to a boy in front of two court officers who had warrants to

take her child.

And they did for no one was there to stop them.

And the hunchback noted the red blemish down the left of the lad's face.

The left foot slightly withered.

Apart from that the boy looked, human.

"My father was right in stopping me having children," he blamed himself for passing bad genes on.

"Ha foot, this is the work of poison carried in her womb, not a hunchback's genes," the midwife chided, and one word sprang to his mind, "Nannaha."

But Leah blamed Mungo's lion spirit for making the foot bad and, face marked.

"Will he grow a mane?" She scared, and her father the hunchback understood grief had her for, the baby was gone.

Only after birth remained and alone the hunchback used cat gut.

"Mungo I will never forget you, please come back for your son Conn," Leah groaned and the hunchback felt history repeated. It was Carman's orders to take Conn

into her house to be a lame Berserka.

A Berserka to hunt down Mungo, the enemy of his Fermanian race.

A boy brought up hating his mother for his foot.

"That's the way the snake works," the hunchback thought and to Leah, "I have money, there are courts, even Carman cannot publicly defy them," naively in hope.

"She is the mouthpiece of Mount Tullos, I am doomed," and Leah cried for her babe.

Somehow a cold shiver broke through the hunchback's defenses.

Leah was costing him his inheritance from mummy but, "She is my daughter."

"I love you," Leah and the hunchback filling with happiness cried, no one had ever said that to him and swore, he did help the humans destroy evil Telephassa City and its false gods. *

Now Leah sat in a dungeon praying to the God that Mungo danced too and found she was afraid. Somehow the hunchback had bribed the jailers to feed her well, allow her privacy for toilet, and bathing and not tortured which was the goalers' whims, when no general orders given.

There had been no general orders concerning Leah, she was a plaything to the jailers if not bribed well.

And the jailers took the bribe and still played with her, ate meat destined for her, tortured and told her to use the hole provided, and Leah blamed Mungo for her fate.

The only thing they did allow was their bath water.

And right now, the hunchback sat furious knowing the goaler's fate now he knew Leah's, for Artebrates had told him:

"She is destined to the vats that gave her birth to be boiled down and recycled."

"My daughter I have failed you," the hunchback.

"And a mazarrat often came and was company for Leah," it was me.

Cathbadh.

Now the Mighty One was enjoying the entertainment

provided by Cathbadh, armed slaves fighting venomous snakes in a tank.

And at a lower table sat Wonder Lord Vinki and friends who saw Cathbadh taking over their influence, something like murder for Cathbadh needed.

So, that night Vinki sent two friends to bludgeon Cathbadh, but they never returned.

Two days later Vinki's cook got instructions from Vinki asking for Mungo's soul, which was a recipe, vinegary sweetmeats and the Fermanians comforted themselves they were eating Mungo spiritually.

Yes, Vinki liked what he ate that night.

And the next day got a letter from the Prefect of Police requesting him to identify two bodies.

Curiosity about his missing friends made him go.

And saw empty craniums and met Cathbadh who said, "Mungo's soul," and Vinki was confused, had he eaten his friend's brains? Vinki asked nothing, but invited to Cathbadh's quarters. Vinki went escorted by men of the mob.

"If I really wanted to, I could turn you all into tripe," Cathbadh told them. Whether he could, Vinki sweated as his escort vanished at the threat. The mob believed Cathbadh was a magician and did not want to become toads, newts and things that ate those creatures.

"Marvelous are they not?" Cathbadh asked and Vinki saw brains in beakers and they were alive.

"NO different from the labs?" Vinki replied.

"The difference is," and Cathbadh pulled one out, "It lives in this aerated solution by filter pumps," then Cathbadh dropped it into a solution of vinegar and said, "Great pickled," and smiled knowingly at Vinki.

During the silence, Vinki knew he had eaten his friends'

brains.

His special friends for were Vinki not called a Wonder Lord?

So, Vinki fled ill and swore he did do the bugger Cathbadh one day. And it was Cathbadh who wanted Leah returned to the labs.

And Vinki sought the resurrected Peelock to eat fresh sweetmeat and plan Cathbadh's destruction.

"And incidentally Leah went crazy, the company of a mazarrat was not enough to keep her sane. I was not a good listener," the singer who sang all the way through Book One, and unfortunately still here.

"I want Lady Leah returned to the vats that bore her out of kindness, for Carman has ordered her destroyed through virus shuttles to turn her into a monster, seeking only the destruction of her great love, Mungo.

It is the kindest act I can do Leah.

But the hunchback thinks my intentions evil and hates me, I am evil, I am Fermanian," extracted from Cathbadh's diary Eclipse Season Month.

"The harlot Moragana I am told successfully poisoned a herd of riding pha and Mungo still lives so has failed me.

Moragana is a bungling baboon in a ballet dancer dress.

I must separate with her and that cousin Serrant before they destroy me from stupidity.

What a foolish man I was to put my trust in lower species, the lesson learned is to do the work yourself," another extract from Cathbadh's diary Eclipse Season Month.

*

Now Peelock, in his castle quite alive repaired by the Incorruptible One before he awoke her, had the computer to tell him what plagues affected

Illustration: Moragana

humans on New Uranus, and the machine programmed to help humans informed him about mustard fever. What he wanted was information to impress the people of Red Town he was still the Red god's chosen one.

There were still thousands of Wendy's out there.

"I have the mustard fever from the wild mustard plant, there is no cure, forgive my sins holy one," he to the perfect woman the Incorruptible One.

And she turned brown eyes upon him, saw through him and knew he had not changed but who was she too judge?

"I will instruct the computer to give you the genetic code for a drug that will save your race."

Peelock used all his cheek muscles not to smile.

Behind him a disc span and paper came out of a laser jet printer.

"I am doomed to remain here forever for if I venture above, I will be killed by Mungo," Peelock faking gloom.

"The difference is that I remain here alive," she replied.

Peelock angry, faked tears knowing she meant natural death would catch him, even with all his youth hormones and transplants, eventually wear would kill him.

"Insanity will come first," he said.

And she knew he was right, she was incorruptible, fixed into the life force that flowed through all, and its pulse kept her sane; and wired into the computer. "No,

one day Mungo will end your misery for you with a lance thrust," she is pitying and told the computer to instruct Mungo she existed.

Existed for this meeting for she was the link between what Mungo danced to and what he must do.

To use the doomsday bomb on Fermanians.

It was obedience, and that is what Mungo lacked, for he was ignorant of the power that visited him.

He was human, his God was human, and the universe was human.

Mungo for all his lust, his weakness was a human, so forgiven, he was also a chosen human.

"I feed too many papyrus books into your INPUT," Peelock snarled.

The incorruptible laughed, felt good, it was the first time she had laughed in ten thousand years.

And it was the same sarcastic laugh when the first human colonists of New Uranus had sealed her in alive in this glass sphere with her computer, to preserve human

knowledge against the Fermanian nuclear fallout.

Sealed because they had rejected human values from lizard wars and The People were sick, dying, thyroid cancer was rampant and leukemia claiming children.

Then someone built a red calf, called it god, and made peace with the lizards, that realized tribute was a better way than having to fight wars for food.

And forgot her and the computer, wired into her brain as a joke, "A computer for the grave," one of the human scientists back then. And the computer was her companion until Peelock chasing a mazarrat that had stolen a vial led him to her.

And now Peelock was happy, he had a germ to infect The People and a cure to offer them miraculously, they would obey Peelock.

As for Mungo he stood still under the red moon with Malachi watching a prisoner from Telephassa and Red Town at his feet.

And about them Fermanian Berserkas and human warriors all armed to the teeth waiting; waiting for what?

"You hardly dance these days?" Malachi asked.

Mungo knew Malachi thought he was not The Wild One anymore because he did not speak to the Unseen unnamed One these days.

"You have become drenched in blood, all day all night we raid blockhouses," Malachi continued, "you are possessed with Leah, don't you hear the mazarrats sing?"

"I will never give her up," Mungo replied feeling an uncontrollable rage in his chest he was managing to control, but still looked at the lizard prisoner with murderous intent.

"We men of Fermanian stock follow The Wild One who is to deliver us from the cruel ways of our queens and kings," and with that Malachi brought his axe through the air and the human prisoner's head bounced on the red grass.

And the Fermanian Berserkas watching where pleased favoritism had not been shown the human prisoner, and now the human warriors waited with sculls upon them faces.

"Our fates are entwined, I will always love you as my Lord and Master, when you die and if it is from neglect from my side, I must fall upon my copper sword," Malachi.

Now Mungo replied," I give you freedom from hate; go save yourself from me Malachi."

"I am brave and fearless," the lizard prisoner which reminded Malachi they were of the same blood.

"Won't save you friend, I am outlaw," and Malachi shoved him forward, so he fell and looked up hearing a lion growl, but saw the man thing Mungo on all fours coming at him.

A warrior was the lizard and he tried to rise, but his hands tied behind his back.

This was an execution for Leah.

And why Mungo tore out his throat lion fashion and, ate his liver and the human warriors watching were satisfied no favoritism shown, the Fermanian.

"*Outlaws they be,*" the mazarrats sang as to why Malachi did what he did, "*Mungo commits murder,*" became their song for Mungo.

"*He is forsaken by the unnamed Unseen One he danced too,*" The Elder added

sadly.

Chapter 3 What The Elder Told Young Mazarrats

"Once upon a time a lizard Berserka carried a message of trade from Peelock to Lord Vinki flying a bright yellow saucer ship across the yellow sky." The Elder telling young,

"why so bright a color was painted shows one cannot fathom lizard minds; it was so bright it is revolting, and looks like a spinning yellow bird, or a sun fallen from the

clouds."

"I know why, it is the color of his knickers he wears, giggle snort," the female mazarrat now earing man's undies and the audience went, *"Oso."*

Then Mungo saw the brightness hovering over a water hole, as the warrior used his sextant to determine his position, and Mungo fell in love with the yellow machine.

Now at Giant Footstep Rock, Mungo climbed for the yellow craft must pass here, and here Mungo dropped into the machine and his falling weight drove his sword through the lizard who collapsed dead.

Now Mungo had no idea how to control the bright yellow machine, and that shows us how dangerous he is. *"More like an idiot,"* **the audience in disbelief.**

And the yellow craft hit the Giant Footsteps' and dented, and Mungo pushed the controls down and the machine skidded on brown sand below. *"And Mungo felt save for he was down,"* the singer back from latrine duties.

"It wants me for tea for I can hear its tummy rumbling with hunger," Mungo shouted hitting the metal engine cover.

"And shows mazarrats know more about technology than lion things, but he is the chosen Wild One and we must help,"

mazarrats sang.

Then the lion left his mind and man's reasoning came banishing fear.

"This button is red and has the Fermanian word STOP. I will pull or press and see what befalls?" And Mungo did and was happy the engine fell silent. But the craft fell straight down and landed on a bush, so saved damage, but Mungo tossed about, so landed on his head.

Now how to start and there was only one other button, green and Mungo pressed and the engine tummy rumbled, and Mungo leapt away, and returned with sword held out, *"just in case."* These humans are idiotic, in high notes a mazarrat girl.

"He is lion man thing do not forget and full of hate, a wounded beast who loves Sasha now for Leah is gone," an unknown mazarrat called.

And Mungo sat at the controls, and saw if he slid the pedals out the wing flaps moved, and the black column stick tilted the head and tail.

"It is only a bird and birds I eat," and confidently waited for the yellow saucer bird to Fly, and it did not.

"WA, WA, WA listen bird fly or be cooked," he shouted, and The Elder smiled and, "you young mazarrats can laugh, for you know a control stick controls speed but not Mungo.

"Yes, it was I who will teach, push the stick forward man lion thing," The Elder from a safe distance and Mungo heard.

"WA, WA, WA, how can a mazarrat know?" Mungo's arrogant reply, but he was a man thing.

"So, I threw ripe fruit at him till he noticed me and chased me, and I would not stop throwing fruit at him till he sat down crossed legged.

We mazarrats know more than anyone, we are the keepers of all knowledge yet do not boast it.

Listen Mungo, comfort is to the least, *from the greatest taken away.*

We have nothing but songs and carving knives to write history on bark, but Mungo sat there as if he had not heard, but he was Mungo with a hunting lion's sense so The

Elder being me stayed put up my tree.

The lever you push forward for speed and pull back to slow and the speaking box tell it where to go and the bird will take you, I added to the stubborn lion man thing.

Still, he sat, and I thought he did not believe me, then he got in and pushed the lever and he went around in circles upon the brown sand.

"Yaw a WA I puke," *for he was not good at flying even upon the sand.*

And I did what all sensible mazarrats do when exposed to the noon day red sun; I slept knowing I was safe from the lion man thing for this lion needed a harpist to soothe

his mind.

And awoke to find him crashed in cacti.

"Oh, mazarrat please help me, come pull the thorns out."

But I would not for he might eat me like he chopped off all heads these days!

"You are crazy, your word is like dung now. I throw stones at you; all you think is Leah, well if you want her that bad, get her but do not expect me to pull thorns out of a

crazy lion," I shouted at him.

But at least I was not throwing ripe fruit at him.

Now my idea took hold, for humans know they think for themselves.

"I will do that," *he shouted back and roared and became excited and I saw how lean and empty his belly was when he arched back roaring.*

Saw how only a mazarrat could fill it.

"Come and show me how to hover like a fly?"

I tapped my head in reply; this was not the same Mungo I knew long ago.

"Do as I say, I am Mungo."

"You are not a king, Red Hide lives and to be like a fly on dung push the red lever this way and that way insect."

And he shot into the sky as a dot.

Now see how we mazarrats obey what Mungo dances too, he must fulfil the papyrus prophesy, that he is royal, must be a king and all I did was plant the idea of Red Hide's death in his mind.

Murderer, he is unfit to lead us.

We all know what drives man things, greed and lust and converting things that they do not own.

And the bright machine slammed to a stop above me.

And Mungo shouted above the engine, "I can fly I can fly."

"Better just speak to the bird and let it fly," I am knowing he would kill himself but he ignored for humans want control. And at the same time, I used one eye to scan me surroundings just in case I needed to jump out of his reach.

"I hunger," *I expected this,* "come, I will fly us home."

"Mungo doesn't dance any more, just listens to voices in his head, one says eat human sweetmeat from Peelock's warriors and he does, another says, make Sasha's belly swell and does."

"Be careful Elder for my voices say you are nice and tender."

"Another voice says wear a crown made of nuts and vines and Mungo does," and I tapped my head and at this he danced from anger, not love, and ripped out the lizard flyer's liver and waving it, he ate and roared like a lion.

"I am king of the lions, he boasted.

"You are king of Moragana's grass bed."

"She loves me."

"Yes, yes, but when will you burn Telephassa to the ground?" And realized me mistake.

"With this yellow bird before the moon is full," *he and I put it down to human* arrogance.

Oh yes, he would show all his warriors the bright yellow machine and they would follow him towards Telephassa, why else had the machine given Mungo?

"Now I tire, tomorrow I will tell you how to attack," and yawned and saw the impatience in Mungo's eyes, and who called me murderer?

*

And the attack was mighty; Mungo flew his yellow bird across the marsh.

Ah the marsh is an unhealthy place. Poisonous snakes and marsh crocodiles, but still thousands came following mazarrat drummers, "Mungo, Mungo, Mungo," chanting, yes this is true for marsh mazarrats witnessed.

And all wondered where mazarrats had learned to make and play drums?

And at the first wall of defense about Telephassa City this horde killed all they found, the young and old, the drunk and poorly armed, and at the second wall of defense

about Telephassa City, hundreds of the horde fell dead from lizard archers, well-armed and armored.

And here a Serrant lived too.

Illustration: The yellow machine

"It was not Mungo's fault," we mazarrats must sing to make sure his warriors see him as a king and don't make a broth out of him."

Nor me and since Sasha gave him young, maybe **I to** and my children will be rulers of this world." Yes, the girl singer, what is she pregnant?

"No, she is infected with Mungo and unfit to sing, hear me little one, unclean," The Elder and because he had judged another clean or unclean, darkness flooded him, and he thought of, "Well if she can dream of being our queen, I can be The Mighty One, as Mungo kills too much, and see I can dance," **and since he was on a cane stumbled and fell off his purple rhododendron plant.**

"Ah Mungo, remember me, it is I the Serrant and know where Leah is?" And Mungo forgot his climbing warriors scaling the second wall for he was obsessed with Leah.

"This city is mine," and forgot the Serrant was evil, "take me in your yellow bird to Leah?" The Serrant added and Mungo imagining beautiful Leah allowed the cousin of the Fermanian beside him, and it bit and threw coils about him.

Perhaps if the Serrant had showed patience it might have had Mungo over Fermanian lines but: who saved Mungo?

Malachi by tail cast the Serrant down the second wall.

"Wah save me," the Serrant hissed in mid-air.

"Mungo," was all Malachi said as blood fountained from Mungo's throat and Malachi flew Mungo to John's surgeons.

"Mungo is dead, Mungo is dead," the warriors of the horde shouted, wept, and fled the attack.

And at John's ranch Mungo was pallid, and John thinking him dying planned no evil, but went and sat on his veranda with Cameron Black drinking under the mazarrat lavender sun.

"Can get rid of the lizard now?" Cameron asked.

"Don't have too; just fell on his sword for failing to protect Mungo his Lord and Master, these lizards surely like dying?" John as Angus Ogg pulled Malachi away from

Mungo.

"At least will hold the first wall," John gloating over the victory, but it was a poor victory for Carman knew the wall defenseless, so offered the weakest of her warriors

there to slow down the horde.

"Why did Mungo not ask Malachi how to fly the yellow saucer bird?" A young mazarrat asked The Elder who replied, *"Because Mungo is more human than he*

realizes."

"Is Mungo dead?" A noticeably young mazarrat.

"Mungo is the jungle, is the jungle dead?" The Elder chided.

And John and Cameron hearing this talk shivered.

Now evil entered their heads, it was time to help Mungo die with the aid of a Pillow.

Cathbadh

"You have done well Serrant, now I can tell Carman my plan worked, and patience is a virtue. She will advance me above

Vinki, and my position in her private chamber secure for she is the loneliest woman I know."

"Hiss, can I go home to my wall?"

"The humans will make shoes and belts of you for what you did too Mungo. One Serrant looks like any other, hundreds of your kind have perished for your crime already, for their cast aside flesh now feeds flies and rodents.

For hundreds of millenniums too come, man will hate the Serrant that lurks in the Grass to bite his ankle."

"Hiss, my crime?"

"You murdered Mungo."

"Hiss," and the Serrant was quiet as outside the window a mob raced on its way to The Mighty One Carman's castle, demanding all tax raising powers given to the

Senate.

"Vinki you are a greedy fool, she knows you are behind this, taking the opportunity of Mungo's attack to divide the city further and weaken it more. Make sure Vinki you do not let the humans in, who will close your Senate and then mount you on a wall as a trophy?"

"Hiss, master you are so wise."

"I know, "and then "argh, I am summoned," Cathbadh as a signal from a star ship reached his thoughts and the Serrant coiled under a rug fearing the god that spoke to

Cathbadh.

"Clinton, yes Clinton, you land in six years."

And Cathbadh sighed, lo of work he could do in six years, who knows he did greet the captain and show them how well he treated humans, and then they did leave him to rule Telephassa.

He did invent new weapons and fight the new arrivals.

Lot to ask, of a disunited Fermanian world where city

states existed all distrusting each other.

And all remembered what Carman did with a little push, and then Ishtar was no more

Chapter 4 Nannaha's bite

Nannaha called, "Fine gentleman want a young girl?"

And the lizard in fine pink silks hurried on afraid someone noticed he had looked at the outcast Nannaha.

And Nannaha cursed Mungo.

"How much Nannaha?" A following dandy asked to be antisocial.

Nannaha smiled, "For your dinner and rent."

So, the dandy with his human femur walking cane lifted her thin black cotton kilt and smiled.

"I see why Vinki loved you," words chosen wisely, and Nannaha rubbed her forehead in submission on his sandals.

She was seeking a new Lord and Master.

And at once the dandy wiped his soles on her hair and was satisfied, "Come," he and stopped off at a dresser and bought Nannaha fancy clothes.

"Beautiful as I remember you," he and Nannaha froze holding up red linen; yes, he was familiar but who? Did it matter; she had had dozens like him seeking to master the mysterious Nannaha.

And he took her to a neighborhood famed for mistresses and greed entered Nannaha, for she saw herself this young naïve dandy's kept woman.

Up a wooden staircase at an inn, as the innkeeper filled

tankards with warm minted beer as a fire sizzled with fat dripping from a spitted slave.

Human of course, for Telephassa was a lizard city.

"I am hungry, I work better on food," Nannaha told the dandy.

He nodded, told her to go to the red door and summoned a server, and ordered six ribs in lemon and broth.

At the door Nannaha found no reply, so entered finding the room warmed by stored solar heat, and a table set with the remains of warm food.

A bath foamed with salts nearby to the solar panels.

And Nannaha undressed and slipped into the bath never noticing in the dim light a man, in a chair.

"It should taste sweet and juicy for she was young," the dandy entering putting down the food, and then helped her wash and he liked, for her skin glowed under the bubbles.

Why Nannaha crooned with pleasure.

"I see you have met my seventh cousin removed," the dandy indicting Nannaha follow his line of sight, and she made turbulence in the bath, so soapy water splashed
onto the floor.

A silent man had watched her undress while she touched her body preparing it for work.

Even one such as Nannaha could be embarrassed.

"Hello love'."

"Vinki," she gasped with recognition.

And Vinki got off the chair and approached dangling a gold torc as a gift.

Now Nannaha remembered who the dandy was, Isisaramman the little dung head who as a teenager pulled her bosoms when she bathed? The little twit who preferred to lose his virginity sleeping with slaves, then with the beautiful Nannaha.

The cruel one who slid a hot lance into her bum for a boil when she slept, and Nannaha feared; *"he wasn't little anymore, run bad girl run,"* my advice in a song, even she needs forgiveness and healing, WA, what am I saying, she deserves what is coming.

Yet her fingers closed upon the gold, and it was hers.

"You will become Cathbadh's comforter," Vinki opening the door on the next chapter of her life.

And a spying mazarrat behind the wall panels, heard, saw, and would repeat so, I heard and knew Lord Vinki had forgotten these words, *"and murder him, strangle him in bed, slip an asp into his soapy bath, that would be fun, just imagine he is splashing and slipping to get out, but just murder him, dead."* The Elder need not worry, I only joked about being dreaming to be ruler of this planet.

*

"It is Lord Artebrates, he sits in his howdah as if Lord of all things," Malachi to Mungo.

"Then we will give him all things," and Mungo signaled so catapults threw packets that at Pteranodons feet exploded.

"What is this?" Artebrates covered in brown dust now.

More detonations killing lizard men and Mungo rode Ono the lioness with Sasha about, to stop the killings.

At once the mass of warriors, human and lizards attacked Artebrates.

"Charge," it was the worst command Artebrates ever gave.

You see if lizards used humans as slaves, they could never realize men things could outsmart them.

And Mungo did what the mazarrats sang later, *"He had trenches filled with spikes."*

Also, *"Mungo left his lions and rode his yellow bird and trailed behind him hooks."*

"Wah I am dead," Artebrates a hook in his left hand.

"And in closed ranks, human Berserkas armed with missile weapons pored death into the lizard charge," the mazarrats. *"And Mungo fired the trenches and Pteranodons burned."*

"Let only the pha riders and lions go after the lizards," and Malachi looked at Mungo above and said, "My little human general."

"One day I will eat that slave," Artebrates as he fled.

"How can a slave defeat you again and again?" **Carman much later** and should have listened to Mungo's roar, "I am a lion thing man thing." *Shuttle genes at work, so there is hope for me, giggle."*

"The answer lies in the inventions that you have used for peaceful purposes, when you should be like men and use your flying machines for war. Are you so afraid?

of change that you still fight the traditional ways?" A mazarrat called The Elder sang.

*

"My belly is full, you must make me queen, when will you kill Red Hide?" Sasha asked.

"What harm has he done me?" Mungo.

"Because your cubs must have an inheritance," Sasha opening her favorite ruby dress of Carman's and Mungo saw her womb was full.

"What have I done thee Leah my sweet?" Mungo and hurt for Sasha was not Leah.

"Leah is dead, you know she was sent to the vats to be boiled down back to lizard broth, you must forget her for now I am new life," but Mungo was not happy for he was

still possessed with Leah and would have fallen upon his

copper sword if Malachi were not present.

"He wants a human woman," Ono from a rhododendron meaning Keira.

Illustration: Ono the black lioness

"I am Mungo, master of all," Mungo and sought Keira who welcomed him.

"He no longer dances to the Unseen name, he has forgotten goodness," Sasha and Ono agreed.

"His manhood rules his head, he is right, he is master of all easy lays," Ono cursing Mungo's sex drive.

And when Mungo had finished his business, he felt as if his head was on fire.

"What ails thee lord?" Keira asked him.

"I see maggots that are the lizard dead come to haunt me, they suggest unclean things and I do them, help me, Keira?" And she held his head on her chest.

Later when Mungo slept, "He is my lord," Keira.

"God Telephassa sends unclean spirits to those who forget him," Malachi sorry for Mungo had not asked to be head of all but was, "He is lion thing and the strongest so the strongest propagate," which was true for Mungo was, The Wild One brought up without civilized values and Malachi wondered what those values were? "It is what I am fighting for, Mungo will follow his fathers and men will call him Mungo the Great, but he is a killer and not great.

He will bring down Telephassa and lizard and men will then live together. And as the scribes say one son will be wise and another mighty and another king, which, Leah's or Sasha's?" And Malachi opened his heart to what Mungo had danced too and cried with joy.

"Malachi tell me the name of Mungo's unknown God?" Keira asked.

"It is Unseen Spirit," Malachi and Keira left him to seek Hamo, Angus Ogg's son for comfort, for she was afraid of the unseen that went bump in the night.

"Mungo come with me," Malachi helping Mungo to his yellow machine bird and instructed a harpist to follow and play, for in Telephassa music quells unclean spirits and Mungo went to Peelock's castle.

"My love be careful, I almost lost you to your own sword, return to my cave," Ono clutching Malachi.

"I will return," and Malachi smiled, and Ono feared Abel and Eve, for they had almost killed Malachi during the battle and she had come across their scent often in the jungle.

"Hunting lions hunt the great hunter; will I have to kill my own children for Malachi my lover in twilight years," she asked watching Malachi depart.

And remembered how Malachi had come to her drunk and asked for a bed.

"Expect me to sleep with the lizard that took my cubs?"

"And replaced them with The Wild One."

And Ono sighed knowing fate had stolen her cubs and her

hate for Malachi crumpled.

"I have always wanted you, at first planned to have you and sell you to harlots for you are beautiful," Malachi.

"You say I am still beautiful; how can this be? I am old."

"I too am old serving your cub Mungo and only want you now for myself. We have much in common, and I have not known a woman since I joined Mungo."

"I have not known a man since Mungo threw me in the cacti, and never a lizard man thing. Your heart is good; you love Mungo my cub and will die for him. You are a true Fermanian, brave and fearless so come Malachi great hunter and take away our lonely hearts."

And that is how Malachi knew Ono whom he had wanted since the first lunar day he saw her.

"Malachi was his friend," and both heard and shivered over the word '**was.**'

*

Now The Elder was mighty sore in spirit for Mungo was not acting how a savior should. He had not swept aside the old ways but indulged in them up to his armpits!

Where was the forgiveness and compassion that was supposed to be with The Wild One of the Unseen?

Instead, he cut heads off and throws the trophies about as if they were watermelons, and the bodies rolled into shallow ditches or dragged out to the fields for the

carrion to eat, to save all the trouble of burying them.

"Dance Mungo, dance again and be filled with the Unseen and know that mercy is First, before the Unseen spits you out like it has swallowed a bitter bug," The Elder

moaned also; *"You are a tyrant Mungo; you sleep where your lust takes you without* conscious. You are no better than Carman and Ishtar who abused you and you love

Leah. What will you come to silence me forever too for rubbishing you? Stop killing and then the spirits of the dead will not haunt you, and you will not need a harpist Mungo

to soothe your brain.

   Mungo the Wild One, how correct for he is so wild he has no boundaries and drags

   all back into the world where strongest rules, the rest servant.

If I ever became this planet's ruler, I would not have Mungo as consort, he ogles Nannaha. "

[Chapter Four

Year 4

"*There was a man lion thing Mungo who took into battle a glass casket in which*

the Incorruptible One lay.

And she no longer spoke for she was not with the computer at the castle for Mungo

had stolen her.

Written in the papyrus books that the Wild One will give rest to the oracle of the Unknown One, and this Mungo fulfilled.

He also deprived Peelock of his source of knowledge for now that evil must rely on darkness to advance his cause," The Elder who instructed the young of his kind.

And he drew a halo above his incorruptible drawing but nothing above Mungo's picture.

And this is how he stole her, "You rose from the dead Peelock, but I am not afraid," Mungo as he rode Ono with lions and Malachi into Red Tower in Lamb Month.

And Peelock raised two vials, "Here is death and hope," and laughed knowing one was mustard fever and one cure.

And Mungo urged Ono to leap upon Peelock, but Ono fell short because of Mungo's weight and Peelock fled terrified.

"Let him go for he has left his door open," Malachi and it was bad advice for none understood what the vials contained, only the dying in Red Town.

So, it was then that Mungo upon the black lion entered Peelock's castle, and went into the vaults and found the computer.

Now machines meant nothing to him for he understood them not, but the perfect woman lying still he had too own.

He was like a monkey, always stealing from others, things it did not understand.

"Malachi was his friend," the computer and Malachi gaped, "what hell, have I entered?"

And the computer displayed a bomb on its screen and Malachi understood what it was.

"No, he screamed and hit the computer with a sword but dented it not.

"Malachi understands what I have to give you Mungo," the incorruptible opening her brown eyes, and Mungo raised his sword.

"You cannot kill me, and I have waited ten thousand years for you."

"You are dead, and I was not a cub that long-ago, liar," Mungo shouted and brought down his sword.

And dented the casings not.

Then CS gas escaped from the computer and covered Malachi and Mungo, and the lions that waited patiently.

"I am blind," Mungo shouted and slashed the glass cabinet

the holy one lay inside.

And an aesthetic spray covered the intruders freezing their limbs.

For even the computer bored with his antics, "*me, I already am.*" The Elder.

"Am I to be eaten now?" Mungo grunted through numbing lips and the Incorruptible One laughed at his innocence or rather, stupidity.

"I will give you the weapon to win the war with the Fermanians, and Malachi do not forget, Malachi was his friend."

"Dam holy bitch, does she expect me to exterminate my own?" Malachi horrified.

"But you already kill lizards, Malachi of no nation," and he felt a traitor, "Your love for The Wild One binds you to fate, and I am fate. Be of good cheer brave lizard

warrior, the doomsday bomb will not kill all your people, only Carman's armies at Nodegamma."

And Malachi knew it well, a dusty infertile valley with a village of that name, goat herders lived there.

Here the armies of darkness will gather for the final showdown.

Here Mungo will stand with his friends, and here fate will triumph and alone Malachi will stand beside his friend."

Then she fell asleep.

"We will take her with us," Mungo mused and Malachi, "Did you not hear her, Alone, alone, alone, simply good stupid loyal friend Malachi again."

And Mungo hugged him.

"Dam you Mungo for there is no escape for me but death."

"*Malachi was his friend,*" a mazarrat sang in the corridors and Malachi said, "The joke is that she will be with us at

Nodegamma," Malachi rubbing his awoken limbs, "I am cold, let us hurry and get out of here Mungo."

*

"When will you kill Red Hide?" Sasha asked suckling a cub.

And the shuttle genes had done a respectable job for the cub looked more human than lion. The cub would have the strength and speed of a hunting lion, and the lethal intelligence of a human.

But Mungo ignored a thousand times, Red Hide was an ageing lion, and could proclaim himself emperor and it would not affect Mungo; he would still be Mungo.

And Sasha rolled across to him and unstrapped buckles, so that her ruby dress fell away.

"I cannot be bribed," Mungo averting his gaze and felt light enter him, for his mercy shown to Red Hide.

"I will see," and Sasha went into her cave and took from it a stolen Fermanian chest of silks, and returned to Mungo, wearing seven long silks.

Now she was cunning, and danced making sure she was in his vision and slowly gyrated till six silks to fall aside.

Now the lion in Mungo was bribable, and he pounced upon her.

And then Sasha pushed Mungo aside and he asked, "What now?" For he lusted for her.

"The broth of Red Hide, his marrow will foam and his sweetmeat I will give to the Fermanians," and "Mungo's word is never broken," Mungo, and he would flee, but she held him, and coiled about him, so all her femininity enveloped.

And he promised his yellow flying machine, but she would not drop the seventh silk till he promised what she asked, and together they joyed, and as soon as his lust left, Mungo felt guilt through him. He was to kill Red Hide, another murder.

And Sasha seeing Mungo holding his temples gathered up her ruby dress and silks, then the cubs, and went to a stream to bath, happy she would be a queen like Carman.

"Where is the harpist?" Mungo yelled but Malachi was not there to answer.

And the dark voices plagued Mungo sore.

"*Murderer*," they tormented, the singer saying chants to protect herself.

*

"*What is this drawing?*" A young mazarrat asked The Elder.

"The killing of Red Hide."

"*Murderer*," The Wild.

*

And it happened that **a storm** crossed the red plains spitting green lighting.

And Red Hide afraid hid in a vacant Serrant borrow.

"Come out Red Hide it is Mungo come to kill you, and claim my kingdom?"

"We will go first," the three companions of Red Hide advised, and he agreed from fear of the storm.

Now Malachi had come with Mungo for he loved him, and feared Mungo's moods could cause harm, and he sat on a grass cutter ant nest six feet high, bow in his hand.

"*No way, Malachi loved what the scribes wrote about him, he got royalties from cheap papyrus books, paid his drinks bill, gurgle not bad this Fermanian liver rot liquid they brew,*" the girl singer on the way to alcoholism.

And green lighting struck brown dust.

And a black lion sped out of the burrow and Mungo sunk his spear in its neck cutting spine so it died.

Thunder rolled.

Then as he freed his spear a white lion hit him, so he rolled and the last a red lion jumped out to land upon him also.

"Help," Malachi as green lighting hit the ant nest, "This is Sasha's greed. Help me unnamed God above," Malachi blaming his misfortune upon Sasha and calling for supernatural help.

And Mungo answered with a roar as he slit the white lion's belly and cut the nose off the red, so both retreated from his anger.

And the night turned green with lighting.

"My little man lion is a good fighter, why do I worry," and Malachi relaxed his bow string and watched Mungo and the red lion, swords both drawn.

And the lion jumped, and Mungo parried and kicked the beast between the legs, and then as the lion doubled, he stabbed its heart.

Thunder.

"Now I will reclaim my kingdom," and he entered the burrow and found Red Hide cowering from thunderclaps.

And ten minutes later he walked up to Malachi as the sky turned green and threw a red mane on the brown dust.

"King at last?" Malachi.

"Sasha is now queen." And Mungo walked on, he did not feel a king, he had killed good fighting lions and would rather have killed dirty minded humans.

"And where did Mungo get the idea, it was his kingdom? Was he born a prince? It was just imaginations put into words that became prophecies and Mungo believed," The Elder sang, and thought about royalties for he was famous, mentioned often in the cheap books; he did see a solicitor along the way.

*

Now Malachi was worried, Mungo had gone alone into the desert, and no one knew if he carried provisions. Gone to where he had hidden the incorruptible, not even Malachi knew where that was.

Illustration: King Red Hide

"You may love me Malachi, but you are still lizard," Mungo had said before leaving and Malachi hurt but understood. The holy bitch had given Mungo a weapon the lion man thing did not understand, and he was lizard, and his race faced a disaster in The Wild One.

Why Oh, why did he have to be his friend?

And Mungo had rent his clothes and covered his head in brown dust.

"*Malachi was his friend,*" The Elder and Malachi angered with sword slew sixteen young mazarrat companions of The Elder, they who were learning how to prophecy.

"*You may kill me, but will you tell Mungo when he returns?*" The Elder, Malachi raised his sword. "*There is no escaping fate for you or even me, if you bring down your sword upon* my skull Malachi."

And Malachi snapped his copper weapon and cried.

"*Go after him, you are the only one he trusts and take the harpist,*" The Elder instructed.

And Malachi's heart broke, everyone thought his little man lion thing was crazy but old Malachi knew better, all this

killing would poison any wild beast and Mungo was
beast.

"He also shared bedding with Ono, remarkably interesting sympathies. Not sharing my bed," our singer wearing pants with a lock on the front.

And as Malachi left, John Wrexham gave the order to crucify the first lizard prisoners, "I must bring Mungo back, he can stop this," and Malachi meant the

crucifixions of six hundred lizard warriors who had surrendered to Mungo who said, "I am tired, John you deal with them," and John hated lizard more than he hated Mungo.

"I only stay because I know Mungo will make things better after the judgement," Malachi breaking a white cloud that filled his lungs with chilly air that smelt of pine, for he had taken the yellow flying machine, "Them scribes have brain washed me, I am only here because of Mungo, I could not care about the others except for Ono.

Judgement, judgement it can't be right?"

So, Malachi found Angus Ogg following Mungo's trail.

"We both seek him?" Malachi.

Angus eyed the hunter sniffing the air with disgust at the strong lizard stink.

Why suddenly Malachi wanted to kill Angus, and Angus wanted to kill Malachi.

"Drop the weapons," it was Mungo.

He also held out both hands to each warrior, and Malachi gripped first, then Angus last, the lizard had scales and a hiss to his words, did he not?

"Let's go put my house in order," and there was something different about Mungo, he was leaner.

But at that moment Abel and Eve the hunting lions of Artebrates landed upon Malachi and dragged him away.

"Brother and sister what do you do?"

"Our fight is with Malachi who stole us from our mother," the lions.

"Malachi is now Ono's husband."

"Wahab our mother has a lizard man as husband, we are shamed by this."

"Not so, Malachi is good for Ono," Mungo but could not stop the lions slashing scales off Malachi, before they ran into the jungle crying out their shame.

"I owe you a life," Malachi.

"Again, I say friend, I give you freedom from the Fermanian customs."

"Malachi was his friend." Mazarrats.

"Did you hear that? Fate says otherwise," Malachi.

Much later Angus Ogg would whisper to Mungo, "Why did you save him, he is only a lizard without a soul." For humans believed how could a lizard have a soul?

In reply Mungo roared out his frustrations; Angus Ogg was appealing to his old prejudices on lizard folk.

And the first thing Mungo did when he got back to the ranch was to free the remaining two hundred lizard prisoners waiting crucified, and took down those who were, still breathing, a hundred.

"Go home," he told them, and they looked at him as if he was crazy which he was, "go home," and slowly they left not believing luck for about them was three hundred of their kind crucified, with carrion birds and bats already feasting.

"What happened in the wilderness?" Malachi asked of him.

"I told that sleeping corpse I am not blowing up half our world and yes, I will take you to her. She is indestructible, therefore dangerous. I tried Malachi, dam it I tried.

I stuck my sword into her, and she just healed again.

I even buried her, and lights glowed over her grave to mark my murderous spot.

I and you Malachi must make sure John and Peelock never get her, or the bomb, we must be her guardians."

And Malachi felt a great weight lifted from him about his conscious playing on him, that he was a traitor to his race.

*

"But it isn't right," John Wrexham complained, and Angus Ogg agreed and John did not stop him leading Lachie, Keira, Hamo and others to pha, and go skinning

freed lizards: lampshades and belts needed making.

He also found a severed red lion's head and stuck it up in his ranch as a trophy, and told all humans he killed Red Hide.

*

"Here my lion sons Malachi, one strong, a lion indeed," and Malachi held up a brown cub at arm's length and it licked his hands.

"It has your face," he said, and the cub peed on his chest.

"Also, your forwardness," and he put it down and picked up a white cub, and it bit him for it knew it was safe as mother was nearby.

"The King," Malachi and put it down, and now Sasha came into the room behind the mud walls.

"One day I will sit on Carman's throne will I not Malachi?"

"Yes mistress," Malachi replied for he saw Mungo as a king already, whom he loved.

And Sasha beamed, she saw lions and mazarrats bowing to her as she passed; "*she* could dream, dream as I do as I dream, I am The Elder," the singer.

"*Yeh, in sixty years hence,*" The Elder and laughed.

Cathbadh his diary

Cathbadh knew things had deteriorated between him and Carman and now planned a dynasty of his own. "I must make her womb swell with a descendant of King Sess, and be rid of her son by Prince Annunaki, Hebat who is cruel and cunning.

The act of killing will be a joy for he is a monster.

And Nudd, who is not a prince but her son with friend Artebrates, who still does not declare civil war on Carman to rid us of her indecision over the human star ship, which she refuses to believe exists, her excuse not to make peace with the humans.

At least Artebrates takes me seriously about it now.

The star ship may get him to act at last.

Oh, gentle Nudd, who is full of a strange light and loves all things and treats human slaves as he treats himself.

I would give life, but you are before my child with Carman who I call a royal harlot, equal to Moragana the ape woman thing that the wicked Serrant has failed to silence.

Chapter 5 Year 5

"I am so sorry," Mungo to The Elder who sat ape like with crossed legs with tufts of growing fur blowing in the breeze.

That was not the only thing blowing for The Elder winded often, and did not make excuses. If Mungo and that ugly lizard Malachi could not accept age, then he was not accepting them.

"I will instruct a mazarrat chiseler to carve the man lion thing on his knees crying under the Heavens," The Elder knowing Mungo wouldn't make the change; he was a man, things like the tufts of new fur following the wind, bouncing from new landing to the next.

"Thank you," Mungo.

Malachi peeled a banana for The Elder.

It went down in one swallow.

"For mazarrats got big gullets." The singer swallowing two bananas in one go and belched.

And then each looked at each as their noses wrinkled, scenting women with perfumes.

That is when the arrow hit dirt and Malachi rolled under a rhododendron bush, whose six-foot yellow flowers hid him.

"Hey cub, you some sort of idiot to stay out in the open?" Malachi called at Mungo.

"Leah," Mungo.

She was there and she was not Leah anymore.

She was bigger, her blond hair entwined with gold bands reaching her knees at the back.

And the solid green eyes peering from bronze helmet slits could be anyone's.

On her belly stretch marks from childbirth, and her charms hidden in silver cups, except when she pulled the light silk cape back with anthropomorphic designs over

them, to use the bow.

"Leah," Mungo pleaded, and The Elder was motionless from shock.

He had cousins inside Telephassa with big singing mouths, and he was about to play dead which all his kind did when confronted with something about to eat them.

"Abel, Eve," Mungo upon seeing them growling for they were Leah's companions, and Malachi cursed as his right elbow stiffened suddenly: arthritis.

"It's only Mungo," Mungo and very slowly Malachi came out with his arrow

pointed at Abel; he would get one of the dung heads first, before he ended up a lizard rump steak.

And Lord Vinki followed Leah chatting with friends all on cloud 9.

"WA," he as Malachi heard his elbow click, click, with painful arthritic resistance, but sent his arrow straight through one friend into a Berserka behind, for so strong was Malachi.

And the friend was a Fermanian dandy and did not die well as expected of Fermanians, who are brave and fearless, for he screamed and screamed trying to tug out

the barbed arrowhead.

A mistake but his entrails were on fire and soon as he tugged, would have none soon.

And something happened, Abel and Eve turned on Lord Vinki. They did not like him for he threw them fish skeletons from the kitchens, as insult to remind them they were domestic cats only.

Now was the time for freedom, like the wild mazarrats that sang nightly from cherry trees, *"It's time for freedom, the Wild One's here,"* and Abel closed his mouth

about a wonder Lord's groin and ate.

Never mind just another friend of Vinki and Malachi grunted satisfaction; they were not Fermanians in his eye.

Now Eve, she chased Vinki away why Malachi seeing the opportunity attacked the Berserkas.

And heard a snake hissing, Leah could speak, "W*ell hiss,"* and the singer made hissing sounds and the jungle too.

"Are you to shame me again Mungo?" Leah asked of Mungo who held her tight.

Then a deinonychus appeared and raked a claw down Leah's back and fortunately,

only her light cape ripped apart. *"A cape so tough it lies its strength, so Leah survived to the dinosaur's amazement. Even we mazarrats did not have that, yet"* the singer.

But she did fall and knock herself unconscious against a rock.

Just as a white object sailed over her.

And Angus Ogg had no other reason to help Malachi apart from self-survival, he did not like lizards just like the other humans.

"And maybe all the new Leah wasn't new, she had remembered?" The singer remembering the human shame.

*

The way the Elder awoke from his fright induced sleep and knew he was still in Hell, for this was Mungo's cave.

About the floor gnawed bones and lion fur and fleas, which were sampling him, so he refrained from a good scratch in case he awoke a lion, and he, The Elder eaten.

And lions and Malachi, and they were facing a large stone

slab.

"What had Mungo been up to in here?" The Elder worried his bones would join the others.

"Mungo dead?" The Elder asked but getting no response, forced his old stiff limbs to work again and got up. It was Sasha lying on the slab, a great gash ran between her bosoms and although attended too, it was obvious she was passing away.

"I always hand Leah to you, my rival in love, why Mungo?"

"Out of love for me," Mungo replied.

Sasha sighed.

"The Elder wondered what Mungo felt." Then found three cubs rubbing at his legs.

"Mungo has broken down prejudice," The Elder looking at the cubs and attracted Mungo over who shouted, "These are my heirs."

They owned Red Hide's entire kingdom, and all that Mungo saw from a red star fruit to a yellow metallic bird, which flew over these lands.

And the smile faded on Sasha's lips as her soul went down a lighted tunnel, and here greeted by Red Hide, her father on the other side.

"Am I late? John Wrexham sent me?" The vet entering the cave just as Mungo roared.

"Guess he was too late," Cameron Black to John hearing the roar, and then the roars of lions down the hill at the ranch.

"Yep, pity we haven't told him we aren't cloning her," John replied and then an earthquake struck.

A high place for human gods crumpled a hundred yards from them, and a priest fell upon his dagger from fear, thinking it was doomsday.

Now Cameron Black had been thinking of using Sasha's skin for a new winter robe.

John about her head as a new trophy.

"Yep, she sure was wasted," John added watching black smoke rise from a quaking nuclear plant nearby.

"Yes, but these three cubs will grow up and then what?" Cameron.

Both humans knew what the mazarrats sang; no lion brat was going to be their king.

And made their way to a group of men holding pha for the vet to return.

And that night Mungo dreamed of a beautiful woman beckoning him to her arms, and when he accepted, she bit him on the neck, filling him with poison.

"I am too late my love," a white lioness coming and passed straight through his Dream, and out the cave walls for she was a spirit.

So, Mungo awoke and tried to fall upon his sword, but Malachi awoken by the shouts stopped him and summoned the harpist.

And Mungo also dreamed of a stone cairn, a hundred feet high for Sasha, built from Fermanian prison labor *"and hoped Fermanians would die, but this last bit he told*

Malachi not." How did mazarrats hear this, do we creep in ears as earwigs, what nonsense, the singer annoyed.

"It was the end of her chosen road," The Elder shouted, but that did not help Mungo's grief either. *"It was her chosen TIME, Mungo, be happy she is home,"* but Mungo's grief denied him this.

Even when Sasha's spirits visited him often, 'as it is said, Blessed are they who mourn,' for this is what it means, his grief denied him seeing her, so Mungo denied knowledge they did meet again in an After Life.

*

It took a month working lunar nights and solar days to build the cairn, and Malachi said nothing as he watched Fermanian prisoners of war labor.

Illustration: Nuclear reactors

"Food for Sasha on her trip over the River of Darkness to Light on the other side," he had heard Mungo and had made sure Mungo kept the harpist near him always.

Just in case Mungo ordered under the influence of bad spirits, which would tell him to destroy the prisoners as it possessed him.

And the cairn filled with Sasha's personal things, her robes and favorite gold torcs and bracelets, both ankle and wrist, The Elder sealed the tomb entrance with carvings of Sasha with Mungo riding into battle, then all went

home as the red sun settled down to sleep the night past.

And none saw a grave robber approach.

"It is yours for Keira, and some land down at Muddy Bend and a herd of pha?" Angus Ogg hopefully for what he had cut off.

"Can't promise Keira, Mungo might object," John mused over Sasha's gold torc.

"He's a past lizard lover," Angus boasted.

"Well since we understand each other, and I want a new white robe for winter," Cameron Black and gave Angus a new laser pistol, and a bag of coins to spend in Red Town.

For he knew what Angus liked to spend his money on, and it would be all gone in

the wink of a night.

"On the pox" a cheeky mazarrat but which cheeky mazarrat, we look the same?

And John put Sasha's head in a large amphora containing cleaning solution before mounting it on his trophy wall.

Mungo and his friends never came visiting so would never see it.

Besides, there were white lions on the Red Plains, *"and this was one of them he had killed with only a single arrow, would be his story."* But a song would be song that you are a liar, and she began to sing.

"So, Mungo's history," John and Angus grunted agreement.

"Maybe John and Cameron had a man at last to do the dirty work, get blamed and take the consequences if he failed or succeeded, Malachi was still about! Mazarrats were still about."

*

Nannaha did not look herself for Vinki had paid for gene shuttle transplant to make her face softer, and voice demure, and figure richer, for Vinki knew Cathbadh

was a lonely man.

"There was no man alive who did not desire the old

Nannaha except one, now even Mungo hopeful of meeting the new Nannaha.," Vinki admiring her who oozed trouble in the form of sexual pheromones and curves?

"Vinki speaks the truth," mazarrats sang from rhododendron trees, *"Mungo lies* with any woman, if she is fair, for he grieves for Sasha."

Now Vinki took Nannaha into Cathbadh's gardens and left her there for Cathbadh, who did eventually find her, for the garden was a peaceful place to think and

have one's heart calmed.

"What is your name?" Cathbadh.

"Nannaha," and she fell so he could wipe his feet on her perfumed hair.

"And now her hair is yuck, but the lustful man will still jump into her duvets. Soles just stood in pet pooh," the singer *hair* sang so, even Cathbadh checked her before stroking it again.

And he found her hair soft and smoothly arousing and said, "Nannaha I hear

is the queen of harlots and more fair than the moon goddess, and is a nymph for she has wings?"

"I hear Cathbadh is a lame blind beggar who sits outside the public baths," she

boldly replied.

And this boldness and dig at gossip spreaders amused him and liked her wit.

And that is not all he liked. *"Her knowledge of astronomy and naval architecture, blah, he was a man so liked the fruit she offered, melons, peaches, bah,"* the singer hateful of men.

For Nannaha knew how to bow, so her spine curved in just the right posture to make it appealing, so her bottom rose in the air rounded and covered in fine muslin only; so Cathbadh lost his reason.

"For he was a stupid man about to catch the pox," and the singer laughed, *"to catch the pox,"* the audience agreed.

And he walked about her admiring all he saw, and lust filled his head and the wax in his ears never heard about her pox.

"I am a single man; the gods have answered my prayers for a companion and who more fitting than the highest comforter in the land, Artebrates thrown aside harlot."

And he took her into his house and joyed with her, and she made sure he thought of nothing but her.

"Hiss" the mazarrat having learned how to.

Chapter 6 Year 6

"I don't think you are my daughter anymore?" The hunch back watching Leah suck
life out of rats.

In reply she offered him a shriveled carcass and when he refused, she opened her mouth dropping her bottom jaw too swallow; true Fermanian fashion as is the way of snakes, their cousins.

And the wily Serrant also.

So slowly, the rodent went down her throat a bulge.

The oily coat allowing it quick passage down to her stomach.

The ringed tail slowly disappeared like a piece of spaghetti.

With the usual wiggle at the end that always sprayed the sauce.

"I am vegetarian these days," he "but did cook you these," and he pushed a silver tray towards her with mice baked in honey or mustard and stuffed with sage and red onion.

Leah hissed and showed her purple snake tongue.

Truly Fermanian!

Fifteen minutes later the tray was empty, and the hunchback finished playing with young Conn, Mungo's child by the original Leah.

"I am satisfied," but Leah thought he meant he had eaten already, but he meant satisfied that the gene shuttles he was feeding them was working, more on young

Conn whose scales under his flesh were dissolving, as they were now foreign bodies as antibodies ate them up.

Leah was not as fortunate as Cathbadh saw her every day in his frenzy to make her more reptilian; a true Fermanian of course.

*

John hefted the head up for nailing on his trophy wall.

"So, Mungo's history?" John as Angus grunted agreement.

*

And Nannaha spied on Cathbadh for her true love, Wonder Lord Vinki and Cathbadh

grew suspicious for he had intelligence, and although he could not prove Nannaha's ill ways, he suspected and one day confronted her.

"Don't you like me anymore?" Nannaha asked making sure she dropped her silks, but Cathbadh turned his back on her to prevent his eyes seeing, then lusting.

"Leave my house," was his firm reply but Nannaha was skilled and wrapped herself about him and he lusted.

But he had warned Nannaha who informed Vinki who had a mob visit Cathbadh, while he mediated in his garden in the early morning hours, when the insects were rubbing their legs together in music and the flowers were just opening spreading their perfumes.

And the mob beat Cathbadh and prepared to hang him from a Rowan tree branch, and his weight would have snapped the branch and brought down hundreds of red berries for birds to eat.

And one Fermanian smirked from a yellow sedan chair watching from the open garden gate.

Wonder Lord Vinki who saw the rope tighten and Cathbadh's face go blue, and Vinki remembered his own blue suspenders, "Such a lovely color!"

Then a mighty sound of carnyx horns, and shields beaten

with steel swords and Vinki saw Lord Artebrates on a shield approaching, that denoted to all he was a general so beware!

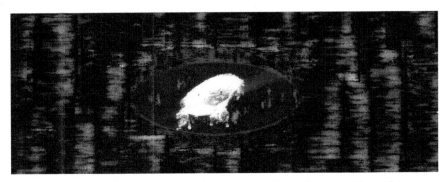

Illustration: Sasha was a trophy on a wall as she was lion thing.

"Release Cathbadh or die?" Artebrates demanded and ignored, so signaled Berserkas to use lasers and one hundred and sixty of the mob died. *"Just plebians,"* a beautiful mazarrat voice sang, *"Yes, addicts, drunks, unemployed, dreamers,"* The Wild.

"Bearers take me away," Vinki cursed knowing this day would cost him treble what he had promised the mob. *"An easy task, even Carman wants him dead. Why? He is a descendant of King Sess,"* and the mob believed Carman would not send Berserkas to stop Cathbadh's lynching and *"she did not, was Artebrates that did."*

And Vinki had forgotten Artebrates a friend of Cathbadh was in Telephassa, and was not on poppy seed as Vinki believed, for Nahanna was busy elsewhere these days.

*

Angus could think of nothing else than owning Keira, which was a mistake, for a woman like her belongs to a man of her choosing, and she had chosen Hamo.

And Angus waited at a watering hole and Mungo approached alone.

And Angus threw his lance and would have killed Mungo if an armed mazarrat had not dropped in its path.

So, Angus withdrew, there would be another time to get his land, pha herd and Keira.

And Mungo carried the unknown mazarrat to Malachi and told what had happened, and as The Elder chanted death hymns, they found a tree hollow and wrapped the body in leaves and placed it within, as is mazarrat custom.

"*The cycle of life goes on,*" The Elder, "*she died so another may live.*"

"*Already hungry eyes are watching,*" unseen mazarrats chorused.

"*Water to the air,*

Elements to the tree," The Elder.

"*Already hungry eyes are watching,*" mazarrats with hands, on the mazarrat in front shoulder perilously walking branches carrying the body.

"*The body goes the way of its father,*

The spirit to the power of all,

Join the elements good woman, your spirit is with the Ceugant Dana the white force," The Elder.

"*Already hungry eyes are watching,*" the vanishing mazarrats taking everything the dead owned, her bow, copper sword, bronze helmet, one red garter, brown loin cloth and silver breast cups.

She no longer needed them.

And The Elder climbed down, an amazing feat for he was old as a green snake from bushes entered the burial hollow.

"*Big fish eat little fish,*" The Elder and walked away.

And none heard Angus told never come to John's house in daylight anymore.

*

"I don't eat them anymore, they should be free like birds or in my cage," Conn said and the hunchback looked into his eyes, *"Didn't the papyrus books say one would be*

wise?"

Neither Leah nor himself took any notice of the firework display outside. Carman was celebrating the hunchback's scientific success, a woman with a pouch could protect her young better than laying free range eggs, the death rate among the new-born would drop, and their race guaranteed survival against mammals now.

They were about to evolve into marsupials.

A pity none listened to Cathbadh and his talk about a star ship that would make them follow the Tasmanian Tiger and Dodo.

*

"Join me Malachi," Mungo holding up a hand to his friend who refused. Once he had danced with Mungo as possessed by something and was afraid. Let whatever that lived in all with no name be content possessing Mungo.

And Mungo threw off his cod piece and danced naked, unashamed for the no name spirit was not interested in flesh but spirit.

But then knowledge set in that Malachi could see his parts, and he wanted to cover them, and he was no longer innocent. He was a murderer among names that

now stuck to him and he grieved, and his spirit pained.

"At least he doesn't need the harpist like this," Malachi and looked down the canyon towards John Wrexham's ranch and was satisfied he saw empty crosses.

Mungo shouted, "no more crucifixions."

And did not see John and Cameron Black standing with

Peelock, and both leaders held papyrus sheets signed with their signatures.

John Wrexham did not want mustard fever breaking out in his lands and Peelock knew it.

And Malachi was wrong about the harpist, Malachi should have been watching Mungo who was not dancing, but on his knees holding his temples, something was roaring in his head telling him to use the bomb, humans in a star ship were coming, this planet was meant for humans, the Fermanian way was over for they were more of an abomination than the humans?

They were dinosaurs that had escaped extinction, but time had caught them up for

time stops for no one.

And when Mungo neared, Malachi saw a resignation in his eyes and mistakenly put it down to a peaceful soul.

Anyway: There was a smacking sound as Angus Ogg drove a dagger up to its hilt in a lizard's stomach. He was one of dozens of lizards tied to cacti hidden from Malachi's view.

"Is he The Wild One father?" Hamo pulling his dagger out of another lizard, and wiping it clean on the next before plunging it home there.

"Even if he was," his work complete, "we are up to Telephassa's third wall and do not forget the scribes say he must die for all of us," Angus eyeing the last few hanging lizards.

"But they are lizard scribes so why they say that?" Hamo protested.

"So, they believe in The Wild One too, that's what makes it so easy destroying these lizards, the fight is already out of them," and he swung round to get maximum power behind his dagger and put the weapon out the other side of the lizard.

But Hamo was not happy, his father was not a great hunter

anymore, he was a crazy killing what he hated most, lizards.

"What about Malachi, I like him," Hamo asked.

"He's a stinking lizard."

Cathbadh

"You were my greatest pupil, and your success is an attribute to me," Cathbadh told the hunchback who could not care as he was going to pull the laser trigger anyway.

First, he would start below the knees just to see Cathbadh crawl about like an insect.

"I am glad I am leaving so hurry, and do your dirty work," Cathbadh and turned his back on his assassin cursing himself for not getting the cloned hand back from the hunchback.

"Look at me," the hunchback didn't want cheated, "this is for what you did to Leah my daughter."

At least Cathbadh knew why he was about to die, and where the genes for Leah had come from.

Then Artebrates arrived like a bad penny again, and the hunchback diverted his attention to the door and never saw what dropped from the beams above flooring him.

"Holy Pterodactyl dung," the hunchback screeched as Moragana pulled his hair out.

So, Cathbadh walked over and took the laser and fired a stream of light into the hunchback's body.

Then walked away and pressed a button to open the door.

"My Lord and Master?" Nannaha asked bursting into the room attracted by the scream, and saw the hunchback in a fetal position holding his abdomen.

"Help the little man out to die somewhere else Nannaha," and Nannaha did so, and pushed the hunchback down an open sewer channel in the middle of the road.

The vermin could finish him nice and slow.

As for the secret conversation between Artebrates and Cathbadh, well she had the room bugged, and this is what she reported back to Vinki her love of her life. *"Perhaps they were soul mates after all?"* The mazarrat sang in a melody of garden freshness.

"He was an abomination to me," Artebrates glad his deformed son killed, after listening to Cathbadh, the reason for the attempted murder was not important, Leah had been a produce of the vats, not a grandchild any general of Telephassa could wish for.

"Bread riots have broken out again," Artebrates now told Cathbadh.

"The supply of humans has dried up; we must find an alternative food source for our people," Cathbadh.

"What about grass?"

"Very funny Artebrates," but the idea stuck in Cathbadh's head, he had time to shuttle genes into everyone if Carman made it law, so all could have a crop grow for

grass eating.

"Always Carman, she refuses to believe in my star ship."

"Is there really a human ship?"

"It will be here soon, time is running out for all of us," Cathbadh.

"If what you say is true then I might as well proclaim for Annunaki's Legion and war?"

"I have told you the truth, the human captain's name is John Clinton, and unless we are prepared to meet him by force, he will condemn us when he sees how we eat his

kind, so we better make peace with our human slaves, and make them our equals,"

sarcastically

"We are a mighty and fearless race," Artebrates haughtily.

"If they can fly across space, they will have weapons only our founding ancestors knew of, we are doomed Artebrates."

*

And Angus saw Mungo dancing, alone, naked, and full of joy.

"Lizard lover," and Angus ran at Mungo with drawn bronze sword but stood on a sleeping cobra, for he was not looking where he put his big feet.

And looked into Mungo's eyes and screamed as he got bit, and covered his own eyes and cut his cheeks in this effort, "WHY?" I will sing a song and you will find out.

Angus Ogg had seen love, it was shining out of Mungo's eyes, and all the filth in Angus had turned to shame.

He just could not look into those eyes and was torn to bits by the knowledge he wanted to commit murder.

"And the Unseen sent a serpent to guard Mungo," a mazarrat sang so all mazarrats knew what had happened.

And Angus fled and Mungo did not follow but danced on, for because he had Repented, The Unseen pitied him and remembered how Mungo could dance, so had

possessed.

"Even with the buffalo mask I know who you are Angus, for the hate you bear me is in your eyes, but I forgive you, for it is your choice to hate or love me, as Malachi does," and returned to dancing.

Now I The Elder witnessed and went and told Malachi who would have stuck his copper sword in Angus's back without warning, and twisted till all bubbled out for

Angus did not deserve an honorable frontal death, the way a warrior dies.

"Mungo has granted life, don't break his word so the broken word befalls on you as blood of a murderer Malachi," and saw

Malachi pained to kill Angus, "just make sure

you are always with Angus when Mungo dances, and think Malachi, how does Mungo tell Hamo, Angus's son whom he loves as a son that he executed his father?

Illustration: And the rest of Sasha became a rug for the winter

Mungo in his present state of mind will hate you Malachi, his faithful friend."

And Angus Ogg was not interfered with as he lay in a bunk house waiting for the venom to kill him, and did not know the snake had empty venom sacks, for it had recently killed rats.

But no sleep came for he kept feeling for his heartbeat to see if he was alive.

And a brave and fearless mazarrat crept to him, it was her first cousin he had killed. *"Now I jump and claw you and drop mumps venom powder on you; suffer Angus Ogg as you die,"* and did not know a snake venom was in him.

Chapter 7 Year Seven

Peelock sat on rusty grass in a red cedar forest watching Mungo lead his hoard against Fermanians under Lord Artebrates, who had insisted he ride his war triceratops

up front to stop criticism he was past it, a soppy poppy popper and out of favor with Mighty One Carman.

"Charge," he shouted his heart thumping so hard it made his rib cage hurt.

Suddenly he felt his youth back, briefly.

Suddenly he felt dizzy and faint.

Suddenly he felt a pain in his chest.

Suddenly he keeled over onto the floor of his howdah.

"Ouch," he was not being sarcastic, then his lips went blue, and his driver fell on

him headless.

"Oh no," Artebrates as he felt himself going down a dark tunnel.

Then he saw light at the end and god Telephassa surrounded like the papyrus books Said, attended by female serpent nymphs.

"I'm coming," and did not know if he meant to his scaly god or to the women whose bottom halves were snakes.

And they welcomed throwing their arms open showing their charms.

Artebrates was not afraid of dying anymore; he was going to paradise where all good Fermanians went for killing humans who did not believe in god Telephassa.

Then something horrible happened, instead of kissing

him and feeding him grapes that hung from trees nearby his god, they showed venomous fangs and went to feed on him.

"Hoodoo." Artebrates screamed for he could hear his god laughing and warriors dying in the real world.

"What is the real world?" The spirit world or the one Carman my cruel lover rules?" He asked himself, see he had had a Near Death Experience, and not all are

about the light, certainly his was not, he had read Dante's! *"I have, so really am pretty and intelligent, not like old scaly there."*

And then light flooded everywhere and the serpent nymphs went off screaming and god Telephassa melted leaving a smell like unwashed underwear.

"I am alive, surely this peace must be Telephassa and the other a demon come to trick me?"

And it came with Mungo looking down at him smelling of unwashed underwear.

"Fighting makes warriors sweat bad, giggle."

And Mungo prodded with lance and drew blood from Artebrates thigh.

"Now I am in hell," Artebrates.

"No, on the red grass plain with the rest of the wounded. Me I did use your skin on my belts and shoes," John Wrexham behind Mungo.

Malachi thought this a bit tasteless; Artebrates was a heroic Fermanian legend, once his own Lord and Master.

"What news about Leah, she was your comforter?" Mungo.

"Where are my warriors?" Artebrates lifting his head up. He did not see any just a computer so large and big, it put those in Telephassa to shame.

"There is a corpse looking at me?" He said fearfully.

"One of Peelock's secrets seems he had her hidden from us," John explained but, that meant nothing to Artebrates who looked dumb.

"We are her guardians," Malachi warned John, who curled up a lip thinking black thoughts where a lizard and a human corpse were concerned. And Artebrates saw

wires came out of whatever she lay upon and went back inside the computer.

"I am very afraid a walking dead is controlling my body," as he saw wires also went into his body from her and the computer, why Malachi grunted over his

superstition.

Men were grunting as surgeons pulled arrows out of them, and dug bullets from bladders.

There were also lizards grunting on the red grass, them left behind as Artebrates army routed.

They were grunting as a herd of Allosaurus, twenty tone monsters with a bullet head were chewing the wounded up.

Malachi had no sympathy for them, they had routed, had not died on battle, now they died the way cowards should die.

"*Malachi, Malachi is there no pity in you,*" mazarrats sang. "*Malachi was all* Fermanian. "

Illustration: Allosaurus, just a big pussy cat.

"*Death is the gateway to Telephassa's paradise where maidens await the brave,*" more mazarrats poking fun at Malachi's beliefs.

"*Fermanians like to die,*" others.

"*Let us poison the lot, giggle,*" in a beautiful voice.

"*Cannot take this woman anywhere,*" The Elder hoping to poison her.

"*Malachi was brought up under a ruthless penal system, boiling for stealing bread and roasting for swearing against your better,*" another.

"*Let them all moan as Malachi's cousins eat them all up,*" one from a bush.

"*Mungo understood, he left the human wounded for Leah wasn't amongst them.*"

"*Humans who were sent by Peelock to help Lord Vinki.*"

"*Mungo and Malachi are brothers in hell,*" a mazarrat sang in bass.

And none asked Artebrates what waited for them on the other side.

And eventually Artebrates told Mungo, Leah was in his house in Telephassa, but not the changes that had happened to her, he was now afraid of dying, he had not led a good life, by Fermanian standards by eating as much human sweetmeat as he could?

And Mungo remembered the house, a castle built by termites and humans.

And The Elder later to his pupils, "*Here fate intervened for Mungo told Artebrates*

this holy woman and her machine, would bring death to his race for she contained a

terrible weapon."

And Artebrates believed and feared, for he remembered the nymphs with fangs

waiting for him. And Malachi grunted annoyed that Mungo spoke too much,

sometimes Mungo pushed his love for him to breaking point."

"*Malachi knew he and Mungo were chosen and controlled not their destinies.*"

extracts from Mazarrat songs.

And Artebrates thought, "I must have this weapon and planned to use it on

humans," for fate had decided how to get Mungo to use the bomb.

"I will take her with me," Mungo but fate had decided ten thousand years ago this

action for the computer allowed Mungo to carry her.

"Dinosaur dung head," Malachi cursed seeing there was no escape from fate.

And fate took John and Cameron to where Peelock sat.

"We couldn't stop Mungo entering Red Town, mustard fever or not. That blasted

baboon started waving his staff and speaking holy gibberish. *"Dance in Peelock's castle and cure the sick, dance Mungo dance, which singed miscreant rat sang,"* John

complained to Peelock who sat motionless.

"Yep, and we cannot just plug Mungo, why man they were carrying him after that Battle, and anyone stupid enough to shoot him would be torn asunder," Cameron Black added.

"Even your riders John," Peelock eventually and pointed at them spearing Fermanians lucky enough to crawl away from the Allosaurus, "you have a lot of work

to undo Mungo's popular victory today."

"Hell, I give them lizards to kill to make them happy, they cannot get enough of them, so just remember I am on your side and keep that mustard fever out of my lands,

and give me the cure," John pleaded giving the answer how to get the people to hate Mungo?

And Cameron did not argue even if he thought they should put a laser into Peelock and hope Peelock did not break any seals on his mustard vials.

"And what gives with this holy corpse that isn't dust?" John asked and not a scientific man knew naught of genes that made a body decay to dust.

"There are laws of an unnamed power existing before humankind said they are scientific laws and dismissed them.

How foolish since the Unnamed One made them in the first place and uses them," The Elder sang to them on the wind.

And none thought their only hope lay in Mungo and the

Incorruptible One for they were humans whose land was under threat, and blinded by Mungo's love for a

lizard, as they could not stand-up wind of Malachi.

Cathbadh

Now Cathbadh looked out the window wondering where the hunchback had fled, if he had any sense out of Telephassa that was burning as hungry rioters broke into

Vinki's granaries, looted and fired them.

The humans on the walls looking in could not fail to notice what was happening.

Artebrates should have removed them when he led his men out to battle Mungo.

"Soldiers from other cities are joining me on the Red Plain, I will return victorious and clean the walls of humans," Artebrates had boasted.

Seeing that smoke was the only thing making him happy, Vinki's suffering and he still felt good granting mercy to the hunchback.

"Let us not forget Fermanian ideas on mercy are different from human," The Elder.

Cathbadh was also happy the mob had broken into Carman's summer palace ransacking,

and the Berserkas guarding it had joined the rioters. It made Carman's position vulnerable and his Sess lineage more secure. He expected news of her assassination or forced abdication at any moment. Things were perilous for his queen.

And he looked at the sky where a human spaceship was.

"Artebrates was needed by Carman, would he come? There was really nobody else to lead the army into *defeat!*" Cathbadh wickedly mused.

*

Now Angus seeing he could not have Keira through John

Wrexham's hands took her by force, and kept her in a hunter's hut three miles from John's ranch, and mazarrats told Mungo and he was wrath and went to save Keira.

"What have you done Angus; I gave your life?" Mungo asked as Malachi and armed mazarrats freed the distressed human woman, for Angus had abused, to make her submit to be his woman.

"My mother gave me my life, and you are crazy and need a harpist," for Angus fancied he could spite Mungo with sword.

"No Malachi bade," Mungo ordered with restraining hands, "he is right, at times I am madder than others and now it is Angus's turn to mock me, just take Keira and

send the harpist to Angus," Mungo and Angus lost his self-control over the remark and drew his sword to slay Mungo, who jumped back and took out his own cutlass.

And a rage of lions possessed Mungo and he overcame Angus.

"Give me life again," Angus pleaded.

And if The Elder had not stopped him Mungo would have killed Angus, "*You* granted life earlier, now it is up to a different power to grant death. Let his blood be

upon another for if you slay him the human warriors will kill you, for they love Angus Ogg and his ways that are their ways."

"One day I will take back the life I gave you, always carry shield slung over back Angus for you will never know what mazarrat will lance your back, listen to me?" And Angus Ogg listened to Mungo.

"*He has the blood of a mazarrat on him, he is a murderer, the dead one sings for justice,*" armed mazarrats sang coming out of red cedars and Angus Ogg was afraid of

Mungo's prowess and planned to kill him by stealth again.

"*Fear me Angus, she was cousin, and it will be me who feeds you to red ants,*" and she showed herself, a pretty thing by mazarrat standards and, The Elder, "*Cousin, so it is you who wishes to replace me, Bah, go home to mummy before I spank you.*"

"*Ha blah blah, The Elder coughed as he saw his replacement, his wonderful, amusing, witty, warrior skilled cousin,*" sang only by her but the AUDIENCE agreed and The Elder, "Mm, better taker this more seriously or will be out of a job."

Book 3
The Elder

Illustration: Triceps and Artebrates charge to war.

Mungo slouched on the red grass hilltop looking down his valley. Behind him rolling to the great yellow river Yathan, and the green grass was Red Town's grazing

pha herds.

Lo a faint stink reached him on the warm breeze as well as fine slit.

"I have got to stop them doing that," Mungo referring to humans skinning Fermanian Prisoners to keep human tanneries working. This had to again stop, or the Fermanians under Malachi would rebel, and he did not need what he danced to, to inspire him to think this way.

The death of the prisoners was a bell ringing the end of Fermanian rule on this planet.

Their numbers were dwindling; even the Berserkas under Malachi knew that, and were nervous, hoping for a new life under Mungo's word.

And Mungo who had been given the land about him by John Wrexham *"knew he owned nothing."* The land men thought they owned, they held in trust form the great Unseen power that made the land.

And his belief in that confirmed when in front of him, a yellow flower with a small bee on it.

"Such beauty I cannot make," and Mungo stood allowing his dusty brown leather kilt to drop, and strode down the red valley taking care not to stand upon any flowers or insects.

He was in one of his close moods with the Unseen.

The Unseen that clothes all not by feathers or cotton but by spirit, so Mungo was naked and unashamed and connected and joyed, leaped high, and somersaulted and screeched strange words.

"Were creature," the humans whispered afraid of Mungo.

This was Mungo's land since John had made peace with Peelock, and John told the people Mungo must go or the plagues of Peelock would visit them......" remember *earlier their conversation! More murderous than Mungo and Malachi his friend,"* in C minor notes.

And the Incorruptible One no longer spoke to Mungo for he refused to use the bomb.

And Peelock had come to the ranch when he was known to be dead, seen alive and the power of god of Red Town his.... *"they were human idiots,"* she sang delightfully.

That the real deliverer, The Wild One, Mungo was a deceiver, a fake. In truth a tomato had genes causing decay removed, so the tomato did not decay, and thus, it had been done to Peelock, legacy of the computer so, he would not decay when Mungo stabbed him and he had made his way to his castle *"for repairs, a cyborg, we mazarrats know what they are but not those silly humans."* She sang not liking Peelock so made sure she was on a wide branch high up.

Peelock was now an incorruptible by science not the Unseen, not by divine intervention.

And the humans had asked Mungo to leave and begged Peelock not to visit them with his plagues, which he did as a demonstration of course.

"I spit at your feet, don't ask me back," for Mungo wanted away to seek Leah not children who once sat at Mungo's feet in hero worship, but now threw pha dung clumps at him.

Mungo also saw pha riders ready to attack on John's orders, and Mungo wanted to fight, but his heart was with Leah, and he did not want Malachi to fight either.

The humans had broken his heart, a heart that should have been strong with the dance of the Unseen. *"He can dance with me."*

"Blah, my stupid cousin needs put in an isolation pad or married off to a young buck mazarrat," The Elder annoyed, ashamed, disillusioned.

And there were flowers on the Red Plain grass, for this was Belinos Month and the year of the Red Lion.

Now suddenly a Fermanian warrior burst into view heading for Mungo, who would give him sanctuary if he managed to cross the Red line, a boundary stream, red from iron oxides that separated Mungo's domains from Peelock's and John's.

And Mungo hoped the Fermanian would make it for hunting deinonychus were hissing, coughing, flowing from Peelock's lands.

And from a corpse of cherry trees in bloom reptilian eyes watched Mungo.

"My Lord Artebrates, it is Mungo, do we kill?" A seven-foot-long soldier with hollow bones.

Artebrates looked at Cathbadh's gene altered coelophysis, a dinosaur built for running on hind legs in its leather armor that was having difficulty standing still, and he was disgusted at the parody before him. It reminded Artebrates from hence Fermanians

sprung from, dinosaur eggs.

"Who told you, you could eat and drink?" Artebrates and slapped the creature with his sword.

Apologetically the beast stuffed the chili dusted fingers into its mouth and quickly swallowed.

And Artebrates eyed Mungo who had stridden four hundred yards and would be at his mud walled hut very soon. It was not the coelophysis fault it was fighting, it was not asked to have its founder ancestor genes sliced so it could evolve a bit faster into a robotic soldier.

It was the Mighty One's Carman's fault in her ruthless efforts to find ways to exterminate humans.

"My Lord, Mungo will cast the lance at the warrior, do we kill him now?" The coelophysis soldier asked.

But Artebrates wanted to see what Mungo would do? Would he kill the Fermanian or help it cross the red line he had heard so much about from Vinki?

"The mazarrats been at work here," he means singing about Mungo's good friend Malachi and Mungo's love for lizards.

And the soldier coelophysis looked about for invisible mazarrats, oh yes, they were there all right, just somewhere too close as usual!

And the Fermanian did not make the stream as the first deinonychus clawed him.

The throw of Mungo's lance had been too late.

Then Peelock's hunters riding pha emerged and one dangled a rope about the Fermanians right ankle, and rode away with the herd of deinonychus following.

Why Mungo walked back to his mud walled hut.

Artebrates sighed, the mazarrats had been right.

"Fire the signal," Artebrates ordered.

And a woman with human anatomy saluted and followed by the coelophysis out of the cherry corpse, and she fired a flaming arrow into the yellow sky and at once

Carnyex horns sounded with metal tubes and gongs, cymbals, and horns.

Mungo looked about himself.

His eyes followed the smoke across the yellow to the bow, "Leah?" He asked of the woman for he could see long blond hair flowing from under her bronze helmet.

And the woman had vision as good as eagles so read his

lips and hissed.

And Mungo saw armored Triceratops pour down his red grass from the hills into the green valley of Peelock's.

"Artebrates again," Mungo seeing this lord appear now.

In answer a flaming arrow thudded next to Mungo's feet.

And the firer hissed and allowed her forked purple tongue to scent wind directions for a better aim.

And Mungo retreated into his mud bricked house to his weapons and cover.

And the female archer wondered why Fermanians feared this naked human, and a faint memory rush of her lying in the grass, with this human and she was slightly confused for the woman felt aroused and did not like the memory.

And she forced herself to show her fangs and drop venom onto an arrow tip.

And Mungo appeared holding sword and was calling, "Leah."

And the sound of bow string twanging as an arrow streaked for Mungo.

And sunk into his left ankle and burned for the venom was fresh and wet.

What else could Mungo do but yank the shaft out.

"Why Leah?" He asked and then held up his hands to stop Lord Artebrates war club descending on his head.

And as the venom clouded his mind, he was aware of lions roaring and Ono coming to his aid.

*

Now Artebrates now released by Peelock from pressure from Vinki who was under pressure from Carman. Therefore, Lord Artebrates was back, not breaking the

peace treaty with Peelock but with John Wrexham.

Now we all know Vinki wanted Artebrates dead, but Vinki did not want to lead the army so was glad Artebrates was on the field, which left Telephassa in his greedy hands.

*

Mungo had left the ranch easily because his heart was sickening for Leah.

And he had asked Malachi to stay and protect the Fermanian Berserkas there for he knew John wanted to skin all and make belts out of them.

Also, Malachi could tell Mungo what events occurred on the ranch, but the Berserkas where not in the thousands as humans, so were at the mercy of John. And Berserkas skinned on this and that pretext, not executed as soldiers, but killed in cruel thought up fashions to remind Malachi he was lizard, something that needed to bask on a rock to warm itself before it could move.

And Malachi knew this was true, the great weakness of his race, that they did become sluggish when the day cooled.

And wished he were human and able to fight even in the chilly rain and freezing nights.

To run fast and not be lumbered by heavy scales." *Do not forget the bouncing tail, not elegant like a mazarrats. Wonder if they clean it after a pooh?"* Oh, I am cheeky?

And the thought weakened him, and made him drink so he was glad to see lizard's skins waiting tanning for his race of reptiles deserved their fate; they were skink lizards that needed to bask under the sun.

A backward evolutionary species that was dying out to make way for the mammalian humans who fate favored.

"Take me next so I may be away from this misery," Malachi.

And mazarrats heard and sang.

"Where is Mungo? His friend Malachi needs a harpist."

*

And Mungo hit from behind by a club from a Fermanian officer, and then the reptile's yellow tail lifted Mungo for the downward sweep of Lord Artebrates club.

"Hiss," the female archer for she was dumb and saw Mungo's head clearly as his bronze helmet fell away.

And thought Mungo beautiful and understood why he was a hero and said, "His hair is his strength."

Also hissing, "Your beauty captured my heart and gave me misery," and implanted fake memories where of Mungo whipping her, before he raped, flooded her mind put there by Cathbadh.

She must kill Mungo.

"Hiss, you must die for the freedom of Conn.

Hiss, if Mungo had been a Fermanian he would be a god after his Death, and his statue joined the heroes of her race in the Hall of Fame.

Hiss, I am Fermanian not human."

And a distant emotion called love saddened her as she saw the club strike Mungo's skull.

Now Lord Artebrates lifted his club again, but Ono bit it in half then tore the neck of the Triceratops apart so, it sank to its knees with Artebrates also.

Now Malachi broke away from the humans and with Berserkas ran to save Mungo his friend.

"Come back Malachi," the humans wanting him and his remaining Berserkas to fight and die for them.

"I am his friend," mazarrats replied as Malachi and his men attacked those about Mungo.

Now he killed his enemy and the last he killed was a coelophysis that fell upon him so, he fell backwards on top of Mungo.

"They are dead, we have nothing to fight for now," the friends of Mungo and Malachi shouted.

"*They are dead?*" Mazarrats alarmed.

"Is Mungo dead at last?" Peelock deliriously happy.

Now he was safe for his followers had new laser weapons and a robotic spy falcon sat next to Peelock, all from Vinki for payment for sweetmeats.

But his happiness went for the Fermanians were attacking his gates using human slaves as shield, and they had charges hanging from poles to blow the gates.

"I am betrayed, today I am lizard food, men light the fuses," and Peelock ordered bags of black powder thrown upon the human slaves, so they died.

Anyway: Mungo's friends took guns and beat back the lizard enemy and closed the gates belonging to a low mud wall about Mungo's mud house.

And Lord Artebrates seeing Mungo dead took a knife to scalp him.

But the fates of Planet New Uranus intervened for Artebrates shot by a friend of Mungo, but Artebrates, shielded by his shield bearers who now fell dead as

they carried their Lord over the small mud wall to safety.

"I have done my duty well, I will be in paradise this day," a shield bearer just before three coelophysis walked over him, then twenty retreating Fermanian in heavy brass plated armor.

But he died happy as his liver ruptured from the weights on him.

And a reptilian fired back a gun at the walls at Mungo's friends.

They had guns too, Peelock traded in all things.

"Hiss," the female archer who felt pleasure that her Lord

Artebrates had not struck Mungo again, and immediately became confused, enough so she mounted her own Triceratops and rode away to the rear ranks where she knew Artebrates would be, and that the Battle of Mungo's Mud House was over.

Compared Artebrates to Mungo and wished her lord dead, and herself the commander of the Fermanian army.

She also found Lord Artebrates waving his house flag when it should have been The Mighty One's Carman's, so had committed treason.

Cathbadh

"The Legion senators declared for the bread rioters; they demand Artebrates be emperor.

Handfuls shout for me, "Let Sess rule, give us Sess," so I fear this crazy world and spend my time assuring Carman I am loyal; besides, I am not to leave her castle so, am prisoner.

Outwardly I obey but use secret tunnels to disobey, I must ingratiate myself with Captain Clinton and he is pleased with the maps I have sent him, for without maps, invaders found years later as skeletons, lost, starved to death, flying mazarrats got them.

"*Traitor,*" I sing so all the world knows.

In return he has granted me my wish of being governor of our lizard people, and to keep them in order, thus I have saved my race and prospered.

A go between.

Now a very bright light seen day and night, it is the star ship coming closer, but Carman believes it is Fermanian so her cruelty to humans increases.

"Of course, it is dear," I lie and croon lover's words to her, Captain Clinton will know what to do with her and Lord Artebrates.

I could do with a nice shiny new belt and shoes!

Chapter 8 Empress Red Sun

And the building was of chewed red dust and tunnels humid and lit by glow worms.

And the termites of Telephassa made it, the original slave workers of the Fermanian reptile ones.

"Are you sure you killed Mungo?"

Artebrates looked at the slim back of his empress trying not to let fear seep into his voice, "I am sure Mighty One," he stuttered remembering waving his house flag and not hers.

And The Mighty One saw from the end of the Royal Observation Tunnel the rose flower below, with humans on sixteen-foot ladders, plucking yellow petals as a

coelophysis sat hunched holding reins to the flying wagon, waiting for it to fill up with petals.

From the coelophysis head dropped a pink skull cap and about his groin a black lion cloth.

"Horrendous," The Mighty One and Artebrates lost to her meaning advanced to see, what, she gazed at?

"The humans?" He salivated, above yellow clouds.

But Carman meant his flag waving exhibition.

"Send for Cathbadh," The Mighty One and left to walk down the Royal Observation Tunnel clapping hands to make the white bulbous termite workers hurry to send her message.

And Artebrates allowed a smile seeing the remains of runaway slaves, dead and moaning for Mungo's deliverance.

"Always Mungo," he spat and Carman now sitting on her solidified gold bee wax throne looked at him with pity. "We let the Death Root vine grow through their orifices and still others join Mungo," The Mighty One.

Artebrates "They out breed us so can afford their losses," and faced his empress relaxing since she showed understanding of his problem, while below twenty-six human prisoners strapped to beams, so young tender Death Root vines wrapped about them, sucking the life out of them.

Flowers opened twenty feet higher up, but it was the roots that yielded the bitter black poisonous gum.

Now and again a piece of human dropped to the ground as fertilizer.

And Carman saw Artebrates as a fragile old man and dismissed his flag waving as an old man's folly, and not a traitor rallying her enemies to his cause. Besides there was no one else to dangerously lead her armies apart from herself.

Why the aged decrypt Artebrates had had enough of war, he would not break her empire by civil war for his son Nudd, whom she saw as the real threat needed being

banished, *their son from a night's illicit fun, He ho*," I am a naughty girl, time I got a boyfriend He Ho.

"Yes, and be married and tied down with dozens of brats," *The Elder relived.*

Silly of her, Artebrates in his youth had been her lover, but now, his skin was wrinkled, repulsive, not just from looks but from his stressful defeats from Mungo.

And now he had authorized the artists to chisel his great victory at Mungo's Mud House in the Temple of Fame. Already human masons who were better at details for

their hands were nimbler had started work.

They had five fingered hands whereas the number of fingers on a Fermanian was decided by the roll of genetic dice, and what reptilian ancestor they hailed from.

handful were still born with claws, and these quickly removed and lain outside the cities never seen again.

"Go ahead Artebrates carve yourself into history," Carman was tired of wars and Artebrates.

At that moment, his age relaxed his bowls and filled the room with wind.

"Mungo's wound and he fell hard to the floor for forgiveness, and hurt himself doing so.

And to be rid of him she kicked him toward the door, and he fearing death managed to leave the room quick enough.

The open-door bringing relief to the stinky room.

When he was gone, she checked her face for wrinkles.

The gene surgeons had done well all thanks to a tomato, **for shuttle genes had been** reversed, not to give her new genes but to remove genes that caused a dead body to rot.

"I am like the human Incorruptible One," she smiled, seeing her body in a mausoleum visited by worshipping Fermanians as The Mighty One who destroyed the humans.

"*Being a cheeky mazarrat I added a wind of well, not mine as girl mazarrats are made of sugar gums, so stank her up good, like I said not mine as girls are made of sugar and spice,*" the singer running for fresh air.

Anyway: Artebrates had no new genes, it was her desire he have none for his flag waving display.

"Die slowly Artebrates," she hissed and Artebrates who wished for life knew she was selfish for selecting favorites for this gene therapy, while men who fought to secure her empire died of old age.

And he hated her now for every bruise she put on his flesh, and outside picked up his new bronze shield bearer.

And knew he was lucky to be still in command of the Southern Army because he had waved his house flag, not Carman's flag and gasped at the numbers who came to it.

As for her flag he had ripped it from her flag bearer and given it to his shield bearer to shred.

And this man Carman publicly blamed for raising Artebrates flag so had him executed, not Artebrates. She was not daft; she was aware of the numbers who had

flocked to Artebrates flag; he would die naturally by old age, and none would blame her.

But a mazarrat had seen.

"The battle had been hard fought and our dead numerous, but Mungo was dead," Artebrates personal letter to Carman who planned Hebat her fourteen-year-old to replace Artebrates and win the armies heart and then she would eat Artebrates.

"Blooming cannibals is what they are," a pretty mazarrat holding her nose.

That was OK she would acquire his general ship by doing so; the public would like that.

And Artebrates knew he had successfully got his empress drunk and bedded four years past by reminding her of their past affair, and when she awoke next day, she was

revolted by the wrinkled prune she had entwined herself about, him. *"A wrinkled prune."*

This union had made the boy Nudd.

With such thoughts he tumbled into his sedan chair and drew the red curtains shutting the world outside.

His hands creaked with arthritis, and he felt the scars of battle Mungo had put on him.

Gone was the spring of his back legs from years of riding the armored Triceratops, replaced by bowlegs from riding the pha saddle.

"John Wrexham and Cameron were bow legged freaks." Not like my handsome boyfriend.

"Hope at; last," The Elder.

Artebrates always summoned to the Mighty One straight from the hunt before bathing in rose scented milk. No wonder The Mighty One favored Lord Vinki?

"Even I had to peg my mazarrat nose, see it was not me that stunk the room but him," the singer expecting believed.

Always Mungo, Mungo and now Mungo was dead and with this thought came fear.

The Mighty One Carman would no longer need him and then?

And remembered waving his house flag and feared.

Remembered the male child Hebat from the union of Carman and her brother Annunaki who had died on the field with Mungo's spear in his back, while Artebrates sat drinking warm green tea in his field tent.

Why by god Telephassa had he allowed Annunaki to lead a scouting party that day?

Why had Mungo been in the area when he should not have?

Peelock had reported him miles away!

"Peelock outsmarted you, old bunion." Our girl.

Why had Carman sent her beloved Annunaki in the first place?

And Artebrates had blamed.

His tongue spliced so he would speak with a dribble for ever more.

But Nudd his lineage to the throne was now secure, and he had nothing to do with it!

Even when they tortured him further and prized off his belly scales so his innards threatened to spill out, he proclaimed his innocence over Annunaki's death.

In the end blinded in one eye from the heat of a dagger and deaf in one ear from a stick pushed in; Carman allowed him life.

"But she knew he was innocent anyway. She was a murderer killing her own brother." The mazarrats had knowledge, wisdom.

She just wanted the public to stop thinking she had murdered Annunaki. Put the suspicion on someone like Artebrates, and have him tortured a little for effect, not too much or the army did revolt.

He was always a useful scapegoat, in the past, present and for the future, scapegoats needed.

And as he made his way through the Companion Tunnel, he prayed to a statue of Telephassa for war against Carman. Nudd could be emperor, his son and because he had served another all his life did not think to make himself emperor.

Now the Mighty One had returned to the observation box and had watched the coelophysis drive the wagon away, cracking the whip on thirty humans pulling it

towards the lunching pha, where dandelion balloons would take the pollen to royal granaries.

"Annunaki had to die," Carman mused not seeing a secret door open behind a bull headed statue of a praying mantis.

And Cathbadh entered, heard, and glided to stand at her back. And knew why she had spared old Artebrates because she had paid Peelock to lie about Mungo, knowing Annunaki was going to his death, and thus one more claimant to her throne gone.

Annunaki had ambitious, wanted the Rose Throne for himself. She knew he preferred his own sex, was more into poppy seed than Artebrates, was a drunk, only

thought of lining his pockets and gambling and had made the mistake of hitting her, and the only difference between them was that she held the power.

And Annunaki was only one in a line of lovers, she had no intention of putting a man on the throne except her son; there had not been a man since King Sess.

Besides no one hit her and that had been Annunaki's big mistake; even his beauty could not save him.

Illustration: Genetically altered to solve the Fermanian problems, but was coelophysis super slave come solder too late?

He also had human blood in him that if became common knowledge would be the end of the Rose Throne.

He also bedded whores, paid them for perversions, and had the pox.

A secret she had had to endure for the empress must be disease free.

Annunaki had had to die.

"One day I will spin around and stab you Cathbadh if you keep entering in unannounced."

"If I were an assassin, I would have killed you Mighty One, I am instead your favorite," and slipped his lilac scented hands about her waist.

At last, she turned and looked into the eyes of her bin.

Cathbadh to rid her mind of bad thoughts against him changed the subject, and concluded she was too infatuated with him to notice his dealings with the star ship. Her Tu, spirit was tired of being in this physical world, he would have to encourage her departure: he was not that worthless drunk Annunaki and would make no mistakes.

"He was just another man in a line of lovers who had thought the same thoughts. Whereas I know how to keep my boyfriend in order, with a whip, a joke." And she laughed at her silly joke and the audience, girls that is, thought about whipping boyfriends.

They were all dead; Cathbadh only lived as he was useful.

And as lust filled his eyes, she read his thoughts for his mental barrier was down.

She would soon have the human masons seal that secret tunnel with Cathbadh behind it, you see she was paranoid, it came with the job.

So Cathbadh better wake up, but he was a man, full of himself, and Carman was a mixed up woman and it never occurred to him she read his body language time and time again.

"Bring on the masons!"

And she saw his ruthlessness as dominance, and no one dominated her.

And in the Tunnel of Fame human masons carved Lord Artebrates riding a Triceratops pushing his barbed lance into Mungo's head.

Another group dusted a six-foot aquaria rock with more pictures showing Artebrates cutting off with his war club six heads belonging to the six companions of Mungo.

And the human stone masons groaned not wanting to believe they had no deliverer any the more the more.

Cathbadh

"Captain Clinton we cannot enter orbit as the main booster has failed," an engineer reported.

Clinton looked at the red ball in front of him and wondered

how humans could have colonized this inhospitable looking planet. It looked too much like the Red Planet back home: he also knew the red sun meant nothing; he had seen blue suns and expected to see other colors before he passed over.

Not all suns burned as Earth's as a nuclear fireball.

He knew black holes existed to take the curious explorer into new dimension of Edinburgh Clark's, magnetic energy, the new worlds of Saint Paul, "We are surrounded by unseen worlds."

"We got too land, Cathbadh said the place is crawling with lizards eating humans, we got to land and save our people," and forgot he was going to make Cathbadh

governor as agreed; Cathbadh was one of them lizards that ate human sweetmeat.

And visualized spanking new reptile leather shoes in his cupboard.

Whereas Cathbadh was visualizing seeing himself sitting on the Rose Throne with human space marines behind him, the real power and if he did what Captain

Clinton wanted, lord it overall.

 Human and Fermanians would live together as equals and that was better than be a lizard latrine cleaner.

And pity he could not see Captain's Clinton's thoughts for the man had just remembered Cathbadh was a lizard, and there was a vacancy for a toilet cleaner aboard ship.

"Skip to my loo, here Cathbadh, a present of loo brushes and cleaners, am I not a kind thoughtful mazarrat, and almost forgot, bleach?"

Chapter 8 Civil War

Lord Vinki rode his riding pha across the grey slate plains towards Telephassa City.

Already feeling sluggish as the red sun sank behind pink clouds beyond the Moon
Mountains.

Beautiful granite outcrops with snow on the peaks that mirrored the moons reflective
light.

The icy glaciers amongst these mountains contained a bluish ice and they glowed like the moon, in the darkness of the night; hence their name, Moon Mountains but Vinki did not see any beauty in them; he was a lizard needing heated up.

And ahead he saw the towers of Telephassa embedded with gems that twinkling proclaimed, "We are rich citizens."

"Curse all human slaves," he shouted and his House Berserka companions understood, the sun was dying for the day and with it their body heat and their running
human bearers would see them as they were, lizards, reptiles, evolutionary backward compared to humans.

"*We mazarrats see everything and sing it loud so lizard hear.*" *That annoyed her.*

Now Vinki must rely upon coelophysis for protection against Mungo's raiders for Vinki had not heard Artebrates had slain Mungo, for he had been trading with Peelock and then off to visit his cotton and tea plantations.

And then the twenty-foot pha stumbled in the greying light in a gopher hole, and Vinki walked air and broke both his human femur bones, which stuck out of his gold helmet.

And would awake later in darkness.

"Bloody humans," his last words.

*

"He has been to Peelock's, look many of the pha are loaded down with goods," Angus pointing at them.

"Then we will take from him what is ours," Mungo replied looking down the hillside in bloom with red poppies.

"Will you lead?" Angus asked.

Mungo touched the side of his head, no, the stitches were sore, and he felt half his scalp missing from Lord Artebrates war club bashing.

"I will go," Angus Ogg beginning to crawl backwards, but Mungo restrained, "It is time for the younger ones, signal them forward or they will never learn fighting skills."

So, Ogg did as bid and soon the red poppies were moving as the young warriors crawled through them.

The Fermanians tired and cold put it down to a night breeze.

And Angus beamed fatherly pride as he saw his son Hamo lead the war party.

And Mungo thanked life Hamo was bright and quick thinking, rather than just relying on brute strength like his father did.

Ivor Novello, was behind Hamo, built like a rock, brown eyed and haired and in his hands a blow pipe, and spear, but around his chest a bandoleer and two handguns.

On his neck a diamond torc that had rubbed with mud so it would not shine under the moon.

Lachie beside him, a small red headed man with a sawn-off shotgun and on his back bow and arrows.

He also had muddied his gold wrist bracelets.

Behind him Kern a man who carried a single shot hunting rifle.

He wore a black leather girdle embedded with gems.

Keira was near him, the woman of the group, her flowing hair kept out of her eyes by a thin gold beaten head band.

In one hand a small axe and in the other an automatic pistol.

And all carried a small shield with a vertical slit for a weapon fired through.

These were young ones sneaking towards cold Vinki and his reptile Berserkas.

They wanted to kill lizards who drank fermented pee as beer. Lizards was disgusting so deserved to die.

They also had lots of jewelry off their corpses, and explains the wealth on these young warriors, Mungo was not paying them!

"Sometimes I think Keira should not be risked," Angus Ogg quietly to Mungo.

Mungo made no reply, his head still hurt, and time enough in the future to settle old scores not forgiven yet.

"For Mungo had not forgotten so how to forgive?" We mazarrats can teach if they sit and be quiet mand have faith in mazarrat teachings, the singer singing.

Now Mungo had let Keira join them because she helped him forget Leah, eight years was a long time since Leah had been with him?

It was good the woman was here, she helped make them a family. The nights were lonely without Keira who went from bed to bed making all one.

Except she never visited Angus Ogg.

"Good odds against the Fermanians," it was Mungo's joke,

but Angus did not laugh,

he was jealous, Keira was on his mind as usual, so he still wished death on Mungo.

But death came to the Fermanians and the coelophysis who were all too sluggish for

the night was, cold.

A night lapwing rose in protest over the noise of gunfire.

Now Mungo ordered Ono and her lions in.

An arrow hit a lion's brass body plates and snapped.

And a hunchback sat with Lord Vinki in the Fermanian camp, disguised as a laborer seeking passage to Telephassa, and there Leah whom he hoped to take back to Mungo, who would reward him with sanctuary?

The hunchback also hoped to assassinate Vinki, by choking him when he slept, by dropping a baby venomous snake in Vinki's shoe, by mixing ground glass in his tea, anyway, if, Vinki died.

"Forward men forward men," Vinki shouted; he did not know what else to shout but did not want them following him the other way.

The hunchback decided it was time to get the heck out of here.

It looked like the humans were about to kill Vinki anyway.

That is when the hunchback on his pha sailed over the palisade walls that were now on fire.

And Vinki recognized him and mounted a pha to follow suit.

"Save us," Fermanian Lords and friends of Vinki begged.

"Useless circus acts," he replied and followed the hunchback.

Then the humans rushed into the camp shooting

anything still standing.

So, Lords tried to follow Vinki on pha but where shoot or pulled off and slain on the spot.

"Mercy, mercy," a Fermanian lord pleaded but Hamo shot him close, he was Angus's Ogg's son all right.

And when the killing done, the looting began. Any Fermanian or coelophysis moaning found alive stabbed, some more when one was cutting money belts off.

Just to make sure the wounded did not have any ideas about shooting you and going to paradise for it.

Then trophies sought, that was worse, trophies taken from the wounded.

"They lost their heads that night." The singer having a joke.

"Humans must not forget why the Fermanian rule is ending, because they are an abomination. Let not the humans become the new abomination," a mazarrat sang

and repeated by mazarrats in B flat.

*

And Angus Ogg was jealous of Hamo for he had gone with Keira and now sought them.

"Give this gold torc to Mungo, he trusts you," Angus and Hamo suspected a foul deed for his father's words were full of acid. And the torc wrapped in lizard skin.

"Open it not Hamo, it is for Mungo."

And Keira covered herself with new silken robes once the property of Vinki.

"He is The Wild One," Hamo.

Illustration: Moon Mountains and poppies

"Tell him you wish to honor him for today's killings," Angus meaning the extermination of Fermanians, "you are my son," Angus reminding that Hamo do his bidding, "Malachi can join him, all lizards can," for Angus was appealing to Hamo's hate of lizard.

So, the boy went, and as soon as he was gone Angus threw himself upon Keira.

And Hamo came to Mungo and Malachi sitting by a river and he spoke his father's words to him and unwrapped the skin from the torc, and oversaw the gold, then threw it at Mungo.

"What is gold to me Hamo?" Mungo asked and with a sword flicked the gold torc at Hamo who caught it from reflex, for he was human, and valued gold.

With gold, "I could buy land from Peelock and build a house for Keira to live with me in."

"You don't need gold for that Hamo, your friends will help you build your house," Malachi laughed.

But Hamo had fallen dying from poison smeared on the torc.

And Mungo roared a death chant and The Elder hearing hurried to Mungo fearing the worse.

"Murderer," Keira spat at Angus, and he laughed and forced

himself on her again.

"Who did this?" Malachi asked the dying Hamo.

He did not reply.

"I hate you," Hamo coughed at Malachi shocked.

"Why I am your friend?"

"You are lizard."

"I am sorry Malachi," Mungo offended and drew his dagger to pierce Hamo with as if by that act he was cutting out the hate humans had for Fermanians.

But Hamo greeted him with a death rattle.

And Mungo plunged the dagger into Hamo, and none knew if Hamo died by the dagger or the poison first.

But dead he was.

And Malachi sickened by hate asked Mungo to kill him also.

And Mungo refused and sat down next to Malachi sickened by all the hate which meant so many brave men killed.

Then Angus Ogg arrived and overcome by shock and grief for it was Hamo not Mungo who lay dead.

"You are banished from my side for ever more, take the body of your son and leave," Mungo and Malachi understood the words and with a sword cut off Hamo's
head.

"When it rots pha hide will cover it as a reminder too would be traitor's death awaits them, be gone Angus," Mungo told the father who dragged his son's body away and he wanted to kill Malachi and Mungo but feared death so did nothing.

And Keira seeing him threw stones at his back hitting him.

The blood of the mazarrat murderer is not on Mungo," mazarrats sang from rhododendron bushes so proclaiming the fulfilment of the prophecy.

"Murderer," one mazarrat added but who had she

indicated, he who poisoned or he who pierced with the dagger?

*

Now the hunchback led Vinki's pha as he rode towards the Termite Castle Zigaratta, **twenty leagues** distance from Telephassa Termite City, and tempted to leave

the sleeping Vinki as dinosaur food but was afraid of being alone in this wilderness.

He was not Mungo of the lions brought up in the country.

The hunchback was a city loving individual so allowed Vinki to live for company.

And next to Vinki surviving Wonder Lords dozing on their pha also, they who had managed to escape, only the brave Berserkas dying as they attempted to make a stand.

Only six miles to reach Ka Zigaratta.

And Malachi saw the pha ride past with Vinki and stood out of the thorn bush and followed them taking short cuts. He had not wanted to be with Mungo as he had been having identity problems; he was a Fermanian who was standing idle as John and Cameron were executing prisoners.

Whenever Mungo stopped dancing to the Unseen Malachi drifted away from Mungo, for it was the Unseen that that kept Malachi as Mungo's friend.

What was Mungo fighting for, to make humans like John the masters of Fermanians, may the lizard gods protect Malachi then.

Three miles to Ka Zigaratta.

And then Malachi collided into Vinki's friends and was disgusted by their feminisms, and they only saw him as an unlucky warrior trampled by them.

"Where are your men to protect us?" One asked.

"Humans everywhere," Malachi and went over to the now riderless pha and led it over to the dismounted prone Wonder

Lord, bent and pretended to check his neck pulse, when he was in fact pressing a thumb deep onto an artery till the pulse stopped.

"One less Wonder to poison society and indeed Malachi was having an identity crisis.

He had just killed another of his race." The mazarrat singer waiting till they moved off and then steal the yellow stockings and sexy stuff.

"We will say he died from another accident, and you have saved us," the Wonder Lords knowing Malachi would suffer for the death of their friend. Now Malachi was also strong and a handsome warrior and they knew how to use their positions to corrupt

young men.

"Were they blind, Malachi was aging, his bump sagged with them, and" she shut up.

Two miles from Ka Zigaratta and there was only two Wonder Lords left in front of Malachi who rode up the back of the nearest and sunk his sword deep into the side of the man's neck.

One mile to Ka Zigaratta and one Wonder Lord left and behind him a grinning Malachi who thought this game jolly playful fun.

He was going home to Telephassa and wondered what changes had occurred, he had heard of his kind no longer ate humans.

And it was not due to the Modernist Party of Vinki for the changes, like Vinki he knew about the spaceship. The future was for humans, anyone with brains was making

friends with humans, trade was possible and were there was brass and Vinki was making it.

And when Malachi thundered across the draw bridge gates at the third wall, he was alone.

"Who are you?" A Berserka asked.

"Egalbenathan cousin of Artebrates and centurion over Decurion's and come to collect Artebrates back to the army camp," Malachi lied thinking what Leah was like these days, and these thoughts helped him to remain calm in front of the guards.

(And the hunchback did not wake Vinki up for he knew the Fermanian who had joined them was Malachi and was doing what he did not have the courage to do.

But near Telephassa they separated, for the hunchback was fearful he might be next, so deliberately took Vinki's pha he was leading and went quickly down a trail leaving the last Wonder Lord to his fate.)

Why Malachi thundered across the draw bridge alone, *"murderers everywhere, better watch my back, I heard The Elder has it in for me,"* and did not sing in case she gave her position away.

"I have not had a single murderous thought on how to get rid of my ambitious cousin," The Elder whose nose did not grow like Mr. Pinocchio.

Chapter 9 Zigaratta

"Mighty One, we are gathered to hear your words of wisdom and obey," the herald shouted to the assembled guests at tables below the Mighty One's Great Table.

WHY Carman looked at her lords and at the herald who spoke the same words every evening.

Well, she had no words of wisdom for them; irritated after her encounter with Cathbadh.

What she wanted was a bath where she could think the future out.

So, the Lords of Telephassa looked at her expectantly, why she did not know? She felt like a dried-up seed husk, they used as balloons.

So, she stood up, Lords anticipating her to start eating spat out mouthfuls of blood wine or dropped their large forks with bits of starters back onto the table.

Carman had stood to utter wisdom and taken them by surprise.

"The humans must die, or we make peace with them, a star ship is here," and she sat down and drank blood wine and nodded to the carvers to begin work on the roasts.

And the carvers began.

The food was squirming on tables below about her Lords and Ladies.

And her carver with assistant with pins skinned her food prepared in garlic butter and then fried the skin to crackling. Outside in the slave quarters a warm breeze took the smells of hogs barbecued, it made Carman ravenous for humans.

And her food tried to push an apple out of its mouth but fainted with shock and pain.

And Carman's guest all smacked lips as their peptic acids went to work in their stomachs, for they loved crackling so much, but none could eat till Carman ate first.

And when she did, none ate faster than Hebat, Carman's fourteen-year-old son and none looked at Nudd with more loathing than he.

Nudd the five-year-old who pushed aside his plate of crackling and ate sweet yam covered in hot runny peanut butter.

And the carver carved and drained blood from food to prepare a broth mixed with sweet red wines and chili peppers to fire lizard blood in this chilly night.

Why Hebat gulped his broth all down and asked for seconds for warmth.

Nudd drank warm buttermilk.

And Carman saw and was pleased Hebat was strong and knew the future lay with him, he was for supremacy over the food that was human.

"What difference between lizards and humans, both roasted their meats, the humble rooster, a living dinosaur, and humans who ate chicken, a cycle, they eat each other, now where did I put that honey melon, yummy found it," the singing mazarrat and her fans ate what she ate.

Then Lord Artebrates late as his arthritis made him slow entered the hall and sat next to Nudd, and the diners went silent at his affront to Carman.

He had made no attempt to apologize for his lateness.

"Never mind he was old and harmless, a joke, let all see The Mighty Artebrates who would lead armies against her, why he could hardly walk." The mazarrats so carman heard.

"Tongue," Carman ordered as the curses and moans of her food were beginning to annoy her as it always did.

And the tongue taken and "Mungo will avenge me," no longer uttered by her food.

The food was weak; Fermanians knew how to take pain, their criminal code made sure, of that, why the way her food withered and squirmed she just could not understand why humans were on the ascent?

"Give me the eyes," she commanded, and the eyes taken so the food could not loath her as eaten.

"Give them to Nudd," and it was deliberate, and her guests fell silent for this boy might be their emperor one day and lead them into battle.

And Nudd looked at his mother whom he longed for a hug and never got.

Now Artebrates still ate humans but not in front of Nudd, so had more brains left to him than Carman cared to admit, took the eyes, and swallowed, belched satisfaction and winded and then waved the carver away.

For the rest of the evening Carman spoke to no one as she watched Nudd and Artebrates, and saw Legion Lords, men from the army bow to Artebrates and Nudd as

they passed, this was not good, Hebat would be their emperor not Nudd.

*

Now later that night she stood at the end of Zigaratta Observation Tunnel breathing in the perfumes of the flower gardens, listening to the quarrelling humans in their slave pens. Fighting over the last of the pig crackling and women, even handsome men.

Looking at the million windows throwing light out of the great termite mounds twenty miles away.

"Bin I am here," Cathbadh corning out of the wall again.

But Carman seethed and reached for a sword hanging from the tunnel wall.

"Angry bin?"

"Pretty soon you will not be my bin," and Carman span and slashed empty air were Cathbadh had been.

Now he stood to her right grinning like a cat.

So, she slashed again then gripped her stomach and dropped the sword.

Illustration: A flower garden, the blood thirsty lizards liked tranquility.

When she moved Cathbadh realized she was pregnant with his child so, hurried to her and got her to lie down.

"Why didn't you tell me?"

"Another heir means another war," she breathed out.

"Yes, that meant civil war but this time the heir was his." What would he do?

"If it is a daughter there will be no wars," he said and at once both knew Hebat would be in danger then.

For ten thousand years only, an empress had sat on the

Sunflower Throne since King Sess had died. And Hupasiyas, the shaman was saying his femurs and molars were aching, predicting troubled times unless an empress found.

A daughter would guarantee Cathbadh's position of influence and Hebat's journey into the purple other world. And pain racked Carman for she loved Hebat but a daughter would change all that, and she knew it.

And Carman took from under her kimono a dagger and struck at Cathbadh, who was so shocked he left her, he would return later when his bin was in better temperament.

Wenches carrying little mins were known to be unpredictable.

"All these babies, these lizards had contraceptives, no excuses, I better not be pregnant?" Our singer and her fans argued over names.

And as Cathbadh slid behind the bull head into his secret tunnel Carman pulled a silk chain hanging from the roof and summoned a Fermanian officer and four coelophysis.

"Centurion Leah."

Leah deliberately showed her fangs emphasizing her reptilian nature for she heard mazarrats, sing she had human blood.

"I am pure blooded mazarrat for we mazarrats built a great wall mentally not to mix with other races, well they have germs, giggle, but Mungo is handsome. "Someone gives me a bow and arrow," The Elder pulling his ears.

She had also thrown caged mazarrats down wells to silence them for good.

"Does Mungo live?" Carman and Leah told all.

"Bring a slave," and one brought, and Leah told to bite him, and he salivated and was sick, fell to his belly and died.

"Why did your poison not kill Mungo?"

Leah shrugged.

Why Carman thought Leah had not poisoned her arrows, and then remembered the incorruptible.

"You must destroy the Incorruptible One, only you can get to her through Mungo,

for the mazarrats sing he still loves you and not Keira.

You may see your son now and Leah left to visit Conn, her eight-year-old puzzled that Mungo still loved her. Why?

Had she and Mungo been lovers, what about Conn? Who was his father, was it Mungo? Such dangerous questions needed traitorous answers.

*

"My darling," Leah hissing wrapping herself about Conn whose long black locks was of human hair, also his blue eyes with only a hint of Fermanian pink retina.

And Leah examined his human skin and like her own had soft scales under it. But disappointed his tail had not grown as her own had, since Cathbadh was her

doctor these days.

"Leah," the hunchback entering and hugging them both.

The boy squirmed; hugging was for girls.

"He is Mungo's child your man thing lover and not by Cathbadh's orders to amuse friends of his as comforter," the hunchback, "that wicked man has inserted shuttle

genes into you to make you more lizard than you were made."

Leah pushed him away, she was Fermanian.

Now Cathbadh had been listening behind a secret wall he now pushed and appeared saying, "She is mine and you have given me much power over Artebrates and your life is forfeit for returning to Telephassa hunchback," Cathbadh.

Now the hunchback drew his dagger and Cathbadh ordered

Leah to defend him.

At once Leah wrestled with the hunchback and Cathbadh laughed.

Of course, Leah succeeded in holding her father still so Cathbadh could play with the dagger upon the hunchback.

Death was a mercy and like all mercies Cathbadh believed waited for. And Mercy came in the form of Malachi seeking Leah and he threw Cathbadh away like

paper.

Now Leah stuck her dagger into Malachi's wrist for she knew him as enemy.

"She is being turned into a monster Malachi, we must take her away from here," the hunchback urgently.

"*And their shouts brought Berserkas for outlaws in traps should be silent,*" mazarrats sang.

"Holy Telephassa dung Berserkas," and Malachi hit Leah on the jaw and knocked her out, then threw her body on his shoulder and threw himself out the cane window, and ignoring his wound bounced, leapt, and fell down vines to the bottom.

Behind him fell the hunchback. "*Poor man, he hit every bit of stem and branch during his groaning descent, landing heavily with a thud, giggle.*"

"Run, only twenty miles to Mungo's camp," Malachi joked but was serious.

"I am going by pha," the hunchback answered back.

None turned back for they did not want to see Conn crying for his mother or they did have seen a smiling Artebrates at the window.

"Leah will bring me the weapon and Mungo's hair," Artebrates for Leah had told him Mungo got his strength from his hair.

Fate was in control, always is.

And Carmen is a murderer too.

Chapter 10 Nodegamma

And Mungo sat on a dandelion flower with The Elder below on red grass alone, for his companions had deserted him after Hamo's death, and Angus's banishment as foretold by The Elder.

And the place was Nodegamma valley and goats grazed here. While smoke rose twenty miles away from Telephassa as civil war raged.

Weakening its defenses.

And Mungo and his teacher were watching pha riders approaching chased by other riders.

Anyway: Once upon a time there was a man called Cathbadh who had wanted to be the greatest scientific mind of his age and race, for into his work he buried his

slumbering thoughts of being emperor one day; he was from King Sess.

And then he saw a human star ship and his mind became unstable and believed his Mighty One must make way for another who could oppose the human star travelers.

"And choose himself as the next emperor, FOR HE WAS unstable, mad, a lunatic, giggle. Think I will declare myself Empress of Mazarrats," yes she and The Elder choked on a fig.

For in frosty winter month, which is October, Cathbadh poisoned Hebat, Carman's fourteen year old *"who was debased anyway, giggle, another Vinki, and my first proclamation would be Banishment for The Elder, giggle,"* and her audience looked for him.

"Who has done this?" Carman with waxen face and Cathbadh fell to his face denying blaming Wonder Lord Vinki or Artebrates.

"Mistress, bring in the infra-red scanners to see if the unseen has been at work," Cathbadh blaming spirit folk.

And in her misery, she did so.

And when the Prefect of Police used the machine Cathbadh shouted, "See a legionary boot print, it is the work of the Legion Senators who want war always."

For Cathbadh had worn them to shift the blame when he had poisoned.

He had dropped yellow cobra venom onto Hebat's sleeping open lips and sent him to nightmare land.

The human slaves would celebrate.

Death to you all," Carman sick of them and summoned Artebrates and all Legion Senators and had Cathbadh held for she suspected him, and to his horror slashed his belly with a short sword so, he gasped frightened for his life.

"My, min, you carry my heir," and so gave himself away and Carman had him dragged to the dungeons and all the way she kicked and stood on his body parts so he

groaned. And behind her followed her court and were smiling for they liked to see great people fall.

And when he swooned, she demanded water to refresh him and then continued stomping him.

"*For she was a demented stomper wearing army boots, giggle. He was a murderer and remember Leah, deserves a good stomping and I will sing accompaniment,*" and she did.

"Carman desires the same fate upon us, we must protect ourselves Artebrates," Legion Senators his friends asking him to rebel.

But the old soldier came to Carman again, "I am needed."

"Needed to see Nudd die," her reply that alienated him for he loved Nudd, "I want your head off now," and Berserkas pulled him to his knees and readied axe.

"She was a mother in grief even if she was a lizard, a reptile, she had feelings," so will forgive HIM a song and her audience clapped happy.

"He is Artebrates, a Berserka refusing to swing the axe and these men let Artebrate go even though it meant their own death from Carman's loyal executioner.

But when Artebrates got home to flee to safety with Nudd, he found the boy with a pillow over his face, very silent and dead.

Illustration: Mungo and The Elder sat on the giant flower.

So, he screamed and wished for the destruction of Telephassa the place of darkness.

And Artebrates led his Berserkas against Carman, so smoke rose over Telephassa City and this are what Mungo, and The Elder were watching.

The War of Radioactivity when King Sess had polluted the land and the cycle was about to begin again.

Karma was visiting the Fermanians, humans beware, and karma will visit also, for what comes around goes around.

And who had suffocated the little boy, who could do such

an evil thing.

"*He was only a lizard,*" a mazarrat sang.

*

"It is Malachi," Mungo still on the flower.

"*Listen Mungo,*" The Elder hearing mazarrats sing so passing one from another what

they saw to The Elder.

An evolved form of the jungle telephone mazarrat style.

"*It is Leah and fate coming.*"

And Mungo jumped down off the flower and ran to meet her, and saw John Wrexham, Cameron Black and Peelock with pha riders with weapons chasing Malachi

and Leah.

So, Mungo roared and Ono with lions ran out of the grass and attacked the humans and died on both sides unnecessary for the humans had Vinki's laser guns.

Now John told a great army of lizards was approaching, and rode hard to see from the valley cliffs, and saw and summoned all his men, and Peelock did likewise.

For as the cloud of dust they saw got nearer, so did the din of horns and drums.

"It is the men of Telephassa and Hurreva City and beyond, a great army of Fermanians, we need all humans here even the wild tribe members of the red grass and

beyond, where is Cadfael?

And Cadfael told to call his people here with these words, "Nodegamma is our Armageddon, ride hard then and fast. A mighty lizard army march here for the

final conflict between human and Fermanian."

And Cadfael rode, the wild tribe members, they who had made him a blood brother he sought.

And above a star ship seen orbiting and none knew if it was human or lizard except Cathbadh, and not believed, and, in a place, he did not want to be.

Therefore, Carman led her peoples to Nodegamma.

A deserted unholy place fit for crows and dung beetles whom the Fermanians used to clean their streets.

And Artebrates also came to this spot, but not to battle humans!

They were Legion men, Legion Senators who hated Carman for Cathbadh was not the only one hanging upside down over a brazier filled with hot coals.

Hebat needed revenged and Carman needed a million blood lettings for revenge, even the street beggars were not safe. Dozens butchered by Carman walking the

streets with sword, slashing any, she vented her grief; of course, she had Berserka guards with her.

"What's the point of being a queen if you cannot excise authority?" A mazarrat sang asking.

And behind these men the camp followers and curious, the sightseers, the souvenir collectors, the mums, and babes of the Berserkas.

So, the battle would take place on three fronts.

While overhead a star ship prepared to enter orbit.

Cathbadh

"Oh, gods of my people save me," Cathbadh begged as his lips cracked from the heat and his hair all singed off.

"What gods, we never see you praying in the temples?" One of his torturers who saw this as an invitation to pull on Cathbadh's tongue with a heated clamp.

"I cannot stand such screaming," a mazarrat complained.

"Are you praying, I cannot hear you, speak up," the torturer and clamped again.

"Maybe the gods cannot hear Cathbadh, but I can," the mazarrat wishing he were not needed to spy for The Elder.

And Captain John Clinton on the star ship above was using **telescopic atom cameras** to watch the battle below.

*"**Even mazarrats have not invented such cameras that seek atoms by heat and then reassemble them as an image,**" **The Elder when told of this camera admiringly but also**

it made him worry, these arriving humans were not slaves.

"Mazarrat be careful," was his advice to his kind.

And a scream broke the night but the night above the dungeon was full of cicada songs and mazarrats singing the news.

And the night in the dungeon filled with a sizzling sound as the torturer pored chilly water over Cathbadh.

The torturer knew Cathbadh was a rich man, Cathbadh still had fingers and could write what he was willing to pay to stay alive.

Of course, the torturer would take the cash and still do his work; Carman still lived

"All murderers."

*"Like you, for dream of replacing me, thinking of pushing me of the toip of ta ree,,mm? Cousins, who needs them?"*The Elder.

"You do for your lineage dies with you," her.

"I have never married, I am a prophet, too busy." T.E.

"Or you prefer your own play and not a beautiful

mazarrat like me, giggle." She was so rude.

"Grrr, where is she," and The Elder hunted
her with murderess thoughts.

"All murderers giggle," and threw an open perfume
bottle at him, so it scented him of women.

"Grrr, where is the?"

End

"It is Carman, and she clutches her belly," Ono in lion tongue for Carman was in danger of miscarrying.

And Ono with what lions still lived attacked her on her howdah triceratops and

speared.

And The Elder let a single tear fall from his left eye.

"What ails thee ape?" Malachi without malice for he was happy, Mungo had Leah back and he hoped they could cheat fate and retire to live happy far away.

He with his Ono and
Mungo with Leah. But Leah
wanted Conn her son with
her.

And since The Elder did not reply Malachi looked and saw Ono lying in a ditch with a spear in her side.

And he rent his brass armored plates from his body so was almost naked. *"Nodegamma,"* The Elder and Malachi screamed knowing fate had won and drew

sword and charged the enemy intent on falling across Ono's body dead.

"My mother is dead?" And Mungo clutched his temples and fell and there was no harpist to soothe but Leah who took his long brown curling kiss curls and yanked his head back and with bronze sword shore them off.

"Each," Mungo and Leah threw his face into the brown dust and waved her trophy.

And Artebrates saw her waving Mungo's locks in the air told his men to look, and they did, and knew without his hair Mungo had no strength and renewed their attack.

Brown dust was everywhere so none could see properly. "Why Leah?" Mungo asked.

"For Conn's sake, now he will be given to me for I have killed his father," she replied.

"He still lives," The Elder behind and hit her with his staff so she fell. "Hit not again for she is my life," Mungo begged.

"Fate is your life," and the mazarrat hit Leah again.

And Mungo roared and The Elder saw he was dead as Mungo lion thing ripped open his belly, so he saw inside and what he had eaten earlier.

Then Mungo picked The Elder up, wanting an end to the prophecies that controlled his life so was to crash the mazarrats against boulders.

Now Mungo saw Malachi also fall with lances stuck in his body across Ono his love.

"Use the bomb now, go to the Incorruptible One," The Elder for now Mungo had no reason not to.

And Mungo listened and paused then threw the mazarrat aside.

At this moment John Wrexham rode up to Mungo, "Your head will decorate my wall."

"Like Sasha's and her white coat makes a fine rug under my cold feet," Cameron Black added also arriving.

"Mungo hated by all but used by all to kill Fermanians," Peelock also here. Now that for which did Mungo have to live?

So, he jumped upon Peelock and opened his throat with his lion teeth, then leapt away before the others could shoot him dead.

And Peelock made strange gurgling sounds as he fell off his pha and none of his new friends attempted to help him.

Anyway, he did not have the Incorruptible One these days to save him.

And Peelock rolled under his new friend's pha, and the hooves went into his soft face.

Now it was Moragana the human ape thing that saved Mungo for she loved him with a burning possession.

"Mungo I always love," she called as she jumped from a wild desert primrose bush and took the white laser light intended for Mungo.

And Mungo fled and that was what Moragana wanted, her love to live.

And John Wrexham was a cruel man as testified by all the Fermanian carcasses that littered the Red Plain shot Moragana with his laser.

He was running to the Incorruptible One.

And behind Mungo the battle was going bad for the humans for Artebrates was in their rear and Carman in the front until Cadfael arrived with twenty thousand free humans and fought Artebrates.

"If only Carman would show herself and lead the reserve into battle," Artebrates hoping his queen would and save the day as human wild men hacked.

"I am sore," Carman for she lay on a couch for she had

lost Cathbadh's daughter from her tummy and the egg lay broken in a bowl so could not help.

Now Vinki ordered by Carman to bring back the head of Mungo for revenge, so he rode pha surrounded by Berserkas to where he had seen Mungo flee.

"I hate the bitch for giving me this impossible mission," Vinki moaned.

"Oh, brave and fearless tailless one your name is Ben Han," the mazarrats sang as he stood with sixty Berserkas in front of Vinki who managed to make the rear as battle commenced.

And Carman knew what she was doing sending Vinki to the forward lines!

Axe against laser but Ben Han stood and still fought with one arm till a laser white light passed across his throat and his head rolled off his body.

And he fell dead and died a brave
man full of valor. But he was dead
and no good to anyone now.

So Vinki came forward again and with his remaining men pursuing Mungo he felt confident for as long as he had others fighting for him, he was brave and fearless as a Fermanian was supposed to be.

And the red sun began to settle on the horizon and the cold of the night felt on

the breeze and **'time stops' for no one** in a battle.

So Fermanians shivered and withdrew from battle and the humans were glad for they could retreat to see to their wounds and get reinforcements, from settlers on the Red Plain.

And the dying screamed for the Fermanians warmed from cooking fires went out and sought sweetmeats to celebrate Nodegamma that was going badly for their enemies.

But the home cities were far from the Red Plain so many did say, "Where do we get reinforcements from and our supply lines long?" And that was the other reason they sought sweetmeats for their rations were cold and besides, "Fermanians always victorious took from the land unopposed," a mazarrat sang but times had changed.

*

"Why didn't we help," a second officer asked Captain Clinton.

"We can now, we have finished entry and a mile up, send down parties to rescue isolated pockets of humans only, make sure they don't bring back any lizards and see if contact can be made with that Cathbadh?

We can rearm the humans and send them back.

No lizards are going to get the better of us humans, see that mass of cooking fires, get the battle computer to lock on and cluster bomb them.

Damn lizards, who do they think they are?

Humans?"

*

Mungo ran through the green lighting illuminated night knowing the gods of the Fermanians or of his own people did not exist.

"But Mungo never danced to his people's gods, just the Unseen One," a mazarrat called to him.

"Damn mazarrat," his reply.

About a mile ahead he could see John Wrexham's ranch lit by the flame of Telephassa City, but he was not going there, he was heading for where he had hidden the Incorruptible One.

Now **three quarters of a mile** and the sky became blue, and Mungo thought he saw a shape running across a boulder.

Half a mile and Mungo saw more moving about the gate houses to the deserted city he headed.

Quarter of a mile and lightening hit a gate house and Mungo heard screams, then the green light from Heaven after the lighting illuminated all and Mungo saw monkey people lurching, those still alive.

And Mungo reached the gate house and did not stop but ran onto the road his ancestors made striding upon dying and dead monkey people hit by the lighting.

Mungo did not hate them; just saw them as disgusting imitations of the humans he hated.

And Ono appeared and Mungo was alarmed thinking this was who haunted him, so he needed a harpist.

"I am not a ghost Mungo."

"I saw you fall; you are a ghost."

"You saw a lion fall and it was not me."

"Malachi was his friend," a mazarrat sang and Mungo saddened.

"Malachi loved you so much he went and got killed," Mungo and Ono saddened. "Why have you come here?" She asked.

"To use the bomb and end the Fermanian war that has taken Malachi and all my loved ones from me," Mungo.

And Ono thought and saw his reason so said, "Ride my back and we shall get the bomb quicker," and together they reached the deserted palace that once housed the governor of New Uranus ten thousand years ago, entered and went down a damp stairway

"Gallows Gate Station,"

written above in big, faded
words in human.

Down went Mungo and Ono never knowing a mile behind raced the hunchback on a pha and on one pha a tied prisoner and on another Conn the boy.

"I am sure he has gone there," the hunchback confident that with Leah back Mungo would be free of the demon that made his mind crazy and not use the bomb.

But Leah hissed and snaked out her tongue, she was going to meet Mungo and part of her mind did not accept she had loved him once, he was enemy.

And nearby an explosion collapsed a fast reactor, civil war was raging.

And The Elder with bandaged abdomen was above Gallows Gate Station and sang, "Artebrates was the tool of Mungo, it was Artebrates who brought down judgement upon Telephassa, the ending of the old to dust and the growing of seeds from the dust of new life, it is the way," and then was told by a young mazarrat Leah was coming, "Will I get to Mungo in time?"

And far below Mungo walked with Ono up to a green marble mausoleum where the Incorruptible One lay.

"Listen Mungo, a ship is coming from Earth your home planet, look into the computer's screen and see," the holy corpse and he did and saw a bright star shaped like a rotating ball.

"My world is here amongst the lions," he replied to the Incorruptible One. "When the ship arrives humans will come in vast numbers because Telephassa

cannot oppose them because Telephassa will be gone, I chose you well Mungo, now you must use the bomb to help them arrive, and I am fate Mungo."

And Mungo always remembered his friend Malachi trying to escape fate and raised his copper sword and struck at her throat, but she was the Incorruptible One and shielded by unseen forces, so the sword flew away.

Then he remembered Sasha and his grief tormented him, so he took a gun and fired at the Incorruptible One who had fated their deaths.

And the bullets went everywhere so Ono was, almost killed.

And he remembered Leah who he had spent a lifetime searching for and all because this Incorruptible One had fated it!

And Mungo saw a large switch and intuition told him to pull it and shut off her power.

And he did so.

The lights went crazy and the earth shook.

*

Now Carman was wanting to leave for Telephassa for she ached for the dead child that had been within her, and looked upon her city far in the distance where it should be; and behold saw a flash there instead and the flash of light soared towards her and in seconds she began to wither and topple and crumple as ash and then was a shadow upon the burnt grass.

And she never knew what hit her and thousands of Fermanians ready to do battle became shadows also as the flash burnt everything in its path.

"The great city Telephassa is no more, gone are the evil Fermanians," mazarrats sang.

And the flash from the doomsday bomb killed humans watching the battle from high ground and those whose land was low survived.

What of Leah, it was luck that she and others were behind embankments and solid walls or below ground.

"Mungo is more than a murderer, he is an abomination for what he has done," mazarrats would sing for now they wanted Mungo to feel so guilty he would throw himself on his sword.

But what were the baboons pretending to be mazarrats scheming?

And back to the Incorruptible One where Mungo threatened the air and walls with his sword.

"She was the bomb Mungo, she chose you well," The Elder too late reaching him.

And now saw The Elder had an army of armed mazarrats behind, above and next to him.

"All Telephassa is gone all ash, a great hot wind blew over them," The Elder and at that moment John Wrexham appeared and fired into the thong of baboons that is how he saw mazarrats without respect, easy kills.

But these were no longer the mazarrats who had always served with their songs and thousands came upon John Wrexham and he knew what terror was when they took hold of him and pulled this way and stretching his body to places it did not want to go.

"They have killed John, what gives with these monkeys?" Cameron asked pleased for he was now Boss and shoot mazarrats, but they numbered like grains of sand on a beach.

And the mazarrats were dying for a secret and they wanted it a kept secret, this was their underground city.

"Argh," Cameron Black as a lasso went about his neck and lifted off his feet.

"And all the king's men couldn't save them," the mazarrats sang, "Humpty dumpy sat on a wall, Humpty dumpy had a great fall."

Rushed the men of the ranch that had followed their leader John Wrexham and although hundreds slain by sheer weight of numbers killed them.

And The Elder his innards bandaged back into his body,

now carried in on a giant leaf by mazarrats shouted.

"The humans haven't landed yet, who knows how humans think?" But he did, "Fall upon your sword Mungo, all your friends are dead," he urged for the secret mazarrat city must be a secret, "This is Experimental Planet 16A, it was us who implemented a war between human and Fermanian and put ideas of a Wild One about for our future domination.

Now the world you knew is gone, all gone above, left to us mazarrats to inherit, fall upon your sword Mungo and be with Leah and Sasha

And Mungo grieved but also angered and picked up the sword.

"This is Planet Mazarrat," The Elder encouraging and ordered mazarrats make a clearing and Mungo saw his cubs from Sasha held above drums of something vile, for drowning.

But at this moment Leah and the hunchback had come behind the mazarrat thong and the hunchback hearing shot The Elder in the head, so his brains flew out.

And a mazarrat threw a lance and it entered the hunchback and stayed there showing it had exited out his back and that is all.

So, the little man crumpled to his knees happy he had sent he who had destroyed the Fermanian race to hell.

Now surely the mazarrats would slay Leah and Mungo for they had assumed the power of the Unseen that Mungo danced too and did exist; because they could not make a lone star yet had destroyed life on a planet.

"I am a probe the voice of Captain John Clinton, lay down your weapons," and those mazarrats that attacked the droid killed by atomic fusion weapons, so a great host slaughtered, and the rest fled for without The Elder were leaderless.

"We are left," Leah hissed and took her son Conn and fell at Mungo's feet so he could wipe his feet on her hair as taught, for she was a comforter, a woman only.

And Mungo lifted her up and for one moment she wanted to bite him for Cathbadh had done his gene shuttle work well.

But love surfaced that love in all and cannot die.

"Carman is dead, Telephassa is rubble, let us live in peace you and I and," he went to get Sasha's cubs, "my children?"

"Are you, my daddy?"
Conn asked. "Yes, I am
the lion man thing."
"Am, I too, kill you?"

"No, I am your daddy."

"That is a good thing for you are a mighty warrior and I like you," Conn and Leah hissed.

A hiss tells lots!

"One cub shall be wise,
which?" "One cub shall
be a king, which."

"One cub shall be a mighty warrior, which?" And Mungo meant all three of his children.

Cathbadh

And the human marines found Cathbadh by using a spectrogram build up resonator so his anatomical make up detected and imaged on a screen.

"How innovating?" Captain Clinton mused seeing what else was in Cathbadh's room for he was in the dungeon.

And The Elder needed to comment but is dead and there are no mazarrats aboard ship.

"What now Long John Silver," a caged parrot sang on bridge, kept as a canary to assess oxygen levels, for assassins could interfere with computers.

"What the heck?" Were the torturers last words as a marine stunned him with a stun probe, but this one designed to kill and electrocuted the torturer with two hundred thousand volts. He jumped, frizzled, and got the human marines in a hungry mood as grilled lizard smelt like chicken.

And Cathbadh taken aboard a cutter and sent back to the human ship.

Captain John Clinton had had a whim, Cathbadh would provide him with everything he wanted to know about killing lizards.

"Many thanks Captain Clinton, I will be made governor of my people?" Cathbadh using a handheld speaker to his throat as his tongue was too swollen to let him speak.

That was all he got to say as he was a lizard so sent to the ship's vet and quarantine.

"I am not a mazarrat," Cathbadh complained as they shoved and squeezed him into a metal cage where dogs usually went and here, he stayed until transported down to Captain Clinton's side in a wheelchair in the ruined palace of Carman.

"Will I be made governor of my people?" Cathbadh asked.

"You will not, you will stand trial for acts of barbarism

against humanity," Clinton replied and Cathbadh looked out the crumpled observation platform and saw a burnt rose tree and a noose and himself hanging there choking, going blue till he died.

"What's it all been about captain? I had plans, we all did, I should be Emperor Sess Cathbadh, my little daughter gone, vaporized.

The Senate Chamber a pile of stone with cuneiform and hieroglyphic drawings, tell me captain please?"

And since the lizard was begging, "The plans of mice and men are nothing," the captain throwing Burns poetry at him, but human culture meant nothing to Cathbadh who was in shock and mourning.

*

Artebrates covered in red dust, and it was hard to notice his military medals and steel breast plates as he had buried a son.

"Egal," carved in a rock slab above the grave.

"You I always thought a monster but died a man to protect his living seed in Conn.

A thing I never did and wish I had, or my children might be at my side.

I cannot say I loved you but should have called you by your name, Egal and not hunchback," and started to pat the soil flat when another spoke to him.

"Remember me Artebrates, it is I Nannaha," and he turned and saw she was still beautiful.

"Desire me Lord and Master and take me into your household?" Nannaha and enticed him so he thought her a harlot seeking his last coins and was not suspicious of her real intentions.

And she bowed and kissed his feet and put his soles on her hair in submission and then lifted her head so he must bend down and kiss her.

And when he bent, and she felt his old, wrinkled lips on her soft full red lips she cut his throat and it made a cutting sound as if hard paper cut.

"The hunchback was worth a million of your kind," so saying epitaph for Egal and she left seeking the remnants of her people who had fled Telephassa and Hurreva for Fermanian settlements still standing at least a year's walk away outside the nuclear blast.

It had been the doomsday bomb, an excessively big bomb.

And she could walk a year whereas a spaceship would get to Huverra in an hour.

*

And Leah hissed and gave Mungo a silver cylinder Egal had given her, and Mungo could not read so gave it back and with his family rode lions into Telephassa and Captain John Clinton told, "A man riding a lion has come to talk with you."

"This must be Mungo whom Cathbadh has told us much, that he is a bandit, whether human or lizard still a bandit, a murderer, one who dislikes the rule of law, so I must see this circus act for myself," Captain John.

Already Cathbadh had woven malice, for Fermanians future revenge? And there indeed was a wild man on a lion and strange looking children rode others. "Bloody heck were creatures?" Captain John and no one laughed at his side for he

was serious,' what the hell were they?'

And that woman with the green eyes, a stunner but she was sticking this snake tongue out of her mouth.

'What the hell was this planet? Hell? A Hammer Horror film set?' Captain John.

And the place soon filled with the smell of wild beasts.

"Needs a bath," Captain John and his junior officers laughed then but stopped when they saw Mungo was not laughing.

And Mungo handed him the cylinder and Captain John ordered a soldier to fetch a lizard who came at the end of a bayonet, fearful and dirty also.

"Enkalla," Mungo roared and Enkalla who was the soldier smiled hope when he saw Mungo; for Malachi was Enkalla's brother remember!

"Read this," Captain John ordered, and he did and grinned, "It is about him, want to know who he is, ask him," Enkalla having his pride back in the presence of The Wild One.

"Mungo and release my friend Enkalla here," was Mungo's reply.

And Captain John observed the savage human here, Mungo gave orders.

"He is The Wild One and did all this," Enkalla waving hands about the destructed city.

"When you tell me what the cylinder says you will be released," Captain John also realizing Mungo was illiterate; an illiterate baboon, now were we heard that before?

"It is the will of Egal, and he gives his mother's inheritance to his daughter Leah, and the inheritance is that she is a descendant of King Sess," and Enkalla fell on his face, "Mighty One," and Leah slipped off the back of a young adolescent lion and fell on her face.

"Sasha's child, Mungo's heir, King of the Red Pride," and wiped Conn's feet on her hair.

Now Captain John thought of ordering Leah's arrest for he wanted an end to lizard dynasties and Mungo saw it in his eyes.

"Mount Enkalla," and Enkalla broke from his guard who lounged at him with a foot long bayonet and Captain John kept silent, but not Mungo who with a roar leapt and landed between Enkalla and the human guard.

"Where is my son Akkad?" Enkalla asked and Mungo asked for him.

"Who the hell is Akkad?" Captain John answered, "Kill them both," an afterthought.

And for answer Mungo leapt at him and had a dagger at his throat before any knew what happened.

"Bring his son to him," Mungo ordered not liking the new humans who did not like him either.

And the smell of Mungo was so close captain John's nose wrinkled. "Take this lizard to the holding pens to find his son if he is still alive, you just about

killed everybody here Mungo with that bomb," Captain John wanting fresh air.

And time does not end on New Uranus and eventually Enkalla found Akkad and rejoined Mungo and they mounted pha.

And Mungo took Captain John hostage till they were outside the first ruined defensive wall of Telephassa, that wall that belonged to a serrant and here let go of Captain John.

"Am I free to go?" Captain John seeing wild jungle ahead hoping he was not to freed here.

A snake at least sixteen feet was slithering into it away from them.

Also, something big and hungry was roaring in there.

"No one harm this human, I give him life and a sword too protect himself from snakish serrants," Mungo shouted.

"Can I trust you?" Captain John not liking the bit about snakish serrants, what where they? "I could have broken my word to Red Hide but did not so kill him for Sasha," Mungo replied.

"Is Malachi alive?" It was Abel the hunting lion. "No Malachi is dead brother," Mungo.

"Then I will fight you for the kingship of the pride now that Red Hide is dead," Abel.

And Eve, Abel's sister sniffed Captain John and licked her lips, so the human knew he was dinner.

And Leah hissed not liking these two lions so near to Conn, and Eve roared at her so Captain John wondered what type of insane asylum he had entered.

He had entered Cathbadh's world of the shuttle gene," a mazarrat in the jungle.

And as Abel and Mungo fought an evil Serrant came out of a burrow and took Eve by the throat for she was watching Abel, dragging her into a burrow.

But Eve was too big to go all the way in. "What was that?" Captain John horrified.

"A Serrant," Abel and begged Mungo to stop the fight so

he could help Eve his sister.

"Who am I?" Mungo asked first.

"Lord and Master and swear to serve thee," Able so Mungo released his bear hug on the lion's neck and Abel begged Mungo to crawl in the serrant's escape hole and free Eve for he was slimmer than Abel.

And Mungo found the second hole and with a lighter, (once he would have used flint, but New Uranus was full of technological advances like abandoned nuclear fast reactors and a burning city called Telephassa and mazarrats living underground armed and dangerous,) made fire and entered the hole.

"WA, WA, WA, it is Mungo again,"
the Serrant hissed. "Thee I will skin
this time," Mungo warned.

And the Serrant let go of Eve's throat and Eve bit the Serrant so hard the Serrant knew it might die now.

"Spare me Mungo and I will tell you where Vinki is your enemy," but Mungo knew the enemy was the Serrant who would bite Mungo as soon as it could.

And Mungo stuck his dagger into the lion bite and twisted so the head of the Serrant came away from its body.

After that since nothing was holding the whole body as one Cathbadh's stitches came loose and all the serrant's interesting inside bits came out and the burrow stunk and steamed.

"Let us go topside," Mungo to Eve who wiggled backwards and was free again in the beautiful world of sunshine and sky and butterflies.

Then Mungo left the damp mysterious world of the Serrant and above rolled boulders over the two holes making it a tomb for his enemy.

"I said I did skin the Serrant, and I will be back," mazarrats

sang nearby.

"Are you Batman or something?" Captain John and Mungo wondered when he did meet Batman?

"We ride," Mungo and mounted a lion covered in brass armored plates and rode away so all Captain John saw was the sun glinting his eyes reflected off the brass.

"Who the hell does he think he is telling me what to do?" Captain John. "Malachi was his friend," a mazarrat.

"Enkalla also," another.

"He isn't your friend," another sang from a giant purple pea flower.

"He will bring judgement upon humans," also added to a new song. "He is The Wild One," another.

"The chosen one."

"This crazy stinking planet," Captain John regretting his orders to come here and walked back as a human scout craft approached.

And they fired at a group of armed mazarrats killing handfuls.

Advanced humans had arrived on New Uranus.

"And the Planet is Mazarra Captain John and belongs to mazarrats," these baboons were able to sing.

*

And Captain John awoke one night and found a papyrus book written by one called The Elder and finished by his young pupils.

The book is, "Mungo,"

Mazarrats were in cages also for Captain John liked the way they sang, so, one added next to the parrot on the bridge and saw wonders and sang about them.

"These baboons build underground cities, don't be crazy lieutenant?" Captain John.

And Cathbadh, "That wheelchair wasn't meant for a lizard to be pushed around in all day, get rid of him," Captain John and the lizard wheeled to the edge of an open sewer one of hundreds that ran through the once glorious city of Telephassa, and here the wheelchair up ended.

And Cathbadh full of sores from beatings rolled into it and lifted his head up from the sludge, his lips dripping the foul-smelling disease ridden affluent.

None would help him out, there was none about anyway for Captain John was executing lizards for crimes against humanity. And what Fermanians Cathbadh did see where emptying their bladders and bowels into the sewer he was in.

He managed to get to the sewer walls, but they were slimy with green mold and wet and steamy with fresh urine.

"Has the world gone mad?" Cathbadh managed and he had guessed right, the Fermanians above where now the slaves; and the slaves were not much elevated in rank for captain John saw them as illiterate superstitious people needing rounded up,

deloused, and educated.

Educated to take orders from him, they were all a long way away from Earth.

He also ordered Cathbadh's body burned, and his ashes

scattered on the wind so cloning would be impossible. Did we mention Cathbadh got diseases that finished him off within a week.

And it was the new slaves who went down and pored petrol over Cathbadh and set him alight.

Well so much petrol used the ashes carried away in the smoke and hundreds of

the new lizard slaves went up in smoke as well.

Petrol was something new to them! Poor lizards and the air stunk of fried chicken! And as for those who died at Nodegamma, their bones bleached and dry. "Where's the hell Nodegamma?" Captain John.

New place names would start appearing and road signs in human tongue and roadside quick food outlets.

'McPherson's Burgers, the best and juiciest ever,' and pet mazarrats played the fool

to get them by their new masters and out in the wilds mazarrats who always learnt new tricks quick sizzled burgers, as well as carried weapons and lived underground and chiseled carvings on tree bark and stones.

Do not worry about the killer of killers and the dinosaurs, the doomsday bomb took care of them, and those that survived, well advanced humans were here now, a zoo built; they would encourage rich tourists from Earth and the rest pushed into the remaining Fermanian lands not discovered by humans yet.

"Pity you got rid of Cathbadh," a cheeky mazarrat and Captain Clinton cursed all baboons.

And what ever happened to Vinki and his remaining Decurion?

"Roll away the boulder," and Vinki's Berserkas did and the Serrant smelt bad. "Cousins help me for I am sore wounded and fear I am dying," the Serrant hissed.

And Vinki allowed the Serrant to come into the fresh air for he had watched events from a distance.

"Take me from this place for you have riderless pha and I will serve you as I served Cathbadh," the Serrant begged not wanting left here for Mungo to return and skin it.

"Cathbadh was my enemy cousin Serrant," and Vinki gave orders to skin the Serrant, "a fine soft skin to make a fine soft body warmer," Vinki holding up the glistening skin and he mounted a pha and rode in the opposite direction Mungo had gone, happy he had got one up on his enemy Mungo who had wanted the skin too.

"There are Fermanian cities still and we can copy the mazarrats how to live underground," Vinki and a mazarrat sang it and all mazarrats knew Fermanians must die, especially Vinki before that Lord got his idea accepted.

There was only room for one specie underground, and it was already there having singing lessons.

And Captain John heard and said, "This is one stinking crazy planet," and saw himself as another Julius Caesar and the place a wild and woolly Gaul to make or break his future and fortune for Gaul was rich in gold mines.

And he awoke when he heard a man lion thing roar.

And The People of Red Town started going to school to read and write and become advanced humans but still saw mazarrats as baboons.

"The Wild One will be bring judgement upon humans," mazarrats sang. "Vinki was his friend," another added.

What was that?

*

"Enkalla was his friend," mazarrats sang.

The troublemakers seemed organized again, they had an idea that Enkalla should take over from Malachi. Why not keep it in the family but who had given them this idea?

Her name was The Prophetess and she had crawled into a laboratory and drunk fizzy liquid in a vial and changed an awful lot.

She looked human and was smarter than The Elder as shuttle genes had given her a bigger cerebellum so she could have bigger dreams like humans.

She dreamed of a mazarrat empire right over the whole Planet Mazarra. Of course, it would need a ruler and saw the job as hers. Since she had human genes in her so mourning for The Elder limited; he would have become a political rival and need done away with. The mazarrat people could see him as a martyr and her as his natural successor.

It was songs that did this for her just as songs helped Bonnie Prince Charlie whip up support for when communication is bad songs do the job. They plant ideas and keep them alive.

"The Prophetess is heir to The Elder," a mazarrat song went.

"Bloody baboons," Captain John said waving to the crowds as driven down a Telephessian Appian Way where Fermanian gardeners were watering imported roses.

And The Wild One headed into the wilderness away from Huverra City that any fool could guess was next on Captain Clinton's hit list.

"Where too?" He asked Enkalla.

"To Sumerkad, a city one month's walk north from here. Wait to you see it Mungo, it is arboreal, highways hundreds of feet off the ground and well hidden from balloon ships," Enkalla replied.

And an eve dropping mazarrat shook its head, Captain Clinton he had heard from a caged mazarrat on a spaceship's bridge did not need seed balloon craft to fly.

Already human engineers had a factory going assembling flying craft, not bright yellow like Mungo's stolen craft; but silver and needle shaped and flew so fast if you blinked an eye, you did not see them.

But they carried weapons that churned up the soil and anything on it.

Yes, the mazarrat shook its head, **time had not stopped** for anyone to catch up with the new human arrivals.

"Hiss," and Mungo looked at his woman and wondered if she still was. He sometimes saw her as a snake and although no longer swallowing Cathbadh's potions, the reversal process would take a long time unless speeded up.

"*And Cathbadh had gone to the gutter,*" a mazarrat would inform Mungo annoyingly.

And Leah was shapelier than ever, and Mungo lusted for her often and did he dance any the more the more?

He was Mungo the man lion thing, there is the answer.

*

The Empress Red Sun was lonely, she only had to watch singers that sang better than her to replace her. She missed The Elder and the heroes, "Yes, the murderers," so was off her food and singing, a dangerous function as already a male mazarrat sang like a Gold Finch, "*The Empress murdered The Elder so is sick, the sickness will spread to all mazarrats."*

How do I get things back the way they were? She asked.

"She does not know what even a mazarrat in nursery knows," the idiot male singer following his cod piece and not his brains as he ogled young girls on the next flower.

"Of course, I will clone them," Empress Red Sun so sang sweeter than him, but the damage done. As female mazarrats preferred the new rival, that male, handsome, single, a pin up for the girls, Pinching locks of his fur as he passed, *"Blooming hell, I will need a wig soon."*

And the sensible matrons wanted stability so, wisdom could flourish and provide ways to topple Captain John, knew Empress Red Sun with a voice as hers could provide, the land would flourish, disease banished and mazarrats build cities under mountains and to travel spaceships.

An easy thing to do as humans caged mazarrats as singing baboons, as favored pets went places, Mars, Earth and beyond.

All the makings of a new story sang by mazarrats.

THE END

ACKNOWLEDGEMENT

Thank my love for dinosaurs, prehistory and lore.
Ask for wisdom and you will be given.

ABOUT THE AUTHOR

Keith Hulse

The story teller was an archaeologist, soldier, jack of all trades, and now Veteran Scottish Warblinded and artist.   He sees ghosts when they visit. He is not a medium.   His house is full of cats. He saw an U.F.O. in the night sky, was so fast, then stopped, then at an acute angle flew towards Stonehaven at sudden speed. At no time was there any engine sounds, just silence and the light, that was the object.   If it was one of ours, our enemies beware.

EPILOGUE EVOLUTION

A defense of this book's ideas
to make creative thoughts
Not a religious book

Frederick Myers and other spirits, said that we belong to soul groups, families and friends grouped together in Heaven waiting to progress into higher spirits *that we see here as orbs of light, bursting energy wanting to communicate and cannot because we will not let them because* what they will say will disturb our views.

These soul groups of human spirits, but others from other dimensions and animals. *Groups of rats and dogs evolving in spirit realms waiting to enter the physical realms to put their lessons learned into effect, and evolve into higher spirit beings; eventually evolving into?*

Is not the Almighty Creator Magnificent in glory and who can visualize the galaxies running parallel to each other, atop, beneath, side by side, visible and invisible?

All Jesus the Christ says is that the married woman will be married to none of her seven husbands: in other words, it is her own eternal progress she deals with.

Jesus The Christ communicated with a fig tree and donkey, they heard his voice, spirit, and mind. They shared the same divine spark and are subject as living spirits to the same spirit laws as us.

Remember Escalates, chats about how to treat animals and eternity, remarkably interesting to all.

Mungo is about evolution and gene shuttling; it is about diversity and color and beautiful creation.

In fact, if you think about it, soul groups on the other side reeks of planned evolutions, a pushing by something Unseen; sure, mistakes made, but the product is? Is creation a result of eternal progress in the spirit realms? As religions say, creation is no accident.

Creation, full of color, diversity, a bursting forth, it is the Mind of God at work and not drab; what is the mind of God, evolution must be a byproduct?

Mungo all about can we cross breed with other types of life?

Now that is very provocative, with the help of gene shuttling and viruses to insert?

In this case is humans and lion humanoid creatures. Humanoids as here we needed to walk upright to free our little fingers to conduct creative brain waves, like rock art, how to herd mammoths over cliffs for diner and make fire, to cook the mammoths.

Lions with fingers who wear brass body armor and can walk on two legs, which mean they are not square moving lumps of muscle, but lion-people who take pride in their bodies. Not worshipping body, but body beautiful.

And since they can walk, they can see enemies and prey easier so have multiplied. And the use of fingers developed the brain so have governments. DEFINITELY WE ARE NOT ALONE IN THESE GALAXIES.

When you think you hear a jet engine roar, it is the sound of a lion-person whose roar **travelled to you on a light wave**. Lot cheaper than building **radio wave transmitters**. It is the **way of the universe to hitch hike.**

Aliens have also learned to use **light waves to send pictures**.

LIGHT WAVES FAST AND CHEAP, CAN THEY CARRY CARGO, SEEDS?
Thick light waves whole beings, a lion-person to you?

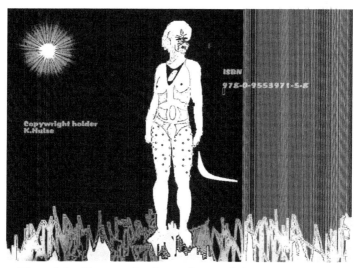

The white lioness Sasha, a hero of mazarrat songs.

BOOKS BY THIS AUTHOR

Ants 169 Illustrations Science Fiction

82652 words 169 illustrations. 262 pages
Adventure with Luke of The Ants, a rival to Tarzan, whereas Tarzan was brought up on ape milk, Luke is raised on Black Ant milk.
Amazing strength and he battles Insect Nobles for the dominant species on Planet World.
Humanoid Insects from chromosome splicing.
Human genes into insects to make them taller, handsome, attractive but cruel masters of Planet World.
A good hero needs a side kick, Luke has Utna, a giant Black Ant he rides, saves shoe leather.

Planet World, Ant Rider Book One, Illustrated

Is Book One of Ants 169, 47619 words, 219 pages.
Ants 169 is so large needed halved.
Book One has Luke finding out his aims and becomes a hero by fighting for human rights.
Full, of adventure, example, Luke ends up a galley rower and saves the ship from pirates.
And like a dog, Utna pines for Luke wondering seashores seeking Luke, his friend, and like a dog, loves his master.

Phoenix, Ant Rider Book Two, Illustrated.

Is concluding part of Ants 169

48439, 187 pages.
Luke concludes his epic struggle against the humanoid Insect Nobles, become this way by gene mixing.
The Insect Queen, Nina and he race to the star ship Phoenix, a human ship that crashed on Planet World in the Time of Myths.
What secrets does it hold?

Ghost Wife, A Comedy Of Errors

74256 words, 159 pages.
Oh, Morag dear, you died so do what ghosts do, Rest In Peace. "not on your Nelly, I am very much alive, and stop ogling the medium Con, dear." Lots of madcap ridiculous fun. Plenty information on the After Life, pity our world leaders would not stop and listen, might be no more wars.

Ghost Romance, A Comedy Melee.

54980 words, 218 words.
A nonstop ghostly ridiculous adventure from Borneo to New York Zoo, with Calamity the orangutan in tow.
Do not worry about the extras feeding the crocodiles, they come under a dime a dozen and are not in any union, and better, made of indigestible rubber.
Not to worry animal lovers, a vet in a shark cage is on standby by for the sweet crocodiles, sea water variety so bigger.

Mungo, Books One And Two.

97334 words 450 pages
A mammoth adventure for Mungo, the boy raised by lions on New Uranus, humanoid, all creatures here are just about humanoid thanks to genetic engineering.
Of his first love, Sasha, daughter of Red Hide, King of Lions, to his war with Carman, Queen of Lizard Folk.

By the way these lizard folk like humans at a barbecue, as the burgers, steaks, and sausages.

No wonder Mungo wars against them.

And no one wins in a war as a human star ship arrives and enslaves the lot.

Advanced humans see other humans as undesirables.

Mungo, Book One.

50632 words, 201 pages.

Mungo travels his world to the floating city of Huverra.

Meet his friends and enemies.

Meet more mazarrats as they provide a parallel story.

Mazarrats a cross between a mongoose and a baboon is said.

Not true, they are cute singers looking for a home.

discover the technological wonders these lizard folks have.

Mungo, Book Two

43887, 232 pages.

Concludes the giant adventures of Mungo, Lion King of Planet Uranus.

By the by, Mungo is based loosely on Bible Stories, so the last battle between good and evil is here too.

Except only new humans on a star ship win, forcing Mungo into the wilds and new adventures.

Printed in Great Britain
by Amazon